a million dirty secrets

a million

dirty secrets

million dollar duet

c. l. parker

Bantam Books
Trade Paperbacks
New York

A Bantam Books Trade Paperback Original

Copyright © 2013 by C. L. Parker

Excerpt from *A Million Guilty Pleasures* by C. L. Parker copyright © 2013 by C. L. Parker.

Published in the United States by Bantam Books, an imprint of The Random House Publishing Group, a division of Random House, Inc., New York.

BANTAM BOOKS and the HOUSE colophon are registered trademarks of Random House, Inc.

This book contains an excerpt from the forthcoming novel *A Million Guilty Pleasures* by C. L. Parker. This excerpt has been set for this edition only and may not reflect the final content of the forthcoming edition.

Library of Congress Cataloging-in-Publication Data
Parker, C. L.
A million dirty secrets: million dollar duet / C. L. Parker.
pages   cm
ISBN 978-0-345-54876-4
ebook ISBN 978-0-345-54877-1
1. Prostitution—Fiction.   I. Title.
PS3616.A74424M54   2013
813'.6—dc23
2013013881

Printed in the United States of America on acid-free paper

randomhousebooks.com

Book design by Elizabeth A. D. Eno

This book is dedicated to my sister, Jessica Neidlinger. She was the first to plant the seed of writing into my head, and she's watered and nurtured that seed to watch it grow into the author I am today. If not for her, I would not be writing. I owe all of my success to you, Jess. Not literally, of course. Ha! I love you for all that you are and all that you make me.

a million dirty secrets

prologue

I am a sex slave—a person held in servitude as the property of another, completely subservient to a dominating influence. Technically, I suppose "whore" would be a more appropriate term to describe what I am. You see, I have made myself completely available to a man, albeit one man, in exchange for money. This would include, but is not limited to, my loyalty, my discretion, and the use of my body in every way, shape, and form that suits his needs.

The irony is that I wasn't forced into this life; I chose it. Well, I really didn't have another choice, as a better opportunity hadn't presented itself in time, but I chose it all the same. He didn't force me. He didn't seek me out. I wasn't kidnapped or brutally beaten into submission. I went willingly.

And I did it all to save a life.

My name is Delaine Talbot, but you can call me Lanie. This is my story.

1

sacrifices we make

Lanie

"You're sure you want to do this?" my way oversexed best friend asked me for what seemed like the millionth time since I'd walked through the doors of the nightclub where she worked—and played—the slut.

Dez was my rock. She held me down when life got too serious, and it was over-the-top serious at the moment. Dez was short for Desdemona, which loosely translated meant "of the devil." She'd changed her name the day she turned eighteen, only because her parents refused to let her do so before then. Seriously, her parents had named her Princess when she was born, but if anyone other than them tried to call her that, it was a bar brawl in the making. Dez was crazy beautiful, the sort of bosomy babe you read about in all the romance novels: long, silky black hair, hourglass figure, legs that go on for days, and the face of a goddess. The only problem was that she carried herself like a biker chick. She also liked to test-ride all the models. Like I said, slut. But I loved her like she was my own flesh and blood. And considering what I was willing to do for my flesh and blood, that was saying a lot.

"No, I'm not sure, Dez, but I have to. So stop asking me before you make me change my mind and I go running out of here like the scaredy cat we both know I really am," I snapped at her.

She never took my drama too personally, because she gave just as good as she got. Boy, did she ever. And she had not an ounce of shame for it.

"And you're really willing to give up your V-card to a total stranger? Sans romance? No wining, no dining, no sixty-nining?" Her incessant questioning grated on my last nerve, but I knew it was because she loved me and wanted to be sure I'd considered everything. We had gone over all the pros and cons with a fine-toothed comb, and I really didn't think we had missed anything. But the unknown was what worried me the most.

"In exchange for my mother's life? In a heartbeat," I said as I followed her down the dark corridor that led to the underbelly of Foreplay, the club where she worked. Foreplay: that was where my life would change. It was the point of no return.

My mother, Faye, was terminally ill. She had always had a weak heart, and it had progressively gotten worse over the years. She had nearly died while giving birth to me, but had managed to bounce back from that and countless other operations and procedures. There was no bouncing back now. Her light was fading entirely too fast.

She was so weak and frail at this stage that she was bedridden, but not before having been in and out of hospitals so much that my father, Mack, had lost his job. He had refused to leave her alone in the name of helping some stupid factory meet its production numbers. I never blamed him for that. She was his wife, and he took his duty as her husband very seriously. She was his to care for, just like she would've cared for him if the roles had been reversed. But no job meant no health insurance. It also meant we were forced to live off the meager savings account my father had managed to tuck away for their golden years. Ergo, purchasing health insurance was a luxury my parents could not afford. Fantastic situation, huh?

Things had gotten even worse. Faye's illness had progressed to the point that a heart transplant was essential in order for her to continue living. That bit of news had taken a toll on all of us, but none more than Mack.

I'd watched my father day in and day out. He had been losing weight, his primary concern for his wife overshadowing his own care. And the dark rings under his red eyes made it obvious that he hadn't been getting as much sleep as he should have, either. Be that as it may, he had always put on a brave face for my mother. She had accepted her imminent demise, but my father . . . he still held out hope. The problem was that his hope was diminishing. It was killing his very soul to watch her die a little more each day. I think a piece of him went with every little piece of her.

I had walked in on him one night after my mother had fallen fast asleep. He was slumped over in his recliner, head in his hands, shoulders heaving from his disheartened sobs.

He hadn't meant for anyone to see him that way. But I had.

Never had I seen him so despondent. There was this nagging feeling tugging at my heart constantly that told me when my mother died, my father wouldn't be far behind. He would literally mourn himself to death. There was no doubt in my mind.

I had to do something. I was desperate to make everything better. To make them better.

Dez was my best friend. My very best friend. I had always shared everything with her, so she was wholly aware of the situation. Desperate times called for desperate measures, and after seeing just how desperate I had become, she had finally told me about the more scandalous business that was conducted beneath Foreplay.

Scott Christopher, the owner, was what one might call an aggressive entrepreneur. Basically, he was a pimp, but not any run-of-the-mill pimp on the streets. No, he'd figured out a way to tap the pockets of those whose pockets were overflowing. His was a high-class operation, an auction where women were sold to the highest bidder. Foreplay might have been the face of his business, but the auction was his bread and butter. It was a big frat party on top, college kids finding their next hookup and getting so wasted they couldn't remember their names, which was the perfect cover for the refined establishment underneath. From what I understood, some of the women—myself included—were participating voluntarily, while others owed Scott in some way. Selling their bodies was their last-ditch effort to repay him, even though it meant losing their freedom in the process.

Dez told me that the clients were always men with fat bank accounts. Even the world's richest tycoons had a thirst for the kinkiest of fantasies—fantasies they would never want to see go public. For the right amount of money, they could find willing flesh and never have to worry about their secret getting out. But it was luck of the draw—I could end up with someone gracious and kind, or a total tyrant who enjoyed dominating his property. If history was any indication, I'd end up with the latter. I hadn't exactly had the best of luck in my life, so why should I believe the powers that be would grant me any favors now?

My mother's illness had required constant sacrifice not only from my father but from me as well. It wasn't like I was resentful, but instead of going to college, I had stayed home with her so that my father could work. Now that he didn't have a job, they saw no reason for me to feel obligated to stick around. I'd never felt obligated. She was my mother, and I loved her. Besides, I still hadn't made up my mind about what I wanted to do with my future anyway. You'd think a woman of twenty-four would have had her life together, but no, not really.

It might have been a pretty low move on my part, getting their hopes up and all, but like I said, hope was something that was lacking in my household, and it certainly couldn't hurt to give them a little. So I managed to successfully convince my mother and father that I had scored a super-sweet, all-expenses-paid scholarship to NYU. Yes, I knew that wasn't something that was likely to happen at this point in my life, but my parents didn't know, and that made all the difference in the world. Being so far away from home meant I wouldn't be able to visit as often, and as much as it pained me to be away from my dying mother for so long, it was absolutely necessary for my plan to work. If I was lucky, they'd never be the wiser. But you remember what I said about my luck, right?

The deal I had made with Scott was that I would agree to live with my "owner" for a period of two years. No more, no less. After that, I would be free to live my own life. Exactly what sort of life that would be at that point was yet to be determined, but I had to remain positive. Regardless, two years was a small price to pay to ensure any amount of time for my mother and, ultimately, my father as well.

The bass coming from the club music upstairs pulsed through the walls and took over my heartbeat, but I tried desperately not to wish I was up there drowning myself in booze and good times, like everyone else who had no clue about the secret outfit that existed right under their feet. The women down here were drowning in something completely different.

We stepped around the club doorman holding a VIP list on a clipboard. He knew who we were and why we were there, so he let us inside immediately. I almost lost my nerve as we made our way past the crowd of women that lined the hallway. They were an assorted bunch, some with a regal air about them and others who looked like this wasn't their first time at bat, but perhaps it was the first time they'd made it to the big leagues. Each woman had a number taped to her bare stomach, and they were standing in front of a mirror that lined the opposite wall.

"Two-way mirror," Dez explained. "Each client who comes in has a write-up on every girl on the auction block tonight. Then they're herded in here like cattle and put on display for the high rollers. It gives them an opportunity to check out the goods so they can decide which desperate girl they might want to bid on."

"Gee, thanks, Dez. That doesn't make me feel bad at all."

"Oh, hush. You know I don't mean it like that," she said, trying to make me feel better. "You're way too good for this sort of thing, and you know it. You're not *them*." She motioned toward the other women in the hall. "But I get it. You're doing it for Faye, and that has to be the most selfless thing I've ever heard of."

Those other women could very well have had their own Faye at home, I thought as I averted my gaze so as not to make eye contact.

We reached the end of the hall, and Dez knocked on the door. A voice yelled for us to come in, but when Dez backed out of the way and motioned toward the entrance, I panicked. Full-on hyperventilation was only moments away, I just knew it.

"Hey, look at me." Dez forced me to face her. "You don't have to go in there. We can turn around right now and walk out of here."

"No, we can't," I said, tremors racking my body no matter how hard I tried to steady my nerves.

"I can't go in there with you. You're on your own from here on out," she said, unable to completely hide her regret and worry.

I nodded my understanding and ducked my head so she wouldn't see the tears welling up in my eyes.

Dez abruptly hugged me to her chest and practically squeezed the air from my lungs. "You can do this. Hell, maybe you'll actually get some good sex out of it. You never know. Don Juan might be on the other side of that mirror waiting to sweep you off your feet."

"Ha! Not likely," I scoffed, and managed to smile a little before backing out of her safe embrace. "I'll be okay. You just make sure the jerk that ends up with me follows through on our deal. If he doesn't, I expect you to send the FBI in here with guns a-blazin'."

"Girl, you already know it. And you know the digits, so you better call me with status reports or I'm coming after you. I have to get back to the bar now, before I lose my job and the inside scoop on you. But remember that I sort of like you and shit." Dez wasn't one for the mush, but I knew that was code for *I love you*. She kissed my cheek and said, "Give 'em hell, babe," before swatting me on the ass and turning to walk away. She wasn't fooling me. I saw the way her shoulders curled in and she dabbed at her eyes with her fingertips when she thought I couldn't see her.

"I sort of like you, too," I said under my breath because she was already out of earshot.

I turned toward the door, psyching myself up before I lost my nerve and backed out. One thought of my mother, and I knew there was no turning back. So I opened the door and marched into that office to finalize the terms of my contract.

Scott's office looked like something I might have expected for a Mafia kingpin. Plush carpet covered the floor, a beautiful chandelier hung from the center of the ceiling, lighted glass cases held various things I assumed cost a fortune, and fine art lined the walls. Classical music wafted from invisible speakers in an attempt to lure me into a false sense of security. The music and elegant décor lent the illusion of a refined establishment, which may have made the clientele feel more at home, but I knew better. You could put a suit and tie on a pig, but it didn't change the fact that it was still a pig.

Scott was at his desk with a cigarette in one hand and a lowball of whiskey in the other. His feet were propped on the desk while he lounged back in his chair, his fingers directing an invisible orchestra like he hadn't a care in the world.

He turned to look at me and grinned before sitting upright and butting his cigarette in a marble ashtray. "Ah, Ms. Talbot. I wondered if you'd grace us with an appearance tonight."

Squaring my shoulders and setting my chin, I looked him in the eye. This was my deal, and I was in control until the money was exchanged. I wasn't about to let Scott Christopher think he was anything other than the middleman he was. "I said I'd be here, and so I am."

He stood and walked toward me, not even trying to hide the fact that he was checking me out from head to toe. "That's a very good thing. I might have had to send out a search-and-rescue team to track you down if you hadn't shown up. You're going to make me a lot of money tonight."

"Can we please just confirm the terms of my contract?" I said with a sigh. I didn't trust him, and with good reason. He sold humans for a profit without an ounce of remorse. How could I trust anyone who did that for a living? If I'd had any other alternative, I certainly wouldn't have been standing there at that moment.

"Right," he said, going back to his desk and opening a manila folder with my name written in bold black letters across the top. "I can personally guarantee that the clientele for this evening will have no issue with discretion. In fact, it's a prerequisite for all who visit my establishment. They're the big ballers, the elite league of gentlemen . . . a real no-nonsense sort with more money than they know what to do with. Their reasons for being interested in the type of merchandise that I deal in are their own, and I don't pry as long as they're paying."

The only solace I took in agreeing to this, other than the fact that I'd be saving my mother's life, was that I knew someone with enough pull could guarantee the payout required to make sure my mom got the surgery she needed and keep his mouth shut about it in the process. No one with that much money wanted the world to know about his involvement in such an operation. And I most certainly didn't want my parents to find out about it. That knowledge alone would be enough to send them to their graves, thereby totally negating what I was trying to do for them.

The other perk, or at least I hoped so, was that anyone who could afford to do this would also be refined enough not to make my life a total living hell. I wasn't naïve; I knew there were some twisted people out there with some sick fetishes, but I held out hope nonetheless.

"I assume you're still cool with my twenty percent cut?" he asked, shuffling the papers.

"Nice try. We agreed on ten percent," I said, not one bit amused by his attempt to hustle me.

"Right, right. Ten percent. That's what I meant." He gave me a wink that made my skin crawl, then he pushed the contract across the desk and handed me a pen. "Just sign here . . . and here."

I scrawled my messy signature above the lines he indicated,

fully aware that I was signing away the next two years of my life. It was a small price to pay.

Shortly afterward, I was ushered into another room where I was told to strip down and put on the skimpiest bikini that I'd ever seen. It really left nothing at all to the imagination, which I gathered was probably the point. The men wanted to see the merchandise before they paid top dollar. I got that, but it didn't make me feel any less exposed and vulnerable. From there, a hair and makeup stylist did her thing, making me look simply elegant and, surprisingly, not trashy.

After that, Scott secured lucky number sixty-nine to my stomach. I kept my head held high as I joined the other women in front of the two-way mirror. The worst part was that while God only knew who or what was on the other side of the mirror looking at me, I couldn't see them. What I could see, though, was myself. I wasn't conceited by any means, but I had to admit that I looked good compared to the other women.

I had never considered myself drop-dead gorgeous, but I was good-looking. My blond hair was long and thick. My eyes weren't anything special, a dull blue, but once upon a time they had been full of life. That was before my mother's illness had taken a turn for the worse. I wasn't perfect in the body department, but I wasn't too fat or too skinny, and I had curves in what I always imagined were the right places. All in all, a good showing, I hoped.

One by one, the women were pulled out of the room. At first, I thought it meant they were being chosen over me, and I felt like the fat kid in gym class who was always the last one to be picked. But then they called my number and I made my way toward the same black door I had seen the others before me disappear through. Once I stepped inside, I was led to the center of the room. All around me there were smaller areas with glass walls. Each room was furnished with one dimly lit table lamp, a telephone, and a cushy red velvet chair. It was obvious that the only thing the occupants of the rooms had in common with each other was money—and lots of it.

The first room was occupied by a sheik with dark sunglasses, a long white headdress, and a business suit. Two of the women who had been in the hallway with me earlier were on either side of him, showering him with kisses while rubbing his crotch and chest. I averted my eyes in embarrassment, only to be faced with a man in another room.

This guy was huge, like big-as-a-house huge. He reminded me a lot of Jabba the Hutt. A picture of Princess Leia chained next to him flashed across my mind, and a shiver ran down my spine. I had never been one to imagine myself as Princess Leia as a child, and I most certainly wasn't going to start now.

In the room next to him was a tiny guy with two huge bodyguards standing next to him. Their hands were crossed in front of them, and I imagined that was probably the closest they had ever come to being relaxed. The little guy had his legs crossed all dainty-like and was sipping on some fruity sort of drink with an umbrella sticking out of it. His white jacket hung casually over his shoulders like he was just too cool to actually put it on. I guessed the male variety was more his type. I couldn't imagine he'd be that threatening. He was probably there to score some pretty young thing to keep up pretenses in the public eye while secretly sneaking someone in the back door, if you get my drift.

I looked toward the last room and sighed inwardly when I saw that the light was out. Apparently whoever had been in there had already made his selection and left, which didn't give me much hope about the remaining assortment.

And then a small orange light flickered from the darkened room like the ember on the end of a recently puffed cigarette. I looked closer and could faintly make out the lines of a body sitting casually in the chair. The figure leaned forward a bit to readjust his position, granting me a better look at him, but not enough to be able to make anything out.

"Gentlemen," Scott said with a clap of his hands as he came to stand behind me. "This is the lovely Delaine Talbot, item number sixty-nine on our list tonight. I believe you have all of her specs, but allow me to highlight some of her finer attributes.

"First and foremost, she has come to us of her own accord. Obviously, she's spectacular to look at, which can make life infinitely easier for those of you who require a partner to attend social functions. She's young, but not too young, so your friends and family will find it more believable that you have a traditional type of relationship, if that sort of thing is important to you. She's educated and well-mannered, has all her teeth, and is in good health. And there's no drug problem to be bothered with, which means no detox period to hold you back from what you really want to do with her . . . and to her.

"And probably the most valuable asset of all is that her innocence is still completely intact. This, my fine gentlemen, is a grade A virgin. Unsullied, untouched . . . pure as the fresh-fallen snow. Perfect to train, no? With that said, let's start the bidding at one million dollars, and may the luckiest bastard win," he finished with a huge fake smile. He turned to wink at me and then stepped off to the side.

The platform that I stood on in the middle of the room began to move, and although it wasn't exactly on warp speed, it still caught me unawares, and I stumbled a little before I regained my balance. Around and around I went while the bidding process began. There were no audible sounds of voices, just the occasional buzz as the lights over the doors illuminated. I could see the men pick up the telephone beside them and speak into the receiver before their light lit up, so I assumed that was their method of placing bids.

I had no idea how high the bids were going. I just hoped that it ended with enough to pay for Faye's surgery. After a while, the sheik and the tiny guy dropped out, leaving Jabba the Hutt and Mystery Man to battle it out. Sure, I had no idea what Mystery Man looked like, but he had to be better than drowning in a pool of Jabba the Hutt.

The bidding between the two of them began to slow down, and I was becoming increasingly dizzy from spinning around on the platform. In truth, I just wanted it to be over with so that I would know my fate and could get on with it. I was still secretly rooting for the mysterious stranger.

Jabba the Hutt's light was the last to flash, and I knew the bid was back to Mystery Man, but he wasn't answering. I started to panic when Scott came back into the room and stood next to me. He smiled at Jabba and then cast a questioning brow in

Mystery Man's direction. I knew it was obvious by the look in my eyes that I was pleading with him, and I had no clue whatsoever if it made a bit of difference to him one way or the other, but I had to try.

The seconds ticked by agonizingly. Everything seemed to move in slow motion, and I felt light-headed and dizzy. I knew that I was going to pass out at any moment if I didn't get some oxygen to my brain, but I was holding my breath, praying that Mystery Man would come through for me and that I wouldn't regret willing him to be the winner.

"It looks like we have a win—" Scott started, but abruptly stopped when the light above Mystery Man's room lit up and the buzzer sounded.

I sucked in a much-needed breath, feeling my brain tingle with the life-giving sensation. My head shot toward Jabba the Hutt. I sighed in relief when he shook his head and waved his hand dismissively in the air before struggling to push out of his chair to extinguish the light on the table.

"You have a new owner, Miss Talbot," Scott cooed, a little too close to my ear. "Why don't you walk on over and meet your master?"

"I'm not calling him master," I seethed, loud enough for only Scott to hear me as he forced me to step down from the platform.

"You'll call him whatever he wants you to call him if you want the cool two million he just paid for you," he retorted, grabbing my elbow and guiding me toward Mystery Man's room.

"Two million dollars?" I asked, astounded. I tried to yank my elbow out of his grip because his manhandling was not part of the deal and he was really pissing me off. However, he grabbed me again, more firmly this time, and pulled me forward.

"What? Not enough? Greedy little thing, aren't you?" Without giving me a chance to respond, he opened the glass door to Mystery Man's room and entered with me in tow.

The odor of cigarette smoke attacked my olfactory sense, but strangely, I wasn't repulsed.

"Miss Delaine Talbot," Scott introduced me to the figure still shrouded in darkness. "Congratulations on your win, Mr. Crawford. I have a feeling she'll be worth every penny."

"Have the contract sent to my address," a deep, sultry voice said from the shadows. The cherry on the end of his cigarette blazed and lit up his features dimly before he disappeared again. "And take your hands off my property, for Christ's sake. I'm not paying for damaged goods."

Scott released his hold on me immediately, and I rubbed at the spot on the back of my arm, knowing there was going to be a bruise there by morning.

"As you wish." Scott bowed unceremoniously. "Take your time with the room, but be careful—she's a feisty one."

I wasn't really sure what I was supposed to do, so I just stood there awkwardly for what seemed like forever.

When I had about convinced myself that he might actually be planning on the two of us staying there for the duration of the two years, he finally sighed and butted out his cigarette. The light clicked on, momentarily blinding me, because my eyes had become accustomed to the dark. When they had adjusted again, I looked at him.

My stomach flipped, and I swear I think my heart skipped a beat . . . or two . . . maybe three.

He was gorgeous. And I was having a really hard time not ogling him. He simply sat there smirking as I took him in. He was dressed in a tailor-made suit, black on black. He wasn't wearing a tie, and the top buttons of his shirt were undone to reveal his collarbones and a brief peek at a sculpted chest with a smattering of hair. My eyes followed the tight tendons of his neck to his prominent jaw, shadowed with the beginnings of a beard. His lips were succulent and the perfect shade of deep pink, his nose was straight and perfect, and his eyes . . . my God, his eyes. Never had I seen a hazel so intense and infused with so many different colors, or a man with lashes that long. His dark brown hair was cut short, longer on top with the front spiked. He was quite possibly the most beautiful man I'd ever seen.

He raised his hand and raked his long fingers through his hair. Whether it was in aggravation at my ogling or out of habit, I had no idea, but it was sexy nonetheless.

I started to question why someone who looked like him would need to go to the extreme of purchasing a companion when he could obviously have anyone he wanted. But then he opened his mouth, reminding me that this was no fairy-tale encounter and things were expected of me—things I had to do whether I wanted to or not.

"Well, let's see if you're worth it," he sighed as he undid his pants and pulled out his massive cock.

I looked at him dumbfounded, because surely he didn't expect me to lose my virginity to him in a disgusting place like that. I mean, I knew I was his property, but really?

"On your knees, Delaine, or the deal is off and you can go home with the lard-ass in the other room. He really seemed to want you," he said with a sexy smirk while he stroked his glorious cock. "Show me your appreciation."

Problem number one: I had never given a blow job in my entire life.

2

gag reflex check

Lanie

"Delaine, you're wasting my time, and apparently my money."

"You want me to . . . Here? Now?" I asked nervously.

"Did I stutter?" Mystery Man asked with a raised brow.

I sank to my knees in front of him and swallowed the lump that had formed in my throat. Thank God the floor was cold, because it wasn't until then I noticed how insanely hot it had become in the small space. Heat rolled off me in waves, and I knew I must have looked redder than a hot iron. Deep breaths of air were vital in order to keep my nerves from making me throw up in his lap. That probably wouldn't have gone over very well.

He sighed in aggravation, and it only made my heart beat faster. "Put my cock in your mouth, Miss Talbot."

I leaned forward and took it, finding that I couldn't even get my hand all the way around it. Sweet Jesus! He couldn't have really expected me to fit something like that in my mouth. I made the mistake of looking up at him. His brow was raised expectantly, and there was a tic in his jaw; for just a split second he looked almost as nervous as I was. I mentally shook my head because surely that wasn't the case, so I went back to the task at hand, which was definitely a task and absolutely something I was expected to get on with.

I was sure I looked stupid as I studied his cock, trying to figure out the best way to go about doing this. All those late-night sleepovers with Dez insisting I practice things like kissing and blow jobs suddenly didn't seem so silly. I knew my way around a banana okay, but then those bananas would've had to have been jacked up with some serious steroids to compare to Mystery Man's cock.

There was a spot of something wet on the head, and I wasn't really sure what I was supposed to do about that, so I opened my mouth and licked at it with the tip of my tongue. I heard him hiss minutely and took that as a positive sign, so then I kissed it, but the kiss wasn't at all sexy. It was more like kissing my uncle Fred on his bald head, only not at all like kissing my uncle Fred on his bald head. Jesus, I didn't have a clue what I was doing, and my floundering was making my mind go to a very silly place. It was my defense mechanism. I recognized it for what it was, but that didn't change the fact it was happening at a very inappropriate time.

I closed my eyes and exhaled slowly, trying to find that very small place inside where I was a sultry vixen. A picture of his face invaded my thoughts, and I suddenly became more emboldened. I wrapped my lips around the head and gave it a little suction. Then I opened my mouth wider and took as much of him in as I could, which wasn't much. Like I said, the thing was huge. I was almost certain I was going to develop a serious case of lockjaw.

"Come on, you can take more than that," he challenged me.

I pressed forward until the head of his dick hit the back of my throat and I thought the corners of my mouth were going to split wide open. This would've been far easier if I'd had one of those snake jaws that unhinge to swallow their prey. And that's about when I really started praying that I wouldn't actually dislocate my jaw.

I pulled back and moved forward again, but this time I guess my gag reflex decided it wasn't going to cooperate. When I gagged on him involuntarily, it set off a chain reaction. In my hurry to squelch the gag and not hurl all over him, my teeth bit into the sensitive skin on his dick. He yelped in pain and then shoved me away before practically crawling up the back of his chair to get away from me and my murderous mouth.

"Goddamnit!" he shouted, and then started inspecting his dick. I hadn't even broken the skin, the big baby. "You've got to be fucking kidding me! Have you ever even sucked a dick before?" Anger marred the features on his face. Even scowling, he was still beautiful. "Because that is undoubtedly the absolute worst blow job I have ever been given."

It was official; I hated him.

"I'm sorry. I just never—"

"You've never given a blow job?" he asked incredulously. I shook my head. "Jesus Christ!" he mumbled as he ran his hands over his face and took a deep breath.

His insensitivity to the situation, or maybe his hypersensitivity to it, set me off. Even though I knew I should probably keep my mouth shut—because, let's face it, he could pretty much do whatever he wanted to me—I just couldn't take it.

"You and your glorious, colossal cock can *kiss my ass!*" I yelled with as much emphasis as I could, but I wasn't done there. "I may not be the type of girl who goes around shoving dicks in her mouth all day—I'm pretty sure you wouldn't have paid two million dollars for me if I was—and I'm sorry if I hurt you, but even if I was experienced at this sort of thing, I . . . There's just no way in hell anyone is going to get something that massive crammed down their throat. You're a freak of nature, but at least I tried, you jerk!"

Me and my nonexistent brain filter had obviously just contracted a hideous case of diarrhea of the mouth. I was probably about to lose the contract and ruin everything. He just sat there and stared at me. His face contorted from surprise to anger, and then he looked confused and maybe a little constipated. He opened and closed his mouth a couple of times as if he was about to say something and then thought better of it. Another moment passed before he turned his head to the side and then back to me.

"So, what you're saying is that you think I have a big dick, and it might be kind of spectacular?" he asked with a smug grin.

I sat back on my heels and crossed my arms over my chest, completely mortified with embarrassment because, yeah, I guess that was what I'd just said, technically. But I wasn't about to admit it for a second time.

"Do you have any sexual experience at all?"

Again I shook my head.

He sighed and ran his fingers through his hair once more. He looked like he was a thousand miles away, probably contemplating whether or not he was going to keep me. And then he finally tucked himself back into his pants and stood up, towering over me.

"Let's go."

"Where are we going?" I was ready to beg him not to sell me to Jabba the Hutt.

"We're going home," was his short reply.

"You're not mad?" I scrambled to my feet and ran to catch up with his long strides as he stormed out the door.

"Oh, I am extremely pissed, but I'm trying really hard not to be." He continued down the hallway without so much as a glance over his shoulder at me. "I suppose if I look on the bright side of things, this means that I can train you to do things the way I like them. But right now, I have a hard-on the size of Texas and I'm not exactly thrilled about it. Where are your things?"

"In some room off the hallway."

We didn't speak another word to each other as we maneuvered our way back to the room where I had changed my clothes and left my things, including my cell phone. He stood outside the door while I changed out of the bandages that were supposed to pass as attire and back into my tank top and skirt. Once I was dressed and feeling less exposed, he led me out the back entrance to Foreplay, one that I assumed was meant for these types of guests only. When we made it to the parking lot, Mystery Man walked over to a limousine where a short, blond-haired man in a black suit and driver's hat stood by the door.

"Mr. Crawford," the man greeted him with a nod and an expressionless face as he opened the back door.

"Samuel," he greeted him in turn as he put his hand on the small of my back and ushered me inside. "We're headed home for the evening."

"Yes, sir," the driver said as Mr. Crawford, aka Mystery Man, slid into the oversized backseat of the limousine next to me. Not that there wasn't plenty of room. Personal space probably wasn't a luxury I'd have much of over the next couple of years, though.

The car was moving through the streets of Chicago within seconds. Mr. Crawford exhaled a long breath and shifted in the seat as he tugged at his pants. Note to self: Don't mess with Texas. I smirked a little to myself.

"Do you live in Chicago?" he asked, breaking the silence.

"No. Hillsboro," was my short response.

I looked out the window, watching the city lights go by. The streets were littered with happy-go-lucky people who seemed to have not a care in the world. I supposed that under different circumstances, and had the world not hated me and my family, I might have been just like any one of them. But as things were, that wasn't the case.

"Why are you doing this, Delaine?"

I wasn't prepared to divulge that information, and it certainly wasn't part of my contract. I preferred not to get too personal with the man who had just purchased me.

"Why are you?" I shot back. Apparently my brain filter still wasn't working.

The scowl was back on his face again, and part of me regretted getting sassy with him when I considered all the ways he could punish me. But only a small part of me.

"You do realize that I own you now, right? You'd do well to remember your place. I'm not a cruel person by nature, but your smart mouth and snarky attitude are testing my restraint," he warned with a stern look.

I was sure I probably looked like a scared kitten right about then, because that was how I felt, but I looked him in the eye anyway, my pride not allowing me to turn away. Or maybe it was fear that made me keep him in my sights and watch for any sudden movements. More likely it was the fact that the man really was a beautiful specimen, and I cursed the needy woman in me for being so weak.

"Look, I know this isn't an ideal situation for you, and you probably have your reasons, just like I have mine," he started. "But the fact of the matter remains that we're bound together for the next two years, so it will be a lot easier on the both of us if we can at least try to get along. I don't want to fight you every step of the way. I *won't* fight you. You will do as I say, and that's that. If you don't want to tell me anything about your personal life before this, fine. I won't ask. But you belong to me and I won't tolerate insubordination, Delaine. Are we clear?"

I narrowed my eyes and clenched my teeth. "Perfectly. I'll do what you say, but don't expect me to enjoy it."

He got a wicked grin on his face then and put his hand on my bare thigh. Slowly he began to caress my skin as his fingertips moved higher, under my skirt. He leaned in toward me until I could feel his hot breath wash over my neck and my skin pebbled from the sensation.

"Oh, I think you will thoroughly enjoy it, Delaine." His

raspy voice made me feel things I should've been too disgusted to feel, and then he pressed his lips to the spot just below my ear in an openmouthed kiss while his long fingers barely pressed against my center. My stupid, traitorous body responded and I became putty in his more than capable hands. I think a slight whine may have escaped my lips when he pulled away abruptly.

"Aw, home sweet home," he said when the car came to a stop.

I was shaken from my Mystery Man–induced haze and looked out the tinted windows. The house wasn't even a house. It was huge. A mansion. I swear he could have fit a whole city inside. If I hadn't already known better, I would've said he was trying to overcompensate, but that obviously wasn't it at all.

Mr. Crawford—God, I hated referring to him by that name—stepped from the limo and held his hand out to help me. I declined his offer and got out on my own. The driveway itself was laid in brick, huge and circular with a stone water fountain in the center that was lit up with soft white lights. Pillars of water shot up into the air and rained back down into the pool of glass. As I turned to look at the rest of my surroundings, I could see nothing but perfectly cut grass and ornate shrubbery that had been sculpted into stags.

Jeez, did Edward Scissorhands live here, or what?

"Right this way, miss," Samuel said, taking my bag from my hands and drawing my attention back toward the house.

Cement statues, also in the shape of stags, adorned the posts on either side of the steps that led to the porch. Their heads were dropped down, as if positioning their giant antlers for battle with one hoof poised in the air. I could've sworn I heard a faint huff of a dare, but I was pretty sure they weren't alive.

Tall white columns bordered the entrance to the house and stretched from the oversized porch to the second story. Samuel thrust open the double doors to allow us to step inside, and Mystery Man gestured with his arm for me to go in ahead of him. The floors were marble, the ceilings tall and dome-shaped.

But the thing that really caught my attention was the staircase. It was centered in the entry and stretched to a landing at the top before it split off into two other staircases that led in opposite directions of the house. It looked like one of those get-ups where the princess appears at the top of the landing and waits to be announced to the awestruck crowd below before she descends gracefully to greet her guests.

Me, on the other hand? I'd probably trip and fall on the first step, my body curled up into a ball as I rolled down the rest and landed with a thud at the bottom. And it would *not* be graceful. At all.

"What do you think?" Mystery Man asked as he gestured with his arms wide open. Obviously, he was proud of his home.

"Meh, it's okay. If you're into the whole pretentious overkill type of thing," I said with a shrug of boredom.

In truth, I was impressed. Very impressed.

"I inherited the house. And I'm not pretentious," he said. "Let's get you upstairs and into something more comfortable so that we can get some sleep. It's been a long day, and I have a feeling it's going to be an even longer day tomorrow—and probably every day for the next two years of my life."

He turned and stalked up the stairs, leaving me to follow behind him again.

"It seems we agree on something, Mr. Crawford," I said.

He stopped abruptly and turned to look at me with a look of aggravation in his eyes. "It's Noah," he said in a solemn tone, and then continued up the stairs. "Only the help calls me Mr. Crawford."

"Well, aren't I the help? You're paying me to be here just as much as you are them," I challenged.

"Trust me, they're not getting paid nearly as much as you are." He turned on the landing to go up the right-hand staircase. "And you will be my nearly constant companion over the next couple of years. People will need to believe that we're the real deal. That's not likely going to happen if you're running around calling me Mr. Crawford."

"Fine then, *Noah*," I said, testing out the sound of it. "Which room is mine?" I asked when we reached a long hallway adorned with large paintings on the walls.

"We're at the end of the hall," he said, still forging ahead.

"Wait. We?"

"You will be sharing my bed. Was that point not clear to you?"

"But we haven't even discussed the terms of the contract," I reminded him.

He opened the door at the end of the hall and I followed him through. The second I was over the threshold, he closed it and pinned me to it with his body. "The terms are pretty simple," he said as his lips ghosted against the skin of my neck. "You belong to me, and I can do whatever I want with you."

He brought his lips to mine and kissed me firmly, but I didn't kiss him back. His movements softened and he grazed his lips over mine, trying to get me to respond.

"Kiss me, Delaine." He pressed his hips forward and that thing in his pants nudged the girliest part of me. "You just might like it."

The thought did not occur to me that he might be right, but I knew I had been pushing my luck with him already and he wasn't likely to keep taking my crap. My mother needed that surgery, and I was sure that we'd be a whole hell of a lot more intimate than this over our time together, so I really had no choice but to suck it up and give in.

I took a deep breath, my chest pressing against his, and then I parted my lips and took his bottom lip between mine. He moaned and repositioned himself so that his thigh was between my legs, his hands on my hips, and his head tilted to the side for better access. I let him deepen the kiss when his tongue swept across my lip, and I knew instantly I would never regret it.

It wasn't like I'd kissed a lot of guys or was some sort of expert, but the things that man could do with his tongue . . .

I placed my hands on his biceps, feeling the bulge of muscle that flexed beneath his jacket. I wanted to be closer, and I thought he might actually appreciate my taking some initiative, so I moved my hands under the jacket to his chest. Then I moved them over his shoulders to force the jacket to slide down his arms. He caught it with one hand and laid it over the chair beside us before grabbing my hips again and pulling me closer. I cupped my hands around either side of his neck and wrapped my tongue around his, sucking ever so gently. He moaned into my mouth and then unexpectedly pushed away, leaving me standing there with my eyes closed, head cocked to the side, hands still suspended in air, and lips puckered in kissing mode.

It was kind of like that awkward moment in *Dirty Dancing* when Baby was still getting her groove thang on with thin air after Johnny walked away and left her standing alone in a room full of strangers.

"See, I told you you'd like it," he said with a half grin.

How was it fair that he could just stand there acting like it was no big deal while I was about to burst a blood vessel willing my body not to explode?

"Don't worry, we'll do that some more, but business before pleasure," he said, taking a couple of steps backward. "The terms of the contract: I will make sure that the money is wired anonymously to the account that you have specified, as you asked. I expect you to be discreet about the details of our relationship, and I will do the same in turn. For all intents and purposes, my family and colleagues will believe that we met on one of my many business trips and that we're deeply in love. You will accompany me to various social functions while conducting yourself as the well-mannered lady that you're expected to be. At my home, you will share my bed and make yourself available to me in whatever physical way that I need. And I must warn you that I have quite the imagination. Have I missed anything?"

Probably, but my head was still swimming from that kiss and I couldn't think straight, so I just shook my head.

"Good," he said as he lay back on the oversized bed (I was

beginning to see a trend with all the oversized things surrounding this man) and propped himself up on his forearms.
"Now, take off your clothes."

"Excuse me?" I practically choked out.

"Delaine, we're going to be seeing a whole lot of each other
in the nude. So you might want to drop that modesty-and-
shyness bit." He looked me up and down and licked his lips
suggestively. His eyes met mine, and the expression in those
piercing hazel eyes nearly brought me to my knees. "You show
me yours and then I'll show you mine."

That was a good deal, right? I slipped off my shoes while
grabbing the hem of my shirt, pulling it quickly over my head.

"Slower," he said in a husky voice, stopping me.

I rolled my eyes because that was so clichéd. "Would you
like to put on music so that I can do the whole striptease for
you, too?"

"Now you're getting it," he said with a wink, and then he
crawled across his bed and grabbed a remote control off the
nightstand. He pushed a button and sultry music began to
play, although I really couldn't tell where it was coming from
because it seemed to be coming from everywhere.

"No! I . . . I can't. I mean . . . I don't—"

"I'm just kidding," he said, turning it back off and returning to his spot on the bed. "Some other time, maybe."

I let out a long breath, then slid down the zipper on the
back of my skirt and let it fall to the floor before stepping out
of it.

"Stop right there." Noah got off the bed and walked toward
me. I crossed one arm over my chest and the other over my

stomach self-consciously before I dropped my eyes to the floor. He walked in a circle around me and I could feel his eyes on me, all over me. And then I felt his touch as he stopped behind me and pressed his chest to my back. The back of his fingertips ran down both of my arms until he reached my hands, and then he took each of them in his and pulled them away from my body.

"Don't hide from me." His lips skirted across the crook of my neck.

He pulled back a bit and let my hands fall to my sides before stroking back up along my arms and over my shoulders to roam down my back. He didn't stop until he reached the clasp of my bra, and before I realized it, he had it undone. He slid his fingers under the straps and slowly pushed them over my shoulders until they fell down my arms, exposing my breasts to him. I could feel the heat of his body against mine again, and his warm breath spilled over my skin as he exhaled slowly. A trail of openmouthed kisses were placed along the length of my neck and over my shoulder, leaving a path of flames in their wake. I shivered, but I was pretty sure it was from his attentions and not from being cold. My body was heating up to the point that I thought I might catch fire.

And then I felt his hands on my hips. His fingers dipped beneath the band of my panties and he began to push them down, oh so slowly. I stiffened, unsure what I should do.

"Relax. I just want to see you. All of you," he said in a comforting voice.

I took a deep breath and tried to relax a bit. It wasn't exactly easy to do, though, because like I said, the man was beautiful, and under normal circumstances I'd want to be all over him.

And then my panties were around my ankles.

I stood there naked as a jaybird, completely exposed and vulnerable to the man who had just purchased me for his own personal pleasure.

"There, that wasn't so bad, was it?" He paused for an answer I didn't have to give, and he knew it. "My turn. You can keep your back to me, or you can turn around and watch."

I knew what he was doing. He was making me choose. Only there really wasn't much of a choice. If I stayed where I was, I'd look like a scared little girl. And if I turned around, I'd look like I wanted this just as much as he did. Win-win for him; for me, damned if I did, damned if I didn't.

So I turned around. If I was going to lose, I wanted my consolation prize. And an eyeful of bonchickawahwah was consolation enough at that point.

Noah gave me that annoyingly sexy smirk again, obviously happy with my decision. Secretly, so was I. I watched as he slowly undid each button of his shirt with his nimble fingers. They were thick and long and, well, porntastic, I believe Dez would say. He pulled his shoulders back as he shrugged off the shirt, revealing one very lucky wifebeater.

Enough was enough. I was there for a reason.

I stepped toward him as he reached for the hem of the T-shirt and stilled his hands. He raised a questioning brow, and I mirrored his expression, daring him to stop me. But he didn't. I placed my hands on his hips and ran them up his sides, tugging at the shirt and dragging it up his long torso. Noah raised his arms and allowed me to pull it over his head, and I tossed it to the floor. Well, I tried to toss it to the floor, but he was quick and caught it in midfall, gracefully draping it over the back of the chair with his jacket and dress shirt.

Before he could face me again, my hands were on his belt and working it loose. Without removing it, I tackled the button of his pants and then the zipper.

"Anxious?" he asked with a sly smile. My only response was to look him square in the eye and shove his pants over his hips. Under the pants? Mouthwatering boxer briefs. Red boxer briefs. Red boxer briefs that were the home of a very proud, helmet-wearing soldier.

Now, I'd seen his marvelous cock up close earlier, but there was just something about the way the man filled out a pair of underwear that really got my gears a-grindin'. You could see just enough detail of what was beneath, while still maintaining an element of mystery; a goody basket waiting to be unwrapped, if you will.

Noah hooked his thumbs under the waistband, maintaining eye contact with me the entire time, and took them off. It wasn't until he grabbed his discarded underwear and turned his back to me that I allowed myself to check him out more thoroughly. He walked toward a set of doors on the other side of the room that I assumed was a closet, and I let my eyes roam over his strong shoulders and down his muscular back to . . .

"You're checking out my ass, aren't you?" he asked without turning around.

I snapped my head to look away before he could actually catch me. "Um, not at all." Of course my voice cracked, forcing me to clear my throat.

"Uh-huh, sure," he said as he shut the doors of the closet behind him. He walked over to his jacket, grabbed a pack of cigarettes and a lighter from the inside pocket, and then strolled over to the couch next to the window and sat down, still completely naked. I wasn't sure what I was supposed to do, so I just watched as he lit up a cigarette and set the lighter and pack down on the table beside him.

I was hypnotized by the way his lips made love to the cigarette with each draw of nicotine. He reached down and grabbed his dick with his other hand and began to stroke it while his eyes raked over my body.

"Come here," he said, motioning to me with a backward jerk of his head.

I hesitated, watching his cock harden before my eyes. With absolutely no shame at all, he never stopped fondling himself as he spoke to me. "It's time for your first lesson. I'm going to teach you how to suck a cock properly."

I'll admit I gulped. With good reason, given my first attempt. But it was his penis's funeral. Knowing there was no other choice, I walked over to where he sat and kneeled between his opened legs to await further instruction.

"You misunderstand. I want you to sit on the couch." He extinguished the cigarette in the ashtray on the table before standing and then pulling me to do so as well. I sat on the couch where Noah placed me, and he was right in front of me. All of him.

"I'm going to fuck your mouth now, Delaine. It's the easiest way I know to show you. Once you see what I like, it should be easier for you the next time. I hope you're a fast learner."

He took his dick in one hand and put the other on the back

of my head, urging me forward until the tip of his cock touched my lips. "Kiss it. And don't be afraid to use your tongue."

I opened my mouth and wrapped my tongue around the head of his dick, letting my lips close over it.

He moaned. "Fuck, that's so good. Keep going. A little suction this time."

I flattened my tongue and took the whole head in my mouth, sucking on it like a popsicle. I could do this. Plus, listening to his instructions sort of made me want to do a good job.

"Put your hand around the base and squeeze just a little bit."

I did as he said and felt him harden further in my mouth. He pushed my head forward so that I took even more of him in while his hips met my movements and then pulled back again.

"Oh, God, yeah. Just like that," he growled, and pushed all the way inside until he hit the back of my throat. Not wanting there to be a repeat performance from Foreplay, I moved my hand up so he couldn't go any further.

Noah wound his fingers in the hair on the back of my head and moved me back and forth slowly. Once my mouth became accustomed to his invasion, he moved faster. The room was silent with the exception of the wet sucking sounds I made and the deep groans that escaped his throat while he watched himself fuck my mouth.

He propped one foot on the couch as his hips pumped his cock in and out. His pace quickened and he began to grunt with each thrust. I was shamefully wet between my thighs and horrified I might ruin his couch. I moaned at the thrill of knowing it was pleasurable for him, which must have been a good thing, because he moaned in turn and thrust harder.

"Fuck! I knew when I saw that fuckable mouth of yours that you'd excel at this." His voice was all breathy and raspy, and he was still fucking my mouth, and I wanted him to touch me because, good Lord, he was sexy.

The more he moaned and groaned and even growled, the more confident I felt. His balls were swinging back and forth and I wanted to see what they felt like. So I reached my other hand up and cupped him gently.

"Shit, shit, shit! You're going to make me come."

I really wanted him to, but I had no clue what I was supposed to do about that.

"Oh . . . God," he grunted, fucking my mouth faster. Long fingers pulled my hair and tugged my head forward and then back again to meet his thrusts. His grip was so tight that it should've hurt, but really, it only turned me on more.

"Let's see if you can swallow." His voice was rough, and before I could register what that meant, he thrust deep into my mouth until he was once again touching the back of my throat. A guttural growl sounded from his chest, and then thick, hot liquid shot down my throat.

I nearly gagged until I overrode my instincts and started swallowing. I'd be lying if I told you it tasted better than chocolate or fruit candy or some other incredulous stuff like that. But it wasn't terrible, either. Common sense told me that I should be thoroughly grossed out, but given the reaction I just got from him—this total stranger who'd paid two million dollars to own me as his personal sex slave so that he could do this to me whenever he wanted—it was tolerable.

He pulled his dick out of my mouth and smiled down at me. "Now that was a motherfucking blow job."

I wiped the leftover wetness from my mouth with the back of my hand and did my best to look disgusted because he didn't need to know that I'd sort of enjoyed it. But he only chuckled in response.

"There's mouthwash in the bathroom."

He stepped away from me and took my hand, pulling me up from the couch and leading me over to another set of doors. We both went inside, and he pulled out a bottle of mouthwash from under the sink and handed it to me. I poured some in the cup and swished it around my mouth while he grabbed a washcloth and wet it and then wiped himself off. Even limp, his cock was stunning.

"Here," he said, pulling out a new toothbrush, still wrapped.

We stood at the his-and-her sinks and brushed our teeth in awkward silence. His reflection kept grinning at me around his toothbrush, and I was pretty sure he was getting a kick out of watching my tits jiggle with my brushing motions. I couldn't stand the smug look on his face any longer, so I averted my eyes and looked around the bathroom instead. It was a bathroom designed for a king, and the centerpiece of the whole room was the bathtub. It was a Jacuzzi big enough to hold at least four people, and it had a bronze faucet on one end. Two steps led to the opening, with two more on the inside of the tub. Inside there were benches about halfway up each side that functioned as a sitting area. I swear he could have easily thrown a party inside that thing. And then I wondered if he ever actually had. For some reason, I wanted to reach out and smack him in the back of the head for that thought.

What the hell was wrong with me? I was standing in my birthday suit, brushing my teeth next to a man I had just met and still didn't know anything about, who had just fucked my mouth royally, and I wanted to smack him for throwing a wild orgy in his gargantuan bathtub . . . in my head. His cock must have impaled my brain, because that reaction wasn't making a bit of sense.

Squelching the overpowering urge to spit my toothpaste in his face, I spat it in the sink instead. My mouth was clean, but I still felt dirty.

"Let's go to bed," he said after he spat and rinsed.

I gave him a death glare but followed him out of the bathroom anyway.

"Um, excuse me," I said, stopping in my tracks as he walked over to the bed. "I'm still naked. Where are my things?"

"I sleep in the nude, and now so do you." He pulled the covers back and slipped under them.

I huffed, then stomped across the room to the other side of the bed and climbed in also, making sure to stay as far on my side as I could get without falling out of it.

"Come here, Delaine."

He had to be joking. It wasn't enough that I was sleeping in the nude? It wasn't enough that he was sleeping in the nude? It wasn't enough that we had just brushed our teeth in the nude after he fucked my mouth in the nude and made me think about him having wild orgies in the bathtub in the nude? Now he wanted to snuggle in the nude, too?

"I said come here." His arm stretched across the space between us and wrapped around my waist, yanking me into his chest. "There, that's better," he said as he nuzzled his face into my neck. "You better get some sleep. You're going to need it."

How was I supposed to be able to sleep with a humongous cock pressed to my ass?

3
rub-a-dub-dub

Noah

I awoke the next morning, my body still heavy with sleep, my dick hard as a fucking rock and wedged between something warm and soft. My hand was cupped around something unmistakably feminine and perky, and I squeezed it to make sure it was real. I hate fake tits, and even though I had seen Delaine's through the scrap of fabric she'd been wearing at the club—and then really saw them when I made her strip for me last night—you just never knew for sure until you felt them. The cosmetic surgery industry was making progress in leaps and bounds, but they could never compare to a perfect set of real tits in your hands.

And make no mistake about it: these were real, and undeniably perfect.

I ran my thumb over her nipple, thoroughly enjoying the way it pebbled under my touch. Delaine might have a mouth on her—boy, did she ever have a mouth on her—but I suspected that once she'd experienced my touch, she'd use that mouth to beg me for more rather than to see how many of my buttons she could push in a single breath.

Regretfully I climbed out of bed, and it didn't escape my notice that Delaine groaned in protest. She was still in a deep sleep and likely didn't realize what she was doing. Had she been awake, I'm sure she would've been relieved.

That fact should've made me feel like an asshole—after all, I, a perfect stranger, was making her do things she didn't really want to do—but she was the one who'd signed on for this. Besides, there were indications that she quite possibly liked being forced to unleash the sexual beast that she'd kept hidden away all of her life. I'd seen the look in her eyes when she had my cock in her mouth last night. She loved it, which was a good thing, because I planned on sticking my cock there a whole lot more.

I trudged to the bathroom and ran a hot bath in my over-sized Jacuzzi. It would be the first time I'd used it since I had found *them* there.

I was the primary shareholder of my father's company, Scarlet Lotus. My mother, Elizabeth, who had been a Buddhist, had named the company. The lotus flower starts as a seed in the mud beneath a body of water and gradually grows upward until it reaches the surface to bloom. The color red symbolizes love, passion, compassion, and all matters of the heart. My father, Noah senior, felt the name suited the company well. Scarlet Lotus was where people could bring their unique ideas—ideas that were near and dear to their hearts, but which they just didn't have the capital to bring to fruition—and watch them grow until they blossomed. For a portion of the proceeds, Scarlet Lotus helped them do just that. My mother had insisted that the company give back to the community, and so charity work had become just as much a part of what we did as idea development.

My parents had died in a car accident almost six years ago, leaving everything to me: the money, the house, and all the shares of the company that my father had owned. None of it could ever begin to replace them, and I was nowhere near deserving.

My father's partner, Harrison Stone, had retired three years ago and handed over all of his stock to his only son, David. David and I had been the best of friends while growing up. With our parents' success, it was nearly impossible to tell who was befriending you because they genuinely liked you and who was just sucking up to you because of the money. David and I had learned the hard way that we could only depend on each other. We were always getting into trouble, spurring each other on to do the most ridiculous stunts. Of course, our parents always cleaned up our messes; they couldn't have the heirs of the Scarlet Lotus fortune all over the tabloids. It would have been very bad for business. Plus we'd be running the company someday, and no one in their right mind would put their valuable ideas in the hands of a couple of punks with a reputation for screwing up.

I'd just never thought I'd be twenty-two and fresh out of college when my day came. David had already been shadowing his father by that point and really learning the ropes. Together we were invincible, and we quickly became the talk of the business world. When we became partners, like our fathers, we already knew we were a good fit.

Or so we thought.

It turned out that David had never agreed with how much money the company was "squandering" on charitable deeds. He was a greedy motherfucker and thought lining his own pocket was far more important than helping the less fortunate. But it had been my mother's passion, and thus my father's, so I wasn't budging. Plus, it made me feel really good to give something back.

About a year ago I had flown to New York to meet with an agency that specialized in community projects to keep kids off the streets. When I had returned, I found David in my Jacuzzi with Julie, my girlfriend of two years.

To be precise, he was fucking her in the ass while she screamed, "Your cock is bigger than Noah's!"

That was a lie. I walked in on them, so I saw for myself. Regardless, I wasn't exactly worried about that point at the time. I was in love with Julie, and David knew it. Well, I'd thought I was in love with her.

He also knew I had planned on asking her to marry me when I got back from that trip, and he'd done his best to talk me out of it. David was a chauvinistic ass. He truly believed that the only thing a woman was good for was satiating his sexual desires.

"Keep 'em naked and on their knees or back twenty-four/seven, and make sure they know their place," he'd said. "There's too much pussy in the world to be tied down to one woman."

He'd told me men like us couldn't trust any woman because they were all a bunch of gold-digging whores anyway; either they wanted a fat bank account or they wanted a fat cock. He thought I was stupid for falling in love, that it made me vulnerable and weak.

He was right. I was broken after I caught him with Julie, but so was his nose, a kneecap, and three of his ribs.

He'd fucked her just to prove a point. And although our friendship was over, the partnership was not. It wasn't that I didn't try to buy him out. I did, but he'd refused to sell. And there was no way I was giving up the company my father and mother had worked so hard to build. So I bit the bullet and went to work every day with my head held high and conducted business as usual.

I learned my lesson and refused to let a woman get close enough to hurt me again.

But I was lonely. And slightly addicted to pussy.

Sure, I'd had flings with several women, but I'd always cut them off the second they got a little too close for comfort. Sex was a very therapeutic way for me to get out my frustrations, but women didn't seem to want to stick around for just that purpose. There were some who had said they understood that it was just sex for me, but inevitably they'd get clingy and want me to feel things I simply didn't and wouldn't, so they had to go.

I could have random one-night stands, but that was like playing Russian roulette with my dick, even with a condom, and I'd grown quite attached to it over my young life, thank you very much.

What I wanted was the same woman in my bed every night and every morning, someone to greet me when I arrived home after a long and trying day at work, eager to please me. Someone who would tend to my every need, no strings attached. Yeah, I knew it was every man's fantasy and that it wasn't likely to come true for most men, but I had enough money to buy that fantasy. So I did.

And that was what had led me to Delaine.

In my world, there was always talk between men. You hear about women gossiping all the time, but men are just as guilty. The difference is that we don't make it as obvious.

One afternoon when I had been golfing with a Scarlet Lotus investor, I'd heard about the auction. I'd done what little research I could on the place, and after speaking to the proprietor, my interest was piqued. Obviously I didn't want to own someone against her will, but Scott had assured me that women on the "menu" were there voluntarily and that on that night in particular I could find a virgin. A virgin was necessary. I was worried about diseases or spending an insane amount of money on a woman only to find out that she was already knocked up with some other guy's baby.

That wasn't the least bit appealing to me.

As I sat in that booth, completely darkened because I didn't want anyone to recognize me, I let every girl showcased go without even so much as a bid. That is, until *she* stood on the podium. Delaine Talbot.

I had read through her specs and the contract she proposed and was intrigued. I had naturally wondered what would make a seemingly wholesome woman like her do such an outlandish thing, but I pushed my curiosity down because, like I said, I didn't want there to be any strings attached. She was offering two years on the contract, and that was right up my alley. Two years of constantly getting my rocks off in any way I could fathom was plenty of time to get it out of my system or find someone else. And when she was gone, I could always cite the age-old reason "We just grew apart."

When I saw Delaine I knew that I had to have her.

Not only was the contract ideal, but she was a perfect specimen. She looked just as wholesome as her specs, not overly voluptuous or fake-looking. I had wavered at the end of the auction, not really sure if I wanted to follow through, but then she gave me this look, like she was silently begging me to keep her out of the grasp of the disgusting tub of lard in the other room.

I might have felt a little sorry for her, which probably should have been the first indication that this was a bad idea. But I made the final bid regardless.

The second indication had come when she had gotten on her knees and sunk her teeth into my dick. That hurt like a motherfucker and let me know without a doubt that I'd bitten off more than I could chew—which was ironic, because she had been the one doing the biting, but whatever. The point is that she'd never even given a goddamn blow job before. Really? I knew she was a virgin, but in my experience most virgins had at least done other things to get off without breaking the seal, so to speak.

And the biggest indicator? That fucking smart mouth of hers.

This was a business arrangement. It was fucked up and like nothing I'd ever done before, but it was a business arrangement nonetheless. I had every intention of abiding by my end of the contract, and I expected her to do the same.

If I was being honest, though, her snarky attitude kind of

turned me on. I don't think I could've gotten as hard with someone who was completely subservient to my every whim. She had fire and ice running through her veins, and she wasn't going to make this easy for me.

Which was exactly the thing that was going to make this even more exciting for me.

I wasn't normally an asshole, but I took business very seriously. Plus I was a horny motherfucker and she showed a lot of promise when I fucked her mouth into submission, even cupping my balls without having been told to do so. Teaching her to do things the way I like them, and watching her sexuality bud and flourish was going to be an awesome sight to behold. And I had a front-row seat.

I shut the faucet off once the tub was full and went out to the bedroom. I pulled back the sheet and ran my hands over the creamy flesh of her ass. Technically, that was my ass now. She shifted a little in her sleep and her eyebrows puckered.

"Delaine, it's time to get up," I said in a soft voice.

"Hmm?" she murmured, but made no attempt to open her eyes.

I leaned in close to her ear. "Get your ass up, or I'm going to ram my cock into it," I said with more assertion and then ran the tip of my finger over her asshole, applying a bit of pressure to accentuate my point.

She shot straight up out of bed then, looking dazed and confused until her eyes focused and she looked at me. I could see the moment that she realized where she was and why she was there. Her hair was a tousled mess of knots and tangles, and what little bit of eye makeup she wore was smudged under her eyes.

"It's time for my bath," I told her.

"So? What's that got to do with me?" she snapped, plopping back onto the bed and covering herself with the sheet.

And guess what that smart mouth did to me at that exact moment? That's right. My cock became instant titanium.

I picked up her tiny frame and hoisted her over my shoulder as I carried her toward the bathroom. She kicked her legs in protest and smacked at my naked ass, but little did she know she was only spurring me on.

I tossed her into the bathtub and laughed when she landed with a thud. The water shot up and doused her hair, causing it to hang limply in her face. She looked like a drowned cat. *Mmm . . . wet pussy.*

"What the hell did you do that for?" she shrieked, smacking her hair back.

"Because you're going to bathe me and I don't want to hear any mouth about it," I answered, getting into the tub as well.

She tried to move away from me, but I grabbed her forearms and pulled her to straddle my lap instead. My dick was wedged between us and she gasped when she realized I was already hard for her.

"There now. This," I said, pushing up so that she could feel my length, "feels so much better. Wouldn't you agree?"

She seethed. "I really hate you."

"I really don't care," I retorted. "Now, wash my hair, and do try to be sensual about it."

She huffed but grabbed the bottle of shampoo anyway. I closed my eyes and just enjoyed the feeling of her hot little pussy perched over my throbbing hardness as she massaged my scalp with her fingers. I noticed she was scraping her nails into my skin, probably to try to deter me from wanting her to do this ever again, but it only had the opposite effect.

I fucking loved the rough stuff, and she wasn't even scratching the surface.

I hummed in appreciation and bucked my hips into her, and I knew I wasn't imagining things; she was pushing back. Her breathing was shallower and I could tell that she was trying to maintain her composure and not let on that she was aroused. And then she leaned forward and rinsed my hair with the spray nozzle, the tips of her nipples brushing across my lips. I opened my eyes to peek and saw her ample cleavage perched right in front of my face, so I stuck my tongue out and flicked her nipple.

"Oh, God," she gasped, and immediately backed away.

"Uh-uh," I tsked. "Bring those pretty titties back up here, Delaine. You're not done. My hair still has soap in it."

She narrowed her eyes at me, but climbed back onto my lap anyway. I heard her suck in a breath as she leaned forward again, keeping her back bowed to keep her tits out of my face, but I put my hand on her back and pressed her forward, capturing her nipple between my lips at the same time.

Again she gasped, and I smiled around her nipple as my tongue got its swirl on. My other hand went to her other breast and massaged it, my thumb running over the hardened peak while I pushed my hips into her again. Her body relaxed and she leaned into me as I sucked on her nipple and then let my teeth gently scrape across the sensitive skin.

She was done rinsing my hair. I could tell because the spray nozzle was just hanging limply from her hands, but she was now arching her back and pushing her tit closer to my mouth. I moaned and released that nipple with a pop to give my attention to the other one. My tongue flicked over the pebbled bud like a serpent, and then I roughly sucked it into my mouth.

I lifted her hips and resituated her in my lap so that the tip of me was right at her entrance. When I pushed forward a little, she stiffened and braced her hands on my shoulders.

"Shh, I'm not going to," I assured her. "I just want you to feel me there."

I shifted forward a bit to apply more pressure and then groaned out loud when the head of my dick barely entered her.

"I can't wait to fuck you," I mumbled into her skin. I pulled her off me and repositioned us so that she was now sitting next to me, because if I didn't, I was going to fuck her right then, and I wanted to prolong the anticipation and play some more.

I leaned in to nuzzle her, placing hungry kisses along the length of her neck while one hand held her by the back of her head and the other ran along the inside of her thigh.

"Have you ever had an orgasm, Delaine?" I skimmed my fingers over the soft folds at the apex of her thighs and heard her swallow hard before she choked out a no.

"Mmm," I hummed at her ear. "I get to be the first at everything. You have no idea how incredibly sexy that is."

My fingers dipped between her folds and I stroked her, avoiding the little bundle of nerves. Her head fell back against the tub, opening her neck up further for me. I removed my fingers and ran them back down the inside of her thigh until I reached the back of her knee to pull her leg over one of my thighs, and then I made a slow and torturous path back up her leg.

"I'm going to make you come, Delaine," I whispered into her ear.

The mounds of her breasts peaked over the water, revealing her perfect nipples with each shuddery breath she took. I made one light stroke from her entrance to her clit, repeating the path with more pressure. She was still with the exception of her breathing, and I lightly sucked at the sensitive spot below her ear.

"It's okay to enjoy my touch. I see no reason why I should be the only one to gain pleasure from our little arrangement." I dipped one finger into her. Her walls clamped down around me and I sucked in a breath. "Goddamn, you're tight. I think the thought alone of sticking my cock into that tight pussy might be enough to make me come so hard I lose my fucking mind."

I pumped my finger in and out of her as my thumb began to make circles around her clit.

"Would you like to see that, Delaine?" I asked, my voice thick with lust. "Would you like to see me lose my fucking mind while the thought of being inside you makes me come?"

She didn't answer, but the way her eyes became hooded and her hips started moving forward to meet the thrust of my finger told me all I needed to know. I inserted another finger and she moaned, her head falling to the side to face me.

And then *she* kissed *me*.

Delaine sucked my bottom lip between hers before shoving her tongue into my mouth to stroke mine. I pulled back because I liked to be the one in control, but I kept my lips just over hers.

"Touch your breast," I whispered. "Help me make you feel good."

I didn't really need her help, but I wanted her to open up more and explore her own sexuality. Plus, watching a woman touch herself just happened to be sexy as hell. I watched as she cupped her breast and pulled at her nipple with her index finger and thumb.

"Goddamn, that's perfect." I groaned and pumped my fingers into her harder and faster.

I pulled my fingers out and stroked along her folds until I could manipulate her clit, softly running my fingers back and forth over the taut bundle of nerves. Then I quickly dipped them back into her pussy and curled them in, finding her special spot.

"More," she moaned against my mouth before she claimed it in another passionate kiss. It appeared I had a very eager beaver on my hands—pun definitely fucking intended.

I shifted my body and turned toward her, releasing the kiss and dipping my head until my mouth was just below the water and sucking on her right nipple while she continued to manipulate the other. I could feel her walls tighten around my fingers, and I knew she was almost there. My fingers moved in and out, curling in to stroke her G-spot. I looked up at her from beneath my lashes and saw that she was watching me. Her mouth dropped open and she arched her back as a moan started low in her chest and finally escaped her lips. The walls of her pussy constricted against my fingers and she tried to clamp her thighs together, but I caught a knee between my legs and held her still.

"Those are my fingers you're getting off on, Delaine. Mine. And this feeling you're having now is going to be so much more intense when it's my cock instead," I told her, and then claimed her open mouth with my own.

She responded immediately, hungrily devouring my mouth in return until her orgasm subsided and she was a heaving puddle of postorgasmic bliss in my hands.

When I removed my fingers, I immediately stood and stepped from the tub, my dick still hard as an iron rod with water dripping from the tip. "Finish your bath," I told her nonchalantly as I wrapped a towel around myself. "I have to go to work. Make yourself at home, but I expect you to be waiting for me by the door when I return at six. Do you understand?"

Her narrowed eyes were back again—obviously she didn't like the change in my attitude—but she nodded her understanding anyway. I might have given her the most intimate moment of her life, but we both needed to remember that this was still just a business arrangement.

"Sure thing, boss," she said snidely, and then saluted me.

"Hey, you know that little slice of heaven I just gave you? Well, if you'd like to be feeling any more of that instead of me simply using your body for my own pleasure, then I suggest you watch that smart little mouth of yours," I warned, running the tip of my finger over her bottom lip. "Of course, I could always just stick something in it to keep you quiet." I knew that pissed her off, and, wanting to piss her off even more, I bent over the tub and said, "Where's my kiss goodbye, woman?"

She reluctantly leaned forward, and I kissed the tip of her nose instead of her mouth.

"Be a good girl today," I said with a smirk and then waltzed toward my bedroom, knowing she was watching my ass again. Before I reached the door, I stopped, flexed one butt cheek at a time, and then looked back over my shoulder and gave her a wink. As I suspected, her mouth was hanging open. When her eyes finally left my ass and she looked up, Delaine grabbed the loofah and threw it at me. I stepped out of the way just as it landed on the floor with a wet thwack.

"I hate you!" she called after me.

"Maybe, but you obviously love my ass!" I yelled back with a chuckle.

She was going to be too much fun to fuck with.

4

double agent coochie

Noah

I couldn't help but smile smugly the whole drive into work. Knowing that Delaine would be waiting for me at home when I returned was definitely going to make the day a bit more bearable. Or unbearable, considering I'd probably be thinking about all the naughty things I wanted to do to my million-dollar girl, and have her do to me, for the duration of the day. Even that millisecond of a thought forced me to rearrange the uncomfortable hardness that seemed to have decided to take up residence in my pants.

But I was a man of business, and business came before pleasure. So the second Samuel opened my door and I stepped onto the pavement that led to the revolving glass entrance of my second home, my smile was gone. Stone-faced Crawford had entered the building.

I was known as a hard-ass around the office. Employees who had been there since my father's day had been shocked to see his rambunctious son morph into a cutthroat wheeler-dealer. But the business world was a cold, cruel bitch, and to stay ahead, you had to keep your guard up or be prepared to have your balls handed to you at the first sign of weakness.

Mason, the only man I trusted around this place, greeted me as I stepped through the door.

Mason Hunt was my right-hand man, my personal assistant, and probably the closest thing I had to a friend. He and his wife, Polly, pretty much took care of every aspect of my life. Mason had my back at the office, and Polly took care of my personal life. She ran my home, overseeing all of the staff and my expenses, so I never had to be bothered with the task. The maids, gardeners, and cooks were there and gone before I got home, for which I was grateful. She was also my personal shopper and made sure I looked damn good for both business and pleasure. Multitasker extraordinaire.

She was really very good at what she did, as was Mason. They worked together like a well-oiled piece of machinery. I'd like to think I had something to do with their getting together. After all, tending to me on a daily basis meant their paths had to cross pretty often. Despite their differences, they complemented each other. Mason was a laid-back, cool motherfucker, tall, southern, and never without his favorite cowboy boots. Polly was just a hyperactive little shit who bounced all over the place. Short and highly social, she apparently never wore the same outfit twice. Not that I'd ever really noticed, but I caught that little snippet of information during one of her rants, which I usually tried to tune out. Polly was the yin to Mason's yang, so it seemed inevitable that they would end up together.

"Hunt," I greeted him as we walked side by side to my personal elevator. Yes, I had a personal elevator. I couldn't stand to be stuck in a tin box with twenty other people crowding me, each one wearing a different cologne or coughing and sneezing all over the goddamn place.

Mason stuck the key into the lock and opened the doors so that I could step through ahead of him. I put my briefcase down and sat on the red velvet couch that stretched along the interior wall. The ceiling and each wall was mirrored to make the small space look bigger. Bigger was always better.

"So, how did it go?" he asked as he pushed the button for the fortieth floor and took a seat on the opposite end of the couch.

I'd been single for quite some time, and Polly had been relentlessly trying to set me up on dates with women she considered to be a good match for me. To stave off her attempts, I finally broke down and told her that I'd been secretly seeing someone that I'd met on one of my trips to Los Angeles. She bought it and stopped trying to play matchmaker, but then she started hounding me about wanting to meet the mystery woman. Usually I could give someone "the look" and they knew to back off, but not Polly. She wasn't the least bit intimidated by me. I'd told her that I was going to ask my mystery lady to move in with me last night—you know, just in case I actually found something I liked at Foreplay and followed through on making a purchase, which I had.

"She said yes," I answered. "I told her to leave all of her stuff behind and I flew her in last night. She's at the house now."

"What? That's great!" He clapped me on the shoulder, his congratulations for the major step I'd taken.

"Yeah, I'm pretty psyched about it," I said with a smile, because it was true. My dick hardened minutely of its own accord to further prove the point.

We spent the rest of the ride in polite conversation. Mason was never one to pry into my personal affairs unless Polly threatened to withhold sex if he didn't at least try to get something out of me. I threw him a bone every now and then to keep him out of the doghouse, but he never pushed me. Today was no exception. He knew *she* was there, but I still hadn't told either of them who *she* was.

Mason reminded me that Polly would be stopping by my house after lunch to tend to the shopping and check on the household staff. That freaked me out. Delaine and I hadn't discussed the specifics of what story we were going to give to my acquaintances, or whether she even wanted to go by her actual name, for that matter. I knew the maids would keep their mouths shut and do their jobs, but not Polly.

I stepped off the elevator and nodded to a couple of other employees in polite greeting as I passed them on the way to my workplace suite in the west corner. Mason's desk was set up just outside my office. All the exterior spaces had floor-to-ceiling windows, red carpets, and white walls with green accents in the décor—the same color scheme as the red lotus.

I swung open the heavy wooden door to my office and closed it behind me before rushing over to my desk and picking up the telephone to dial my own home. I had to talk to Delaine and make sure we hashed out some details before Hurricane Polly showed up. Polly would start her supersleuthing and would put two and two together, and the truth about our arrangement would be out before I'd even had the chance to get my dick wet. In hindsight, I probably should've had all this figured out before I decided to purchase a woman, but you know what they say about hindsight.

There was no answer at the house.

Of course there was no answer. Delaine probably didn't feel comfortable answering my phone, but I was now beginning to sweat in my suit, imagining all the ways this could blow up in my face when Polly arrived to do her job.

In a panic, I picked up my briefcase and walked back out the door, dialing Samuel on my way past Mason's desk and telling him to swing back around to pick me up. Mason stopped me before I could make a break for it. "Daniel called and said he's waiting for you to let him know if you're dropping by today," he said, confused.

Daniel Crawford, my uncle the doctor.

"Shit, I forgot all about that. I'll call him from my cell. Not sure what time I'll be back, but I have to take care of some things," I said as I pushed the door open and slipped out into the hall.

You'd think Delaine had sucked out all of my fucking brain cells last night, the way I was screwing up. Maybe she had.

And there was that damn hard-on again . . .

"Crawford!" David's voice boomed from the other end of the hall, where his office suite was located, before he started making his way toward me. "What the hell is this about?"

I sighed and turned toward him, my hand already balling into a fist and ready to rebreak his nose if he started trying to push my buttons. For the most part, we were able to stay out of each other's way, but because we were partners, it was impossible to avoid each other entirely.

"What?" I asked with my teeth clenched.

"Ten percent of what we earned last quarter was sent to charities!" He held the quarterly report out toward me as if I hadn't already seen it.

"Yeah, so?"

"We agreed on five percent."

"I don't know why I bother having the same discussion about this every time I turn around, but here goes nothing," I spat out in irritation. I really wasn't in the mood to deal with his shit right now, but then again, I never was. "With the bad economy, charities need our help more than ever right now, Stone. The huge tax write-off, not to mention the fact that a good deal of our clients sign on because of our generous charitable efforts, proves even further why donating is not only the right thing to do, but a smart thing to do. Besides, we have more than enough money to spare and you know it."

It wasn't until then that I noticed the employees had stopped their daily routines to watch the showdown. It wasn't the first time, and probably wouldn't be the last. Of course David would take full advantage of the audience.

"Then maybe you should sell some of your shares to me, and donate that money." His ugly face smiled smugly before he turned his back on me and walked toward his end of the building.

As much as I was trying to get him to sell out to me, he was doing the same in return. Both of us were too damn stubborn to let the other one win.

His abhorrent behavior in front of our employees and the fact that I knew he didn't really give a shit about my mother's dream for Scarlet Lotus to pay it forward, so to speak, made me entertain the thought of knocking every one of the fucker's teeth out of his oversized head. But I'd learned as a child that two wrongs don't make a right, and I really was in a hurry, so I slowly counted to ten to regain my composure and forced my feet to move in the opposite direction. I'd deal with him later if need be.

I made my way to the lobby and outside and was relieved to find Samuel already waiting at the curb. Chicago rush hour traffic can be a bitch, but somehow Samuel always seemed to outmaneuver everyone else, and in a stretch limo to boot.

Lanie

Oh . . . my . . . good googly-moogly!

Never, and I do mean never, had I ever felt something so insanely pleasurable in all my life.

The wicked things that man did with his fingers and the seductive way he looked at me from under those long, lush lashes, hypnotizing me and my body into obeying his every command. The dirty things his sinful mouth said that made me feel like slapping him and riding his face all at the same time, and don't even get me started on that tongue and the malevolent way it sang to my nipples. I swear, I think he was speaking in tongues even though not a sound was made, but I sure as hell felt it.

The man was evil incarnate, Satan's immortal son, and I

was doomed. I could feel what little religion was left in my traitorous body being sucked from my soul, turning me into a backsliding sinner. I was going to hell, and I really hoped his fingers met me at the gate.

I sat there in my postorgasmic bliss, my skin shriveling up and the water going cold. Back and forth he walked from the bedroom to the bathroom as he got ready for work. I watched him brush his teeth in his underwear, and then he disappeared back into the bedroom only to reemerge in a pair of black slacks that hung low on his hips and accentuated the delicious V of his abdomen. The belt on his pants was hanging open, he still didn't have a shirt on, and he was standing there barefoot. I was mesmerized by the movement of his back muscles as he looked into the mirror and did absolutely nothing but put a dab of gel in his palm before he ran his fingers through his sexy hair. He looked over at me, winked, and did this half-smirk thing while he applied deodorant in a way that made it look pornographic. I seriously wanted to nuzzle his pits.

There was an air of confidence about him that made me want to lick him from head to toe, and then maybe suck on all his little piggies.

While a part of me was relieved that he was leaving, my inner miniwhore wanted to beg him to get back in the tub and show us that magic trick he'd done with those porntastic fingers again. Just like that, Double Agent Coochie was born. All it had taken was my very first orgasm to bring her to life. And she was apparently a very shameless hoochie. Great.

It wasn't until I heard Noah shout that he was leaving and the door close behind him that I finally forced myself to get out of the bath of sin. My bags were sitting just inside the door; I assumed Noah had brought them up. Once I was dressed and feeling a bit modest again, I decided to leave the bedroom in search of some sustenance. I hadn't even eaten the night before because my nerves had been all over the damn place and I'd been worried that I'd end up puking right in the middle of my auction.

The house was eerily quiet, but oddly warm and cozy given how big it was. I slowly made my way down the hall and toward the staircase, checking out my surroundings in awe. It was tastefully decorated with large paintings that looked like they cost more than what my father had made in an entire year at the only factory in Hillsboro. The floors were carpeted a regal red, but the walls were kept white. Most of the doors to the other rooms were closed, but I didn't bother to open them because I was hungry and I knew I'd eventually see them over the next two years.

Once I made it down the staircase, the eerie quiet went out the window. There had to be at least half a dozen women in gray uniforms with white aprons scurrying about like a colony of ants united in the task of making Casa de Crawford immaculate. All of that stopped the second they sensed my presence, every pair of eyes trained on me in surprise.

"Um, hi," I greeted them.

A short, pudgy woman stepped forward with a smile as bright as the sun. "Excuse me, miss. We didn't mean to disturb you. We can come back later if you'd like." She waved her hands at the other women and they started gathering their supplies.

"No, it's fine!" I said, probably a little louder than necessary. "I mean, you know . . . you're not bothering me. So just do whatever it is you're here to do, and I'll try to stay out of your way."

The lady turned back to me again, same smile in place. "We shouldn't be long."

I furrowed my brow. "Pfft, yeah. Take your time." She bowed slightly, which was weird, and then turned again, but I stopped her. "Um, can you point me in the direction of the kitchen?"

She waved her hand toward a long corridor. "It's just down the way and through the dining hall, miss."

I thanked her and headed in that direction, convinced I had given the help plenty to speculate and gossip about the second I was out of earshot. Not that I blamed them. I'd probably do the same if I were them. And then I wondered if maybe I looked different now that I'd had my first orgasm. Could they tell? Surely not.

I wandered toward the back of the house and through a huge formal dining room with a table in the middle that had to seat at least fifty people. Okay, that might have been a slight exaggeration, but I swear it looked just like that table in *Indiana Jones and the Temple of Doom* when they served chilled monkey brains to the guests.

There was a door at the other end, and I swore to Christ that if I pushed it open and found myself in some ancient tunnel filled with booby traps and every insect known to man, I was so out of there. Thankfully, it was only the kitchen. But I wasn't really sure you could even call it a kitchen. That just seemed like such a small word for the restaurant-style food preparation center that was before me. Everything was stainless steel and more sterile than the inside of a gallon of bleach. However, a quick glance around showed no sign of monkey brains or those brass cuppy thingies they were served in, so it was all good.

I looked around until I finally found a pantry that was as big as the entire first floor of my house back home, and boy, did I ever hit the mother lode of junk food. Seemed Mr. Crawford, aka King of the Finger Fuck, had a sweet tooth. I grabbed a box of Cocoa Puffs—because I seriously was coo-coo for Cocoa Puffs—and some chocolate syrup and did the happy-time dance out of the pantry and back into the kitchen.

I remembered seeing bowls somewhere during my search, but it was going to be like a massive game of Memory to find them again. After opening several cabinets, I finally scored a win and squealed, "Yay, me!" while I did a fist pump in the air.

I was my biggest fan.

The refrigerator was obvious and, you guessed it, huge. Imagine my disappointment, though, when I opened one side of it to find that it wasn't a walk-in cold storage unit. I wouldn't have been surprised to find a butcher living inside there with a whole herd of cattle, but I guess Noah skimped on that part.

I grabbed the milk and went back over to my stash, filling my bowl with cereal and licking my chops when I poured the moo juice over the cocoa yumminess and it turned all chocolaty. I was careful not to pour too much and make a mess, even though there was probably some little flute thingy around there somewhere to blow on to command a group of little orange men with green hair to scurry in and clean up before retreating back to the dungeon of doom and gloom with the rest of their little pals.

Yes, I had an overactive imagination, but it was totally warranted in a place as big as this.

I knew exactly where the glasses were from my previous expedition for the bowl, so I grabbed one and squirted a crazy amount of chocolate syrup into it. I swear I could hear my dentist tsking at me from somewhere deep in the recesses of my conscience.

And then it was time to start another game of seek-and-find to score some silverware. A plastic spoon would've been okay at this point . . . heck, I'd make do with a spork. *Score!* First drawer I opened, I hit the jackpot. Which was a good thing, because I loathed soggy cereal.

Milk and syrup back to the refrigerator, cereal box back in the pantry, and I was on my way.

And then the phone rang.

I looked around the kitchen and finally spotted it hanging on the wall next to the stove, but there was no way I was going to answer that thing. Firstly, because that would mean I'd have to leave my sugar haven. Secondly, because I had absolutely no idea who it could be, and it wasn't my house. Plus, how would I explain who I was or why I was answering Noah's telephone?

Um, hi. I'm the piece of virgin ass for whom Mr. Crawford paid two million smackeroos to have his dirty, dirty way with. In fact, he just fucked my mouth last night, but that was after I nearly bit off his dick and before he finger-fucked my whore of a pussy into oblivion this morning. He's not here right now, but I can take a message if you want.

Yeah, that conversation was not going to happen.

So I ignored the incessant ringing and dug into my goodies.

As much as it was irritating me, the sound of the phone did remind me that I needed to call Dez and check in with her. I had stashed my cell phone away in my things, hoping whoever purchased me wouldn't do something like take it away and forbid me to have any contact whatsoever with the outside world. Noah hadn't said I couldn't, so I assumed it would be okay.

Not that I really gave a rat's ass what he said. I'd sold him my body, not my humanity.

Once I'd scarfed down my breakfast, I rinsed my dishes, put them in the dishwasher, and then I stood there like an idiot. I had no friggin' clue what I was supposed to do with the rest of my day. I thought about going upstairs and finding my cell to call Dez, but I'd just eaten a Jethro Bodine–sized portion of Cocoa Puffs, so that would be too much like exercise. In an epic light bulb of a moment, I decided to hunt down a television set and get my Maury on instead.

After I had roamed around for what seemed like an eternity, and was really wishing I had left a trail of bread crumbs to find my way back, I finally found what was obviously an entertainment room. It was like a testosterone-filled playground for men. Video game consoles, air hockey table, a massive stereo system and dance floor, theater seats and a leather sectional, a poker table, a wet bar, and the biggest television I'd ever seen.

Well, it was more like a wallevision. Seriously, it took up a whole wall.

I wondered if Noah ever sat in here with his hand shoved down the front of his pants in a classic Al Bundy pose.

Can someone please tell me why I suddenly envisioned shoving my own hand down his pants?

Double Agent Coochie smiled knowingly and nodded at me in answer.

"Shut up. You are out of control, missy," I mumbled to my crotch.

Anywho, I had no clue how to turn the monster of a television on, but I did manage to find a giant remote control on the bar. I picked it up with both hands and sat in one of the theater seats to study it. The thing had a gazillion buttons on it and not a damn one of them was labeled.

This should be fun.

I closed my eyes and did that thing where you swirl your finger around in the air and just let it drop down on a button and hope it's the right one. Nothing. I opened one eye and looked around, finding rainbow sparkles reflecting off the walls as they spun around the room. I looked up and . . . He had a disco ball in his man cave? I giggled to myself and tried again. This time Eminem started blaring out of the surround-sound speakers at a decibel level that was probably going to cause me to go deaf in a matter of minutes. I tried to turn it back off, but of course I'd had my eyes closed while I was pressing buttons, so I had no clue which one it was. That probably wasn't the best idea I'd ever had.

By this time I was frantically pushing buttons, trying to find the right one to stop the insanity, but only causing more insanity instead. I kid you not, the dance floor started rotating, lights were flickering on and off in a multitude of colors, the seat I was sitting in started vibrating and giving me a massage and . . . What the hell? Was the blender seriously controlled by the damn remote?

One more button and the bastard of a television finally clicked on.

I threw that remote across the room and sank back into the molester seat with the super friendly fingers because, as shot as my nerves were, I could really use that massage.

"Calgon! Take me away!" I shouted at the top of my lungs so that I could hear myself over Eminem's "Not Afraid." "Screw you, Slim Shady! I am afraid. Very afraid."

"What the hell is going on in here?" someone's voice yelled.

My eyes shot open and I lurched forward, my heart nearly pounding out of my chest in shock. There stood Noah in the doorway with a look of utter confusion on his face.

"Make it stop!" I yelled back.

He walked across the room, picked up the remote from the floor where it had landed, and expertly pushed a few buttons until there was finally silence and my molester chair stopped feeling me up. Well, that part hadn't been so bad, and I sort of wished he had forgotten to push that button.

"I'm sorry!" I yelled, because apparently my brain hadn't quite processed the fact that I didn't need to anymore. Noah raised a brow at me. I lowered my voice and started again. "I'm sorry. I just wanted to watch TV . . . and who uses a remote with no labels anyway?"

"It takes some getting used to," he said, putting it back on the bar.

"What are you doing home? I thought you said six."

"Yeah, well, having never done this sort of thing before, I may have forgotten to go over some details with you, and Polly will be here today." He opened his suit jacket and pushed it back to put his hands on his hips.

I wanted to bite his belly. Obviously Double Agent Coochie had taken over my brain, traitor that she was.

"And please," he continued, looking sexy as hell with that red silk tie, "don't play with shit if you don't know what you're doing. We wouldn't want there to be another mishap, now would we?" He seriously petted his Wonder Peen through his pants as if he was consoling it. I wanted to grab that sexy tie of his and strangle him.

"Pfft, that was soooo yesterday," I scoffed. "Get over it already. Besides, I kissed it and made it all better for you last night."

Those words did not seriously come out of my mouth. And that quick, I was thinking about him coming in my mouth. *Jesus, Lanie! Pull it together. You hate him, remember?*

Him. Not the Wonder Peen or those orgasmically long fingers, which he was currently drumming on his lick-me-right-here hips.

"Fuck you! I hate you," I said and then gasped immediately, covering my mouth. Not because I was afraid I'd offended him, but because dropping the F-bomb wasn't something I normally did. I also didn't normally think about fingers in the very sluttish way I had been mere seconds before. I decided to blame the chocolate and sugar overload for my temporary mental breakdown.

"Oh, you are going to fuck me." He stalked toward me. "A lot. Just not right now. We've got shit to do. Let's go."

"Go where?"

He grabbed my wrist and hoisted me up and away from my super-duper molester chair, keeping me in tow as he led me out of the room.

"I'm taking you to your appointment."

"What appointment? I don't have an appointment," I said, trying to pull free from his grasp.

"You do now. It would be quite irresponsible of me not to have you checked out by a physician before I pillage that sweet little pussy of yours, wouldn't it?"

I stopped dead in my tracks, forcing him to as well.

"You're taking my kitty to the vet?" I asked, insulted.

"I don't know you well enough to trust that you are everything that you say you are." He pulled me roughly against his chest and cupped my ass. "I bought a virgin, and I intend to make sure I got what I paid for. Plus you'll need birth control, because when I finally do get inside that tight little gold mine you're sitting on, I want to make sure I can feel everything."

My jaw hit the floor.

"Close your mouth, Delaine. Unless that's an invitation for me to stick something in it," he said, and then lifted my chin with his fingers to close my mouth before stepping away with a smile on his face.

A minute or two later, I found myself sitting across from

Noah in the back of his limousine and on my way to the twat doc.

Noah lit a cigarette and blew the smoke toward the window he had cracked open. Normally I'd be all up in arms over the lack of consideration for my lungs, but the way he wrapped his lips around that filter . . . well, it made me think naughty, naughty things.

"You can kiss me, you know," he said as he took another draw from his cigarette. "I'm here for your pleasure just as much as you are for mine."

I crossed my legs, trying to find the friction that I now suddenly craved, and threw my arms across my chest defiantly. I didn't say anything in response. I mean, what was I supposed to say to that?

"This," he said, making long strokes over his cock through his pants, "is for your pleasure as well. You shouldn't be too shy to ask for what you want, Delaine. Or take what you want, for that matter, because I'm sure as hell not going to be."

I turned my head and looked out the window, trying to ignore the throbbing in my girly bits. Said girly bits, however, were salivating with the visual that his words provided. From the corner of my eye I saw him put his cigarette out before he said, "Here, let me show you."

He immediately crawled across the space between us and roughly uncrossed my legs before burying his face between my thighs. Then he cupped my ass with his hands and pulled me forward to give himself a better angle. I gasped in surprise when I felt the warmth of his breath seep through the thick material of my jeans while he worked his mouth back and forth over me. I watched the movement of his head in shock, and then he looked up at me and made a show of letting me see his long tongue lick from back to front. He bared his teeth and gave me a crooked grin before he nipped at the place just over my clit and winked.

"Oh, God," I moaned, and then grabbed two handfuls of his hair roughly and shoved his face between my legs.

Noah's mouth increased the pressure on my pussy. "Mmm . . . I love a woman who knows what she wants, Delaine."

The way he purred my name made my insides quake, threatening an eruption the likes of which Mount St. Helens had never seen. But then the bastard's hands moved over mine and forced me to release my hold on his hair before he pulled back and placed one light kiss over my clit.

"That was . . . promising." He sighed. "I can't wait to see your reaction when there are no clothes in the way, but unfortunately, that's going to have to wait until later."

I sat there panting and completely unable to get my inner whore under control, but Noah sat back in his seat and straightened his clothes like he was totally unaffected by what he had just done to me. He ran his hands through his hair to repair the damage that I had done, and I screamed internally, wanting to yank it all out.

The passenger door opened and Samuel greeted us with a smile. Noah stepped out onto the pavement and reached a hand out to help me. I accepted his offer, but only because I wanted to squeeze the hell out of his fingers, which I did, but he seemed unfazed by that as well. Bastard.

Through my sexually frustrated rage, I barely registered that we were entering some sort of medical building and Noah was leading me down the hall and into an office area. The receptionist at the front greeted Noah in a professional manner, but she was undressing him with her eyes the whole time, seemingly oblivious to my presence. I knew I had no claims to him or anything, but she didn't know that, so her shameless flirting rubbed me the wrong way.

She probably wouldn't have been the least bit deterred if I'd boasted that he'd just had his faced buried between my legs, the shameless hussy.

Before my inner bitch could rip those fake lashes off her eyelids, we were escorted into an exam room, where the nurse took my vital signs and then told me to strip, handing me a paper gown to slip on. She also handed me some form that she said they needed me to complete for all my basic information, but Noah took it from her instead.

"My uncle Daniel owns this practice," Noah said when the nurse left the room. He was scribbling some information on the form. "He's not a gynecologist, and I didn't want you to feel uncomfortable around him later, so one of his colleagues, Everett, will be doing your examination."

I nodded, really hating what was about to happen.

"Do you have any health issues they need to know about?"

I shook my head in response, and he handed me the form to sign. When I gave it back to him, he motioned for me to undress and turned his back while he continued to talk. "I've told my family and friends that you and I met some time back on one of my trips to LA. They all think we've been secretly seeing each other for the past seven months and that I've finally convinced you to move to Oak Brook to live with me. I haven't told any of them your name, so it's up to you if you want to use your real name, or something else."

"Well, since you already put my real name on that form, I guess we'll go with that." I stepped out of my pants and folded them neatly before reaching for the blue paper gown. I heard him murmur an expletive under his breath. He apparently hadn't thought of that before he filled out the form. "Besides, if we use something else, I'm probably just going to mess everything up. And thanks, by the way."

"For what?"

"For at least coming up with a halfway decent story about me so that I don't look like the whore you and I both know I really am."

He turned around then and took two long strides toward me until his body was so close to mine that I could feel the heat rolling off him in waves. He put his finger under my chin and lifted it so that I looked him in the eye. "I'd hardly call a virgin a whore."

I didn't have a chance to respond because there was a light knock on the door. He stepped away from me before calling for whoever was on the other side to come in.

"Noah, my boy!" A jovial man wearing a white lab coat came into the room and hugged Noah. "It's so good to see you. How have you been?"

"I'm surviving," Noah said with a genuine smile on his face as he hugged him back.

The doctor turned to me then with an apologetic look.

"I'm sorry, but there was no file, so I'm afraid I don't know your name."

"Delaine. Delaine Talbot," I told him, and then suddenly became very fascinated by the plain white tiles on the floor beneath my feet.

"Well, it's very nice to meet you, Miss Talbot." He shook my hand and then motioned for me to sit on the exam table as he sat on the little rolling stool in front of me. "Now, what can we do for you today?"

"Delaine just needs a routine exam, and she'd like to go over her birth control options," Noah answered for me.

"I see. Well, the form of contraception you're least likely to forget to take is the shot. Is that what you'd like to try?" he asked me with a polite smile.

"Um . . ." I'd read some material on it during my last visit to my own doctor, but this was sort of last-minute, so I wasn't really sure.

"Each shot lasts for three months, and one of the perks for most of my patients is that it normally makes your cycle lighter or stops it completely. It's been a pretty popular form of contraception over the last few years."

"Yeah, okay. That sounds good," I answered with a shy nod.

"Well then, let's get started, shall we?" His smile was genuine and comforting.

I lay back on the table and Noah came and stood by my head before I put my feet in the stirrups. It wasn't like I'd never had a Pap smear before, but having all your goodies sprawled out like that in front of a perfect stranger was always unnerving. I mean, crotch docs saw a lot of snatch, so you had to wonder if yours looked any different from the others or if it had some kind of deformity of which you weren't aware. Before I could even complete all my inner ramblings, he was backing away and patting my leg to tell me he was done.

"There will be some cramping over the next few days. You can take some ibuprofen for the pain. And you might experience a little bit of bleeding, given your particular circumstance, but all in all, you should be fine." He stripped his gloves off and disposed of them. "Make sure you come in if you experience anything irregular."

His assistant came up beside me and wiped my arm down with alcohol before she gave me a shot.

"I'll just leave you to get dressed now and then you're free to go," he said as he turned for the door. "Noah, it was great to see you again."

"You too, Everett, and thanks," he said before turning back to me. "I'm just going to go settle up on the bill and I'll meet you outside."

He followed the doctor and his assistant out and I jumped up, instantly regretting the fast movement because I was already feeling sore. I dressed as quickly as I could, wanting to get the hell out of there, and when I opened the door Noah was waiting for me.

"You okay?" he asked, probably because I had an arm over my abdomen.

"I'm cramping a little, but if I can just go home and lie down, I think I'll be all right."

"Okay," he said with a nod, and then pulled out his cell

phone and pushed a button. "Good morning to you too, Polly," he said into the phone. "I need you to wrap up whatever you're doing at the house. I'm on my way there and my guest and I will need some privacy. . . . Yes, Polly, it's her." He rolled his eyes, but held my elbow and guided me out of the building and into the waiting limo. "She's not up for visitors right now. Maybe in a couple of days. Call Mason and tell him that I'll be back in the office within the hour. Thank you, Polly."

With that, he ended the call and sat next to me, draping his arm around my shoulders. "Polly takes care of all my personal business, including the household. She means well, but she can be a bit much to handle sometimes," he explained. "It'll be harder to fool her with our little secret than anyone else, so keep on your toes around her. She's a sneaky little shit."

I nodded my understanding, and he cupped his hand to the side of my head and nudged me to lie over on his chest. It was probably too intimate a thing for him to do since we'd just met each other the night before, but considering the intimacy we had already shared, I supposed it was okay.

I listened to the thrum of his heartbeat as we rode along in silence. And for the first time I actually paid attention to the way he smelled. I recognized the scent of his body soap and deodorant from this morning, but I also caught another scent that was more distinctive and so very . . . him.

His fingers stroked my hair, and I closed my eyes, just enjoying the silence and his tender caresses. The action was so soothing that had I not been in a good deal of discomfort, I probably would've fallen asleep.

All too soon we were home. Noah stepped from the car first and held his hand out to me, dismissing Samuel's attempt to do his job. I slouched over because I was really starting to cramp a bit more by then.

"Shit, are you okay?" Noah's voice was frantic.

"I'm fine. Just a bad cramp," I said, trying to keep as much strain as possible out of my voice. I didn't want him to think I was a big baby who couldn't take a little bit of pain.

Without warning, he scooped me up into his arms and carried me bridal-style through the front doors, which Samuel had already opened wide. I tried to get him to put me down, but he wouldn't listen. Instead, he carried me all the way up the stairs and into his bedroom. He sat me down long enough to pull back the covers so that I could slide beneath them and then he was gone again.

"Here, take these," he said when he returned, handing me two pills and a glass of water.

I took the offering and swallowed the pills down. Noah took the glass from my hands and put it on the nightstand beside me.

"Will you be okay if I go back to work?" he asked, worry evident in his voice.

"I'll be fine. I just need a little nap," I said through a stifled yawn. "Go. I can relax better if you're not here anyway."

"Ouch, that hurt," he chuckled lightly, with his hand to his chest. "Glad to see you haven't lost that attitude. I'm sure you'll be fine and ready to make another attempt at biting my dick off in no time flat."

He leaned over to kiss my lips and then stood up.

"Do you have a cell phone?" he asked.

"Yeah, it's over there in my purse. Why? You're not going to take it away from me, are you?" I asked, panicked that he might.

"Not unless you give me a reason to," he said, walking over and grabbing my purse.

He handed it to me, and assuming he wanted my phone, I pulled it out and gave it to him. He pushed a few buttons before handing it back to me. His own phone started ringing then, and he pulled it out of his inside jacket pocket and silenced it.

"I programmed my cell number into your phone, and now I have yours, too. Make sure you keep it on you at all times. Not only for your safety, but also because I won't be happy in the slightest if you keep me waiting when I need you." He put his phone back in his jacket. "Call me if you need me for anything. I mean it."

Although he was trying to be stern, I could see the sincerity in the expression on his face. I rolled my eyes and nodded sarcastically, because I just really loved to piss him off, and then turned my back to him, mumbling, "Go away already. Your face is making my uterus hurt."

It was true, but only because his face was so pretty and I wanted to ride it but couldn't. And here was the odd thing about that: not only had I never given head, but I'd never been on the receiving end either. Now, all of a sudden, I couldn't get the picture of his face between my legs out of my mind. Crazy.

I'm telling you, it was because he was so damn pretty.

"Mmm-hmm, okay then," he said, like he didn't believe a word of it. "I'll see you later this evening."

I heard the door close softly behind him and I snuggled into his pillow, inhaling his scent once again. While part of me was glad nothing would be expected of me for at least the rest of the day, I had to admit that another part, my budding inner miniwhore, was super bummed that apparently I wasn't going to get another round with the King of the Finger Fuck either. With that depressing thought lingering in the back of my mind, I slowly drifted off to sleep.

5

dessert à la mode

Lanie

"Delaine," a husky voice sang into my ear as I fought my way out of a sleepy haze. I faintly registered the feel of a rather large, warm hand stroking the inside of my thigh and I moaned involuntarily.

"You should be more careful about the sounds you make in your sleep. Moaning like that might make me lose what little control I'm maintaining. It does unspeakable things to me."

Hot breath washed over the skin of my neck, and the most delicious shiver ran down my back when I felt his tongue suck my earlobe into his mouth and then his soft lips closed around it. His hand began to knead my thigh as it gradually moved higher, causing me to squirm in an attempt to find the perfect placement for optimal advantage.

"Shit," he cursed, and then pulled away all too quickly.

My eyes shot open and I gasped, realizing the traitorous response his touch, coupled with his sultry words, had evoked from my body.

Noah ran his hand through his hair, nervous and obviously

aroused. "Dinner is ready. You should probably get up and try to eat something."

Really? I had lost a whole day?

I buried my face under the covers, because seeing him looking all breathless and horny was making me react the same way, and now was not the time to lose my composure over him.

"I'm not hungry," I mumbled into my pillow.

"Regardless, you need to eat. Now, either you can get up on your own and join me in the dining hall, or I can throw you over my shoulder, carry your ass downstairs, and force-feed you. Which is it?"

I growled in frustration and hit the pillow with my fist, but I made no move to get up.

"Have it your way, then," he said, yanking the covers back and starting to reach for me.

"Wait!" I sat up quickly and pulled my knees to my chest. "I'll get up. God, you're such a Neanderthal! Just give me a little bit of privacy to get myself together and then I'll meet you down there. Okay?"

"Fine," he said, backing away. "But don't keep me waiting long. I detest eating by myself."

I nodded in understanding and watched as he walked out the door, my eyes immediately going to his ass. God, I was such an ass slut.

As soon as he left the room, I grabbed my cell phone from the nightstand and pressed the speed dial for my best friend.

There was no hello on the other end, but there was no mistaking she'd picked up either. "Well, it's about fucking time!

What the hell happened to you?" Dez shouted over the bass thumping in the background. Apparently she was at work. "Are you okay?"

"My cooch hurts, but other than that, I'm fine." Except I really needed to pee, badly. So I rolled out of the bed and made my way in that direction.

Dez laughed. "Dayuuum! He put it on you like that?"

"Actually, my hymen is still intact, but I don't know how long that's going to last." I stopped short when I caught a glimpse of myself in the mirror. "Oh my God. I look like crap."

"You always look like crap. So give me the deets. Who bought you? Is he hot?"

"Um, Noah Crawford. And yes, he is hot to the nth degree. Actually, I don't even think 'hot' is an adequate description. The man is a raging inferno of flaming hotness," I admitted, mostly because even though I couldn't lie to my best friend, it would be blasphemous to lie about Noah Crawford's level of hotness. The dude was off the charts.

"He's flaming? So that means he's gay? Aw, I'm sorry, hon," she laughed.

"No, he's not gay. At least, I don't think he is," I said, trying to smooth out my hair. "He buried his face between my thighs, so I'm guessing he's really into girly bits."

Dez gasped, obviously excited by this news. "He got his carpet munch on? Oh my God! Did you love it? You loved it, didn't you? Wasn't it the best thing—"

"Dez! Focus!" I said, trying to get her attention. "My pants were still on, so I still don't have a clue, nor do I have much time on the phone. Let's spend it talking about something important, yes? How are my folks? Did the money go through to the account?"

"The money is there, and damn, bitch . . . you went for two million? You'd think those pervs would want a woman of the world who knows how to show them a good time, but no, they want little Miss Innocence. I can't say I understand that logic."

"Dez," I said, trying to rein her back into the conversation before she could go off on one of her tangents. "How is Faye?"

"I went by there earlier today to check on her. She's the same, sweetie. No change," Dez's voice was more solemn. "But now we have the money for the operation, thanks to your courageous effort." Dez sighed. "I really admire you, Lanie. Sacrificing your goodies like that and all? That's really heroic. I'm serious as a heart attack."

"Well, as long as it helps Mom it's worth it, right?"

"Mmm-hmm. And there's no shame in enjoying a little rat-a-tat-tat on your vag while you're at it."

I smiled and gave her a half laugh. "Yeah, I guess you would see it that way. Look, I have to go. Tell my folks that I'm swamped with freshman stuff, but I'll call them the first chance I get, okay? And I sort of like you."

"Sure thing, babe. And I sort of like you, too," she said with a hint of sentimentality to her voice. At least, as much as she was capable of. "Clit licks and tit nips, bitch!"

I hung up the phone and decided to grab a quick shower. When I was done, I walked into the bedroom to dress, but I couldn't find my things anywhere. I even looked in Noah's massive closet and still nothing. So I grabbed one of his dress shirts, which thankfully was long enough to cover my nakedness. Yeah, I knew it was probably going to tick him off, seeing as how he was all OCD over his clothes, but surely he didn't expect me to walk around naked all the time.

I brushed my teeth and looked myself over in the mirror, satisfied that he was going to flip his wig, but he would definitely tell me what he did with my things if for no other reason than to get me out of his. Then I hightailed my ass down the stairs before I ended up pissing him off for keeping him waiting so long. Again, not because I cared, but because I wanted to see his pretty, pretty face when he did get pissed.

He was sitting at the head of the table when I entered the dining room—er, excuse me, dining hall. The placement to his right was set for me, I presumed, and I took my seat. Noah looked me over from head to toe, taking in my current state of undress, and I watched him swallow hard.

"I hope you don't mind. I really had no choice since all of my things are gone. What did you do with my clothes?" I asked.

"I'd planned on taking you shopping this afternoon, so I had the help dispose of your other things," he said, picking up his napkin. "I didn't realize you'd be sleeping all day. My apologies."

He *disposed* of my things? "You can't just get rid of my stuff!" I screeched.

"I didn't get rid of everything. Just the clothes," he said dismissively. "They weren't up to par with my lifestyle."

"Well, aren't we just the elitist? I'm sorry I didn't come prepared for your ritzy lifestyle."

"No apologies necessary," he said, quite seriously. "We'll

take care of that tomorrow. Although I have to admit that you do look rather delicious in my shirt."

The way he was looking at me, you'd think I was an all-you-can-eat buffet and he hadn't had a meal in days. It was at the point where he licked his lips that I forced myself to look away, suddenly becoming very interested in the actual buffet before me. All three courses of the meal were already laid out: salad to start, a juicy steak and baked potato, and a slice of three-layer chocolate cake with a side of vanilla ice cream for dessert.

I unfolded the napkin and laid it in my lap. "Did you make all this?"

"I'm a multimillionaire. I don't have to cook," he said, picking up his fork and stabbing his salad. "I pay people to do this for me."

"I see. Sort of like how you pay for pussy?" I asked, and then took a sip of water from the goblet in front of me.

Noah choked on the bite of salad he had just taken, and I gave myself a mental high five while smirking around the rim of my glass.

"Why is that, anyway?" I asked, not the least bit concerned for his welfare.

"That subject is not up for discussion," he said, taking a drink of wine. "How are you feeling? Any bleeding or cramping?"

Until he mentioned something about it, I'd almost forgotten about my little excursion to the twat doc. "Well, that's a personal question, but if you must know—"

"I must, and nothing about your body is a secret from me

for the next two years. The sooner you get used to that idea, the better this situation will be. Now, you were saying?"

I gritted my teeth together, trying my damnedest not to tell him to go fuck himself, even though that might have actually been sort of hot. Mentally picturing that scene, I needed to do a quick count to ten in my head before I felt reasonably calm enough to answer his question. "The cramps have subsided, and I haven't had any bleeding at all. So does that mean you're going to fuck me now?"

"Yes. How about right here on the table?" he said facetiously as he made a show of testing its durability with a shake. He gave me a crooked grin to make sure I knew he was only joking. "I think I can allow you to have the evening off to recuperate. I know you hate me and must think some pretty terrible things about me, but I'm not a monster. I am capable of showing a little compassion every now and then, you know."

Double Agent Coochie was already strapping on her hooker heels to perform her table dance and was beyond disappointed when he took it all back. She was threatening a revolt, but I mentally stomped that slut in the face and told her to simmer down.

"Have you called anyone to let them know you're okay?" he asked, cutting into his steak.

I wasn't really sure how I was supposed to respond to that. If I told him the truth, it might piss him off enough that he would decide to take my phone away from me. But he hadn't established any rules regarding having contact with family or friends, plus he knew I had my cell. I hated to lie, because one lie almost always led to another, which led to another, until you'd woven one heck of a web of deceit that was near impossible not to get caught up in. Plus I was still looking forward to watching his pretty, pretty face in one of his pissy tantrums. So, screw it, I told him the truth.

"I talked to my best friend, Dez, before I came down to dinner."

"And your parents?" he asked, his face not showing any indication that he was upset by my admission.

I was disappointed, to say the least . . . and I also had to snatch Double Agent Coochie's hooker heels from her and grind one into her sassy little mouth.

"They think I'm away at school. I'll have to call them eventually, but they can't know where I am or what I'm doing. It would kill them."

Noah nodded and tented his fingers under his chin. "That's understandable. But I want you to feel free to keep in touch with whomever you need to. As long as you're holding up your end of the deal and not trying to break our contract, you'll have most all the freedoms you enjoyed before you came to me."

"Most?" I asked, arching a brow in question.

"All except for your body, of course. That belongs to me," he clarified.

"So I can leave the house whenever I want?" I asked, testing the limitations.

"I expect you to be here when I am here, unless I have preauthorized an outing. I say preauthorized because I want to know where you are at all times. Plus, there may be times when I feel the need to come home during the day for a little stress relief," he said with a crooked grin.

Let me clarify: that wasn't just any crooked grin. My pussy was leaking at an abnormal rate and I feared for the safety of the expensive fabric that lined the chair I was sitting in. My nipples were at full attention and I pulled my shoulders forward, hoping my hussified reaction wouldn't be noticeable. But it didn't stop there. Oh, no, I was apparently on a roll with my newfound whorishness.

"And are you feeling stressed now?" I asked in a sultry voice.

Don't ask me where that came from. I didn't even recognize my own voice. Apparently I had let my guard down just enough to allow my hoochie of a coochie to get the drop on me, going straight for the verbal function of my brain and setting up camp. That was my story, and I was sticking to it.

Noah chuckled and licked his bottom lip, which really sort of pissed me off because I kind of wanted to do that. "Let's see. I have an incredibly sexy woman in my house, whom I've paid some major dough to have my way with anytime I want, yet I can't because I've brought a bit of discomfort to her. So, yeah, I guess you might say I'm a tad bit stressed."

Double Agent Coochie found the part of my brain that controlled my motor skills and planted her flag. I had lost all control of my own body. I laid my napkin next to my plate and pushed away from the table. Noah kept his eyes trained on me the entire time. As I walked toward him, he sat back in his chair and tilted his head to the side with his eyebrows furrowed in question, waiting to see what I intended to do. I slid between him and the table and sank down to my knees.

"What are you doing, Delaine?" he asked, his voice deep and husky.

"Stress management." I smiled, unfastening his belt with an unbelievable amount of confidence.

"I thought I told you that you have the night off," he said, scooting his chair back a bit to give me more room.

"You did." I unzipped his pants and laid the flaps open as I kissed along the bulge just under his Calvin Kleins.

Noah ran his fingers through my hair and then cupped my chin, lifting it so that I met his gaze. "If you keep that up much longer, I'm not going to be able to stop you."

"Then don't," I said, dipping my head down to continue my previous actions.

He pushed his chair back further until he was out of my reach. "Not until I've had my dessert."

Without warning, he lifted me up and sat me on the edge of the table, pushing the dinner dishes away. His hands were on both of my knees as he spread my legs and pulled himself closer. Then he moved up my thighs slowly, dipping under the hem of his shirt and pushing it up along the way.

We both watched as he revealed my nakedness beneath, and I gasped when I heard a feral growl from deep in his chest. I had always kept myself sufficiently groomed in that area because, well, you just never knew when you might end up in some sort of freak accident and someone might have the need to see something down there.

He licked his lips while ogling my cooch, and then he finally lifted his eyes to mine. "I'm sure you won't mind if I kiss this and make it all better."

Without waiting for my response, he spread me wider and began to suck the skin on the inside of my left thigh.

"Um, Noah?" I started in a shaky voice.

"Hmm?" he hummed as he continued to work his way up my thigh.

"Do you really think the dining room table is the best place to do this? I mean, it can't be very sanitary."

"I eat all my meals at the table," he mumbled against my thigh.

I suppose he had a point, and I probably wasn't going to win that argument, even if I really wanted to. Besides, it didn't matter because by then, he'd reached my center and his nose was nuzzling my love nubbin. I felt his tongue run along my folds and I grabbed on to the hair of his head to hold on because it felt like the world was spinning way too fast.

"You smell so good, Delaine. And you taste even better." He moaned against my pussy, and then his hand ran along the underside of my thigh to lift my leg, draping it over his shoulder. I watched as he lapped at my center, and then he captured my clit with his lips and sucked chastely before flicking it with purpose. He looked up at me and winked while his serpent-like tongue sped up, and a pleasure like I'd never known shot through my body and my head dropped back.

"Look at me," his husky voice commanded. "I want you to watch me feed on you."

"Oh, God," I groaned, lifting my head to obey.

First one and then another finger disappeared inside me and began to move in and out while the fingers of his other hand spread my lips apart. He sucked my clit into his mouth, latching on and doing this unbelievable thing with his teeth and tongue that I couldn't see, but I sure as hell felt. Then he pushed his fingers all the way in to the knuckles and curled them back and forth, and I couldn't help the porn-star-like moan that came from somewhere in the back of my throat.

"Mmm, you like that, don't you?" He flattened his tongue out, taking a long lick from my opening to my clit, where he resumed his suckling.

"That's . . . sweet Jesus. So amazing," I groaned through heavy pants.

My chest heaved and my grip on his hair tightened as I pulled him toward me with each grind of my hips into his face. He hummed in appreciation, apparently approving of the fact that I was showing him what I liked most. His fingers left my opening and I whined in protest, but then I saw that he had a spoon full of ice cream. He smirked before dropping a small dollop right on my clit. I gasped at the chilling sensation against my overheated nub and nearly lost all of the control I had. Noah bit down on his bottom lip as he watched my reaction and then surged forward, roughly devouring my pussy and licking it clean of the sweet cream.

A coil was beginning to tighten in the pit of my stomach, and I recognized it from the bath earlier. Every muscle in my body tensed and my thighs were involuntarily trapping his head between them. Seriously, it was like my pussy had morphed into a Venus flytrap, unwilling to let the awesomeness that was Noah Crawford's face escape.

Noah sucked harder on my clit and then shook his head back and forth, which just about sent me over the edge, but then he buried his face as close as he could between my legs, licking, sucking, moaning, and humming. His fingers moved in and out, curling back and forth. I couldn't take it anymore.

Feeling him, seeing him, hearing him—it was too much. Like sensory overload or something equally mind-numbing.

My whole body shuddered as the coil finally sprang free and my eyes squeezed shut. Blue and black spots flickered behind my eyes as I bit my bottom lip and moaned out my orgasm. Wave after wave pulsated through my body as Noah continued to lick and suck. When the intense pleasure finally subsided and my body relaxed, he stopped and looked up at me while licking his lips.

"There. All better?" he chuckled with the sexiest grin on his face.

"Mmm-hmm," I barely eked out, nodding my head like only an idiot would.

He sat back in his chair, remnants of the ice cream and my juices glistening on his chin. I was so mortified that I actually blushed. I mean, that much wetness couldn't be normal, could it?

"Pussy à la mode—my favorite." He grabbed his napkin, wiping his mouth and chin.

I pulled the shirt down to cover myself and hopefully some of my embarrassment, and blurted out the first thing that came to mind.

"You still haven't had my cherry," I said suggestively.

Noah let out a hearty belly laugh, rubbing his hands over that pretty, pretty face, which had been buried in my vajayjay just minutes before. I'd come down those stairs wanting to see him pissed, but this was so much better.

"Eager, are we?" he asked. "Well," he shrugged his shoulders and then slapped his thighs as he stood and hooked his thumbs under the band of his fuck-her-wear. "If that's what you really want . . ."

Realization smacked me like a Mack truck and my eyes widened as my legs instinctively snapped closed. "No!" I shouted, louder than I probably needed to. "I'm . . . I'm still sore."

It was an outright lie. I knew it. Double Agent Coochie knew it. And, more important, he knew it.

"Is that right? Hmm, well I could always make you," he said, using that husky voice that made my insides dissolve into a puddle of goo.

He took a step toward me and lifted my chin to give me a soft kiss, and then another, and one more. His hands roamed over my shoulders, down my arms, and around my waist as I fought to keep my whorish thighs from opening up to invite him in.

Noah broke away and trailed kisses along my jaw to the sensitive spot below my ear. "Soon," he whispered as he cupped my face in his hands and took my bottom lip between his.

He pulled away and cleared his throat. "I have some work to do tonight if I'm going to be able to take you shopping tomorrow," he said, running his hands through his hair. "You can do whatever you want in the meantime."

With that, he walked away and left me sitting on the table, stunned to silence, in a postcoital haze, and wearing nothing but his shirt.

Noah

I had to get out of there.

Her taste and smell were everywhere, and she was sitting

there in my goddamn shirt, looking sexier than she had any right to be. And to top it all off, she was offering me her fucking cherry.

Did she not have any clue whatsoever about the amount of restraint it took for me not to impale her with my cock right then and there?

But she had to have still been sore, and ramming my dick into her unabashedly wasn't going to do anything but make that situation worse. Which also meant I'd have to wait even longer to do it again. And once I had her there was no way I was going to be able to keep myself from taking her over and over again, on every surface in the house. And my house, much like my cock, was pretty damn big.

Control. I had to maintain control and have a little more patience. All good things come to those who wait. Right?

I sat down at my desk and brought the fingers that I'd had inside her tight little pussy to my nose, inhaling her scent once again. Yes, it was a masochistic move, worse than any other sort of torture imaginable—other than maybe having to watch someone else fuck the shit out of her right in front of me—but I couldn't resist the allure of eau de Delaine.

I suddenly became aware of the massive hard-on I had been sporting since she walked into the dining room wearing nothing but my fucking shirt. I groaned at the pain my rock-solid dick, twisted and mangled into a very uncomfortable position, was causing me at that very moment. I reached my hand into my underwear and winced as I pulled my cock out. I could've used it to drill a railroad tie.

I couldn't very well let it stay like that. I'd never get any work done with that thing waving in my face, especially with

Delaine's taste still on my tongue and her smell still lingering on my fingers and in my whiskers.

I reached inside the top drawer of my desk and pulled out the bottle of lotion I had stashed there.

I squirted a generous amount into my palm and ran my hand up and down my shaft. I closed my eyes and imagined my million-dollar baby, still clad in my shirt, on her knees in front of me while I sat at the table. My thumb swept over the head of my dick and I hissed, picturing the flat part of her tongue making the motion instead as she scooped up the pre-come. She closed her eyes and moaned as she tasted me.

Her tongue swept across her bottom lip in anticipation of more while her greedy little mouth devoured my cock and swallowed me down. I could feel the back of her throat constrict around the tip of my dick as she moaned and bobbed her head up and down. My hand kept time with the imaginary Delaine's movements. Faster and tighter I stroked myself, and I recalled the night I fucked her mouth, my cock sliding back and forth through her perfectly pink and pouty lips.

Imaginary Delaine looked up at me, and I squeezed the base of my dick tighter, bucking my hips into her mouth. My free hand grabbed on to the edge of my desk so hard I thought I heard the wood crack beneath my fingertips. But her eyes—blue and vibrant with life, so warm, so hungry—they never left mine. She sucked me hard and fast. Then she let my cock go with a pop of her mouth before she tossed her hair over her shoulder, licked from the bottom of my shaft to the top, and then took me in as deep as she could go with a moan of satisfaction.

I grabbed the back of her head and held her there as the heat of my release radiated through my body and my movements became jerky before I spilled my seed down her throat. When I milked myself of all the seed I had, I opened my eyes. She wasn't there, and my hand was covered in my own spunk.

I sighed and reached inside the desk drawer, pulling out a wet wipe and cleaning up my mess.

Once I was sufficiently germ free, I turned on my computer. I queued up the security system and found Delaine in the kitchen. I'd told her she could do whatever she wanted, and this was what she chose to do? She was washing the dishes by hand while dancing around to a beat that was obviously in her head. I'd have to try to remember to buy her an iPod on our shopping excursion. Her hips swayed to and fro as she hopped around and tossed her hair back and forth. Soapsuds floated in the air about her, and she turned in a circle with her head thrown back, spinning and laughing like she didn't have a care in the world. I couldn't help but chuckle when a strand of hair got caught in her mouth and she spat and swiped at it, succeeding in inadvertently landing a clump of bubbles on the tip of her nose. Blowing a puff of air out of her mouth, the bubbles went flying and she went back to work on the dishes.

I closed out the program, knowing the distraction of watching her would keep me from reviewing the files I needed to go over and writing an email to Mason to be forwarded to the board members in the morning.

A couple of hours later, I was seeing double before I was through with my work. I powered down my computer and turned off my desk lamp before heading up to bed.

Delaine was already fast asleep when I reached the bedroom, looking angelic. But I knew she was actually the devil in disguise. I took a quick shower and slid under the covers, pleased to find that she was nude, as requested. So I snuggled into her backside and wrapped my arm around her stomach. She shifted a bit in her sleep and murmured something unintelligible before she settled back down and her breathing evened out.

The thought occurred to me that I might have bitten off more than I could chew with Delaine, and that would never do. Tomorrow I would reassert my position and remind her and myself of the reason she was here.

Tomorrow . . .

~$~

I woke the next morning, my cock in the same precarious position between her creamy thighs as it had been yesterday. Today would be different, though. She was here for a reason, and although I wasn't a total bastard, I did have needs.

My left arm was draped over her waist, my hand cupping the awesomeness that was her boob. (*Seriously, did I just use the word "boob"?* asked the grown-ass man who apparently reverted to a seventeen-year-old kid when he was touching boobies. Dear God, my mind was turning to mush over her tits.) The pad of my thumb swept over her nipple and . . . nothing. Well, that would never do. So I made another pass, pinching it slightly between my thumb and finger with each sweep.

Houston, we have pebbling!

She squirmed a little in her sleep, and I hoped it was because I was making her feel good and not because she could actually hear my overly immature inner ramblings. Her squirming called attention to the iron rod attached to my body and how insanely amazing it felt when it slid back and forth between her warm thighs.

I just needed a wee bit of lubrication and I should be able to sufficiently get off without ever dipping my wick into her virginal pussy. She wasn't ready for that yet, even though I was dying to get in there.

I kissed her bare shoulder and made a slow trail of follow-up kisses along the width of it until I reached her neck. All the while I slowly pumped my hips back and forth and rolled her nipple between my fingers. Delaine gave me a little moan and brought her hand up to cover mine. I froze for a second, concerned that she might protest against what I was doing, and then I realized that I really didn't fucking care if she wanted me to continue or not.

To my surprise, she didn't try to remove my hand. Instead, she started massaging it, encouraging me to knead her breast more aggressively. That one not-so-simple act caused my hips to buck forward, and I could feel her go rigid when her hand shot down between her legs and she found my cock.

"Not yet," I whispered against her neck, and then I began to suck at her skin there.

She shivered in my arms, and that shot straight to my dick, making me impossibly harder. I needed more friction. I moved my hand down her stomach and between her legs and opened her folds to allow her wetness to coat my cock. I slid back and forth a couple of times and couldn't stifle the moan the warmth of her juices elicited.

"You feel so good . . . just . . . like . . . this," I said with each gentle thrust of my hips against her.

Delaine arched her back and changed the angle I was rubbing against, but I knew it still wasn't what she needed. I took her hand and guided it lower so that she could feel us moving together. The arch in her back became even more pronounced as I pressed our hands tighter to the underside of my dick, and because my fingers were longer, I stretched my thumb to press the head of my cock to her clit.

"Oh!" she gasped, and rolled her back to glide along my length until she hit the spot again.

"More," I moaned against her shoulder.

I pulled back and thrust forward again, the head of my dick pressed so closely to her that it inadvertently pressed against her opening. The tip barely entered her before I pulled away and thrust forward again. What surprised the shit out of me was that she was pressing back and didn't even go stiff when I was at her entrance.

Her hand kept me pressed against her as I slid back and forth between her wet folds with more urgency. She didn't need me to keep her in place any longer, so I pulled away and grabbed her hip for leverage. She felt so soft and warm and slick. My cock was swimming in her wetness and I couldn't get enough of it. Harder and faster I thrust, her slick thumb brushing over the slit on the head of my dick and then flicking over the pronounced ridge. She was driving me insane.

I had to slow down, so I made long strokes against her,

purposely letting the head of my dick push against her opening again. She pushed back and I forced just the tip inside. Instantly she froze. She held her breath and tensed up every muscle in her body.

"Relax, baby," I whispered in her ear. My breathing was out of control and I was nuzzling her neck trying to compose myself while the head of my cock was still just barely inside her. Fuck, she smelled so good and she felt even better.

"I want you so fucking bad," I panted, still not moving for fear that I would take her. "Goddamnit, why do you feel so fucking good?"

My cock throbbed with the need to pound into her tight pussy. A little voice inside my head screamed for me to thrust, grind, pull, thrust, grind, pull. Maybe if I just allowed myself a tiny bit more . . .

"Don't move, kitten," I murmured against the nape of her neck.

I inched forward minutely, feeling her walls constrict around me as I allowed the entire head of my cock to be encompassed by her. A minuscule amount of movement was all I allowed myself.

"Don't . . . move." My voice was practically begging her as I squeezed my eyes shut and fought back the urge to give my cock exactly what he wanted.

A tiny whimper escaped her throat and I felt her hand slip between her thighs to stroke me.

"Fuck!" I pulled out of her abruptly and shot out of bed.

"What? What's wrong?" She sat up, confused.

"Goddamnit! You can't do shit like that, Delaine! It's tak-

ing every ounce of control I have not to fuck the living day-
lights out of you right now, and you go and encourage me!
What were you thinking?"

She bowed her head and let her hair fall like a curtain to
shield her face from me. She rocked back and forth with her
forehead on her knees as she mumbled. "I don't know. I guess
I thought you'd like it. You just felt so good," she groaned.

Well, what do ya know? She fucking wanted it, too.

A giant smile spread across my face, and I stalked back
toward the bed, my dick still at full mast and ready to give her
what we both wanted. And then my cocksucker of a goddamn
motherfucking son-of-a-bitch cell phone started ringing. I had
half a mind to chuck the fucker out of the damn window, but
I knew I couldn't.

I groaned and walked over to the nightstand where it sat,
my dick bobbing up and down with my movement. "Crawford!" I barked into the phone.

"Good morning, Mr. Crawford. I hope I didn't wake you,"
replied the nasal voice of David's secretary.

"What do you want, Mandy?"

"Mr. Stone wanted me to let you know that he's called an
emergency meeting of the board members in light of the re-
cent crisis," she said.

"What crisis?"

"Have you not seen the news? The stock market is plum-
meting all over the place due to the oil spill. Scarlet Lotus's
holdings have taken a real hit."

"Son of a . . . ." I started, wiping at my face. "Fine. I'll be in
right away. Tell Mason to wait for me downstairs with the lat-
est reports."

I hung up the phone without another word and turned to Delaine. "I'm sorry, but I won't be able to take you shopping today."

"What am I supposed to do about clothes? Wear more of your things?" she asked with much attitude as she finally looked up at me.

"As much as I love to see you wearing my clothes, I don't really have anything small enough for you." And then I got an idea. "I'll have Polly take you instead. She has great taste."

I pulled my wallet out of the nightstand drawer and took out the gold card. "Here. Don't be worried about how much you spend; I'm sure Polly won't be. I'll call her and let her know what you'll need, but you can get anything else that you'd like."

"And in the meantime?" she asked, looking down at herself. "I can't exactly go out looking like this."

"I'll have Polly bring something of hers for you to borrow."

I dialed Polly on my way to the bathroom and filled her in on what Delaine needed in her wardrobe, saving the lingerie shopping for me to do with her, of course. There would be parties that we would need to attend, and I wanted to be sure she was dressed appropriately. Of course Polly was all too happy to take Delaine on a shopping spree on my dime. I warned her not to be too pushy with Delaine and to let her pick some things out on her own. I also gave her explicit instructions not to pry. Anything Delaine wanted her to know, she'd share of her own accord.

When I had finished getting dressed, I gave Delaine last-minute instructions. "Don't tell her anything about our arrangement, no matter how hard she digs for the information.

Tell her what you want of your personal life, but as far as anyone knows, we met in LA. I should be home around six. Make sure you're waiting for me at the door."

With that, I picked her up, accosted her mouth with a rough kiss, and let her fall back to the bed. "I was really looking forward to having you model lingerie for me today. Another time." I winked and playfully smacked her ass before grabbing my briefcase and jacket.

I hated having to leave her like that to deal with Polly alone on their very first meeting, but I had no choice. Hopefully she'd be strong enough to deal with Polly, or evasive enough to keep her at bay for the time being. Plus I was really hoping the whole shopping spree thing would soften the blow by keeping Polly too distracted to pry.

I could only hope. . . .

6

dastardly duo

Lanie

"Hello? Is anybody home?" I heard a singsong voice call from the entryway. "Delaine? It's me, Polly, personal shopper extraordinaire, here to whisk you away to what I consider to be paradise."

I hurried down the staircase, wearing the same shirt I had put on the night before for dinner. And, as embarrassed as I was to meet a stranger for the first time in nothing but my john's shirt, I really had no other choice.

"Make sure the silver gets polished this week, and tell the cook to change tonight's menu to pot roast." Polly scribbled something on a paper attached to a clipboard and then handed it back to the same maid who had given me directions to the kitchen yesterday morning. "Thanks, Beatrice. You're all doing a wonderful job, as usual."

She looked up then and saw me. "Oh, hey!" Obviously she was one of those cheery morning-person types. Her hair was platinum blond and bouncy, and she was so smiley and unbelievably gorgeous that she reminded me of a high school cheer captain in an eighties movie. It was almost infectious, and part of me wanted to punch her for making me feel like that.

"Um, hi," I said awkwardly. "Lanie Talbot."

"Polly Hunt," she said with a wide smile. "I'm so ecstatic to finally meet you!"

I stuck my hand out in a friendly gesture, but she rolled her eyes playfully. "Oh, please!" She snorted softly through her pert nose as she waved off my somewhat formal greeting. "We're going to be shopping all day together. In my world, that's like having sex." She giggled and then grabbed me for a quick hug. "This is for you, by the way," she said, handing me a pink bag.

"Clothes?" I asked, just to be sure.

"Yes, ma'am. Say, what happened to all of your clothes anyway?"

"About that . . . ," I hedged, not having a clue how to answer. "My moving here to be with Noah was kind of a rushed decision, and I didn't really have time to pack very much. What little I did bring didn't seem to be up to par with the styles and trends you guys wear around here, so I got rid of them."

There. That sounded like fashion-speak, right?

Polly arched a perfectly manicured brow, and I could see the wheels turning in her head. She squinted her eyes at me in doubt. "And you were naked when you did this?"

"Um, no," I half laughed. "Of course not, silly. The clothes I had on are just dirty. Yeah, they're dirty."

"Uh-huh." She eyed me suspiciously. "Well, why don't you go ahead and get changed and we'll get going?"

~$~

Riding in Polly's little red Beamer scared the shit out of me. Multitasking was a gift, but I wasn't so sure it was a gift that should've been used while driving. She was doing well over the legal speed limit while bopping along to the radio and talking even faster than she drove without taking so much as a breath that I could tell. Every now and then she honked the horn and cursed at a fellow motorist for going too slow or changing lanes at a time that wasn't convenient for her.

"It's Chicago. Learn to keep up or get off the road, ass-holes!" She looked at me and shook her head while rolling her eyes. "People who are obviously scared are dangerous and have no business behind the wheel of a car."

I agreed, but hyperactive, road-rage types who were strung out on caffeine shouldn't be allowed behind the wheel either, for that matter.

She whipped into a spot just vacated by another vehicle. And when I say "just vacated," I mean the other car was barely even out of the spot before she parallel-parked without slow-ing down, running up on the curb and forcing some of the pedestrians walking on the sidewalk to scramble out of the way.

I managed to wrench my fingertips out of the dashboard, where I was sure there would be lingering imprints, and got out of the car. I would have been perfectly willing to kiss the ground had it not been so grotesque. Public streets and side-walks were like petri dishes cultivating death cocktails.

Polly popped her sunglasses on, threw her purse strap over her shoulder, and said, "Let's go, *chica*." Her three-inch heels and short dress, which looked like it was made for a little girl instead of a grown woman, would've been a big no-no for me, but she pulled it off without a hitch. Seriously, the woman was too cute with a side of come-here-lovah-boy.

We went into the first shop, and the ladies behind the counter recognized her immediately, even calling her by name.

"Friends of yours?" I asked.

"Professionally, not socially," she said under her breath. "You might say I'm a frequent flyer here. Plus I tip very well."

"Ladies," she said, turning back to them and holding up Noah's gold card, "if you would be so kind as to hook my new friend up with your finest."

I was rushed into a dressing room to strip, and before I even had all of my clothes off, garments were being slung over the door. I groaned inwardly, because shopping just was not my thing, but I had to admit that I felt sort of like Julia Roberts in *Pretty Woman*, being fussed over like that.

Polly stood outside the door praising things she approved of and scoffing at things she didn't. I thought I was safe in my own little room, closed off from the rest of the world, but Polly wasn't having that. She pushed open the door and strolled right on in like I didn't have anything she hadn't ever seen before. I supposed I didn't, but still, I might have wanted to retain a wee bit of privacy.

I was beginning to learn quickly that in Noah's world, apparently my body was a free-for-all. So I gave up caring and let what my mama gave me hang out like I was a centerfold to be envied, though I was far from it.

"So," Polly sighed as she sat down on the bench in my dressing room and watched me. "Tell me all about how you and Noah met."

"Um, I guess like anyone else does," I said, trying to figure out the contraption of a dress that she'd handed to me to try on next.

"No one meets in exactly the same way. Everyone has a story. Give me the details, girlfriend," she said, helping me with the dress.

And then I got giddy because her curiosity was going to let me play with Noah a bit. He had told me to say as much as I wanted. "Well, he'd probably kill me for telling you this, so I'll have to swear you to secrecy."

"Bitch's honor." She put her middle and index fingers directly under her eyes like Samantha on *Bewitched*. She won me over completely with that little maneuver—a psycho after my own heart.

"I met him outside a drag queen show," I said in a hushed whisper. "He was so pretty that I thought he was one of the performers."

"Noah Crawford was at a drag queen show?" Polly shrieked, and then started giggling when I cupped my hand over her mouth and shushed her.

"He *said* that he wasn't familiar with the area, wanted a drink, and wandered in there by mistake," I embellished. "He was outside smoking a cigarette when I showed up, and I've always secretly wondered if it was because he'd just gotten his rocks off."

Polly and I laughed together, and it felt really nice.

"Then what?" she asked, hanging on my every word.

"Well, I might have given him the 'uh-huh, like I'm going to believe that' look, at which point he proceeded to ogle the girls," I said, flexing the boobage. "Just to prove a point, I'm sure."

"You do have nice tits." She shrugged, as if to say, *That makes sense.*

"So anyway, he asked me out for a drink, and because he was so cute, trying to prove how manly he was, I let him fuck me. I haven't been able to get rid of him since," I laughed.

"Well, I'm glad to hear he's finally decided to settle down somewhat, especially after what happened with Julie," she said, adjusting my tits in the dress. I think she secretly wanted to grope them. I wasn't the least bit offended, if that was the case, but I *was* curious about what she'd said.

"Julie? Who's Julie?" I asked, eager for any intel on Noah's past. Not because I cared, but because I wanted the ammunition should the need for it arise later.

"No one. Never mind. I shouldn't have said anything," she said quickly. "Hey, you are absolutely smoking in this dress."

Way to change the subject, little sneaky one. I'll have to keep my eye on you, I thought.

~$~

I couldn't even begin to tell you how long we spent shopping. I let Polly choose the majority of the clothes, and all of the shoes. I wasn't opposed to looking nice, and I actually really loved all the cute shoes she picked out, even though I knew they were a safety hazard for someone like me. She refused to let me buy any underwear because Noah wanted to do that part. But really, couldn't a girl just get some regular cotton panties?

Finally Polly decided we should break for a late lunch.

"So, tell me a little bit about yourself," she said, digging into her salad.

"What do you want to know?"

"I don't know. The basics, I guess. Where are you from? Who are your parents? What do you do? That sort of stuff. I mean, Noah even kept your name hush-hush," she said with a roll of her eyes, clearly aggravated by his refusal to give her any details about me.

"That's because I'm in the witness protection program," I said nonchalantly before I took a bite of my sandwich.

"You're what?" She dropped her fork.

"Yep," I said, doing my damnedest not to crack a smile.

My attempt was futile because the look on her face was simply priceless, and I lost it, practically spewing bread crumbs all over the place.

"You little liar!" she laughed. "You almost had me there. Now, tell me the truth."

"Okay, the truth is I'm from Graceland and Elvis Presley is my father."

"Elvis and Graceland?" she said with an arched brow. "Aren't you a little too young to be his kid?"

"Uh-uh. Haven't you heard? He isn't really dead. He's off with Tupac and Biggie, popping pills and smoking ganja."

Polly sighed and rolled her eyes.

"Would you believe Michael Jackson and the Neverland Ranch?" I asked in my best Maxwell Smart impersonation. "I'm white enough for that, right?"

"All right, smartass," she said, throwing a cucumber slice at me. "I get it. You obviously don't want to talk about yourself. But why is that, Lanie? What are you hiding?"

"Oh, no, you don't." I pointed an accusing finger at her. "Noah already warned me all about your conniving little ways. Don't try to go all supersleuth on me. I'm really just not that interesting. I come from a small town, and I moved out to LA because I had big dreams of breaking into the porn industry. It just didn't work out." I shrugged.

Polly choked on her water and I couldn't help but laugh at the look of shock on her face.

"I'm kidding . . . about the small town." I giggled.

That earned another huff from Polly, but she finally dropped the subject when I asked her to tell me about herself. Apparently she had no secrets whatsoever. She even told me about the sexual position she and her husband had tried out the night before, and said I should try it with Noah. But what she didn't know, and could never know, was that I was a virgin hooker and really had no say in what Noah and I did in the bedroom . . . or on the dining room table . . . or in the limo . . . or in the bathtub, for that matter. Not that I'd know what the hell I was doing in the first place.

At last lunch had been eaten, the little black strip on the back of Noah's gold card had been worn down, and the trunk of Polly's car was almost too full to close. We were on our way back to the Crawford estate and I hadn't given up one morsel of information, so I was pretty darn proud of myself. I wasn't sure Polly had actually believed anything I'd told her all day, except maybe the drag queen show tidbit. Honestly, she wasn't as tough as Noah had led me to believe.

We pulled to a stop in the circular driveway, and Polly stopped the car right in front of the door. She didn't get out, though. She turned to me and pulled her sunglasses down, looking over the top rim. "I like you, Lanie. I really do. And I can already tell we're going to be great friends," she started. "But let's get something clear. You need to understand that Noah is more than just a boss to me and Mason. He's our friend, and Lord knows he doesn't have many of them. He's been hurt before, and I can't stand idly by and let something like that happen again. So as long as you're being good to him, I won't pry into your personal life."

I put my hand on her shoulder and gave her a serious look. "You're a terrible liar, Polly, but I'll try not to hold it against you."

Her mouth dropped open as if she was offended, but she knew she'd been called out. Just then Samuel came out to help us with my bags. I gave Polly a wink and got out, leaving her sitting there with her mouth still hanging open.

I thought it was sweet that Polly was so protective of Noah. If only she'd known the truth behind our relationship, she wouldn't have been so quick to give me the "if you hurt him, I'm going to have to kick your ass" speech. She never actually threatened me outright, but she was most definitely warning me.

"This isn't over, Lanie!" she called from the car as Samuel and I made our way into the house.

"See you tomorrow, Polly!" I called over my shoulder with a giggle, then disappeared inside the house.

I went up to Noah's bedroom and started going through the bags. I had no clue where to put my things, but something told me that most of what Polly had picked out wasn't supposed to be balled up and stuffed in a drawer somewhere. I went to his closet and opened it up. I'd like to say I was shocked by the meticulous way he had everything stored there, but I wasn't. I saw neat rows of shoes, each pair polished to perfection; his dress shirts were arranged by color, as were the suit pants and jackets, all sheathed in plastic dry cleaner's bags. But the real kicker was that everything was spaced so that nothing touched anything else.

He was such a super freak.

So what could I do? I grinned and bit the corner of my mouth. Then I shoved all of his clothes to one side and hung my clothes up alongside his. If he didn't like it, he could just give me my own room.

~$~

By quarter of six, everything was put away and I was waiting by the front door, as Noah had instructed. Kind of ridiculous, if you asked me, him expecting me to just stand there like June Cleaver, waiting for him to come walking through the door. I supposed he'd probably get a real kick out of it if I took his briefcase from him, handed him his sweater, and kissed him on the cheek before leading him to the den to sit in his favorite chair where his slippers and pipe were waiting. Not bloody likely, Ward.

The click of the doorknob brought me out of my TV Land fantasy, and I stopped biting my cuticles. Noah looked like hell warmed over, but the smile on his face was instant.

"Hi, honey! How was your day?" I asked with the biggest, fakest, most sarcastic smile I could muster.

Noah huffed out a laugh and set his briefcase down on the

table. He ran his hands through his hair as he cocked his head to the side and regarded me. "It was shitty."

"Aw, poor baby," I cooed, poking out my bottom lip to mock him. "Sitting behind a desk all day in a cushy air-conditioned office while other people wait on you hand and foot sounds absolutely grueling."

"You know, I like your mouth better when it's got something in it." He reached for the front of his pants and undid his belt. "So why don't you come here and make my day a little better?" he said as he pulled out his cock.

My mouth dropped open, and I imagined I had the same look on my face that Polly had had in the car earlier.

"Yeah, just like that, only on my dick."

"Right here? In the entryway? But I'm not sure the cook is gone yet. What if someone sees us?" I said with a frantic rush of words. I may have been panicking, but Double Agent Coochie was already on her knees with her hands raised in prayer, begging me to just go with it.

"Well, now, that would be part of the allure, wouldn't it?" He reached out and pulled me closer to him. I could feel the movement of his hand against my stomach as he stroked himself. Noah's hot breath washed over my face, his lips mere inches from mine. "I bet that turns you on, doesn't it, Delaine? The fear of being caught on your knees with my dick in your mouth?"

The tip of his tongue snaked across my bottom lip and barely flicked at my upper lip, teasing me beyond distraction. "I'm going to introduce you to things you never even dreamed of doing before," he murmured. "Forbidden things that I guarantee you're going to love."

I suddenly remembered that I was still without panties, and Double Agent Coochie was now drooling all over my thighs. The man had a wicked way with words.

Caught in his trance, I sank to my knees in front of him and took his cock in my hands. He groaned when I licked my lips and then gave the head a sensual kiss, capturing the little pearl drop of pre-come on the tip. I made a big show of swallowing it, like I was savoring his flavor. That earned me yet another moan.

"You like that, Noah?" I asked in a deep, sultry voice.

He stroked my cheek with the back of his hand and then gently entwined his fingers in my hair. With one swift motion, he pulled my head forward and pushed his cock into my mouth.

"Yeah, I fucking love it."

I made fast work of him, sucking and licking and bobbing, practically swallowing him whole, just the way I remembered he liked it from my first night there. I grabbed his hips and pushed and pulled him, faster and faster. His head dropped back and he balled his hands into fists in my hair.

"Too much. Too quick," he grunted as he tried to pull away, but I wasn't having it.

I grabbed his cock again and pulled him forward. If he was going to pull away, he was going to do it without his dick attached to his body, and I was pretty confident he didn't want that. I could feel his pulse throbbing in my mouth and I relaxed my throat, taking him as deep as I could, while desperately trying not to gag on him.

He growled, and then I felt the hot semen spurt down my throat. His movements became jerky and I looked up at him, seeing his face scrunched up like he was in pain. Looks could be deceiving. As much as I hated to admit it, he had a very sexy come face.

When his grip on my hair loosened and his body began to relax, I slowly backed off, licking him along the way. Then I let his cock go and watched it bounce lifeless.

"You were paying attention. Good girl." And then he patted me on the head like a dog before tucking himself away in his pants.

That arrogant son of a whore!

"I don't know about you, but I've really worked up an appetite. Let's eat," he said, clapping his hands.

Noah

All fucking day long I'd been trying to conceal the constant hard-on in my overly expensive pants. Christ, you'd think if you paid that much money for something, it would come equipped with some fancy gadget to help out a dude with just this sort of situation—Go Go Gadget Cock Block or something.

Pfft, whatever.

I kept imagining Delaine naked, trying on different outfits and spiked heels . . . all . . . damn . . . day. Plus, David Stone wasn't exactly my favorite person in the world to hang out with. The fucktard jumped to conclusions and acted like every little dip in the market was the end of the world. Scarlet Lotus was a resilient company and had always stood strong. This little crisis would be no different.

So I was glad to finally be home, and I was even happier to see that Delaine was waiting by the door. Truthfully, I'd never thought she'd follow my instructions and be there, but she was. And she was running that smart-ass mouth of hers, making my dick even harder than it already was.

Not a very wise move on her part. So I stuffed something in it to shut her up. I deserved a big pat on the back for thinking quickly on my feet.

And it had felt incredible, too. When I tried to back away and she grabbed me and forced me to stay put? Goddamn! My million-dollar baby was learning to crawl, and I think I might have gotten a little tear in my eye.

I was perfectly aware that my patting her on the head like a dog was going to piss her off, but that was what she deserved for acting like a bitch.

As my punishment, I suppose, she was silent during dinner. She wouldn't even answer outright questions, and that pissed me off more, but I let that shit go, because I was planning some punishment of my own. Eager to get to it, I insisted she join me in bed right after I rushed her through dinner. She was stripped buck naked and waiting for me under the covers when I finished in the bathroom. Just as she should be. Just as I had paid her to be.

"Are you angry with me?" I asked as I sauntered across the room, wearing nothing but a smile.

She didn't answer. In fact, she actually rolled over and turned her back to me. Fuck that. I would not be ignored. Not in my house, and most certainly not in my bed.

I slid in next to her and rolled her on her back. "Don't ignore me, Delaine. I don't like it. Especially when I've paid millions of dollars to be lavished with attention."

Her eyes flickered to mine. "I'm not your bitch."

"You're anything I want you to be," I reminded her.

Before she could say anything else, I covered her mouth with my own. Her lips were unyielding and her body stiff. She was going for the dead-lay play. I had to hand it to her because it was a brilliant plan, but I'm sure she must have forgotten how traitorous her body could be when at the mercy of my capable hands.

Her punishment: bring her right to the edge of ecstasy without ever letting her fall off into it.

I pulled back and smirked at her, ready and willing to play her little game. Then, without taking my eyes off her face, my hand went to the inside of her thighs and I pushed her knees apart before quickly cupping her pussy in my hand. She gasped only minutely, doing her best not to show any sort of reaction. I kept watch over her as I slid my fingers between her folds, feeling them become slicker and slicker with each pass over her entrance.

"Your body betrays you, Delaine," I told her in a low voice.

I inserted one finger inside her, slowly moving in and out. Her chest rose and fell with heavier breaths and her mouth was agape, but she met my gaze and made no sound. I took my finger out and circled her clit instead, feeling the muscles in her legs twitch as she fought to keep them under control. Two fingers dipped inside her. I curled them back and forth, masterfully manipulating her G-spot. I knew it. She knew it. But she refused to show it.

I pulled my fingers out and brought my hand to my mouth. They were glistening with her juices and I could smell her arousal. She still hadn't averted her stare, so I knew she could see her wetness.

"You're trying to act like you're not affected, but you and I both know differently. And this . . . this is the proof." I stuck my fingers in my mouth and closed my lips around them. She was so delicious I had to close my eyes to savor her taste. When I opened them again, her once vibrantly blue eyes had darkened and her cheeks were flushed.

She grabbed me by my ears and pulled me to her, crashing her mouth to mine. I would've laughed out loud at how easy it was to break her, but she was kissing me so greedily, her nipples pressing against my bare chest with each of her labored breaths, and she was writhing around, trying to ensnare my legs.

In short, my shit backfired on me, and I couldn't play games with her anymore. I wanted her. I fucking needed her.

Without breaking the kiss, I rolled on top of her for that prime position to bring us both pleasure. Her legs opened to me eagerly and I stroked her tongue seductively with my own in thanks. I had no more settled between her legs than she was lifting her hips, grinding against my cock while moaning into my mouth.

"Slow down, baby," I said with panting breaths as I broke the kiss and tried to ease her urgent movements. "Don't worry. I'm going to make you feel good."

I kissed her softly as I began to shift my hips against her sweet spot. Delaine's back arched off the bed and I wrapped my arm around her to hold her to me. Then I moved along her jaw and down her neck, finding the place where her neck met her shoulder, and sucked gently, all the while grinding slowly against her.

She was so wet, so receptive. Her hands drifted down my sides and over my ribs until she was finally cupping my ass, urging me closer. I could feel her warm breath brush over the shell of my ear, and her tiny whimpers of desperation sent shock waves straight to my dick. She buried her face in my neck, sucking and licking at the skin there. Oh, God, I just couldn't take any more. I needed her to come, and I needed it now.

I lifted myself off her but kept contact with my hips, still moving back and forth between her slick folds. She was biting her lip so hard I thought she was going to break the skin. A look of pure concentration was etched in her features as she pulled and pushed against me with longer strokes. She was almost there.

I leaned down on one elbow and cupped the back of her thigh with one hand and hoisted her leg over my hip. Back and forth I rocked with long, thick strokes, feeling her clit rub over the head of my dick.

"Come on, kitten. Talk to me. It feels good, doesn't it? So fucking good. Don't you just want to lose control? Let it go, baby. Let it go."

"Holy shit! I'm going to . . ." She moaned loudly, her eyes rolling to the back of her head.

I felt Delaine's body go rigid in my arms and I knew she was feeling the bliss of the orgasm I brought her. Without hesitating, I lined myself up with her opening and pushed my cock into her, stealing her virtue with one short, swift thrust.

Her back arched off the bed with a sharp intake of breath. Her mouth hung open, shocked as her eyes found mine.

I'd hoped taking her virginity in midclimax would make it easier, but I couldn't tell if it actually had. I mean, I had mirrors. I knew how big my cock was.

"Breathe, kitten," I whispered. "Just try to relax. It won't hurt for very long."

I didn't know whom I was trying to convince, me or her, but I didn't move, either. Even though every primal urge inside begged me to thrust into her over and over again, I didn't. If I couldn't get myself under control and allow her to acclimate to my size, I'd end up ripping her to shreds. Then I wouldn't get to do this again for quite some time. Plus I'd feel like an ass for causing her more pain than necessary.

Delaine exhaled slowly as her body began to relax and sink back onto the bed. I pushed forward, further sheathing myself inside her tight little pussy. She clenched her eyes shut and bit down on her lip again. I knew I shouldn't have given a damn about whether or not I was hurting her, but I was a man, and most men actually want the woman they have their dick buried inside to at least enjoy it. However, this was her first time, and given my size, it wasn't likely she was going to be getting off.

I pulled almost all the way out and pushed back in slowly. I had to stop again. My legs shook with the effort not to move, sweat dripped from the tip of my nose, and I think I may have actually stopped breathing. I seriously thought I was in danger of exploding from the inside out.

"Fuck, you feel so good. So fucking tight," I moaned.

"Then what the hell are you waiting for?" she asked in a challenge. "Fuck me and stop acting like a pansy. Unless, that is, you're worried you'll come too soon. Jesus, if I didn't know better, I'd think you were the virgin here." It was the most she'd said since greeting me when I came home. Her voice was off, betraying her exertion, but she was determined to push my buttons.

You'd think a comment like that would obliterate my erection. But it didn't. It just made me unbearably harder, if that was possible. There was just something about her mouth and the way she challenged me that turned me on. I was a sick bastard. But I didn't really give a fuck because she was feeding my already scorching need for her.

"Oh, you really shouldn't have said that," I shot back, then pulled all the way out, only to thrust back into her again.

She hissed between her teeth and squeezed her eyes shut. I made short movements in and out, not really wanting to hurt her, but not caring if it felt good to her, either. She was mine, there for my pleasure, and I was going to make sure she knew I hadn't forgotten about that.

"This is my pussy, Delaine. My fingers were the first to touch it, my mouth the first to taste it, and my cock will always be the first to fuck it. And for the rest of your life, the memory of having me this deep inside you will always be on your mind. No other man will ever compare. I have officially marked my territory. *My* pussy. Do you understand?"

Her nails were digging into my skin where she was holding on for dear life, and her teeth were clenched, but she still managed to eke out, "Last time I checked, it was attached to my body."

"Wrong answer." I thrust deep, not hard enough to hurt her, just enough to get her attention.

She gasped. "Jesus Christ!"

"I think you know that's not my name. Try again."

I kept moving inside her, feeling the pressure build up within me quickly. My balls were aching, begging for the release, but I couldn't give in yet.

Her nails dug into the skin on my back and she pushed her hips upward with a growl. Her teeth were still clenched and her thighs clamped down on my hips as she met my thrusts. I had to give it to her—I was impressed. I knew she was uncomfortable, possibly even in pain, but she wasn't giving in.

"Say . . . it!" I growled back at her, punctuating each word with a deep thrust.

Her breath caught, but she met my eyes in challenge. Another hard thrust and I heard her whimper. "It's yours! My pussy is yours, Noah Crawford!"

That was all I needed to hear. With one more deep thrust, I came, grunting out my own orgasm. I let all of my weight fall on top of her and kissed her, groaning into her mouth as I pumped my hips sporadically until I had no more seed to give. She kissed me back hungrily, attempting to dominate the kiss, to prove a point that didn't even need to be proven, as much as it pained me to admit it. She could keep up with me, tit for motherfucking tat. And if she could do that her very first time, I was in a whole hell of a lot of trouble.

Lanie

That hurt insanely! Do you hear me? Insanely!

It wasn't so bad when he first pushed into me. Having been

in midorgasm and caught totally unaware that he was planning to do it probably helped. I was just stunned. But I was relieved that the whole popping of the cherry thing was finally done, even though the Cooch had taken quite a beating.

It was when Noah kept stopping that I got pissed off. The longer he took to get it over with, the more uncomfortable I was going to be. Or so I thought. Because once he got going, that feeling of being completely filled was actually pretty close to the best thing I had ever felt. I had known it was going to hurt because he was inhumanly huge and all, but feeling that raw power between my thighs and taking it like a trouper made me feel like a superwoman.

And then I had to go and open my big mouth and challenge him. I guess I was a nitwit with a penchant for punishment; one of those sickos who just couldn't admit defeat, even though I knew I was being outscrewed, as it were. Like a rookie cop on the scene of a bloodbath in progress who rushes in with their gun all half-cocked, thinking they're going to take down career criminals.

A supercop I was not, but Double Agent Coochie was donning her cape and knee-high red leather boots like she was some kind of superhero, complete with neon blue unitard and gold belt with a flaming red *C* emblazoned on her chest.

I guess she missed the memo that we'd just had our asses handed to us.

Noah rolled over onto his back and pulled me into his arms until I was half lying on his chest. "Are you okay?" he asked softly.

I nodded, not really sure what to say. I didn't want to admit that it had hurt. I didn't want to admit that it had been a complete turn-on. I didn't want to admit that there were parts of it that I had really and thoroughly enjoyed. So I stayed mute.

Wonder Cooch, on the other hand, was already kicked back with a cigarette, blowing smoke rings with a satisfied smile on her face.

"It'll get better," he said, tenderly running his hand up and down my arm, which only made me curl my leg over his thigh and snuggle into him. Like the two-faced whore that I apparently was.

I could hear his heart beating hard and fast in his chest, and my head rose and fell with his heavy breathing. A light sheen of sweat covered his skin, and without thinking, I tasted him with an openmouthed kiss. That kiss led to another, and then another until I had his nipple in my mouth.

"You probably don't want to do that, Delaine," he said, all breathy and sexy-like. "I have a pretty quick recovery time, and I'm sure you're nowhere near ready for another round."

Noah's fingers drew lazy patterns down my spine and over my ass before retracing the trail on the way back up to my neck. His breathing was becoming normal and his heartbeat, although still prominent, was evening out.

"I need a cigarette." He sighed and moved a little beneath me, so I backed away from him so that he could sit up on the side of the bed. He grabbed a cigarette and his lighter from the nightstand and lit it, exhaling the smoke as he turned toward me.

"You might feel better if you take a hot bath. I'll go run some water for you." He got up and strutted toward the bathroom.

There was something in his face that I couldn't quite discern. Did he regret what we had done? Part of me knew that couldn't be it, but I'd seen him in this mode before, after the gyno visit. And then it occurred to me: he might not have regretted taking my virginity, but he sure did feel responsible for my discomfort, and now he was trying to take care of me.

Now why did the bastard have to go and act all sweet like that? I don't know about the rest of you ladies, but I found it incredibly hard to hate someone who was being nice to me.

Double Agent Coochie thought we should show our appreciation. Benedict Arnold was switching sides on me in favor of the O. And there you have it—Super Cooch was hopelessly addicted to the Wonder Peen, and they were joining forces to form the dastardly duo.

baby did a bad, bad thang

Lanie

I woke the next morning to find that I was lying on my back, which wasn't how I usually slept. Something warm and heavy was on my stomach, and I cracked an eye open to investigate. Dark, tousled hair tickled my skin with each rise of his head forced by my inhalation. He was on his side, his face positioned just far enough down my body to allow his hot breath to spill across the sensitive flesh of my nether region. I closed my eyes and swallowed thickly at the sensation, feeling more like a woman than I ever had. It was a very good feeling.

Noah shifted in his sleep, and it drew my attention to the warmth of his hand on the inside of my thigh, dangerously close to my center. I moaned at the dual sensation of his breath and touch and then clamped a hand over my mouth to stifle the sound, hoping like crazy he hadn't heard me.

Double Agent Coochie had most definitely heard me. She was waggling her brows and motioning for me to shove his head between my legs. *Please go back to sleep, Slutty McSlutterson.*

Noah mumbled something and turned his face into my stomach. His movement actually brought his head closer to my pussy, and I arched a brow at Coochie, wondering where she'd gotten the superpowers to actually make that happen. Shameless hussy.

He cupped my thigh and slid his hand up far enough that his fingers were resting against my slit, and I instinctively pushed my hips into him. I didn't mean to. It just sort of happened, a reflex or something like that.

"Mmm," Noah mumbled in his sleep. At least I was pretty sure he was still asleep.

And I'll be damned if that sound, coupled with his proximity to my girly parts, didn't make me all horny. I started doing some mental calculations, wondering if I could possibly get off on him while he slept, with him never being the wiser. But of course that would've depended greatly on how heavy a sleeper he was. And let's face it, I wasn't exactly experienced in that area.

But then I suddenly remembered his words from the limo: "I'm here for your pleasure just as much as you are for mine."

So I decided to test the validity of what he had said. You know, to see if he was a man of his word and all. It was purely for experimental purposes, so don't get all judgmental on me.

With one hand I ran my fingers through his hair, while the other brushed along his broad shoulder and down the length of his arm until I found the hand between my legs. Noah stirred a little more, snuggling into my stomach. I couldn't see his face, which meant I also couldn't see his eyes to know if he was awake. Regardless, I kept going.

I laced my fingers through his and lifted his hand to cup my pussy. The weight of his hand there sent shivers through my body and I was instantly wet. His palm rested over my clit, providing a delicious pressure that forced a tiny mewl from my lips. I covered his fingers with mine and manipulated them to move how I wanted them to between my wet folds. I thought I heard Noah take a sharp breath, but to be honest, with all the other sensations I was feeling at the time, I couldn't actually be sure that it wasn't all in my head.

Pushing his middle finger lower, it circled over my opening before I forced it inside my body along with my own. I was a little sore from the previous night, but not terribly so. In and out I worked his long finger. It wasn't the same as when he actually had control of his own movements and touched me the way *he* wanted to touch me, as only the King of the Finger Fuck could. Frustrated, I removed his finger and moved it along my wetness to tease my clit instead.

Both of our fingers were drenched in my arousal, effortlessly moving over the tight knot of nerves at the apex of my folds as I worked myself into a frenzied state. I could feel him twitching, definitely awake and wanting to move of his own accord. But he didn't. He left me in control, and I wasn't sure that I even really wanted it at that point. I just wanted to get off.

So I dipped two of his fingers inside me and brought them back out, hoping to entice him into taking over. When that didn't work, I lifted his hand and brought the same fingers to his mouth, dragging them across his lips, teasing him, practically begging him to want more than the taste.

I felt his lips brush against my fingers as he drew his own into his mouth. He hummed his gratification softly, the delicious sound sending another gush of arousal from my center and down my trembling thighs. I started to pull away, but his unrelenting grip on my wrist was like a shackle. With quiet determination he then brought my soaked fingers to his wicked lips as well, repeating the action as he greedily sucked one into his mouth until my skin tingled in pleasure at the thoroughness of his tongue. After lapping up all of my juices on that one finger, he moved his attention to the other. The man had mad Hoover skills that went directly to my clit, and it pulsed in response.

"There's more where that came from," I whispered suggestively. Then I pulled at his hair with my free hand and nudged him forward.

"You're actually giving me an open invitation?" His husky voice was thick with sleep.

"I'm giving you what we both want," I said as I lifted my hips in unspoken invitation, hoping to entice him to respond.

Before I even had a chance to lower myself to the bed, Noah had flipped over and was now between my legs, his nose skimming my swollen clit while his lips hovered dangerously close to where I wanted him to be.

"You fucking make me crazy, Delaine," he groaned. "You shouldn't offer yourself so willingly to someone who's supposed to disgust you. It doesn't make any sense."

I sighed. "I do believe you said you love a woman who knows what she wants? Well, right now, what I want is your mouth on me." Don't ask me where or how an inexperienced, recently de-virginalized person such as myself got the nerve to say something like that. It was just as much a mystery to me, but it felt natural nonetheless.

I rolled my hips toward his face to accentuate my point.

He growled, baring his perfect teeth at me. Then he closed his eyes and took a deep breath. "No."

"No?" I asked, confused.

Double Agent Coochie's mouth dropped open in shock.

He opened his eyes, and the intensity of the now darkened steel gray color that had replaced the hazel almost startled me. "If we do this right now, I'm going to want to fuck you. Hard." He growled the words with heavy breaths. "I won't be gentle, and trust me, your pussy can't handle the kind of beating I'd be putting on it. Yet. So you might want to stop trying to seduce me."

"Don't even, Noah," I scoffed. "What's so different now from when you used me as your dessert bowl the other night? You had enough control not to fuck me then."

"I hadn't had you then. I hadn't felt you wrapped around my cock, squeezing me. God, you felt so good," he said with his eyes closed, apparently reliving the feeling in his mind. Then he shook his head and hoarsely whispered, "I can't."

With the finality of his words still ringing in my ears, he leapt out of bed and raked his hands through his already sleep-disheveled hair—which, just for the record, resembled his I-just-fucked-you hair, and that made Double Agent Cooch ache to run her fingers through it as well.

I brought my addled attention back to him and saw that his cock was still hard as a rock, large and in charge. Damn, his arousal alone was almost enough to make me want to beg for it. Almost.

"You can't do shit like that, Delaine! I could bend you over any available surface in this house and fuck you hard and fast, anytime I want. Don't forget that." He ran his hands over his face and then perched them on his hips. "All right, look. I'm going to go take a dip in the hot tub so that I can try to settle down some. You might want to make sure you're out of my bed and dressed before I get back up here."

"So you're just going to leave me like this?" I asked incredulously as I motioned between my open legs.

His eyes were drawn down to my core like a magnet, and I didn't know if I wanted to giggle over his lack of control or hand him a bib to help with the drool on his chin.

"Fuck!" he growled. "Yes. I'm leaving you like that."

He yanked the door open and was gone. His glorious ass practically smirked at me as he disappeared from sight.

I slammed my head back on the bed and grabbed his pillow, covering my face with it to smother my scream of frustration. Noah Crawford made no sense to me whatsoever. He'd purchased me for exactly this sort of thing, had told me to not be afraid to take what I wanted, but when I swallowed my pride and attempted to do just that, he told me I couldn't, and then he ran away like a scared little girl.

Had something happened in the middle of the night and the roles somehow gotten reversed? Maybe I'd slipped into an alternate universe. And why on earth was I all of a sudden so horny for him? Well, I knew the answer to that one: Double Agent Coochie. The slut had taken over my life.

My pussy was throbbing with need, and I groaned.

I jumped out of bed, still naked as a jaybird, and went after him, hoping I wouldn't get lost in that monster of a house trying to find the hot tub. Also, I might not want the help to see me naked if I were in my right mind, but I wasn't, so it was cool. Besides, it seemed they were never there when Noah was, so it was a safe bet we had the house to ourselves.

I somehow managed to find him despite the size of the house. He was outside; the early morning sun had just made its appearance over the horizon and the sky was bathed in rich oranges and pinks. The backyard was vast and I noticed there was a rather large swimming pool there, but my mind was elsewhere, so I paid little attention to any of the other details. Noah's back was to me and his broad shoulders were stretched out, his arms draped over the side of the tub, as thick steam swirled around him. His head was back and his eyes were closed as he took deep breaths in through his nose and out through his mouth.

I walked toward him, careful not to alert him to my presence. He didn't stir at all as I carefully slipped into the hot tub and slowly inched toward him. His muscled neck was stretched out invitingly and his chiseled chest glistened with water droplets. He was beautiful—a perfect specimen of a predator able to lure its prey by his appearance alone.

I could've stayed like that, ogling him. But I hated him, so you've probably already guessed what I did. Before he could become aware of my intentions and attempt to stop me, I placed my hands on his sides and straddled his lap, immediately nuzzling the spot between his neck and shoulder.

Not what you expected? You try to see if you could pass that opportunity up.

"Delaine, what are you doing?" He grabbed my shoulders and tried to push me back, but I pushed back harder.

"I'm taking what I want, Noah. You don't get to renege on your offer." I positioned myself against his still-hard cock.

"Stop!" he ordered, persistently pushing me away.

I was caught off guard and lost my balance, which in turn made me fall heavily into the heated water. A chlorinated deluge splashed around me, drenching my hair. I huffed in frustration and crossed my arms over my chest, giving him the major stinkeye. Enough was enough. Both the cooch and I were hot, horny, and waaaaaay pissed off.

"What's your problem, Crawford?" I threw my hands into the air and slammed them back down into the water, showering him.

He calmly wiped the drops of water from his face, but his chest was heaving, indicating he was anything but calm. "I'm trying not to hurt you any more than I already have," he said between clenched teeth. "A feat you're making insanely hard for me to do at the moment."

I lunged toward him and scrambled back onto his lap. I grabbed his cock and placed it at my entrance, prepared to do all the work myself. He tried to fight me off, but I was a persistent little minx when I had my mind set on something. And at that moment I needed to prove something to myself. Noah had walked away from me earlier that morning after I'd shamelessly thrown myself at him, and that didn't sit well with me. Rejection sucked.

"Fine! You want it? You got it," he snapped, and then he grabbed my hips and pushed down hard.

"Fuck!" we both yelled at the same time. Only mine was more like a "son of a whore, this shit fucking hurts" kind of a fuck, where his was an "oh my God, this feels so fucking good" kind of a fuck. It was a lot of F-bombs, but completely warranted.

I sucked in a breath and held it as I buried my face in the crook of his neck, my fingertips digging into his shoulders. I tried so hard not to move because doing so would've made it hurt even more.

His hot breath was on my ear. "See? I told you, but you just have to be so stubborn, so defiant, don't you?" His hands rubbed up and down my back in a soothing motion as he continued. "Will you please let me decide when you're ready now? I might have a little more experience than you at this sort of thing."

I nodded in acquiescence, still holding my breath and unable to talk. Noah lifted me off him slowly and cradled me in his lap. He pushed my hair out of my face and stroked my cheek. "I promise there will be plenty of fucking over the next two years, and I really appreciate your eagerness to please both yourself and me. It's what made it too hard for me to take care of you back there in the bedroom."

Normally his assumption that I was all hung up on him and his dick would've earned a snarky response from me. But to be honest, I didn't have it in me. It really did hurt and I felt defeated. Plus, he was right: I was all kinds of hung up—on his dick, not him.

I wasn't stupid. I knew it wasn't normal for me to feel that way about someone I was supposed to hate. I did still hate him, but something totally messed up was going on in my brain and body. Maybe it was Stockholm syndrome or something. I guessed my not exactly being his hostage ruled that out. And I wasn't really being forced to do anything against my will; I'd signed the contract, even decided the terms of said contract. I didn't know whether I was coming or going, but I really wished I'd been coming.

He lifted my chin and softly kissed my lips. "I'm sorry I hurt you," he whispered with his forehead against mine. "This whole thing was supposed to be about pleasure, not pain."

"Yours, not mine," I reminded him.

Noah closed his eyes and sighed before sitting up. "At first? Yeah." He sighed again and watched as his hand caressed the swell of my breasts. "I want you to feel good, Delaine."

Me too. What did he think I'd been trying to do all morning?

I lifted myself from his lap and turned to face him. My fingers twitched, wanting to touch his hair, so I granted them that small favor. He reached for my hips and pulled me to him, his mouth suckling my breast. But I needed more. So I put one foot on the bench seat beside him and nudged him on the shoulder until he released my nipple and sat back. Then I did the same with my other foot and hoisted myself up into a standing position, my body dripping wet. Double Agent Coochie was directly in front of his face, and she puckered her lips for a kiss.

Noah cupped the back of my thighs to offer further support

and keep me from falling. He looked up at me, his hazel eyes a kaleidoscope of colors questioning my intent.

I gave him a half smile and said, "Make me feel good, Noah." Then I laced my fingers through his hair and nudged his head forward.

He smiled at me, his eyes lighting up with desire as he bit down on his bottom lip and shook his head. "Where did you come from, Delaine Talbot?"

He didn't wait for an answer. His mouth was on me, placing openmouthed kisses on my folds, sucking the skin into his mouth while his tongue did that magical thing it did. My head dropped back and I moaned loudly, letting him know just how good he was making me feel. His fingertips were firm against my thighs, demonstrating his strength and assuring me that he wouldn't let me fall. My fingers worked through his hair, urging him closer. Then his very talented tongue dipped inside me and I loosened my hold to allow him movement to thrust it in and out.

"God, I should be paying you," I moaned.

His tongue swirled around my clit and then he lightly grazed the swollen bundle of nerves with his teeth before gently sucking on it.

"Right there," I mewled, pushing my hips closer while pulling his hair to keep him in place.

He kept sucking on my clit while flicking his tongue over it quickly. That inexplicable glorious pressure was building in my girly bits as my legs started shaking. Noah brought his hands up to cup my ass and held me to him. He maneuvered until his fingers were grazing my opening, but he didn't enter. Instead, he went to the puckered skin of my ass and pressed until one finger was inside me.

"Holy fuck!" I screamed out as I came.

My insides exploded and my body started to convulse. I might have been afraid that my knees would buckle and I would fall if I hadn't been so completely overwhelmed by the sensations radiating through every molecule of my body.

"That's right, kitten." His husky voice dripped with lust, even though his mouth was still on me. "Feel good for me. Feel good, only for me."

My hands had such a tight grip on his head, shoving his face into my pussy, that I wasn't sure how he was able to make any coherent sounds. I wasn't even sure how he managed to breathe, let alone talk. He sucked my clit into his mouth again and moved his finger slowly in my ass, causing another orgasmic wave to shoot through my body. I was seeing little tongue-shaped stars by that point and I didn't know how much more I could take, but I wasn't going to stop him.

However, I did let my fingers relax in his hair so that he could regain some freedom of movement. He apparently thought that meant he had permission to stop, because that's exactly what he did.

Note to self: the next time Noah Crawford has his face buried in your pussy, do not let go of the back of his head.

"Come down here, baby," he urged me as he put his hands behind my knees to help me down.

I sank down onto his lap and immediately claimed his mouth with my own, wanting to show some appreciation for the pleasure he had given to me.

"That . . . felt . . . so good," I managed to get out between kisses.

"Yeah?" he asked with a conceited grin.

"Yeah," I said, pressing my sensitive pussy against his hard-on. "I want to make you feel good now."

"Delaine . . . ," he warned.

"I know, I know, but I don't think it will hurt. If it does, we'll stop, okay?"

I wanted to do it, plus I was still so horny for him, even though he'd just gotten me off. I didn't know how to explain it. All I knew was that I really wanted to make him feel good, and I didn't think that sucking him off was going to be enough to show my appreciation after what he had done for me. I wanted him. I wanted his cock buried deep in me.

"Please?" I begged pathetically.

"I want to . . . really fucking bad," he said, squeezing my hips and moving me against him. "But we shouldn't. Not yet."

His hands stilled on me as he turned his head away. And then in this really detached and commanding sort of voice, he said, "We're going shopping today. Go on up to the room and get dressed. I'll use one of the other bathrooms."

What had just happened? He was all Richard Gere sexy and chivalrous one minute, Attila the Hun tyrannical the next.

"So I guess now we're back to the whole 'I bought you and you'll do as you're told' thing?" I asked, stung once again by his rejection.

"We never left there. I said I want you to feel good, but that doesn't change anything. I just wanted you to know that I'm not a total bastard." He still refused to look at me.

"Yeah, well, I disagree," was my only response. If he could act the part of the authoritarian boss, then I could certainly act the part of the disgruntled employee.

I removed myself from his lap again and climbed out of the hot tub. In my rush to find him, I hadn't thought to grab a towel, so when I saw his draped over the back of a nearby lounge chair, I took it for myself. I heard him mutter an expletive behind me, but I didn't think it was over the stupid towel. Regardless, I didn't bother to look back at him before I wrapped it around my torso and went back into the house.

Of course he was right. Not about him not being a total bastard, but about nothing having changed. I had been stupid and naïve to think that his kind words during his momentary lapse meant he actually had a heart. I mean, what sort of knight in shining armor runs out and buys a whore for his own selfish purposes anyway? Regardless of the fact that he wanted me to feel good as well. That was only something else he got off on— knowing he was so good that he could command total control of my body when I'd lost all ability to control it myself.

Back in the room, I jumped into the shower, leaning against the wall as the water washed away my tears of rejection. What the hell was I doing? I'd thrown myself at him, practically attacking the man who was supposed to disgust me. And why? Because he gave great head? I was the disgusting one. He was supposed to be the predator and me his prey. Yet I was carrying on like some crazed nymphomaniac.

And where did I get off, getting off while my mother, the sole reason I'd done this in the first place, was lying at home in her bed, probably dying? I hadn't even called to check in, for

Christ's sake. I didn't think it had anything at all to do with the distraction that was Noah Crawford, but maybe more with my shame, with a fear that if I talked to my folks they'd somehow know what I'd done. Of course that was silly. The fact of the matter remained that I had no clue if they'd found my mother a donor or if the surgery had been scheduled yet. I knew Dez would call me if there was something seriously wrong, but for all intents and purposes, my parents thought I was in New York getting an education, not right under their noses in Chicago getting my freak on. They were probably worried to death that I hadn't called.

I shut the water off and stepped out of the shower. I could hear Noah mumbling a string of profanities from his closet, and I stifled a giggle. Apparently he didn't like my organizational skills. Within minutes, I heard him slam the closet door.

"I'll be in the goddamn car! If you know what's best for you, you won't keep me waiting!"

With that, another door slammed and he was gone.

My towel still wrapped around me, I grabbed my cell phone and sat on the side of the bed. Just one push of a button and two rings later, my father's voice came through on the other end.

"Lanie, sweetie. What's wrong?" Mack's tired voice sent a pang of guilt through me, and I wanted to cry.

"Nothing's wrong. Can't I just call my parents to check in?" I asked, trying to sound irritated, in an attempt to keep the sadness out of my voice.

"Er, yeah, of course you can. How's the Big Apple treating you?"

"Fine. My classes are intense, and one of my professors is a gigantic bastard," I answered, only slightly lying. Okay, so I was doing some serious lying, but technically, there really was someone in authority over me who was educating me. Just not the sort of education my parents thought I would be getting.

"Yeah, well, keep your nose to the grindstone and stay away from all those frat parties and you'll do fine, kiddo."

"Mack, you sound tired. Are you getting any rest at all?"

"I get enough." He sighed, used to hearing me nag him about his own health. "She needs me, ya know?"

"Yeah, I do. How is she?" I asked in a more somber tone.

"Mom's hanging in there. She's awake if you want to talk to her. It might actually make her feel better. In fact, she's got some good news for you."

"Yeah, I'd love to hear her voice." He didn't need to know just how true it was.

I could hear him saying something in the background and then the shuffling of bedcovers as he handed her the phone.

"Lanie? Is that you, baby?" My mother's voice sounded weak.

"It's me, Mom. How are you?" I choked out.

"Meh, I'm not so bad," she laughed lightly. "Hey, I've got good news. An anonymous donor deposited a huge sum of money into our bank account. Can you believe it? Mack says it's a scam, but I think it's an answer to our prayers."

"Oh, wow! That's great, Mom," I said, genuinely happy that I'd brought her a little bit of sunshine when all her days had been filled with gloom.

She started a coughing fit, and Mack had to take the phone

away from her, but not before she managed to cough out, "I love you, baby."

"Is she okay?" I asked my dad, concerned.

"She's fine. Those fits hit her sometimes when she tries to talk too much."

"So, good news about the money, huh? Do me a favor and don't try to overanalyze it or anything," I said. "She needs that money. I don't care where it came from. When is she scheduled for surgery?"

"That's the thing, Lanie." I heard a door close in the background and assumed he had left the room, not wanting her to hear the rest of our conversation. "Having the money is great, but it doesn't do a damn bit of good if she doesn't have a donor. There are so many people ahead of her . . . I don't know if it will be in time."

My God! That thought had never even occurred to me.

"Don't worry, Dad. Miracles have a way of happening when we least expect them."

"You might be right." I could still hear the doubt in his voice.

"I know I am," I affirmed. I'd managed to get the money; somehow I'd manage to get her moved up the transplant list, too. There had to be a way. I refused to believe that the universe would let me put myself through all this only to let her die in the end.

"I've got to get to class. Give her a kiss for me, and promise you'll get some rest."

"Yeah, yeah, yeah. You do know it's the parent's job to worry, right?"

"I'll always worry about you guys. It's killing me that I can't be there right now."

"Don't go all sappy on your old man, Lanie. Get off the phone and go live. Love you, kid." With that the line went dead. I was shocked because Mack rarely ever expressed his feelings. It wasn't like I ever questioned that he loved me. I knew he did. It was just a shock to hear it.

Suddenly I felt a renewed strength in what I was doing. Talking to my parents reminded me of the reason I had been so hell-bent on doing it in the first place. And the truth of the matter was, I would've done this even if Jabba the Hut had been the one to purchase me. As infuriating as Noah was, it could've been worse.

Now I just had to figure out what to do about that transplant list.

Noah

It wasn't right.

The girl was killing me, one raging hard-on at a time. Blue motherfucking balls!

She was too willing, too enticing, too hard to resist. But I'd done it. God help me, I'd done it. Even when she'd stuck out that voluptuous bottom lip of hers, I had resisted. *Welcome to sainthood, Noah Crawford.*

The night before had been great. Really great. But I'd felt like shit afterward. I'd stolen the girl's virginity, for Christ's sake! Everything that should've been in place for something that monumental just wasn't. There was no romantic setting, no vow to love her until the end of time. Only pure animalistic fucking. I'd fucked her. Plain and simple.

And while it had been great for me, I had a hard time believing it had been the be-all-and-end-all for her. Yet she wanted more. Delaine Talbot was a glutton for punishment.

But it was what I wanted, right? Someone there to fulfill all my sexual desires and fantasies, a woman who would cater to my needs, while I wouldn't have to give a shit about hers. No emotional ties, no arguments over where we were going to have dinner, no awkward first kiss or meeting the parents, no chance in hell of catching her in my bed with any so-called best friend, no strings attached. Period.

With Delaine and that contract, that was exactly what I had. So why was I questioning it?

Because somehow it felt different. Different was good. And when different was wrapped around my cock, it was really fucking good.

Okay, that solved my mysterious momentary lapse in direction. With my head screwed back on straight again and motivation rekindled, I waited for Delaine to join me in the limousine for our shopping trip. Lingerie shopping. I was really looking forward to it, too, even though I knew it was only going to add to the permanent rise I was sporting in my Levi's. But that was okay because I was wearing the loose-fit ones, commando. That should keep me from busting through the zipper, right?

Wrong.

Samuel opened the door for Delaine when she finally came out to join me, and I swear I could have killed Polly Hunt with my bare hands. Or maybe I should give her a raise.

My million-dollar baby was wearing a little black cotton skirt that barely covered her ass, and a blue tank top, the same color as her eyes, sans bra. Judging by how hard her nipples were, I'd say the limo was a little chilly and I needed to have Samuel turn the air-conditioning down. Or not. A high ponytail and black peep-toe heels completed her ensemble, and I mentally noted both as things to hold on to while fucking the shit out of her again in the very, very near future.

"How was your date with Polly?" I asked, trying to get it together because I was about five seconds away from the very near future, figuratively and literally.

"I had a lot of fun with her," she said. "But you were right. She is extremely nosy. Lucky for you, I'm quick on the draw."

She laughed, and it sounded almost dainty, so unlike what I'd seen of her so far. I wasn't sure how I felt about that. I mean, if she started acting all innocent and shit, that could potentially make me feel worse about what I was doing. I needed to piss her off or get her to piss me off.

"Mmm-hmm, that's nice," I answered quickly. "So you don't have anything on under that skirt, do you?"

"What?" she asked, taken aback. "Um, no. You threw out all of my clothes, remember? And you wouldn't let me buy any underwear when I went shopping with Polly."

"Let me see," I said with a nod.

"Let you see what?" she asked with a slight edge to her voice.

"That pretty pussy."

She arched her brow at me defiantly, but I met her stare.

"You're serious?" she said incredulously.

"Yes, I'm serious. Lift the skirt, goddamnit!" I was an ass, I knew it. But I had to raise my voice to really piss her off.

"You're such a jerk," she mumbled with a roll of her eyes, but she begrudgingly pulled up her skirt to reveal my toy anyway.

Delaine was looking at me like I'd lost my fucking mind, which, admittedly, I probably had. But her expression changed when I undid my jeans and pulled out my cock.

"What are you doing?"

"Come here and spit on it," I said, ignoring her question.

"I *tried* to sit on your dick in the hot tub, and *you* said we couldn't do that yet. But now when we're in a moving vehicle, with someone sitting on the other side of a thin glass barrier and hordes of people all around us outside the car—now you want me?"

"I said 'spit,' not 'sit,'" I corrected her, and then she got a look of disgust on her face. So of course I had to clarify the purpose. I mean, I didn't want her to think I was some sort of fetish freak. "I need the lubrication."

"For what?"

"My dick is harder than a fucking titanium rod and I can't fuck you, but you come out here with your nipples all pert and your skirt barely there and I can't take it anymore! I need some release. So if you don't mind—and even if you do, I really don't give a shit—I'm going to jack off before I end up taking you like some savage caveman. Because I most definitely cannot even think about you in fucking lingerie in my current state."

"Oh," she said simply, her mouth keeping the O shape for longer than was necessary.

I felt like a dirty old man paying for pussy. Oh, my God, I'd paid for pussy.

"Why not just order me to suck you off?" I could always depend on Delaine's sassy attitude to pull me out of my funk and set me back on track. "After all, you did pay an awful lot of money for me to make you feel good."

I smirked. "Because I think you're starting to like my cock in your mouth a little too much."

She reached across the space between us and slapped me. Hard.

Finally we were getting somewhere.

I grabbed her wrist and yanked her into my lap, turning her over to lie across my legs, with all the rounded, creamy glory of her bare ass staring me in the face.

"Obviously you forgot your place in this relationship, Delaine, and you must now be punished like the little brat that you are." I raised my hand and brought it down hard on her pert ass. A red palm imprint grew across her flawless skin and I felt my balls draw up tight. I'd fucking branded her, and damned if that didn't turn me on.

She was mine.

She jerked in my hold and tried to scramble away, but I slapped her ass again, reveling in the way it bounced with a slight jiggle.

"You bastard! Let me go!" she screamed, her face red with anger.

"Tut, tut," I reprimanded her. "Name-calling is another no-no, naughty girl."

I smacked her ass again, harder this time, and then rubbed my hand over the pink wheal that was beginning to rise as a result. She flailed her legs, inadvertently spreading them wide and giving me a fantastic view of her sweet pussy. I angled my wrist and smacked her bare lips next. Once, twice, three times. And my little naughty girl moaned.

"You like that, huh?" I asked in that husky voice I happened to know she couldn't resist.

I smacked her ass again when she didn't answer. Afterward I leaned forward and caressed the mark with my tongue to ease the sting of pain. While doing so, I gave the folds between her legs a gentler slap, feeling and hearing the wetness that had developed there. I moved the pads of my fingers in a circular motion, earning another moan that she dragged out between clenched teeth.

Three wet fingers slapped at her opening in rapid succession before two dipped inside.

"Unf . . ." She wiggled in my lap.

"Be still!" I ordered her, and then removed my fingers, spanking her ass hard again.

She yelped in response, but stilled her movements as ordered. That deserved a reward, so I slipped my fingers back between her slick folds and massaged her clit before dragging her wetness up and between the cheeks of her ass and circling her other opening. When I applied a slight pressure there, she rolled her hips, pushing back into me.

To say she was receptive to my touch there would be an understatement. I bit down on my lip, barely able to contain my excitement, because I knew I was definitely going to slide my cock into her pretty little ass.

"You want me to make you come, don't you?"

"No. I hate you." And then she moaned, the sound a total contradiction to the words she spoke.

"Do you?" I asked with a devilish smirk.

I gently patted her pussy again, making sure I hit her swollen clit. She lifted her ass into the air, trying to angle herself so that she could reap more of the benefit on that little bundle of nerves. I gave her what she wanted, but when I felt her body tense, signaling her impending orgasm, I stopped and gave her ass one last, hard slap. Before she could even register what was happening, I lifted her and sat her back down in the seat across from me. She was panting pretty damn hard, her chest heaving, as she dropped her chin and looked at me. Anger flashed in her eyes, which only amused me.

I felt the car stop and knew we had arrived at our destination. I still hadn't been able to get off, but we were out of time and it would have to wait. No matter; I happened to know the shop had private dressing areas, and I knew one of the saleswomen personally. She was a real hellcat in the sack, very eager to please and willing to try anything once, or even five times.

I tucked my dick away in my pants and leaned across the space between us. Cupping Delaine's chin in my hand, I forced her to look at me even though she was trying to pull out of my grasp.

"For future reference, slapping me only turns me on. And judging from the way that pretty little kitty purred when I spanked you, I think it's safe to say the rough stuff turns you on, too. I'll have to remember that."

I bent to kiss her and she curled her lips in, denying me. I tugged on her chin and gave her a stern look. "Kiss me, or I'll take all your lovely new clothes away again and make you walk around the house naked for the next two years."

"Polly will just—"

I cut her off in midsentence and claimed her mouth with mine. That must have pissed her off because she bit down hard on my lip. A low growl echoed from my chest, but I continued and shoved my tongue through her parted lips. She pushed on my chest as I smothered her cries of protest, ignoring her attempts to get free.

I finally released her and gave her a cocky smile. "I told you, I like the rough stuff. You can pull your skirt down now."

She looked down at her lap and tugged on the minuscule piece of cotton just as I tapped on the window and Samuel opened the door for us. "Le Petit Boudoir," I said in a flawless French accent as I stepped from the car. "Come, Delaine. Let's shop."

She huffed and climbed out of the car to join me on the sidewalk. "Whatever. Let's get this over with."

I turned to face her, fed up. "You know, you might be a little appreciative of the things I do for you. You knew what you were getting into when you signed up for this gig. So it makes no sense to me whatsoever that you feel like you constantly have to cop an attitude with me. I'm not exactly mistreating you. In fact, I think you've been treated pretty fairly, better than most other women in the same situation."

"Yeah, well, I highly doubt you'll find many other women in the same situation, Mr. Crawford, so you don't really have any evidence to validate that statement." She swung around, her ponytail smacking me in the face as she stalked past me. "You fucked my mouth, you threw away my clothes, you made me greet you at the door just to give you head, and you took my virginity. So you'll have to excuse me if I'm not exactly compelled to apologize for hurting your feelings."

I noticed she didn't mention the ass spanking I'd just given her.

She reached the door and swung it open a little harder than necessary. Without even looking back at me, she stepped inside and disappeared from sight.

"Yeah? Well, you liked every minute of it!" I yelled after her, but of course she didn't hear me. However, the half dozen or so people walking by on the sidewalk did.

I was Noah motherfucking Crawford, Chicago's most eligible bachelor, and she made me look like some psychotic lunatic shouting at thin air. I looked back at the car just in time to see Samuel trying to conceal his smile.

"I'm glad this is entertaining you. Wait here. We won't be long," I snapped, and then followed after Delaine.

My eyes scanned the shop in search of her, and I found her rummaging through some of the undergarments in the center of the room.

"Noah Crawford," a sultry Latin voice cooed from behind me.

Delaine looked up right as a pair of hands encircled my waist from behind and warm breath trickled over my skin. "I've missed you, lover. Where have you been hiding?" Fernanda whispered in my ear.

I turned my head to the side and gave her my best smile,

never taking my eyes off Delaine because her reaction was too priceless, comical even. The lift of her brow and the way she defiantly raised her chin exposed her jealousy.

Well, now, this could get interesting.

"Fernanda," I acknowledged my onetime mistress as I turned and gave her cheek a lingering kiss. "How have you been?"

"Lonely," she said with a pout.

I thumbed the pout and then stroked her cheek. "Aw, a beautiful woman like you? Lonely? I find that very hard to believe."

Delaine cleared her throat, and when I looked up at her, she tossed her head to the side and continued to browse, acting as if she hadn't been paying attention to the interaction. She wasn't fooling anyone.

I took Fernanda by the hand and walked her toward my girl. "I'd like to introduce you to someone. Fernanda, this is Delaine. Delaine, meet the very voluptuous Fernanda."

I threw that in there on purpose. But she really was voluptuous: long legs, jet-black shiny hair, full lips, and a figure that made grown men cry. Le Petit Boudoir was just a little side job. Her main income came from nude modeling for various prominent magazines aimed at refined gentlemen.

"It's very nice to meet you, Delaine," Fernanda said with a pleasant smile as she offered her hand in greeting.

Delaine looked at me and then back to Fernanda before she finally shook her hand. "You too." Her words were curt and her tone sharp enough to cut glass.

"So," Fernanda said, retracting her hand and sliding it

around my arm while pressing her other hand to my chest possessively. "Are you treating the lovely lady today?"

Delaine narrowed her eyes, focused on the familiar way in which Fernanda touched me.

I gave Fernanda a flirtatious smile to further taunt Delaine's little green-eyed monster. "As a matter of fact, I am. Do you have a private room available?"

"Anything and everything I have is available to you, Noah Crawford. You know that." She laughed and tossed her long hair over her shoulder enticingly before leading me toward the back.

Delaine was left to trail behind us, and I had to hide my smirk. Payback was a bitch, and she was seething with jealous rage. I could feel it rippling off her like heat off a desert highway.

We were escorted into a private dressing room. Three of the four walls were covered in mirrors, and there was a smaller room for the lady to change into different outfits before coming out and modeling for whomever she brought along for the show. Two racks of the top-selling lingerie were stationed in one corner beside a minibar. In the opposite corner there was a red velvet-covered bench. Fernanda led me to the center of the room and sat me down in an oversized armchair that was in the perfect position to see everything.

Delaine sat on the bench seat with her arms crossed over her chest. "Pick something that you like and try it on," I told her, motioning toward the rack of garments.

"Noah, I don't think—" she started.

Fernanda cut her off. Of course she sensed the tension and

wanted to help out. "You know what? You look like my size. Why don't I pick something out for you? I know what he likes."

Delaine's claws shot out like she was the daughter of Wolverine. Or it seemed that way to me, anyway; I might have been seeing things. Without waiting for an answer, Fernanda left the room to go back into the shop. Delaine turned on me immediately, not even bothering to lower her voice.

"Did you fuck her?"

"Does it matter?" I stood and walked over to the bar to pour myself a drink.

"Yes, it matters."

"Why? Are you jealous? Because I fucked you, too, and you get the benefit of a whole hell of a lot more fucking than she ever got. Does that make you feel better?" I took a sip of the scotch I'd poured for myself.

"You're disgusting!" she huffed, and then turned away from me again.

"I'm insatiable. Big difference."

"Why did you even need to spend millions of dollars on me when Little Miss Cuchi Cuchi Charo was willing to make *anything and everything* available to you?" she asked, mocking Fernanda's accent. It was kind of cute.

"Charo is from Spain. Fernanda is Argentinean," I corrected her. "And while Fernanda is quite pleasing to the eye, a lot of eyes have been pleased by her." I winked and tilted my glass toward her. "It wouldn't work between her and me in public. But she's cool. She understands."

She started to say something in response, but Fernanda

came back in and started hanging garments up in the smaller dressing area. "I picked out a few things I thought would really accentuate your figure."

"Go ahead, Delaine," I said, taking my seat again. "Show me."

She sat there, stubborn and unmoving. Fernanda looked at her and then back at me in question.

I shrugged. "She's shy."

"Oh, well, that's okay. I can model them for you, if you want."

God bless Fernanda and her eagerness to please. This couldn't have turned out better if I'd planned it.

"You know, I think that's a fantastic idea, Fernanda," Delaine spoke up. Her voice was hard and sarcastic as she stood up with a huff. "I'm sure Noah would prefer to see you in them, anyway. In fact, let me give you two some privacy." She turned on me and narrowed her eyes. "I'll be waiting in the car."

With that, she stormed out of the room, slamming the door behind her.

"Did I do something wrong?" Fernanda asked.

"No, it wasn't you," I assured her. "Just wrap up whatever you picked out and charge it to my account. I'll take it all," I said as I stood. "It was good to see you again, Fernanda."

"You too, Noah." She hugged me close and kissed me on the cheek. "I'll have them delivered first thing in the morning. Go get the girl, sweetie."

I nodded my thanks and headed for the car. When I got inside, Lanie was sitting with her arms crossed over her chest and her face turned to look out the window. "Home, Samuel," I directed him before he closed my door.

"You mind telling me what all that was about?" I asked Delaine.

She whipped her head around and glared at me. "In the future, if you want to go visit one of your old girlfriends to get your freak on, please have the decency not to make me go along. I'm not into that."

"She's not an old girlfriend."

"Girlfriend, plaything . . . same difference." She studied my face and then shook her head before turning away. "You might want to wipe that hooker red lipstick off your cheek."

I swiped at the side of my face and looked at my hand. Sure enough, Fernanda's lipstick was smeared on my fingertips.

"Look, I didn't bring you there so that I could get my freak on with an old girlfriend. Although I'd be perfectly within my rights to do so, if I wanted. The contract states you can't be with any other men. It says nothing at all about me."

Her head snapped around again. "You bastard! If you think for one minute that I'm going to sit around while you're out fucking every woman you come across, just so that you can carry some freakish disease back to me, you've got another thing coming! I will hightail it out of that house so fast it'll make your head spin!"

"And then I'll sue you for breach of contract," I stated matter-of-factly. "However, we don't need to worry about that because I don't plan on sleeping with anyone else, for the next two years anyway. You are the only woman I want to fuck,

Delaine. Now, will you please stop throwing these childish tantrums so that I can enjoy you?"

The expression on her face softened minutely to a pout, but she still held her defensive posture as she looked away from me again. I took her lack of a response to mean she was reluctantly agreeing to my request.

"Good. Now for your punishment for acting out in front of a good friend of mine and embarrassing me," I started. She looked back at me again and was about to say something, but I cut her off before she could. "I was trying to buy you some nice lingerie, but now you will be required to be panty-less for me at all times." I smiled smugly at the way she opened and closed her mouth. "I should probably thank you for not being able to control your temper, because that actually works out better for me. So thank you, Delaine."

"Oh . . . you . . . ugh!" she huffed, and then turned away again.

The rest of the drive was spent in silence. She refused to look at me, but I couldn't take my eyes off her. I was disappointed that I hadn't gotten to see her model the lingerie for me in the shop, but I had a possessive streak as well, so I guess I could understand why Delaine was upset. She had been throwing herself at me all morning, and with the exception of the little gift I'd given her in the hot tub, I had been rejecting her attempts to do something for me in turn. I had to admit I would've been a bit miffed if I'd been in her position, too. But where I was used to her reluctance to let me have my wicked way with her, she wasn't used to mine.

What she didn't understand was that I was trying to be

gentle with her. For now, anyway. But all that was going to change as soon as that pretty little kitty of hers had had time to recuperate. After the beating I was planning on putting on her, I was sure she'd be begging me to go "get my freak on" with an old girlfriend.

8
fire, bullets, and vamps, oh my!

Lanie

Noah left me alone after the epic fail of a trip we'd made to the lingerie shop.

I wasn't jealous. I swear. It was the Cooch. She was royally pissed and throwing up picket signs all over the damn place. The Wonder Peen was going to have to kiss some major ass to win her over again. He might have been able to get away with another one of those spankings, but I couldn't say for sure.

I went to bed before Noah, but I was only faking sleep when he crawled under the covers. My feelings were a tad bit hurt that he kept his back to me and an insane amount of space between us. No naked spooning or forking, no gropage, nothing.

The next morning, I woke before he did. He was still sleeping when I got out of my shower, and that was even after I made as much noise as I could to purposely wake him. Don't ask me why I did it, because I really didn't know. I might have sort of missed the bastard.

I even strolled into the bedroom naked, rummaged around

in his closet for something to wear, accidentally on purpose knocked a couple of pairs of his shoes to the floor (and left them there), and then closed the door harder than necessary. Nothing. So I had to check the man's pulse, right? I mean, who could possibly sleep through all that?

But then my stomach made this noise that signaled feeding time, and I distinctly remembered having seen a box of Frosted Flakes in the pantry, so Noah whoremongering Crawford's well-being was quickly forgotten.

I had just slurped down the last of the sweetened milk from my cereal and put the bowl in the sink when Noah finally emerged. God help me, he was standing there with towel-dried wet hair, a pair of distressed low-rise jeans, and absolutely nothing else—except the little black band of his Calvin Kleins underneath. So let me say this: naked Noah was glorious, but half-naked Noah, in nothing but a pair of blue jeans . . . thud.

The little trail of hair that led from his belly button to the wonders beneath? Totally lickable. And by wonders, I meant his morning woody was apparently still in full effect, because that was one gargantuan bulge beneath that denim.

The Cooch crossed her arms defiantly and turned her back on him. She refused to look at or even acknowledge the Wonder Peen's presence.

"Good morning, Delaine," he said as he ran his porntastic fingers through his hair.

"Good morning, Wonder Peen. Um, I mean, Noah."

Noah arched an eyebrow at me and then shuffled his bare feet in my direction. The closer he got, the further I backed away, until I was all the way up against the sink. He placed his hands on the counter and caged me in before he dipped his head and gave me a toe-curling kiss.

Double Agent Coochie turned to look over her shoulder and then quickly turned back around, remembering that she was still pissed at him.

He tasted minty fresh and I seriously considered sucking on his tongue, but that would give him the impression that I wanted his attention. And although I knew that was true, he didn't, and I saw no reason to clue him in.

He rounded out the kiss with a suckle to my bottom lip and then dived straight in on my neck as he leaned his body into mine. The gargantuan bulge pressed into my girly region, and the Cooch's resistance wavered. Strong arms wrapped around my waist, and Noah held me to him as he continued to wantonly knead my flesh. His neck was on display in front of my lips, the tendons taut and alluring. I couldn't help myself. I had to taste him.

I leaned in and sucked on the skin between his neck and shoulder, and he moaned into my ear. I sucked as hard as I could, because for some unknown reason I was still pissed about the day before and feeling a little possessive.

"Are you trying to mark me, Delaine?" his husky voice asked against my ear.

I ignored his quiet chuckle and bit into his flesh to aid in my attempt. He apparently liked that because he pressed harder into me until there was no space left between our bodies. His head fell back and to the side, exposing more of that gorgeous flesh. I wasted no time in devouring his offering with my wet and demanding mouth. My hands curled through the longer locks of hair on top of his head and gave a none-too-gentle tug. I could taste the coppery flavor of his blood as it rose to the surface of his skin, and it set off a feeding frenzy inside me. Mindlessly I dug my nails into his scalp, scratching at the tender flesh. Harder and harder I sucked, reveling in the saltiness of his skin. And still I wanted more. I swear I must have been a vamp chick in my past life, because I could visualize my teeth sinking into his flesh and losing myself in his very essence.

"Enough!" he finally barked in a commanding tone, and yanked his neck away before quickly stepping out of my embrace.

Both of us were panting hard, and I could still taste him in my mouth. I'm not ashamed to admit that I whimpered a little bit. I had been denied the chance to live out one of my naughty vamp fantasies. But then my eyes locked onto his neck and Double Agent Coochie giggled in glee.

Noah Crawford had the mother of all hickeys.

The skin on his neck was already turning a beautiful shade of dark crimson, and a welt was beginning to rise, marring his perfect skin.

One side of his mouth turned up into a smug smile as he looked me over. He lifted a long finger to brush my cheek and watched my heaving breasts with rapt fascination. "I let you mark me, only because I plan to mark you later." The back of his hand barely swept over one of my breasts. "My mark won't be a simple hickey on the neck, though. Everyone will know that you belong to me."

A shiver ran down my spine and I could feel the gooseflesh rising on my skin. Noah's gaze went to my nipples, and he sighed when he saw the evidence of how much his words had aroused me.

"Very nice," he said before rolling one bud between his fingers. "No bra?"

I rolled my eyes at him and crossed my arms over my chest.

He pulled them away and stepped toward me. "Let's take a closer look, shall we?"

His hands slipped under the hem of my shirt and slowly slid over my stomach and ribs before he found the bare flesh of my breasts. He cupped them in his hands as his thumbs passed over their hardened peaks.

"I like this. Makes it so much easier to do this." He lowered his head and took one nipple into his mouth for one chaste suck, and then he gave the same attention to the other one.

That might have had something to do with equal-opportunity employment, or whatever. I mean, technically, I was working for him. Well, at least my body was. The Cooch used to be a model employee before the whole Noah-slobbering-all-over-the-Latin-whore thing. She was a real go-getter; always going for the "greatly exceeds expectations" on her annual evaluation. Pfft, brownnoser. I guess her theory was that if she was successful, she might get a raise.

"What about panties? Let's see if you're obeying the rules of your punishment." His hand slid down my abdomen. With one flick of his fingers he had the button of my shorts undone and was slipping a hand inside. I should've felt like a heifer at a cattle auction being felt up by some lonely and very desperate farm boy. But you remember what I said about the porntastic fingers, right? Yeah, they were still porntastic.

He deftly maneuvered two fingers between my folds before slipping them inside me. His fingers curled back and forth, hitting that little spot of awesomeness until my eyes nearly rolled to the back of my head and a moan escaped my lips. Then he pulled them out, gave the love nubbin a few quick strokes, and slipped them back inside me quickly. My knees nearly buckled.

Noah quickly withdrew his hand. "You might need to change those shorts now," he said with that smug look. Then he stuck his fingers in his mouth and sucked them clean.

I was quite perturbed by his tease. "Are you finished? Did I pass inspection?"

"You did," he acknowledged, and then turned toward the refrigerator. "I have to run out and pick something up today, but I'm expecting a package to be delivered. Samuel can sign for it, but the contents belong to you, so feel free to open it."

"What is it?"

"A gift." He shrugged his shoulders as he poured himself a glass of milk.

"You spent two million dollars on me and you're buying me gifts on top of that?"

"It's as much a gift for me as it is for you." He kissed my forehead and patted my ass before he walked back out of the kitchen and left me standing there by myself.

I had no idea what sort of gift it might be, but my curiosity was piqued. What woman didn't enjoy getting presents?

I found out a little later. The doorbell rang—and, by the way, it was one of those snooty doorbells that seemed to go on forever—and Samuel signed for the package. "Here you go, Miss Delaine," he said kindly, and handed the package off to me.

"Please, Samuel, it's Lanie," I said, and smiled at him. He nodded respectfully and then took his leave.

I'm not ashamed to admit that I felt sort of like a kid on Christmas morning when I knelt on the floor in my skirt—yes, I changed—and ripped into the box. It wasn't an easy task, either. Whoever packaged that thing had sealed it up like Fort Knox. I even had to leave it in the entryway and retrieve a knife from the butcher's block in the kitchen. No worries; I was careful so that I wouldn't destroy the wee bit of treasure on the inside.

All that went out the window though when I finally got into the stupid thing and looked inside. "Le Petit Boudoir" was written all over the tissue paper, and there was a note from none other than Fernanda. I opened it up, and I'll be damned if her handwriting wasn't every bit as beautiful as she was.

> Dearest Delaine,
>
> Noah asked me to send these over. He's going to absolutely love them on you. I have to admit that I'm a bit jealous. So sorry we didn't get a chance to play.
>
> Enjoy!
> Fernanda

That bitch!

And Noah had obviously lost his mind, thinking it was okay to have this stuff sent to me. You'd think he would've gotten the clue when I walked out on them yesterday. He couldn't have actually thought I wanted to put something on my body that would remind him of her.

I wadded the note up and crammed it in my pocket.

In a fit of rage, I punched the box. Of course, that didn't quite quell my anger, so I stabbed it with the knife that I was still clutching in my fist. I didn't stop stabbing the damn thing until my arms got sore. Bits and pieces of lace and silk lay unrecognizable in the cardboard box, but I wasn't satisfied. I could still see it, and I knew what it was and what it represented.

I jumped up and ran with purpose to the supply closet in the laundry room. Sifting through its contents, I finally found what I was looking for: lighter fluid.

I ran back, grabbed the matches out of the kitchen pantry, and dragged the offending box out into the driveway. I doused it with every last drop of lighter fluid left in the tin, struck a match, and dropped it into the box. I had to take a step back when a ball of fire ignited and shot up into the air.

Yes, I knew I was exhibiting irrational behavior. Yes, I knew my reaction was a bit on the psychotic side. But damn it all, I was not about to wear something one of his whores had picked out because she knew what he liked. And I wanted there to be no doubt in his mind how I felt about it, either.

As they say, hell hath no fury like a woman scorned.

I turned my back on the inferno and walked away. Even though the fire was relatively small and contained, in my mind it was huge. In fact, I was sure I looked just as awesome as little Drew Barrymore in *Firestarter* with flames engulfing everything around her, because Samuel stepped onto the porch with his mouth hanging open and his eyes wide in awe.

"Are you okay, Lanie?" he asked frantically.

"Oh, I'm just perfect . . . now." I heard the gentle purr of an engine as I stepped past him and across the threshold to the house, so naturally I turned around to see who had come to pay us a visit. It was Noah, and he was actually driving. His car was a sleek, shiny black sports number that looked like it cost him more than I did and reminded me of a leopard on the prowl.

He threw the car in park and jumped out, not even bothering to shut his door as he stalked over to my little bonfire. He looked at it and then up at me.

"Your gift was tainted," I said matter-of-factly before I set my chin and walked away.

Of course Noah chased after me. "Samuel, get the extinguisher and put out that fire!" he ordered.

"Let it burn, Samuel," I called in a bored tone over my shoulder.

"Delaine!" he shouted, but I kept walking. "Delaine! You stop right this instant or I swear to God I'll—"

I spun on my heels to face him. "You'll what?"

I watched his face contort in shock. The muscles in his jaws flexed as he ground his teeth, obviously trying to come up with a retort and failing miserably.

"That's what I thought," I said, and then turned and continued up the stairs. "You know, something's seriously wrong with you, Noah Crawford. You saw that I was infuriated when we were at your girlfriend's little shop. And yet, for whatever asinine reason, you thought having a woman who obviously still has the hots for my man send over something that she picked out was a good idea? And you're supposed to be some huge business mogul?" I laughed incredulously and shook my head. "Soooo messed up. Oh, and by the way—" I stopped at the top of the stairs and turned to look down at him while digging in my pocket. "She left a note."

I threw the wadded piece of paper, and it hit him in the chest before falling to his feet. He snatched it off the floor and unfolded the crinkled page before looking it over.

"Oh, for the love of . . ." he started, and then sighed. "Delaine, Fernanda is bisexual. She wanted to see you in the lingerie and was disappointed because she had hoped that you and she . . ." His voice trailed off.

"That we . . . ?"

He lifted his brows and gave me an expectant look.

Oh. *Ohhhhh* . . .

"You're not serious," I said with a humorless laugh.

"Well, she didn't come right out and say it, but I know her well enough to feel safe in saying she was hoping for a little two-on-one fun."

A Lanie sandwich. I had to admit, I was slightly flattered. I mean, Fernanda was beautiful and all. The hetero gal in me was a tad bit curious, but I didn't think I could ever actually go through with something like that. I was strictly dickly. Period. But Dez?

"She's going to get such a kick out of this," I mumbled to myself.

"What?"

"Nothing. It doesn't change anything. You bought that lingerie, even after you knew how much it upset me. End of story. I'm still angry." With that, I turned and walked away.

I heard him growl in frustration, and I think he might have hit a wall with his fist, but I couldn't be sure.

~$~

I felt awful about an hour later and decided to hunt Noah down to apologize. When I got to the bottom of the stairs, sure enough, there was a fist-sized hole in the wall around the corner. I rolled my eyes because it was completely uncalled for, but then again, so was the little tantrum I'd thrown with the lingerie.

I could admit when I was wrong.

He wasn't in his office, or the kitchen. I thought I heard the television blaring from the entertainment room, so I followed the sound and gingerly poked my head through the doorway.

Noah was reclining in one of the theater seats with his shirt tossed to the side. It was the most relaxed I'd seen him since the day I'd met him. I cleared my throat to alert him to my presence.

He turned his head to face me, and although I expected his expression to be angry, it looked more like he was waiting for me to warp into bitch mode again.

"I'm sorry," I choked out, because apologizing to the man who'd purchased me as his sex slave wasn't exactly an easy thing to do.

He sighed and patted his thigh. "Come sit with me for a bit."

I walked across the room and perched myself on his lap while resting my arm around his shoulders.

"I'm sorry, too," he said, rubbing my thigh soothingly. "I didn't think. I just thought you might like the lingerie, and truthfully, I really wanted to see you in it."

"I guess I'm sorry I set them on fire," I mumbled.

"Don't be. Your feelings were hurt, so I understand why you did it." He chuckled. "You're a little hellcat, you know that? It sort of turned me on. Especially when you called me your man."

Damn. Had I done that?

"Well, you are for the next two years," I said, covering, and then diverted my attention to the television. One of those popular vampire series was on, and I did my best to conceal my inner girly girl. "I love this show. There's something about vampires that's just so sexy and forbidden."

He laughed. "Oh, really? What's so sexy about them?"

I looked at the television again, and the vampire had some human chick strapped spread-eagled in a standing position while he fucked her with his vamp speed. "That's the reason," I answered, pointing to the screen. I was getting pretty worked up at the sight of the vamp's naked ass and the way he pounded into the poor girl, but she wasn't complaining.

"I knew I had you pegged right. You really do like the rough stuff, don't you?" he asked as he moved his hand up my thigh and nuzzled the side of my breast. He took my clothed nipple between his teeth and lightly teased it. "Hmm? Do you want me to do that to you?" he continued, nuzzling the bud with the tip of his nose. "Have you spread-eagled in front of me while I pound into that beautiful pussy?"

Yes, please.

"I can do that, Delaine. I can fuck you like that."

I drew in a stuttering breath and he looked up at me from beneath his long lashes.

"Lift your shirt up for me, baby," he said in that husky voice.

Double Agent Coochie stood up and took notice.

I slowly did as he asked, and for once I wasn't the least bit disgruntled about it. He made this moaning sound that caused the Cooch to shiver and then melt into a pile of goo. His lips wrapped around my left nipple while his hand moved closer to my center. Slowly his tongue circled the raised bud before he scraped it with his teeth. I could feel his hot breath wash over my skin as he exhaled in contentment. Then his lips closed over the nipple and he suckled it as he moved his head back and forth. With one long suck he pulled away, elongating my breast before releasing it and watching it snap back into place.

I was gushing full-on, Niagara Falls style, between the legs at that point.

Noah inclined his head and placed sensual kisses along the underside of my jaw until he reached my ear. "I've got something for you," he murmured. When I pulled back and gave him a warning scowl, he rushed to explain. "I picked it out just for you. I promise. And I've never given any other woman anything remotely close to it."

"Okay . . . ," I said warily.

He reached beside him and picked up a black box with a slim emerald ribbon tied around it and sat it on my thigh. "Open it," he urged when I stared at it.

I took a deep breath and released it slowly as I picked up

the box and tugged on the end of the ribbon. Then I lifted the lid, and my mouth went agape. It was a silver cuff bracelet with an oval in the center that was decorated with a diamond-encrusted stag. Just beneath it, there was a banner with the name "Crawford" inlaid with even more tiny, shimmering diamonds. It was breathtaking.

Noah took it from my hands and secured it around my right wrist. "It's my family's crest," he said with a shrug. "This will let everyone know that you belong to me. I want you to wear it at all times."

"It's too much," I said, shaking my head.

"There's a certain standard of living that comes along with being my girl, Delaine," he said. "Although we both know that it's contractual, no one else does. It makes sense that you would wear this sort of jewelry. Besides, I happen to think it looks sexy as hell on you."

I nodded reluctantly.

"Lift the bottom," he said, nodding back toward the box. "There's more."

I reached inside the box and pulled at the little silk tab on the bottom, trying to guess what more there could be.

Holy speeding bullets, Batman!

I'd seen this type of thing before; Dez had dragged me along to more "fun" parties than a person should ever be forced to attend in one lifetime. Honestly, I didn't get what all the fuss was about. And now I found myself staring down at the mack daddy of all silver bullets. The same Crawford crest was carved into its side, but thankfully there were no diamonds. And then I had an epiphany. They said diamonds were a girl's best friend, but the silver bullet sure could give them a run for their money in that category.

The Cooch perched her hands on her hips, insulted that he hadn't given her diamonds as well, but grateful all the same that she wouldn't have to worry about it shredding her girly bits.

"The bracelet is so that everyone else knows that you belong to me," he explained as he took the vibrator from my hands. "This . . . is so that you will."

He turned the switch on and slipped his hand between my legs to press the bullet against my clit. "Oh, God," I gasped, and my head fell forward.

"Well now, that wasn't the reaction I was hoping for," he whispered into my ear. "We've been through this before, Delaine. This little toy is supposed to remind you of whom you belong to. So tell me, Delaine, who is that again?"

He pulled the bullet away so that it lightly touched that little bundle of nerves, and then he started working it in excruciatingly slow circles.

We're his dirty little slut! Say his name! Tell him anything he wants! Just get me more! the Cooch screamed at me.

"Please . . . Noah," I said on a moan, and then arched my hips up to close the distance.

He grabbed my hip with the hand he had snaked around my waist and held me down. "Please what?" he teased.

The cocky bastard had asked me to say his name and I'd complied. And he was still teasing me?

"More. I want more," I moaned pathetically.

"More what? More of this?" He pressed the bullet closer and gave me what I craved.

"Oh, God, yes." I realized my mistake a little too late. Noah pulled the bullet away again and gave me a scowl.

"Let's try again. In fact, let's make a new rule. Every time you feel the need to say the name 'God,' you say my name in place of it. And I guarantee you're going to love my version of heaven."

Noah pressed the bullet to my clit again and then quickly slid it between my folds before slipping it inside me.

"Oh . . . Noah!" I cried out.

"Very good, Delaine. You're a quick learner," he said in approval, and then he rewarded me by taking my nipple into his mouth again and sucking it vigorously while working the bullet around inside me.

I didn't know which sensation to concentrate on, and I wasn't even sure why I was trying to differentiate between the two. Because together? Oh my Noah, it was euphoric.

And then it was over. No bullet, no suckling, nothing. I looked at him like he was crazy. Then I found my little Crawford bullet back in the box and on the table.

"You're not sore?" he asked.

Again I looked at him like he was crazy. "Hell no!" I said with a raised pitch to my voice.

He slid out from underneath me and stood, forcing me to land with a thud in the chair. I was about to protest his quick disappearance when he knelt before me and pushed my knees open. As he leaned forward and hungrily claimed my mouth with his own, his hands pushed my skirt up. I eagerly lifted my hips to assist him, although I didn't know why he didn't just slide the damn thing off my legs. This way was kind of hot, though. There was something intensely erotic about being so in the heat of the moment that you didn't even want to take the time to completely undress.

Noah did not disappoint. I heard the clink of his belt buckle, and then he sat up, unfastened his jeans, hooked his arms under my knees, and yanked me forward until my ass was barely perched on the edge of the seat.

"I want you so fucking bad." His voice was strained as he pulled the Wonder Peen free of its confines. "And I refuse to wait any longer. Give me what's mine," he demanded.

"Take it," I challenged.

I wasn't actually trying to be difficult. He knew it, and I knew it. This was just what we did. We challenged each other, and then reveled in the possessiveness we both felt. As much as I'd like to deny it, I couldn't. It was a guilty pleasure that we both thrived on: raw, animalistic, wild. The hickey that I'd put on him earlier was a stark reminder of that. I reached a hand forward to touch the mark and then looked him in the eye. He knew the message I was trying to convey: *Mine* . . .

Noah let out a feral growl and leaned over to attack my mouth with a passionate and brutal kiss. I laced my fingers through his hair and gave him everything I had in me, because if you were going to tango with Noah Crawford, you'd better bring your A-game. He didn't even bother to shove his pants over his hips before he lined up with my entrance and pushed in slowly.

He broke the kiss abruptly and hissed. "Jesus, kitten. You're so damn tight."

The Cooch squealed in delight when she was finally reunited with the Wonder Peen. I could almost see the two star-crossed lovers as they ran across a field of daisies to finally be in each other's arms. He whispered his apologies; she forgave him of all his transgressions.

It was disturbing, but very gratifying.

Once he was completely sheathed inside—and trust me, it was no easy feat—he hooked his arms under my knees and pushed until I was spread as wide as I could go.

"Oh, Noah," I gasped, still playing his name game. "Yes . . . yes . . ."

He pushed forward so that his hands were gripping the ends of the armrests for further support. His forearms held my legs in place as he bent at the elbows and leaned into me.

"I'm going to fuck the shit out of you now, Delaine," he warned with his lips hovering over mine. His breaths were my breaths and I tilted my chin to kiss him, but he pulled out of reach. He let his lips ghost over mine as he finished torturing me. "If I hurt you, tell me, and I might stop."

"Bring it on," I said with narrowed eyes, then leaned my head forward and bit his bottom lip.

Noah growled and smashed his lips against mine. I could taste a slight hint of blood, and I knew it was his. It drove me insane with want, so I sucked on his lip, provoking him further. He pulled out of me quickly and then pushed back in a little slower, but it was enough to draw my attention away from his lip. I dropped my head back and arched as he withdrew again and pushed back in harder.

When I looked back at him, I could see the cut and trickle of blood on his mouth. I licked my bottom lip, wanting to taste him again. It was sick, I know, but if you'd ever tasted Noah Crawford, you'd understand why I was jonesing for more.

"I'm supposed to be the vampire, Delaine. Not you," he reminded me with the increased speed and intensity of his thrusts.

I reached for him and managed to get hold of his hair before he could pull away and deny me what I wanted. I pulled and tugged on his thick locks until he finally submitted and let me force a kiss on him again. I went straight for the blood that was pooling on his lip and scooped it up with the tip of my tongue. Without breaking stride in his thrusts, Noah captured my tongue with his before I could bring it back into my mouth to taste him. We fought for dominance over the kiss and the blood, and it was so goddamned, er, Noah-damned erotic that I nearly came right then.

He broke the kiss and looked down at the place where we were joined, and I followed his lead. His jeans were just barely hanging on to the top of his thighs. That coil in the pit of my stomach kept winding tighter and tighter with the image of his cock slamming in and out of me. But, damn it, he was moving so fast and I wanted the sensation to never end. As if reading my mind, he slowed down so that we could both see better. I watched him lick his lips as a bead of sweat trickled down the slope of his nose and dropped onto my abdomen.

"That's a beautiful thing, isn't it?" he asked as he watched me. I looked back down between my legs and was immediately entranced by the sight. "My thick cock fucking your beautiful, wet, tight pussy. I'm going to come all over that pretty little kitty of yours, Delaine."

He drew in a long breath and then started pumping his hips faster and faster. It wasn't exactly vamp speed, but it was pretty damn close. Yes, I felt some discomfort, but no, I didn't care about it at all.

He gave me one of those sexy crooked smiles and then lunged forward with his teeth bared. I felt them graze across the flesh covering the artery in my neck, and then he sucked hard. The illusion that he'd created, a vampire tasting his mistress in the throes of passion, made me feel like I'd been picked up and slammed into an ocean of orgasmic bliss. It hit me so hard that I couldn't make a sound; I don't even think I was breathing. My mouth dropped open, my eyes rolled to the back of my head, my back arched, and I dug my nails into the skin of Noah's back to hold him to me.

He slowed his movements and did that unbelievable thing where he rolled his hips with each thrust, causing a delicious friction on my clit. The whole while, he moaned into my neck, and the vibrations from it shot straight to my core. I was sure my body was convulsing at that point, but he kept going. He finally released the skin on my neck and looked down on me with a devilish grin.

"My turn." He pumped his hips feverishly. Each inward thrust made a smacking sound as skin met skin. I was acutely aware that his efforts were actually moving me back up in the seat, but it didn't matter. I felt my walls clamp around him again as I was tossed on another wave in that ocean of orgasms.

"Goddamnit," Noah muttered. And then he dropped my left leg and pulled his cock out of me just before his semen shot out in spurts. It was hot and thick against the smooth skin of my pussy, and I watched in rapt fascination as he slid his hand back and forth over his length. His chest heaved and his head fell back while a low moan reverberated through his chest.

I wanted to fuck him again, just so that I could see the replay.

When he'd emptied all of his seed, his head fell forward and he looked me in the eye. His pectoral muscles flexed as he inhaled deeply to settle his breathing. He blew out the air in a quick gush and then tilted his head to the side before he leaned forward and gave me a soft, lingering kiss.

"You okay, kitten?" he asked as he cupped my cheek with one hand and swept his thumb over my kiss-swollen lip.

I kissed the pad of his thumb and nodded lazily because that was all I could muster.

He rose to his feet and pulled his pants up enough to keep them from falling around his ankles. When he turned and walked toward the bar, his back dimples smiled at me and the Cooch gave them a coy wave. I guess the little hoochie was thinking of two-timing the Wonder Peen now.

Noah disappeared behind the bar, and I pulled my shirt down. Within seconds, he came back to me, carrying a wet towel.

"One of the many benefits of having a wet bar in the entertainment room," he said with an amused look on his face. He cleaned up my girly parts with tender wipes against my flesh. "Are you sore now?" he asked as he stood and walked back toward the bar.

"Gaw, Noah!" I huffed and yanked my skirt down. "I appreciate your concern, but . . ." I trailed off, seeing the look of expectancy on his face. He was hoping I was sore.

"Yes, Noah," I conceded. "You put a serious beating on the Cooch. I won't be able to walk for days."

Truthfully, my legs were sore, and the Cooch really was licking her wounds, albeit in blissful contentment.

He got a huge, conceited grin on his face and I knew I'd stroked his ego exceptionally well.

"Hey, Noah?" I said, getting his attention.

"Yes?"

"All those superhot vampires on TV with the tight little tushies, sex hair, and faces so beautiful they can make you orgasm with a single glance?" He quirked a disapproving eyebrow at me. "They don't have a thing on you. You're far sexier and way more exotic, and although I haven't seen theirs, I'd find it really hard to believe any of them could have a bigger cock. You're gold, baby."

He laughed at me, then bit the corner of his lip. "Aw, shucks," he said demurely. "You're only saying that because it's true."

I laughed and shook my head at him. "You're such a conceited ass."

"There you go, talking about my ass again. You know this obsession of yours is bordering on being unhealthy." He grabbed both of my hands and pulled me to stand in front of him before wrapping my arms around his neck and encircling my waist.

I reached up on the tips of my toes and kissed him softly. He was no longer bleeding, and he didn't wince in pain, so I swept my tongue across his bottom lip. He granted my non-verbal wish to deepen the kiss and softly stroked my tongue with his. It was the sweetest kiss we'd shared since my arrival. I hoped we'd have more of them, and found I didn't hate myself for doing so.

Our business arrangement might not be so bad after all.

9

i smell bacon!

Lanie

My name is Lanie Talbot, and I . . . am an ass addict.

In my defense, Noah's ass was ridonkulous. It was all round, firm, and perky. Two little dimples were perched right above it on his lower back, and then there was this little smooth slope that rounded out deliciously into two muscular cheeks that hollowed out when he flexed it. Add to that the creamy yumminess of the skin, and you had a vision of divine assness.

It was morning and Noah was lying on his stomach while I was perched on my side next to him. He was still sleeping, and I was gawking at all his naked glory. He had kicked the covers off sometime during the night, and when I woke I was immediately greeted with the glorious sight of his delicious body in its untainted form. He was magnificent. Although I loved the way his clothes hung on his frame, this was so much better.

I watched as his back rose and fell with his even breaths. Every muscle was defined, and my fingers twitched, wanting to reach out to trace them. His face was turned toward me, and I marveled at the length of his dark, thick lashes. The lack of shaving over the weekend had left a delectable shadow of a beard on his strong jaw. I rather liked it and made a mental note to try to find some way to convince him to wear it like that more often, corporate America be damned. His lips were slightly puckered and there was a tiny mar to the bottom one, a reminder of our erotic session from the day before, when he'd more than fulfilled my wicked little vamp fantasy.

A smile crept onto my lips and I reached forward to gently cup his face. As I delicately ran the pad of my thumb along his lower lip, he moaned before finally stirring. I knew I probably shouldn't wake him before his alarm went off, but I couldn't help myself. Lips like those had to be touched.

His eyes fluttered open and immediately met mine: swirling pools of green, brown, blue, and amber so rich and deep, you could drown in them.

"G'mornin'," his scratchy morning voice greeted me. He puckered his lips and kissed the pad of my thumb.

"I'm sorry. I didn't mean to wake you," I lied, and pulled my hand away.

"'S okay. What time is it?" He propped himself up on his elbows and looked at the alarm clock on the nightstand beside him. He groaned when he read it and flipped onto his back. "Fuck. I need to get up and go in to work." He sighed and ran his hands over his face.

"Do you want me to make you some breakfast?"

His hands fell from his face and he looked at me in surprise. "You can cook?"

I giggled at him, because apparently I was going soft. "Yes,

Noah. We simple blue-collar folk actually have to do that sort of thing, unless we want to die of starvation."

"Can you make bacon and eggs?" His face wore this adorable little hopeful expression.

I rolled my eyes and nodded. "How do you like your eggs cooked?"

"Over medium?"

"I can do that, Noah. I can make you breakfast like that," I said seductively, making a play on his words from the night before. You'd have thought I was offering him the same damn thing he had been offering me, because I swear he got a hard-on.

"Sweet! I'll just go grab a shower and get dressed." He was out of bed in the blink of an eye, and I was left to stare after him. Yes, I was ogling the ass masterpiece, the assterpiece.

I slid out of bed as well and threw on a pair of shorts and a tank top. It would do until I was able to take a shower myself. Once downstairs, I grabbed a skillet from one of those fancy-schmancy thingamabobs that hung over the center island and put it on the stove. The stove. Let me tell you about this thing. Gordon Ramsey himself wouldn't be able to figure it out. There were buttons and knobs that went on for days, and I'll be damned if I knew what any of them were supposed to do. So, much like with the universal remote, I just started pushing anything I saw. I had a brief flashback to that day and shuddered, but I was relieved when I pushed the right one on the second try. The first try? Let's not even go there. My eyebrows were still relatively intact, and there was only a slight smell of singed hair lingering in the air.

I danced my way over to the refrigerator and had to push a

few things aside to find the—get this—butcher-cut bacon. Mmm-hmm. Apparently Noah Crawford did not do run-of-the-mill meat. I shook my head at the absurdity and grabbed the eggs. After washing my hands thoroughly, I prepared my station.

The bacon was in the skillet and almost in need of a turn when Noah's arm encircled my waist from behind. I felt a brush of his hand against my shoulder, and my hair was pulled back to reveal my neck. Instinctively I cocked my head to the side to tempt him and shivered in his arms when the tip of his nose ran along the length of my neck and he inhaled deeply.

Noah

"God, that smells good," I whispered into her ear. "And the food doesn't smell too bad, either."

It smelled fucking delicious, but there was something about seeing her at my stove, cooking breakfast for me, that made me want to taste her more. I sucked her earlobe into my mouth and teased it with my tongue while my hands began to roam over her silky skin.

"Noah, I'm trying to cook." She giggled, and the sound sent shock waves to my cock.

"So cook." My hand slipped under her shirt and I played with the waistband of her cotton shorts. I could feel her pulse quicken under my tongue as I placed sensual kisses along the tender flesh of her neck.

"Unless you like burnt bacon, you might want to stop that. It's incredibly distracting."

"Don't burn my bacon, Delaine." My voice was seductive

yet commanding, the way I knew she secretly liked it. I slipped my hand inside her shorts and cupped her with my massive hand. She gasped and tried to turn to look at me, but my hold kept her in place.

"No, no, Delaine. You need to watch the skillet," I reminded her. "Because if you burn my bacon, I'm going to have to punish you."

She gave me a seductive little half smile. Yeah, she wanted to be punished almost as much as I wanted to fucking punish her. Jesus, I loved our little games.

I parted her lower lips and slid my long fingers between the already wet folds. I loved the way she was always so receptive to my touch. So I pressed my entire body against her back to give her more of it. I knew she could feel my dick hardening against her, and I also knew she got off on that shit every bit as much as I did. I continued my assault on her neck, letting the fingers of my other hand do the walking to find a pert nipple. She arched her back and pressed her ass against my erection when I gave it a slight tweak.

"Noah—"

"Shh . . . bacon," I whispered against her ear.

I wanted to play with her, see how good a multitasker she was. So I withdrew both of my hands and slowly pushed her shorts over her curvy hips and down her legs.

"What are you—"

I answered her question when I spread her legs and inserted two fingers into her from behind. As I worked her with my right hand, the left made fast work of my pants and my cock sprang free. I was perfectly aware that I would probably forever associate the smell of bacon with what was about to happen. And much like Pavlov's dogs, I'd likely get a massive hard-on anytime the scent permeated the air around me. But it was a chance I was willing to take.

"What about my eggs?" I asked as I curled my fingers back and forth inside her. "Come on, Delaine. I'm starving."

Shaky hands picked up the two eggs and cracked them against each other to break the shell of one. She was going to play. I loved how adventurous she was.

I pulled my fingers out as she carefully dropped the first egg into the skillet. She cracked the shell of the other egg against the rim while I pulled her hips back and lightly pressed down on her lower back to get the perfect arch.

"Don't break the yolk," I warned, then pushed into her at the same time as she dropped the second egg into the skillet. She jerked and nearly broke it but recovered nicely, managing to keep the yellow center intact.

Fucking Delaine was un-goddamn-believable. In all my past endeavors, I had never come across a pussy as sweet as hers. It was hot with silky flesh that hugged my cock tighter than any other I'd had the opportunity to infiltrate. It drew me in and squeezed possessively like it never wanted to let me go. I was a slave to it, which was ironic since she was supposed to be my slave. She played her part well, make no mistake, but that little pussy of hers owned me. And I didn't mind one motherfucking bit.

I bent slightly at the knees and held her in place as I slowly moved in and out of her. She felt so amazing wrapped around my cock that I wondered if I would ever be able to get enough of her. When she turned her head and looked over her shoulder at me while biting down on that goddamn bottom lip, I knew the answer was fuck no, I would never get enough.

I grabbed a fistful of her hair and pulled, forcing her to arch her back further until that delicious little mouth was within my reach. I claimed it in a heated kiss and she moaned into my mouth.

"Is that bacon I smell burning?" I asked against her lips.

She turned back toward the skillet and flipped it over with shaky hands. I kept my hand in her hair, and the other on her hip as I increased the pace and urgency of my thrusts. The cheeks of her perfect little ass jiggled with each smack of my hips against them and I found it impossible to look away. Wanting to see the treasure trove hidden between those two heavenly dollops, I grabbed her hips with both hands and used my thumbs to spread her open. I groaned when the garden of forbidden pleasure was revealed. Her back entrance teased me with its tightness and I felt my dick grow impossibly harder.

"Fuck, baby," I moaned. "Your ass is so beautiful. I can't wait to put my cock in there."

I felt her body stiffen and she looked back at me again.

"Not now, Delaine, but soon," I assured her. "Trust me, as freaky as you are, you're going to love it."

I ran my thumb over the entrance and pressed until it slipped inside. She gasped, and then I felt the walls of her pussy constrict around my cock. I could feel the pulse of her orgasm as her head fell forward and she held on to the counter for dear life, a purring moan growing louder and louder with each pulse.

"Yeah, that's just a sample of what it will feel like."

I bit my bottom lip and grabbed ahold of her hips as I pounded into her sweet little cunt, increasing her pleasure. My balls tightened and an awesome feeling of euphoria soared through my body until it exploded out of me like fireworks. The grip I had on her hips grew tighter, but I didn't have the sense about me to worry about bruising her in that moment.

A long, feral growl clawed its way out of my chest when Delaine rolled and pushed her hips back into me over and over again until she'd milked me dry. I released her hips and placed my hands beside hers on the counter and then pressed forward to cage her in place, panting against her shoulder. Between much-needed breaths, I managed to drop a few chaste kisses here and there. Mostly because I couldn't get enough of her, but also as a form of thanks.

Yeah, look at me. This woman was required to fuck me, and I was thanking her for letting me do just that. It was better than nothing, though, right?

Her soft voice broke the silence. "Um, Noah? I think I burned the bacon."

I lifted my head and looked into the skillet. Sure enough, the bacon looked like charcoal and the yolk on the now rub-bery egg was broken. I dropped my head and laughed against her shoulder as I wrapped my arms around her. "That's okay, baby. I wasn't really all that hungry anyway."

"But . . . you're still going to punish me, right?" God bless her, she actually sounded hopeful.

"Oh, hell yeah."

~$~

By midday, I found myself sitting at my desk, unable to concentrate on a damn thing because I couldn't stop thinking about Delaine.

A knock sounded at the door before it popped open and Mason waltzed inside. "Four slices of bacon, two eggs over medium, and toast," he said with a quirked brow as he set a to-go box in front of me. "Breakfast for lunch?" Mason had been looking at me funny all day, and it was really beginning to piss me off.

I shrugged. "What can I say? I had a craving."

Polly bounced into the office and sidled up beside him. "You're lucky the diner down the street serves breakfast twenty-four hours a day."

I gave Mason a questioning look.

"She was on her way in anyway, so I asked her to pick up your lunch." He shrugged. "You're always saying I should learn to delegate."

"Hey!" Polly said in mock protest as she playfully punched his arm. "You don't delegate to your wifey, ass."

"Yeah, well, why don't you and your *wifey* run along and play so that I can enjoy my lunch in peace?" I suggested as I popped the lid of the container open.

The smell of the bacon immediately brought back the memory of this morning, and the front of my pants tightened. I could almost feel Delaine's hot wetness constricting around my cock as I moved inside her. Damn, I missed her.

"Actually, I have something I want to talk to you about," Polly said, yanking me out of my fantasy world.

I looked up at her and motioned toward my lunch. "Can it wait? This isn't going to taste very good when it's cold."

"No, it can't," she said as she took a seat in front of my desk. "Go ahead and eat. It won't bother me."

And because I knew she'd just be pacing outside my door while I ate, with several interruptions to see if I'd finished yet, I gave in. Polly could be a pushy little shit when she wanted something.

"All right, what's so important?"

Mason cleared his throat and started walking backward to the door. "I'll be at my desk if you need me."

I saw the look of apprehension on his face, and that clued me in that I wasn't going to like whatever it was she wanted to talk about. Like I said before, Mason is Polly's opposite. He knew when to leave shit alone, whereas Polly pushed until she got what she wanted.

I picked up a piece of bacon and took a bite while I waited for her to begin.

"So I was balancing your checkbook this weekend, paying the utility bills and whatnot, when I ran across an entry for a rather large sum of money that had been transferred from your personal account to an account in Hillsboro, Illinois," she started in a questioning tone.

"And?" I took a bite of the eggs. They needed salt.

"And . . . two million dollars? Noah, I know it's not my place to ask, but what the hell?"

"You're right, it's not your place to ask," I said, suddenly losing my appetite. I'd known she'd see the transaction, but she'd never questioned me about my outlandish splurging before. Then again, the last time I'd dropped a load even remotely similar to that, it had been for my Hennessey Venom GT Spyder.

Polly narrowed her eyes suspiciously. "Are you doing something illegal?"

"Polly, I'm warning you. Back off," I said in my most menacing tone. "The last time I checked, I was the employer and you were the employee. So don't come in here like you're going to interrogate me over something that is none of your business."

"You don't scare me, Noah Patrick Crawford," she said as she stood and waved a finger at me. "Something's up, and I don't know what it is, but you know I'll just keep digging until I figure it out. And don't think I didn't notice that the transaction just so happened to take place at the same time Lanie showed up."

She was pissing me off. I could feel the vein in my forehead bulge.

"Delaine," I corrected her.

"No, she asked me to call her Lanie. I guess she prefers that to her given name, but you should know that since you two are so in love," she said, crossing her arms over her chest. "What's the deal between you and her? 'Cause I'm not buying the whole 'we met outside a drag queen show in LA and fell in love' bullshit. You're a lot of things, but into dudes you are not."

My eyebrows shot up into my hairline and I nearly choked on my own saliva. "She told you we met at a drag queen show?"

It sounded like something Delaine would say. I wasn't really all that surprised. In fact, it was kind of funny. That was when I got an idea that would help me fuck with both of them—Polly for snooping when she should have been mind-ing her own damn business, and Delaine for making the drag queen comment in the first place.

"Did she tell you she has a penis?"

"Shutthefuckup!" Polly's mouth dropped open in shock, and then she quickly snapped it shut as she got a thoughtful look on her face. "Wait a minute." She narrowed her eyes suspiciously and put a hand on her hip. "I've seen her naked. She definitely does not have a penis."

"Not anymore," I added. "What do you think the money in the account was for?"

I could practically see the hamster running on the wheel inside her head as she processed what I was saying. "Oh. My. God! Lanie's had a sex change?"

I shrugged. "I don't see what the big deal is. Her name was Paul. She looks pretty convincing now, though, doesn't she?"

"But you're not into dudes."

"She's not a dude . . . now." I laced my fingers together and cupped the back of my head as I reclined in my chair. "Any more questions?"

Polly stared off into the distance, dumbfounded, until finally she shook her head. She started for the door, but I stopped her before she could leave.

"Oh, and Polly?" She turned to look at me. "This has to be our little secret. You can't say anything to anyone, especially not to Delaine. She's pretty sensitive about the subject and just wants to be accepted as the woman she's always felt she was on the inside."

"Oh yeah, right, no problem." She nodded vehemently while giving me a look that said "pfft, as if," then grabbed the doorknob to leave.

I was pretty damn proud of myself for being able to think so quickly on my feet. When Delaine found out what I'd done, she was going to be mega-pissed. For me, that translated into another epic sexcapade. Ding, ding, ding, ding. Triple whammy.

I stopped her again. "One more thing. I'm fucking kidding."

"About what?"

"The whole thing, Polly. I made it all up. Delaine has never been a man named Paul, and she most certainly does not now, nor has she ever, had a penis." I laughed. "But God, you should've seen the look on your face."

"Ugh! Noah Patrick Crawford!" She seethed between clenched teeth as she marched toward me. "I should knock the piss out of you!"

She swung her purse and smacked me in the back of the head.

"Ow!" I laughed, and ducked to avoid further blows.

"I'm going to tell her about this!" she said, taking another shot at me.

I was hoping for that.

She backed away and the coast appeared to be clear. "Look, it doesn't surprise me that she said she met me at a drag queen show. She has a very odd sense of humor, Polly. You never know if what she's saying is true or if she's bullshitting you," I explained. "It's one of the many things I love about her. But the truth is, we met at a conference."

The real truth was that most of what I said actually *was* true.

"Apparently she's not the only one who bullshits around

here," she said with her hands on her hips. Then she sighed and said, "Okay, confession time. When I saw that big transfer, I started thinking, and nothing was adding up right. So I did some research, and lo and behold, I couldn't find any trips that you've booked to LA over this supposed time you've been seeing her. And even though I had no last name to go by, I also didn't find anyone named Delaine or Lanie on any of the flights from LA the day she showed up." She took a breath. "What I did find was a receipt from a very posh club that just so happens to be owned by one Scott Christopher. A further background search on him revealed charges for trafficking. Human trafficking. Women, to be specific. So," she concluded with a sigh, "you wanna tell me who Lanie really is?"

Fuck my life! The motherfucking jig was definitely motherfucking up.

"It's complicated, Polly," I said, defeated. Damn it, I needed a cigarette and a shot of Patrón.

"Noah." Her voice was much lower, and she gave me this pitying look as she took a seat in front of me again. "You bought her, didn't you?"

I gnawed on the inside of my cheek and just looked at her. She obviously took that as an affirmative.

"I'm not going to ask you why, because I'm pretty sure I know the answer to that one already. But Lanie . . . she's a good girl. Why would she do something like that?"

"I don't know," I answered honestly. "We agreed not to discuss it."

"Well, don't you think you should find out?" she asked incredulously, flailing her hands in the air. "Just because you can't discuss it with her doesn't mean you can't do some digging on your own. Jesus Christ, Noah. Use the head on top of your shoulders instead of the one between your legs. Who knows what sort of trouble she might be in?"

She was walking a very thin line with the way she was talking to me, but if anyone could get away with that shit, it was Polly. She was just too cheery and cute to go all ballistic on. It would be like attacking a fourth-grader.

Plus she was right. And if I hadn't been so distracted lately, I would've done exactly what she'd suggested. Delaine had this way of making me forget who I was. It wasn't like I didn't have the connections to find out more about her, possibly even the reason she'd agreed to that contract in the first place. Maybe part of me only wanted to live in the fantasy world I'd created with her.

I mean, it didn't change anything. I'd bought her fair and square. But if she was in trouble, maybe I could help her out. After all, a large part of what I did at Scarlet Lotus was managing our charitable donations. My mother would've helped her. She wouldn't have purchased her or taken her virginity, and she probably would've killed me if she'd known I had, but nonetheless . . .

"So?" Polly asked, obviously waiting on a response from me.

I sighed. "I'll do some digging," I relented. "Now will you please go away and stop bothering me, you little pissant?"

"Sure thing," she said, back to her normal cheerful tone as she practically skipped toward the door. "I was about to go over and visit with Lanie anyway. I'm sure she can use the girl time."

"Don't bring this up with her, Polly. I mean it."

"Okay, okay," she said with her hands raised in surrender.

"And you're fucking fired, by the way."

She rolled her eyes, knowing it was a lie, and said, "Mmm, okay. I dropped your laundry off at the dry cleaner's. So I'll see you tomorrow?"

"Yeah, see you tomorrow."

As soon as she was gone, I picked up the container of my uneaten lunch and chucked it in the trash. I slammed my fist down on the desk in frustration, mostly aimed at myself. I should've been smarter about this. I should've been a little less selfish, a little less perverted—a little less hard up.

I opened the contacts list on my computer and found the number I was looking for. Brett Sherman was a ruthless private investigator who I'd hired when things turned sour with Julie. I thought for sure she'd try to pull some stunt and blackmail me or something, so I'd commissioned him to do some digging to get the dirt on her before she could even try. I'd used him on occasion since then. The fucker charged an arm and a leg, but the work he did was worth every inflated penny.

I dialed the number and was pleasantly surprised when he answered on the first ring.

"Brett Sherman."

"Brett, Noah Crawford," I greeted him.

"Mr. Crawford! What can I do ya for?" He was obviously happy to hear from me.

"I need you to find out everything you can on a lady by the name of Delaine Talbot from Hillsboro, Illinois," I said. "Do you need anything else?"

"An age would be nice."

I felt even more disgusted with myself because I'd violated her in so many ways, with plans to violate her in even more ways in the future, and I didn't even know the answer to that simple little question.

"Early twenties," I guessed.

"That should be enough to go on. I'll call you by the end of the week," he said, and hung up the phone abruptly.

Sherman didn't have the manners for pleasantries, but I was fine with that because I knew he'd go right to work the second the call ended.

"Noah!" David barged into my office, un-fucking-announced and un-motherfucking-invited.

"What do you want?" I said in a voice that conveyed that I wasn't in the mood to deal with his shit.

"Do I have to want something to come have a chitty-chat with my friend?" he asked with an arrogant grin as he sat down in a chair and propped his feet on my desk.

"You and I haven't been friends for a long time, David. And I doubt we ever really were." I leaned across the desk and knocked his feet down. And I was none too nice about it, either.

"Oh, don't be that way, Noah," he said with a mock pout. "You don't still have your panties in a twist over that Janet girl, do you?"

"Julie, and fuck you."

"No, fuck you," he said as if he was insulted. "I can't be-lieve you let a chick come between us, man. Whatever happened to bros before hos?"

"Chitty-chat time is over, Stone. Get out or I'll throw you out," I said between clenched teeth.

David stood and started for the door. "I swear, I don't know why you're still so bent out of shape over that slut. I told you, man. Or at least I *tried* to tell you. They're all gold-diggin' whores. Hit it and quit it, love 'em and leave 'em . . . whatever," he said with a shrug. "Just don't get emotionally attached, and never *ever* let them see you sweat, my brother."

I scoffed. "Like I'd take relationship advice from you."

"Say what you want about me, but the ladies are clawing at each other to get all up on my jock." He grinned and then grabbed his junk. "Just wait until you see my date for the ball. Whew! She is one hell of a looker," he said with a wink.

"Hooker is probably more like it," I mumbled as he walked out.

I could hear the smug bastard boisterously greet Mason like they were old college buddies, and it made my eye twitch in aggravation. I really hated him. Our whole lives, he'd just had to have anything I had. I'd thought it was one of those things that best friends did, but David took that to a whole other level. My friends, my girl, even my company—he wanted it all.

Well, I had something he could never have. I had Delaine. And I'd be damned if I'd ever let him anywhere near her.

I'd had enough for the day, so I picked up the phone and told Samuel to bring the car around. It wasn't like I was getting anything done anyway. I packed up and told Mason to call me if anything needed my immediate attention. I couldn't wait to see Delaine for a bit of stress management, and I was pacing like a madman by the time Samuel arrived.

He opened the door of the limousine for me to step inside and asked, "Where to, sir?"

"Home, and when we get there, make sure the staff take the rest of the day off," I told him. "I'd like a little bit of alone time with Delaine."

"Mr. Crawford, sir, Lanie left with Polly. They went shopping for a gown for the ball, I believe."

"Samuel, have you forgotten your place?" I asked in a calm voice, because he'd just called her Lanie and that wasn't at all like him. "Her name is Delaine."

"My apologies, sir, but she asked me to call her Lanie."

My jaw clenched and I reached out and slammed the door shut myself. I shouldn't have been upset with him, because it wasn't his fault. He was just doing what he'd been asked to do, as usual. But damn it all to hell if I wasn't royally pissed the fuck off that it seemed everyone else on the damned planet was calling her by such an informal name, yet she'd never asked me to do the same. You'd think the guy that was getting balls-deep in her would be awarded that privilege.

It was around five o'clock that afternoon when Polly finally dropped her off and she strolled through the door. I hadn't bothered to call and tell her that I would be home early, so she was surprised when she opened the door to find me sitting on one of the benches in the foyer. My knee was bouncing like crazy and my hair was mussed from my having practically pulled it out by the roots in my impatience.

"Oh! Noah," she said with a look of shock. "I wasn't expecting you home so early."

"Obviously," I said with a bit of resentment to my voice. "Where the fuck have you been, Delaine?"

"I went shopping with Polly. She said there's some sort of company function this weekend and insisted I have a new dress tailored," she said with a roll of her eyes.

"I told you that I wanted to know where you are at all times. Why didn't you call me?" I realized that I sounded like a madman, but damn it, I was pissed.

Silence fell around us as she continued to stare at me like she expected my head to explode. "Bad day?" she asked after what seemed like an eternity.

I dropped my head and looked at the floor. "Yeah, you could say that," I mumbled.

Delaine set her bags down and walked over to where I sat. When I wouldn't look up at her, she knelt down in front of me and searched my face. Without a word, she cupped it in her hands and pressed her lips to mine. What started out as a sweet kiss that was meant to calm me down quickly spiraled into a heated exchange of desperation.

"God, I missed you, too," she mumbled between kisses. I let pass without comment the fact that she hadn't said my name in place of "God," because I couldn't really make myself care about that shit when she was rubbing all up on me and pressing her tits as close as she could get them to my chest.

She shoved my jacket off my shoulders, and as I shrugged out of it, she went straight for my belt buckle. Then she made quick work of my pants and pulled the waistband of my boxer briefs away to reveal my cock. Of course I was already hard for her because that was what she did to me.

A tiny mewl escaped her luscious pink lips when she looked me over. Then, without even pulling my underwear down, she grabbed me by the base of my dick and plunged it into the hot, deliciously wet cavern of her mouth. I hissed when I felt her teeth barely scrape my length. She was looking up at me and her plump lips were wrapped around my cock, moving back and forth like she was starving to death. Then she closed her eyes and hummed like my dick was the best damn thing she'd ever tasted. It was a divine sight.

"Delaine," I said on a breath, caressing her cheek with the back of my hand.

Saying her name like that reminded me of how I was apparently the only motherfucker who called her that. But again, I let that shit go, because I could feel the head of my dick hitting the back of her throat with each pass she made. Plus her moans, intermingled with the wet sucking sounds coming from her efforts, echoed through the empty space that surrounded us. The foyer had really great acoustics.

"Harder, baby. Suck me harder."

She moaned around my dick and then met the challenge. She repositioned herself so that she had a better angle and went to fucking work on my cock. Faster, harder—and, son of a bitch, she was even going deeper. I could've put my hands on her head to help her, but it was all her. I wanted her to do it on her own.

She abruptly slowed and sank as far down on my dick as she could go. Then I felt her swallow around my cock, taking it even further into her throat. My baby could deep-throat like a motherfucker.

"Goddamn, goddamn, goddamn," I chanted as an orgasm came out of nowhere and commenced to kick my ass.

My release was fierce and forceful as it shot out of my cock and down the back of her throat. She hummed and closed her eyes, swallowing my come and still taking my cock in further with each gulp.

"Fucking . . . shit . . . Delaine!" I gasped between pulses of my release. My heart was pounding in my chest, hard and furious.

With one long, last suck, she released me. She kissed the head of my dick, and that made it twitch, which apparently amused her because she giggled and then did it again.

"Where the fuck did you learn to deep-throat like that?" Maybe I should've waited until I could actually breathe again before talking, but I wanted an answer to that question immediately. "I didn't teach you that."

She shrugged and wiped the corner of her mouth. "Polly told me how to do it, and I thought I'd try it out. Why? You didn't like it? Did I do it wrong?"

Polly may have redeemed herself just a little bit.

She looked so worried that it was cute. I grabbed her and kissed her hard before putting my forehead to hers. "You were perfect, Lanie. I fucking loved it."

Yes, I called her Lanie. I wanted to see what she would say.

Her eyes went wide and she backed out of my embrace. "Delaine," she said curtly, and then she stood, grabbed her bags, and started to walk away.

I quickly shoved my dick back in my underwear and took off after her. "Oh, so Samuel and Polly get to call you Lanie, but I can't? What the fuck is that shit about?"

"They didn't pay millions of dollars to own me for two

years. They are not my boss. They are my equals, just lowly servants paid to cater to your every need."

"That's fucked up." I put my hands on my hips. The action drew her attention to my crotch, and her eyes lingered on the spot, my pants and belt not yet secured back in place.

"It is what it is, Noah. It is what it is." She turned and continued up the stairs, effectively ending the conversation.

10

easy does it

Lanie

That bastard had some nerve. Using my name like that? What the hell?

I heard him taking the stairs two at a time as he ran after me, so I walked faster.

"Delaine!" he yelled, but I just kept walking. Well, I was sort of jogging by that time because I really wanted to get away from him. All of this, everything I'd been dealing with and continued to deal with, was hard enough without him making it harder. I had to get away before I totally lost it in front of him.

"Wait, goddamnit!" he yelled as I dropped my bags and took off at a full sprint.

I opened the door to a random room and slammed it shut behind me. It was pitch black in there and I had no clue where I was, but I knew that I was throwing up a blockade between me and Noah and that was all that mattered. I fumbled in the dark until I found the locking mechanism on the doorknob, and I secured it in place before turning my back and leaning against the door.

He was already there, pounding on the other side with his fists. I heard him growl in frustration, the sound almost frightening me. "If you don't open this door, I swear by all that is holy I *will* break it down!"

"I don't want to talk to you right now! Go away!" I said as loud as I could so that maybe he could hear me over the beating he was putting on the poor, defenseless door.

"Fine. Have it your way."

The pounding stopped, and I sighed in relief that he had given up. I had begun to sink down to the floor when I heard what sounded like a strained battle cry from the other side, followed by a loud crash against the door that sent me tumbling forward. I managed to catch myself on my hands and knees and whipped my head around as light from the hallway spilled into the room.

Noah stood in the center of the doorway, his arms hanging at his sides, his shoulders rising and falling with heavy breaths. A shadow fell across the front of him, but I could still see the menacing look on his face. He looked almost lethal.

"You accuse me of treating you like any other employee, yet you never listen when I give you an order," he seethed.

"Yeah, well I'm insubordinate. Fire me," I said, getting to my feet to storm past him.

He grabbed my arm and swung me around until my back was pressed to the wall just inside the door. His body was pressed to mine, his forearms flush with the wall and rendering me immobile. He forced my legs apart with his knee and I could feel his hot breath against my ear as he ground the bulge in his pants against my stomach. He wasn't kidding when he said he had a lightning-quick recovery time.

"Why? Why can't I call you Lanie?" He buried his head in the crook of my neck. The sound of his voice was a mix of desperation, anger, and frustration, and for the life of me, I couldn't figure out why. He dragged his lips across my skin sensually and then lifted his head to look me in the eye. Piercing hazel orbs reflected an intensity that both shocked and made me want to give him anything he asked.

"I've treated you well. Better than you could've possibly hoped for in your situation. And I've always made sure you've been adequately taken care of in other ways as well." He reminded me of his meaning by bending at the knees and slowly grinding into my very center. A traitorous moan escaped my lips. "So, why? Give me one good reason."

How about five? Because it made all this too personal. Because it would be too hard to leave him at the end of the two years. Because it was going to make it too easy to fall in love with him. Because I just couldn't . . .

That was the truth. But if I told him any of those things, he'd send me packing and demand a full refund.

"Because you want to," I said, giving him the fifth reason.

"I want you." He leaned forward and gently tugged at my bottom lip with his teeth. His hands left the wall and he began to run them up and down my sides desperately. "Why are you torturing me?"

I was torturing him?

"I'm not torturing you, Noah," I sighed. "Not giving you permission to call me Lanie means that for once in your life, you can't have something you want. And you only want it because you can't have it. And it's killing you because you have no control over it whatsoever. You're overly privileged and spoiled rotten. And it's pretty obvious that everything in your life has been handed to you on a silver platter. But this one? This one is personal. You have to *earn* the right, and only I get to decide when you have adequately done so."

I could feel the vibrations of his growl against my chest, reminding me of how enticingly close we were. Obviously he didn't like my answer. "You're mine. Maybe you forgot. Here, let me remind you."

His body kept mine pinned against the wall, but his hands yanked my skirt up over my hips before he pulled the front of his underwear down and released the beast within.

I understood perfectly what Noah was doing. I had stripped him of the control he thought he possessed and had made him feel like less of a man. This was his way of regaining it. I expected it, even coveted it. We both knew my body would react. That went without saying. But my mind, my soul . . . those were mine to give, only when I felt him worthy. And that was never going to happen. This was no fairy tale. This was me, being owned by a man who had paid big money to ensure my physical submission. Nothing more. And I wasn't about to put myself out there like that, because I could definitely see myself falling for the likes of Noah Crawford, which guaranteed a broken heart for me.

"Do it. Fuck me," I challenged. "That's what I'm here for, right?"

He stopped and searched my eyes. Then he leaned in until our lips were barely touching and asked, "Why did you sell your body to me?" His cock was pressed against my entrance, but he didn't move.

"You were the highest bidder." The tip of my tongue made brief contact with his lower lip and I arched my back to try to entice him to just put it in already.

"That's not what I mean, and you know it. Why did you put yourself up for auction? Why did you need the money?"

"Boy, you're full of questions today, aren't you?" I ran my hands through his hair teasingly and tried to maneuver my hips so that his head could enter me, but he pulled back enough to thwart my effort.

"Answer the damn question and stop trying to fuck me," he said forcefully.

"Why? Don't you want to fuck me?"

He hooked his hands behind my thighs and lifted me off the floor, and then he thrust his cock into me. In one swift move, he was totally submerged inside my body. I gasped and clutched his shoulders.

"You tell me. Does it feel like I want to fuck you?" He rolled his hips to grind into me. "It's damn near the only thing I think about lately. I'm so fucking addicted to your pussy that I can't think straight. Now, stop trying to distract me and answer the question."

He kept his hips still and refused to move any more, even though I was doing my best to get some friction going.

"Noah, please," I begged like a shameless hussy. I could feel his thickness stretching me and I wanted more.

He leaned forward and his husky voice permeated my ear, sending shivers down my spine. "Answer the question and I promise I'll give you what you want. Because you want it, too. Don't you, Delaine? You want to fuck me just as much as I want to fuck you. Goddamnit, just think about it—my thick cock moving inside that tight little cunt of yours. In and out until you feel like you're going to explode."

I moaned and slipped my hands under his arms and down his back until I could slide them down his boxer briefs to grab a handful of his ass. Then I rolled my hips the fraction of space allotted to me, desperate to feel the mind-numbing orgasm I knew he could give.

"Yeah, you like the thought of that, don't you, kitten?" He sucked my earlobe into his mouth and nibbled it teasingly. "All you have to do is answer the question."

I was already teetering on the edge of losing control, and then he just had to go and call me "kitten." He'd been doing that a lot lately and every time he did, it shoved me right on over into the abyss of insanity. I wanted him so badly I thought I might cry. And he smelled so good that I swear I probably could've gotten off on his scent alone. I whined out of frustration because I knew I couldn't give him the answer he wanted, just like I knew he wasn't going to give me what I wanted if I didn't.

"You're not going to tell me, are you?"

"No," I answered, and he let out a frustrated breath. "Like my name, my reason for the contract is also personal."

He shut his eyes tightly and I could see his jaw muscles working as he ground his teeth. Abruptly he pulled out of me and set me on my feet. He made quick work of tucking himself back into his pants and then secured the belt in place. It had to hurt because he was still hard as granite. He hissed in discomfort, confirming my suspicion. When he was done, he looked back at me, shook his head in disappointment, and then walked out of the room without a word.

I sank to the floor with my knees drawn up to my chest and my face buried in my arms. That was when everything came crashing down on me. My mother's illness, my father's despair, the stupid contract—and Noah. The pretenses I had to keep up with him; pretending that I was so much more unaffected by him than I actually was. It was too much and it had made me numb.

I was lying to my parents. I was lying to Noah. And I was lying to myself.

Oh, what a very complicated web of deceit I'd spun.

I was so out of my league. No way was I going to come out of this unbroken.

I was falling for him big-time already. I meant what I'd said earlier; I had missed him today. I couldn't stand being away from him. And then when I walked in and he was waiting for me, looking exactly like I felt—spent and anxious from the separation—I needed him. I needed him to need me.

Yes, I said needed. Not wanted, *needed*.

I sat there on the floor for hours, mulling it all over in my head and generally feeling sorry for myself. But I couldn't stay there forever. Eventually, I'd have to face Noah, so I hauled myself off the floor and decided a nice, long dip in the pool would probably be a good idea. Maybe by the time I was done, Noah would already be fast asleep. I still wasn't even sure he wanted me in his bed. Unless he ordered me otherwise, that was where I'd be. Great. Double Agent Coochie wouldn't give me issues with that at all, I thought sarcastically. Yep, a nice dip in a cold pool was exactly what I needed to sober me and the Cooch.

Luckily, the house was big enough that I didn't bump into Noah on my way to the bedroom. He wasn't there. I did a quick change, putting on the scrap of cloth Polly had sworn up and down was a bikini, and made my way outside to the pool. I may have also sent a silent prayer in thanks to the powers that be my father didn't have to see his baby girl in that ludicrous getup. However, I soon realized exactly how much God was punishing me for this life of sin I had stumbled upon when I found Noah swimming laps in the pool.

I was momentarily stunned when I caught sight of his sinewy muscles as he sliced through the water like a hot knife through warm butter. His movements were smooth and fluid, like he was part of the water himself. When he reached the end of the pool, he grabbed on to the side and pulled himself out. Water cascaded off his frame and his wet hair shone black as night, reflecting the light of the moon. My eyes trailed over his shoulders and down his lean back to his . . . Oh. My. God. He even swam in the nude.

The Ridonkabutt was flexed and more chiseled than any butt had a right to be. I wanted to bite it. Hard.

"You're staring at my ass again." His voice dripped like liquid sex and knocked me out of my drunken stupor. Yes, I was drunk on the badonkadonk. And he had eyes in the back of his head? Maybe those little back dimples were actually an extra pair.

I gasped when he turned around, and he quickly covered himself. He shrugged and, completely uncharacteristic of him, looked embarrassed. "The water's a little cold."

Well, you could've fooled me. I mean, he wasn't as colossal as I was used to seeing him, but there were plenty of men out there who only wished they were as large when they had a raging hard-on as Noah was when he was limp.

"Sorry, I didn't know you'd be down here. I'll just . . ." I turned to go back inside.

"No, don't. Stay."

I turned back around and he was walking toward me with that towel wrapped around his waist and beads of water clinging to the fine patch of dark hair on his chest that stretched into a trail leading to the object of my affection. The towel did nothing to dissuade my ogling. The Wonder Peen was bulging under there, and if he got excited, I knew the massive tent he'd pitch would be big enough to shelter the whole damn Von Trapp family. Kind of made me feel like singing, except my singing voice really sucked. So much so that it had been outlawed in my own home. But I digress.

Cooch was threatening to gnaw her way through my bikini to get at him, and I smacked her on the head to get her to settle down. Apparently it wasn't a mental smack, because Noah looked at me with a raised brow.

"Um, I thought I felt a mosquito, and well, that would be a really uncomfortable place to have the itchies," I said. It wasn't a very good cover.

"Uh-huh. Well, you're free to use the pool. But if you don't mind, I'm going to relax in one of the lounge chairs for a bit while I dry off. I'm feeling a little tense and could really use the fresh air."

"I could give you a massage if you want," I blurted out. "I mean, I'm pretty good at it."

He looked just as surprised as I was by my offer, but he tilted his head to the side as if he was considering it. He nodded and then gave me a crooked smile. "Yeah, that would be really nice."

I followed him over to one of the lounge chairs and waited while he reclined it all the way flat and lay down on his stomach. He folded his arms so that his chin rested on them while I stood there like a complete idiot trying to think of the best way to approach him.

The assterpiece looked like the best seat in the house, so I straddled him and perched the Cooch right on top of it. Like the ass whore we all knew she was, she got herself a little better acquainted with him right away, flirting unabashedly with him behind the Wonder Peen's back.

"Um, this usually works better with lotion. Do you want me to go get some?" I asked.

Noah lifted his head a bit and looked back at me. "Not really. I'm pretty comfortable and would prefer you stay right there."

The Cooch and I were in agreement on that one.

I started on his neck and shoulders, kneading the flesh as firmly as I could without pinching his skin. He moaned in approval while I worked the tense muscles until I could feel the tension melt away under my fingers. He kept his eyes closed and I did my thing, making my way across his shoulders and down his back. I couldn't help myself—I leaned forward and gently kissed his neck. He moaned again and shifted his hips, causing a delicious bit of friction between my legs. I figured since he liked that, I'd do it again to see if I could get the same reaction. Noah did not disappoint.

I kissed a trail down his spine, all the while continuing to massage his muscles, craving the feel of him beneath my fingers and palms. He arched his back, which brought his ass even closer to my center like an offering. So I slid down his legs and made a pit stop to swirl my tongue in those little dimples above his ass, dragging my arms and hands along the flesh of his back as I did so. When I reached the towel, Noah lifted his hips and I slowly peeled it back, exposing God's gift to ass whores everywhere.

My tongue slipped out to wet my lips as I ogled it, feeling suddenly ravenous. Then I slid my hands over the two luscious mounds and palmed them greedily.

"Your ass is so perfect." I leaned forward, gave it a quick flick of my tongue, and then bit him.

Noah flinched with a hiss and I bit him again, but on the other cheek. He was delicious. I took a hunk of his skin into my mouth and gave it all the suction I had. Oh, God, I was finally getting what I wanted most, and it was so worth the wait. My moans mixed with Noah's hisses and then some stuff went down seriously fast.

Somehow Noah was able to flip over without bucking me off him and onto the ground. I found myself straddling his chest with my legs over his shoulders, the Ridonkabutt nowhere to be found. I was kind of miffed about that, but I quickly settled down when I felt Noah's mouth frenching the Cooch.

"Shit . . . ," I said with a sharp intake of breath when I realized he had also managed to pull the strings on my bikini bottom and had me bare. When Noah Crawford wanted something, you couldn't bat a lash around him or you were going to miss seeing how he got it. Not that I was complaining or anything.

He looked up at me from between my legs. "Take your top off for me. I want you to feel the cool night air against those beautiful little pink nipples."

I reached behind my neck and pulled at the string and let the top fall forward. He kept his eyes on my every movement while he gently kissed and sucked at my clit. My nipples were already pebbled and I wanted to give him a show, so I palmed my breasts and rolled the rosy peaks between my fingers. He hummed in appreciation and then I released the tie at my back and tossed my top to the side.

"Lie back, baby. Let me make you feel good." His arms came up to my sides and he helped ease me back until my stomach was flat and I could feel his cock under my shoulder. Then he slid his hands back down my sides and grabbed my hips. The sky was clear and the moon was full and fat overhead. I could see each and every single star in the night sky, and it felt like I had been warped into another universe. Noah was doing that otherworldly thing with his mouth as a gentle breeze washed over my skin, and I could hear all the nocturnal sounds of crickets and other bugs and animals around us. It was serene and exotic.

I felt Noah's tongue enter me and I suddenly wanted more, to feel him inside me right in that exact place at that exact moment. Not that what he was doing didn't feel simply awesome; I just wanted more.

I didn't want to argue. I didn't want to think. I didn't want to do anything but feel.

So I sat up, and after a brief protest from Noah, I broke up his little make-out session with the Cooch.

"Did I do something wrong?" he asked, confused.

I simply shook my head as I straddled his waist. "No talking. Just feeling," I whispered against his lips, then kissed him passionately.

His arms wrapped around my back and he held me to him, answering my kiss with an equal fervor. This was what I was looking for. Our bodies said things our mouths would never admit. There was no competition, no challenge, just two people giving and taking in the most natural way, fulfilling a basic need.

I put my hands on his chest for leverage and raised myself up. His eyes were locked with mine as I rolled my body and slid my wet folds along his length. I had no idea if I was doing any of this right because I'd never been in control before. I only did what felt nice to me and hoped he liked it, too. When his lips parted and his eyes became hooded, I had my answer.

My hands traveled down his chest and over the defined muscles of his abdomen until I found his monstrous cock. I lifted myself off him and positioned him at my entrance, but then I hesitated. God, I so did not want to mess this up.

Noah must have sensed my unease because he caressed my thigh and in the most tender voice said, "Just ease down slowly, kitten, or you'll hurt yourself."

I took a deep breath and let it out slowly as I followed his instruction, feeling every bit of his massiveness fill me inch by magnificent inch.

"That's it, baby. God, you feel so fucking incredible."

"I don't know what to do," I confessed once I had taken him all the way in. His cock was so much deeper from this angle than it had ever been before.

"Move your hips, up and down, back and forth. Ride me, baby. Do whatever feels good to you, and I promise it'll feel good for me, too." Then he licked his luscious lips and said, "Come here and kiss me."

I leaned forward and he craned his neck up to meet me. As he did so, he held my hips and slowly began to move back and forth inside me. Then he swiveled his hips and I felt him grind against my clit. I gasped when a shock wave of pleasure shot through my body.

He broke our kiss. "See? Just like that."

I kept my eyes on his and my hands on his chest as I sat up a little and rolled my hips to re-create the same sensation. I could feel the ridges of the head of his dick, the throbbing of his pulse, the pressure of his hands as he pulled me back and forth. His thumbs were pressed to the sensitive spot over my hip bones and I moaned and dropped my head back. The stars and moon were looking down on me, and I was convinced that this was the most perfect I had ever felt in my entire life. I felt alive, no longer numb.

"What are you thinking about, kitten?" Noah's voice was raspy and filled with desire.

"How perfect this feels," I answered honestly, and then looked back down at him.

He rose up into a sitting position and cupped my face in his hands, pulling me in for a languid kiss. It was deep and sensual and perfect for the moment. Neither of us rushed. We took our time and enjoyed the feel of each other without any thought of contracts, illnesses, or reasons.

He wrapped one arm around my waist while the other massaged a breast. Then he broke the kiss and his mouth latched on to my other breast to gently suckle me. I ran my fingers through his hair and held him to me, my own locks falling forward and creating a curtain around him. I moved my hips faster and rode him with more purpose than when we had begun. The tip of his tongue flicked at my nipple, and I closed my eyes as that familiar feeling in the pit of my stomach spiraled out of control. My orgasm released like tiny molecules exploding through my blood. His name spilled from my lips and echoed through the otherwise silence of the night, and I heard him growl.

When the moment had nearly passed, Noah lifted me up and put me on my back. Then he put my arms above my head and linked his fingers with mine to hold my hands in place, lying flush with me. In and out he moved, intensifying my orgasm and bringing it back to life.

"Goddamn, you're beautiful, Delaine. Do you know that? So fucking beautiful."

He gripped my hands tighter and thrust deeper, but not faster. The look in his eyes was intense and his lips were slightly parted as he looked down on me. "I'm sorry . . . for everything. I'm so sorry."

Before I could ask him what that was about, his lips were on mine. He hummed and moaned and grunted, assaulting my mouth with a ferocious hunger. I answered the best I could, but he was simply out of my league on that one. It was a desperate kiss, like he couldn't get enough, which was just fine with me because I never wanted that moment to end. But I was concerned. His movements became more erratic and I heard that familiar guttural growl that always preceded his release. Then, as forecasted, he broke the kiss and came inside me. His eyes never left mine.

"Oh, fuck—so good," he ground out between clenched teeth. His thrusts became uneven and staggered as the last of his seed sputtered forth. When he was done, he collapsed on top of me before he clutched my body to his and rolled us over onto our sides.

Noah was still breathing heavily when he pushed the hair back out of my face and gave me an adoring look. Then he leaned forward and kissed me gently on my swollen lips.

"Why did you say you're sorry? For what?" I asked, because I had to know.

He sighed and shook his head. "For badgering you about the name thing. I was being unreasonable. It makes sense that you would want me to call you by your given name instead of one that's so much more familiar."

"Oh. Well, you definitely made up for it." I laughed lightly.

"No, that was all you. You're incredible."

"I am pretty spectacular, aren't I?" I joked. The Cooch popped her collar.

At least my uncharacteristic arrogance got a laugh out of him, and it was surreal because he didn't do a whole lot of laughing. He pulled me closer, and I nuzzled into his chest to listen to the heavy thud of his heartbeat while looking up at the sky. I think I made a comment about how beautiful the stars were and I heard him murmur his agreement, but for the most part we were silent. I would've given anything to hear what he was thinking, but I knew it would probably just turn into another one of those petty arguments we tended to have. And I really didn't want to ruin the moment. So I kept my mouth shut and basked in the feeling. Because between Noah and me, both of us stubborn as mules, who knew what tomorrow would hold?

11

what the . . . ?

Lanie

I was dreaming. I could feel Noah's body against my back, holding me under a star-filled sky and whispering sweet nothings into my ear as I drew his arms tighter around my waist.

"I'm so sorry. I didn't know," he whispered. "But now that I have you here, I can never let you go. Never, Delaine. You are a part of me now. I can't let you walk away from me."

"There's no place else I'd rather be, Noah," I sighed, and nuzzled closer. "I want to be here like this with you forever. Hold me tight and don't ever let me go."

"Never. I love you, Lanie. Please tell me you . . ." His raspy voice faded out and the scene around me became fuzzy and melted away. I desperately tried to summon it back with my mind, but it was too late. I was rousing from my sleep, and it was simply gone.

"Please tell me you don't lie around and sleep all damn day."

"Huh?" I sat up and blindly looked around the room, which really didn't work well when my hair was all over my face like

Cousin Itt from *The Addams Family*. My hands clumsily swiped at the rat's nest, enough to part the curtain of mane so that I could see the little pissant that dared disturb my slumber. Because that sure wasn't Noah's voice.

"Go away, Polly," I huffed, then fell back onto the bed in dramatic fashion. I grabbed Noah's pillow and hugged it to my chest as I inhaled his scent and sighed contentedly. "I'm sleeping." There was still a chance I could recapture my dream if she'd stay quiet and just disappear.

"Not anymore, you're not," she said, and then I heard her skip across the room to do God only knew what, but I swore if she jumped on me, I was going to give her a thunder flick to the forehead, followed up by a wet willy to the ear. She was way too bubbly in the mornings, and probably deserved it for that fact alone, but I was biding my time so that I'd have the element of surprise on my side.

"What do you want?" I half whined as she pulled the drapes back and let the bright morning sun assault my comfy-cozy surroundings. I practically hissed and buried my face in my pillow. Then thoughts of vampires filtered into my brain, which then led to thoughts of the vampiric sex Noah and I had had in the entertainment room.

We should so do that again.

The Cooch perked up like ten thousand milligrams of caffeine had been pumped into her. Slut. I guess she was seconding the motion.

"Well, for starters, I'd like for you to do something with that godawful stuff you call hair," Polly said, and I felt her delicately lift one tangled lock of it before dropping it again and rubbing her hands together. You'd think she thought I had cooties or something. "And then we need to have a talk."

"About what?" My sleepy voice was muffled by the pillow, and I almost gagged when my morning breath came back at me. The hair could wait; I needed some toothpaste and a toothbrush.

"Stuff. Now get your little butt up before I go get a pitcher of ice water and throw it on you," she said, and smacked me on the ass.

I sat up with a huff and narrowed my eyes at her before I got right in her face. "I really can't stand you, Polly. You know that?"

Once I'd showered—pleasuring myself twice with the help of my nifty little Crawford bullet—shaved, and, yes, brushed my teeth, I went back out into the bedroom, where Polly had already made the bed and evidently picked out my clothes for the day. I dressed and threw my hair up into a messy bun before I made my way downstairs.

"Polly?" I called, having no clue where she would be.

"In here!" she yelled from the kitchen.

When I entered, I found she already had coffee made and had poured me a cup. "Wow, you almost look human."

"You may have just saved yourself from getting your butt kicked," I countered, because the best part of waking up really was Folgers in your cup. However, I highly doubted the rich aroma I smelled was Folgers. Noah would've had nothing but the best gourmet coffee known to man in his house.

I took a seat across from her at the kitchen island and started shoveling sugar into my coffee. "So what's so important that you had to disturb my beauty sleep?"

"We'll get to that. First of all, I want to know if you tried the deep-throat thing," she asked, ready to dish.

"Yep. And I do believe you'd make one hell of a Yoda, and not just because you're vertically challenged."

"A quick learner you were, young Skywalker. Or should I say, young Streetwalker?" she said in her best Yoda impersonation. We both laughed, but then Polly abruptly stopped and cleared her throat. "Um, sorry," she said with a ping of guilt on her face.

"For what?" I asked, confused.

"Oh, um, nothing." She took a sip of her coffee.

"Uh-uh. No way. You spill. Now." I pointed a finger at her.

Polly set her cup down and heaved a great sigh. "Oh, God. He's going to kill me. I just know it," she said as she nervously wrung her hands.

"Who? Noah?" I knew that was whom she was talking about. "For what, Polly?"

She scrunched her face up like she was about to say something she didn't really want to say. Then she covered her face with her hands and peeped out at me between her fingers. "I know, Lanie. I know everything."

"What's everything, munchkin? You're not giving me anything to go on here," I said with a roll of my hand, hoping to encourage her to keep the deets coming.

"I know about the contract that you and Noah have. I know that he paid two million dollars for you to come here to live with him for the next two years. I know that you two aren't a legitimate couple. I know about the sex. Oh, God, Lanie, I know about everything, and I really wish I didn't because it's just too much, too overwhelming for someone like me to handle," she blurted out in one long strand of frantic words.

My hands were shaking so badly I had to set down the coffee mug I was holding, for fear that I might drop it, or throw it across the room at a wall, or whatever. "He told you?" My voice was relatively calm, which surprised the heck out of me.

"No, no, no, no, nooooo. Please, Lanie, it's not his fault," she pleaded desperately, like she was trying to fix everything. "See, I do all his household accounting, and I saw the money transfer and confronted him about it. I put two and two together and ascertained that the money was transferred around the same time you showed up. And then, well, you know how I am already. I started to do some digging. But, to be fair, if you had just told me the truth when we first met, I wouldn't have had to. I mean, you were talking about Elvis, Tupac, MJ, drag queens . . . And Noah wasn't any help, either. When I asked him about the money, he said you used to be a man and it was for your sex change operation, and—"

"Ho, ho, hoooo!" I belted out, stopping her. "Wait, what did you just say?"

Polly took a deep breath. "Which part? Or do you want me to start all over again?"

"God, no. I don't think my brain could take that a second time." I pinched the bridge of my nose because I had a massive headache threatening to break loose courtesy of all the yammering and revelations that were being thrown at me. "Polly? Did you say Noah told you I used to be a man and had a sex change?"

"Yeah, but he also said he was joking," she said with a shrug and then her eyes got wide as saucers. "He was joking, right? You didn't really have a schlong, did you?"

"Yes!" I screeched.

"Yes, you had a schlong?" she asked with an expression of shock—and, possibly, even a wee bit of curiosity—on her face.

"No, Polly. Yes, he was joking," I clarified. Noah Crawford had it coming big-time.

Vengeance would be mine.

"Good. I mean that's . . . good," she said with a sigh of relief. And then she propped her elbow up on the table with her chin in her hand. "Lanie, honey, why did you do it? Why did you sell yourself for sex?"

"It's personal, Polly. And I don't want you to go snooping around to find out. If you do, I swear I'll kick your scrawny little ass," I warned. She crossed her heart in a silent promise not to. "Besides, Noah doesn't even know."

"Yeah, and I'm sure he hasn't pressed the issue with you, either, especially since that would mean he'd then have to tell you about Julie. The cow," she murmured.

"Wait, that's the second time you've said her name. What's the deal with this chick? Is she an ex-girlfriend or something?" If anyone was going to spill the beans, it would be Polly. She had probably told me more than she was supposed to in the first place.

"I swear if he ever finds out about this, he's going to fire me for real, and probably Mason, too. You know, the whole guilt-by-association thing. And then we'll be homeless with nowhere to go, no money to shop with—"

"Tragic," I muttered sarcastically.

"I know, right?" she said as if it really was. "Okay, look; I'll tell you, but only after you tell me what the real deal is between you and Noah."

I thought about the dream, but that was all it had been. Right? Noah could never feel that way about me, no matter how good I was at deep-throating his colossal cock. "The real deal is that it's a business transaction, Polly. Nothing more," I said matter-of-factly.

"I'm not buying it, Lanie. You can lie to Noah, or even to yourself for that matter, but I don't believe it," she said, calling me out. "I heard you. Before I woke you up. You were talking in your sleep, and from the sounds of it, you've got it bad for the boss man, sister."

"Goddamnit, Polly! Is there ever a time when you're not being nosy?" I asked, offended by the invasion of privacy.

"Hey! Don't you use the Lord's name in vain with me!" she chastised me, her finger wagging.

I put my elbows on the table and ran my hands through my hair in frustration. "I'm sorry, Polly. Look, this isn't exactly an ideal situation for me. I'm falling for the man who paid enough money to feed a starving village for longer than I have any knowledge of, just so he can get in my pants anytime he wants with no strings attached. And try as I might to hate him, I can't! What's wrong with me? It's not Stockholm syndrome, because I haven't exactly been kidnapped and I'm not being kept here against my will. I signed on for this, but it's getting to be too real. You know?"

Polly nodded with a sincere look on her face as I continued to ramble on. "And with all the stuff I have going on back home, all I can do is throw up my hands and say, 'Jesus, please take the wheel'—which isn't going to do me a whole hell of a lot of good, because the life I'm living isn't exactly saintly—but I have no clue what I'm doing here. And I seem to be digging myself in further and further. I mean, I know I'm just a whore to him, and that he could never feel anything for me that's even remotely close to the mad crush I have on him, but . . . ugh!"

I took a deep breath. My face was flaming hot and I thought I might start crying at any moment. No way was I going to do that because it would make me look weak and even more vulnerable. But I was thankful that I could get at least some of it off my chest before a complete and total mental breakdown crept up on me. Because I was seriously close to that happening.

Polly seemed to really get me, though, and contrary to her usual manner, she simply listened and let me vent without trying to force me to go into any more detail. There were no words to describe my gratitude.

She stretched an arm across the counter and took my hand in hers with a comforting smile. "You're carrying a pretty big burden, huh?"

"I don't want to talk about it."

Polly and I both started laughing at the same time. Not a full-on belly laugh, one of those laughs where we both recognized how ridiculous my statement sounded after the huge load I had just dumped.

"Don't worry, sweetie. You're going to get through this. And you never know what might happen. I mean, Noah isn't incapable of having feelings. At least, I don't think he is. I'm sure that nasty little debacle with Julie was only a minor setback and not something that will leave him emotionally scarred for the rest of his life."

"Yeah, you were going to tell me about that. What's the deal with him and that chick?"

"Well, she's a total bitch, for one," she started with a disgruntled sneer. "Noah dated her for two years, give or take a lifetime. Her father, Dr. Everett Frost, is a really close friend of the family and that's pretty much how they hooked up."

"I, um, I met Dr. Frost," I said, remembering his name from the appointment.

"Yeah, Everett's a good guy. I don't judge him by his offspring," she said. "Anyway, Noah went away on a business trip, but he'd decided—against all better judgment—to propose to her when he got back. For some unknown reason, he thought he loved her. I'm not so sure he really knew what love was, and I'm still not convinced that he does even now. But anyway, he came home only to find his beloved Julie getting rammed in the ass by his best friend."

I gasped and put my hand over my heart. I wasn't doing it for dramatic effect; it was a completely natural reaction to my shock. "Oh, no . . ."

"Yeah, 'oh, no' is putting it mildly," Polly said. "Needless to say, Noah's heart was crushed, or maybe it was just his ego, but either way, he was devastated." She paused and looked at me with this fearsome, overprotective mother-bear expression in her eyes. "And Lanie, I simply don't know if he can take any more. So if this thing between you two really does advance to another level, you keep that in mind. We clear?"

How sweet was that? She was about as big as a mosquito and every bit as annoying, and there she was, sounding all authoritative and issuing a thug's warning. Somehow, though, I didn't put it past her to follow through. Not that it was anything she'd have to be concerned about, because Noah Crawford didn't feel that way about me and I was going to fight against every urge I had to make sure I didn't put myself in front of that train either. Any type of feeling I was developing for him would have to be buried somewhere deep inside, lest my heart get ripped to shreds in the hands of the one man with enough power over me to do so.

"Perfectly clear, Polly. No worries. Although I really don't think Noah is the one you're going to have to worry about getting hurt in this equation."

"Yeah, I get that. I know he seems like a hard-ass on the outside, but when he lets the real him shine through . . ." She sighed. "He's got some real potential to be all that and a bag of chips. So I can absolutely see where there's cause for worry."

"Ah, don't say that, Polly," I whined, and put my head in my hands.

"Sorry, babe." She stood and patted my shoulder. "Keep your chin up, and believe for all you're worth that what's meant to be will be." She winked at me before grabbing her clutch and tucking it under her arm. "I have errands to run. I'll talk to you later."

She gave me a chaste kiss on the cheek, and then all I heard was the clip-clop sound of her heels as she walked away, leaving me there to dwell on all my issues. The funny thing was that I didn't dwell on it. I was more concerned about Noah and the horrible stuff he'd been through.

Yeah, my problems were probably tons more pressing, what with my mother dying a little more each day, but it was the nurturing side of me—and probably my perpetual state of denial—that made me push that aside for the time being and just feel for him. I couldn't imagine walking in on my best friend and my guy going at it like that.

I cursed myself when an image of Dez and Noah together flashed behind my eyes and sent a shiver down my spine. Hell would freeze over before that would happen. I knew it, but if it ever did, Hell still wouldn't be anywhere near as cold as my heart.

Poor Noah. That explained why a wealthy man with looks to kill and a body to die for would stoop so low as to purchase a woman—so she could never pull something like that on him again.

Stoop so low . . . that would put me on the bottom of the barrel then, wouldn't it? Of course it would. Even though I wasn't good enough for him, I pledged to make sure I took care of him the way he needed and wanted me to, if only for the couple of years I was bound to him.

Noah

Ten minutes to purchase her.
One hour to get her lips wrapped around my cock.
Three days to taste her juices.
Four days to pop her cherry.
Two weeks to lose my fucking mind.
Shit.

Just over two weeks. Fifteen goddamn days.

That was all it took for one purchased virgin to get me all kinds of wrapped around her cute little pinky. In the two years that Julie and I had been together, she never once managed to pull that off. But Delaine? My whole world had been turned upside down in just two motherfucking weeks.

It wasn't at all how this was supposed to go down. How in the hell was I going to last two years when I'd already give her anything she asked for on a silver platter? Fucking Candy-Ass Crawford, that was what I should've changed my name to.

Goddamnit.

I had done nothing but think about her all day at the office. And that was exactly why I pulled a desperate move like having Samuel bring her with him to pick me up. Yeah, I could've easily had him break every traffic law there was in the state of Illinois to get me to her quicker, but when I started to entertain the thought of purchasing a helicopter so that I could avoid the delay of rush hour traffic, I decided having her brought to me was probably the best alternative.

I was sick in the head. And I probably should've looked into some sort of twelve-step program for my new obsession because there was no way it could have been healthy.

Samuel pulled up to the curb where I was waiting impatiently, and before he could get out and open the door for me, I held my hand up to stop him. I'd get to her so much faster if I opened the door myself. I wrenched it open, and there she was . . . my million-dollar baby, wearing nothing but my robe and a pair of spike heels, just as I had requested when I called her earlier in the afternoon. And fuck me running, she was lounging back on the seat with the black silk of the robe open and hanging off her shoulders as it pooled around her body. Which was all her doing; I hadn't requested that, but I was overjoyed that she'd taken some initiative.

She was all cream and silk, and goddamn it, she was fondling her breast with one hand while the other caressed the flat plane of her stomach. Her naked flesh had only ever been touched by one other person like that—me—and it almost seemed to be beckoning me once more.

My lips curled back into a protective snarl I didn't even realize I was emitting as I scanned the area around me to see if anyone else had gotten an eyeful of my woman. I had to have her, had to mark my fucking territory, and I could not and would not wait until we were back to the seclusion of the house.

"Home, Samuel," I growled. "And take the scenic route or whatever. Just don't disturb us."

"As you wish, sir." He nodded, then got back in the driver's seat.

I quickly stepped inside and closed the door to shut the outside world out and keep Delaine's hidden treasures all to myself. Because I was a selfish bastard and I never shared. Ever. I didn't even want anyone else to see what I'd laid claim to.

I knelt before her, threw my briefcase and the jacket I was holding to the side, and quickly undid my belt and pants before shoving them over my hips. My dick sprang free and I grabbed it to keep it from bouncing around all awkwardly.

"Get it wet for me, kitten," I said as I angled myself so that I was right in front of her face. God bless her, she licked her lips and eyed me hungrily before leaning forward and opening her mouth to take me in.

I stopped her. "Not like that. Lick it, baby. I want to watch your tongue work me."

She gave me a sexy smirk and then flicked her tongue out to gather up the spot of pre-come on the tip. My dick twitched of its own accord and I hissed through my teeth. She kept her eyes on me as she wrapped her hand around the base of my cock and flattened her tongue out to give it a long lick from bottom to top.

"Son of a bitch," I groaned.

Out of my peripheral vision, I caught her movement as she closed her thighs and worked them back and forth to create friction. I had to see her, needed to see the evidence of her arousal.

"Let me see that pretty pussy, Delaine. Spread your thighs wide for me."

She made this greedy little sound, swirling her tongue around the head of my dick, and then she put one foot on the floor, opening her legs for me. Goddamnit, she was so fucking wet already. I cupped her bare sex with my hand and slid my fingers between her silky folds. She arched her back and rolled her hips to get closer, but I pulled away, wanting to tease her.

"Don't be mean," she protested in a deep, sultry voice.

I gently smacked the bundle of nerves at her apex once, twice, three times before applying pressure with three fingers and massaging it slowly. Delaine rolled her hips in a circle and pushed back against my fingers. Then I felt her hot mouth engulf my cock. I sucked in a breath of air as I watched her work me. My fingers slid down her center and I pushed all three inside her. It was a hell of a tight fit, but she moved forward to meet them regardless. I eased them out and reinserted two so that I could curl them back and forth over her little magic G-spot, which really sent her into a feeding frenzy on my cock.

Two weeks ago she'd been a virgin. Today I'd have sworn she was a professional.

"Oh, fuck! Easy, baby. You're gonna make me come," I warned her. As good as it felt to release in her mouth and watch her swallow me down, that wasn't what I wanted this time. I needed to mark her, from the inside out.

I tried to pull away, but she had a tight grip on my cock. So I removed my fingers and pushed against her shoulder to get her to release her hold. She gave me a pout, and it was so fucking sexy I had to lean forward and suck on that bottom lip. She wound her fingers through the hair at my nape and pushed her tongue past my lips to seek out mine. I gave it to her without putting up a fight, but only briefly, because I needed to be inside her and didn't want to waste any more time.

So I broke the kiss and grabbed her roughly behind her knees, yanking her forward until she was slouched in front of me with her ass hanging halfway off the seat. I spread her legs and positioned myself between them, my cock straining to get inside. Delaine rolled her body, trying to get closer, but I still wanted to play.

"Watch, baby. Watch my cock while I fuck you." Her eyes drifted to the space between us and her mouth dropped open when I took the head of my dick and rubbed it back and forth between her folds and over her clit. She was so wet and her pussy felt like hot silk.

I pulled back the skin of her folds and watched as her entrance stretched. She was so fucking tight that it amazed me that I could ever fit inside her. She couldn't even get her hand all the way around my thick cock, yet I'd had it inside that tiny little opening.

I swirled the head of my dick around her entrance and then lined myself up. "Fuck, I need you. I have to be inside you." Slowly I pushed into her a little at a time, watching as my cock disappeared bit by bit.

She made this incredibly sexy sound.

"You like the way that looks? It's sexy as hell." I realized I was rambling, but I really didn't give a shit, because Jesus, it was incredibly erotic to watch.

"God, yes," she answered, and then I arched my brow at her because she'd said "God" instead of my name.

I pulled out of her and made another pass over her clit until my cock lay between her folds. Then I held her lips in place and moved to and fro in a stroking motion. My cock was bathed in her wetness, glistening in the little bit of light that filtered in through the windows. I couldn't take it anymore. I pulled back and thrust deep inside her, eliciting a gasp from her strawberry-colored lips.

"Oh, fuck, Noah," she moaned as I gripped the tops of her thighs and thrust in and out of her at a steady pace. I noticed she only ever used the word "fuck" when I was making her feel good. That might have been a bit of an ego boost for me.

We were both watching, both breathing through parted

lips, both fascinated by how perfect we looked joined together. I could feel her walls gripping my cock tight as if her beautiful pussy was claiming me, unwilling to let go. My balls slapped against her ass cheeks with each thrust forward, creating a dual sensation. It was fucking heaven, and I needed her to come because there was something else I wanted to do before I had my release.

"Touch us, kitten. Cup yourself with the palm of your hand and spread your fingers around my cock," I instructed her.

With the hand attached to the wrist bearing my bracelet, she timidly reached forward and did what I said. Her head fell back, exposing that creamy neck in open invitation, and there was no way I was going to turn it down. I leaned forward and lightly scraped my teeth across her flesh before sucking it into my mouth. Then I kissed my way up to her ear, all the while pumping my engorged cock into her gorgeous body.

"Did you miss me today, Delaine? Because I fucking missed you. I had to jack off three times because I couldn't stop thinking about how good you feel wrapped around my cock." I accentuated my point by thrusting faster. "Did you? Did you play with yourself while you thought about fucking me? Maybe you even pulled out my gift for some practice rounds? Did you get yourself off, kitten?"

She nodded, but that wasn't enough.

"Tell me. I want to hear you."

"Twice," she admitted. "And it was nowhere near as good as the real thing."

"That's . . . what I'm . . . talkin' . . . 'bout," I growled, emphasizing each word with a deep thrust of my cock.

She whimpered in response and wrapped my tie around her fist before yanking hard and pulling me to her mouth. I ravished her with a hungry kiss, laying claim to what I already knew was mine, but reaffirming it just in case. Our tongues moved deftly against each other as I gripped her hips harder and fucked her faster.

My cock pumped in and out of her and I could feel the walls of her pussy constrict around my thickness with each push and pull. I broke our fevered kiss and dipped my head to capture a pert nipple between my lips to lightly graze it with my teeth. I felt the nails on her free hand scrape my scalp as she held me to her, and I regretfully had to break that shit up so that I could sit back because I wanted even deeper. I watched as my cock appeared and then disappeared inside her over and over again, aided by her arousal.

"Put your fingers in my mouth, kitten. Let me taste you."

The way Delaine played along and followed every single one of my directions was just fucking great. She slipped her fingers between her folds, gathering up her juices before she brought them to my mouth. She ran the tips along my lips teasingly and I flicked my tongue out to gather up her offering before I opened my mouth and allowed her to push them inside. I groaned loudly when her taste hit my tongue. She was so goddamn delicious. I licked her clean before releasing her fingers again.

"Do I taste good?" Fuck me running. The way she looked at me and licked her lips and said those dirty, dirty words . . .

"See for yourself," I said, and pulled out of her. She wanted to talk dirty, so I was going to show her how dirty I could be.

I raised myself as much as I could with the low ceiling of the limo and pushed her head down toward my groin at the same time. She got the message and greedily took me into her mouth. And I'll be damned if my little prized possession didn't fucking hum when she tasted herself on my cock. I pumped my hips back and forth a couple of times and then took it away from her again.

"Time for fucking, not sucking," I said, and plunged back into her pussy. She was mewling and moaning, arching her back, whispering my goddamn name, biting on her bottom lip and rolling her head from side to side. It was an awesome sight to see.

"Shit. I need you to come." It took everything in me to restrain myself from blowing my load inside her.

"Harder, Noah. Fuck me harder." I would have, gladly, but in our current position, it was easier said than done. Not to worry, I had a solution.

I pulled out of her. "Turn around, kitten. I want to go deep."

She groaned in protest, but I knew what was best for the both of us, so I wasn't budging an inch.

"Turn the fuck around, get on your knees, hold on to the back of the seat, and spread your legs," I ordered hurriedly.

She looked confused but did as I said. I helped her get on her knees in front of me, but facing the rear window. Her plump ass was perfectly round and her back was arched at the perfect angle to allow me free access to that delectable little pussy. But when she saw the traffic moving all around us at a slow pace, she turned her head away as if to hide.

I slid inside her from behind and leaned forward to whisper in her ear sensually. "Don't worry, Delaine. We can see them, but they can't see us. Pity they can't watch me fuck you. I'd like the whole world to see what they can never have."

With that I sat up and pounded into her. And oh shit, I was so much deeper from this angle, and her cheeks were spread with her asshole teasing me. Delaine grabbed on to the back of the seat, her knuckles going white with her grip as I fucked her as hard, as fast, and as deep as I could go. Sweat poured off my brow and dripped off the tip of my nose, and it really didn't help that my tie had been drawn tighter around my neck when Delaine grabbed it to pull me in for a kiss. But the one sensation that was dominating all others was the feel of her constricting around me.

Fuck the outside world. I had everything I needed right in front of me.

Remembering how well she had liked it before, I stroked the center of her ass with my thumb, applying pressure to her back entrance. She moaned loudly and arched her back, right on motherfucking cue. So I took it a step further and pressed until my thumb was inside her up to the knuckle. Her head fell between her shoulders and she pushed back into me.

"Yeah, baby. Feels good, doesn't it?" I said as I pulled my thumb out partially and then reinserted it. "I'm going to fuck you here. I'm going to put my dick inside your tight little ass and you're going to fucking love it. Soon. Very soon."

I felt her walls tighten around me in rhythmic waves as she came undone and gave in to her orgasm. "Oh, Noah!" she cried out.

God, yes. My girl wanted me in her ass just as much as I wanted to be there.

"Look at them, Delaine," I said, talking her through it. "Look at all those people out there, going about their mundane lives with no clue about what's going on in here. They can't even fathom feeling what you're feeling right now, what I'm about to feel."

"Son of a . . ." An indescribable feeling surged from my balls and shot up the length of my cock as I finally came.

"Oh, I can feel that," she said with a breathless moan. "I can feel you coming inside me, and it feels . . . it feels . . ."

"Fuck, tell me, baby. What does it feel like?" I managed to ask through my orgasm because I really liked hearing dirty words come out of her fuckable mouth.

"Like nothing I've ever . . . I'm going to come again," she moaned out, and then her body began to clench up, every muscle at attention and every nerve ending throbbing as she called my name. I increased the pace of my thrusts, praying I could stay hard long enough to see her through her second orgasm. By some small miracle I did, and when we were both done, we collapsed onto the seat with me lying on her back.

"Damn," I mumbled as I rolled off her. "You're going to be the death of me, woman."

She giggled and rolled over to kiss me softly on the lips. "So how soon is very soon?"

"What?" I asked, pulling my pants up.

"You know . . ." Her voice trailed off as she looked toward her voluptuous ass. "You said 'very soon.' How soon is very soon?"

I was shocked, and what came out of my mouth was, "I

fucking love you . . . ," which was a really stupid thing to say, so I had to fix that shit by adding, "You-rrrr enthusiasm."

Before I could shove my head any further up my asshole, I grabbed her and kissed her deeply, deep enough to make her melt in my arms and hopefully forget my faux pas. Me, on the other hand? I was ready to cut my own nuts off and take them to a butcher to grind into tiny morsels of meat to be fed to vicious dogs. Because it was the most idiotic thing I could've said, but something in the pit of my desolate heart told me it was right.

What the fuck was that all about?

I pulled back and looked into her eyes—another stupid move—and I felt myself falling. For real. And that wasn't kosher. At all.

I was weak, and she was bringing me to my knees.

Two weeks. Two motherfucking insignificant weeks that had somehow become very, very significant.

Goddamnit.

~$~

We finally made it home, relatively unscathed as far as the human eye could tell. On the inside however, I was a fucking mess. And now, more than ever, I needed to know everything about her. I needed to know why she was here in this situation in the first place. When I'd first started all this I had convinced myself that her personal business didn't matter. But Polly was right: Lanie was a good girl, even if she did act like a raging bitch at times.

I had excused myself to my study after dinner, where I did

quite a bit of pacing and a whole lot of knee bouncing while I contemplated what to do. Sure, I could wait for my man Sherman to call me with his findings, but I was impatient, so I picked up the phone and made the call. Yeah, there was a whole hell of a lot of nail biting going on as I waited for him to pick up.

"Sherman," he answered on the third ring.

"It's Crawford. Do you have anything for me yet?" I asked, not really sure if I wanted to know the answer, but needing to all the same.

"Actually, I just got the last of everything I needed. I was going to call you first thing in the morning, because I didn't want to disturb you," he said. "So what do you want to know?"

"Everything."

12

tickling the ivories

Noah

"Okay, here goes," Sherman said. I could hear him settling in his seat and flipping papers while I anxiously awaited any bit of information he could give me about the puzzle that was Delaine Talbot.

There was a timid knock on the door to my study, and then it opened wide. Delaine positioned herself there rather seductively, her arms stretched above her head as she arched her back against the door frame. Her wet hair was tossed back off her shoulders and her long legs were angled so that one was bent at the knee. She was wearing black wrap-around heels, the cuff with my family's crest, one of my black dress ties, and nothing else.

"I'm sorry, am I disturbing you?" Her voice was a purr of erotic lust. She seductively fingered the tie that hung loosely in the valley of her fuckawesome tits. "I can leave if you want."

My heart thumped erratically in my chest, and I was sure my mouth had to be hanging open. She was a vixen, a porn star . . . a goddess.

My cock strained against the zipper of my suddenly too tight khaki pants, all the blood having raced there within a millisecond. I thought for a moment that maybe my little soldier was trying to burrow a hole so that he could have a look-see for himself, but that couldn't actually happen—could it? I was quickly learning that whenever Delaine was around, anything was possible.

"Crawford?" Sherman's voice was a vague echo in the background. My focus was trained completely on my million-dollar baby, her body the siren distracting me from my previous obsession. She was all that mattered. Everything else faded into nothingness.

"I was just in the shower and, well, all that hot water was washing over my skin with the most delicious pressure, and it made me think about your body pressed against mine and that magical thing you do with your fingers . . . and your tongue . . ." She closed her eyes and reclined her head while caressing her bare throat with one hand, the other slipping between her legs as she sighed. "I need you to touch me."

"Helloooo? Are you still there, Crawford?"

I shook off the haziness the best I could and cleared my throat as I forced myself to look away from her. "Um, yeah. I have someone, er, something to do. Call me first thing in the morning."

I didn't wait for a response before I hung up the phone. He'd call me because he wanted to get paid. And I figured I'd gone more than two weeks without knowing the information I wanted, so surely I could wait ten more hours.

With lightning speed, I was standing in front of Delaine with both hands fisted on the door frame above her. I didn't dare touch for fear I might bruise or break her. "You can't fucking say stuff like that without—"

Unable to finish my thought because she was standing there, all sinfully naked and smelling wickedly aroused, I lost all resolve and sank down on one knee, perching one of her delicate feet on my shoulder before I leaned in to give her the tongue-lashing of her life. Of course it was merely a punishment for interrupting such an important business call. It was going to hurt me far worse than it was going to hurt her.

Yeah, even I called bullshit.

"Uh-uh-uh." She pushed ever so slightly on my shoulder with the spiked heel of her shoe to force me to sit back away from her. "So I was just wondering . . . You don't happen to play piano, do you? Because I found this sexy little black number downstairs, in what I assume is your music room, and I was thinking about how incredibly erotic it would be if I were to be, oh, I don't know—on display for you while you played for me. I mean, take a look at this black tie. I am dressed formally, after all."

'Nuff motherfucking said.

Without uttering a word—because, like I said, none were needed—I threw her over my shoulder and headed toward what she so adequately called my music room. The acoustics in there were even better than the acoustics in the foyer, and I couldn't wait to hear the echo of her screaming my name. And she would definitely scream.

Lanie

Men were so predictable.

All I had to do was show up virtually naked and insinuate I wanted a little bit of attention, and I had him eating out of the palm of my hand. Well, maybe it wasn't exactly the palm of my hand that he wanted to eat out of, but either way, I got the desired result.

I'd been thinking about the whole cheating-whore-of-an-ex-girlfriend thing that Polly had told me about earlier, and I was determined to shower him with the attention he craved, to make sure he knew that I was all about him. Because when it came right down to it, that was the whole reason he'd stooped so low as to buy a woman in the first place. I was a sure thing: guaranteed to cater to his every whim and desire, guaranteed to want him and *only* him.

Not that I was complaining. Sure, I should have been disgusted with myself for basically being a willing participant, and I was—to an extent. But I was a woman with needs that I hadn't ever realized I had before all this began, needs that were most certainly being met by a man who under normal circumstances would've been able to get me into his bed without having to ask twice. Besides, I'd signed on for this, right? I'd known what I was getting myself into. Actually enjoying the "work" had to be an added perk. I mean, I could've just as easily been stuck with Jabba the Hut.

The Cooch was nodding emphatically in agreement until I had to go and mention that fat, nasty bastard, which sent a shiver down her spine.

Noah threw me over his shoulder like a sack of potatoes and I giggled like a school girl when he turned his face and nipped me on the ass with those gorgeous white teeth of his. Apparently I wasn't the only one with an ass-biting fetish.

We finally made it into the music room. I could tell because his saber-toothed purr had become more like a constant humming vibration that I not only heard but felt. As gently as he could, he sat me on top of his baby grand and stood between my parted knees.

"This what you had in mind?" His voice was a deep, sultry rumble that traveled through his body and out through his hands, which were perched on the piano on either side of me. I actually felt the vibration of it against my girlie bits, making me reminisce about my new bestie, the Crawford bullet.

"Actually, I was thinking something more along the lines of you sitting on the bench, letting those talented fingers of yours molest the ivories," I said while running my hands up and down his chest. "You think you can do that for me, Noah? Play me a little something inspired by the vision of my . . . your . . . pussy?"

I pressed my lips to his reverently, but he made no move. He was still as a statue, an Adonis of a statue. I had begun to think that maybe my dirty talking hadn't come off as sultry as I'd hoped when he leaned in closer to my ear and whispered.

"Delaine?"

"Hmm?"

"I think I just came a little." Before I could formulate a response, he pulled away abruptly and went to sit on the piano bench.

With my chin perched on my shoulder and angled toward him, I watched his hands softly skate over the keys without making a sound. The look in his eyes was one of pure awe and concentration, a man who obviously revered his instrument. I couldn't blame him; I thought his "instrument" was pretty awe-inspiring myself.

He licked his lips and shifted to a more comfortable position before he looked back at me expectantly. "You promised you'd provide the inspiration if I'd play."

One problem: if I tried to swing my ass around on his glossy piano, which was nowhere near as slick as it looked, it was more than probable that there would be some skin squeakage. And I just didn't know if my dignity could handle a major blow of embarrassment like that when I was trying to be sexy and seductive. So I did the only thing I could.

I hopped down, amazingly remaining upright on the insanely high hooker heels that I was wearing (the Cooch had picked them out because they matched the nearly-there outfit), and then strutted my nearly naked ass toward Noah, channeling every runway walker I could remember from the countless fashion shows my mom had forced me to watch.

I think I was pretty successful at it, because Noah eyed me like he was a wolf in one of those Looney Tunes cartoons, licking his chops like I was a prized lamb. Feeling probably more confident than I should have been, I put one foot up on the bench beside him. You know how they say, "If looks could kill . . ."? Yeah, well if looks could feel you up, I swear that was exactly what Noah had done to my legs, my ass, my boobs, and the Cooch—heck, his eyes had just as many appendages as an octopus.

Speaking of puss, mine was positively sopping wet. Go figure. It wasn't because Double Agent Coochie was salivating; it was because the twisted slut was crying tears of joy over what she knew was to come. Well, lots of tears, actually. So I made a big show of perching my ass on the top of his piano again and crossing my legs to conceal that little fact. Even though I'd come to learn that was a major turn-on for Noah, I wanted to tease him a little bit. After all, he needed some incentive to give me what I wanted before I gave him what he wanted.

Noah looked up at me and then slowly began to undo the studded buckle that was wrapped around my ankle. When he was done, he leisurely pulled my shoe off and placed a lingering kiss on the top of my foot.

"Can't have these on my ivory babies, kitten," he said in a hushed voice as he dropped my bare foot and went to work on my other shoe. "By the way, remind me to give Polly a raise."

"Just buy her a pair of these bad boys, and she'll say you're even."

Placing my shoes down on the floor beside him, he kissed a trail along my shin until he reached my knees. Then he pushed them apart and set my feet directly on the keys, as far on each end as they would stretch. The sound that came from them depressing the keyboard was really quite hideous and we both cringed at the same time, but then he was eyeing the Cooch and that expression changed quick, fast, and in a hurry.

"I fucking love how wet you get for me." The Cooch was busy oiling herself up and spraying Binaca in her mouth, warming up for the big show. "You should probably know that no one has ever laid a finger on my baby grand, Delaine, let alone their feet."

"I'm sorry. I can move them," I said, but before I could lift so much as a pinky toe, he stopped me.

"Don't." The quiet stillness of his voice carried more weight than if he had barked the order.

Noah never took his eyes away from my center as he rolled the sleeves of his shirt up to his elbows. When he was done, he straightened his back and curved his shoulders in slightly to position his fingers on the keys.

"Um, I haven't played in a while," he said nervously with a shrug of a shoulder. "So I might be a little rusty."

I already knew that. Right before Noah had called to tell me to be in the car when Samuel picked him up from work, Polly had phoned to check on me. We talked for quite some time while I wandered around the house. That was when I had stumbled upon the room we were in. That was also when Polly had told me that he used to play all the time before the whole Julie debacle. When she told me that she didn't think he'd played since, I knew I had to at least try to get him to again. After all, they said music soothed the savage beast. I wasn't so sure I wanted him soothed right before he fucked the life out of me, mostly because I thought he needed to release some pent-up frustration or rage or whatever, but maybe if he got reacquainted with something that had made him happy once upon a time, it would still be all good.

Was it risky? Yes. But I figured if I had any chance whatsoever at succeeding, appealing to his sexual nature was definitely the way to do it. Polly thought I might be a weak spot for Mr. Crawford, and while I had no intention of exploiting that tidbit of knowledge for personal gain, I definitely wasn't going to deny myself any pleasure that might come my way from helping him learn to live again.

I was a puddle of goo the moment he made that piano sing the first chord. His fingers moved quickly and expertly along the keys, stringing together a melody that I didn't think I'd ever heard before but which was beautiful nonetheless. I was afraid for the cleanliness of his piano, because if he kept playing like that, I'd come big-time, without him even having to touch me. Although, I guess in a way, he was; the fingers making that beautiful music that was vibrating through the piano and across my girlie bits belonged to him, after all.

"Lean back on your elbows, kitten," he said without missing a note.

At least I didn't think he missed a note. It wasn't like I was any kind of expert at that type of thing, but it sounded right. More than right, really; it was erotic. I wouldn't exactly call it a soundtrack to a porn flick, but considering that music was obviously another extension of Noah—much like his fingers, his tongue, and his colossal cock—it made sense that, by extension, it would rock my pussy also. It more than rocked my pussy, in fact. It moved me, made me feel things that were probably illegal in forty-eight states. Plus, the way his digits worked those keys, it was obvious where he'd gotten the practice in for other things. So I realized that the King of the Finger Fuck had apparently changed his name from the King of the Piano Fuck.

I leaned back on my elbows, but kept my eyes on him. Noah was looking right back at me. And when I say he was looking right back at me, it wasn't the Cooch. It was me, my eyes. He was looking at me so intensely I thought I might spontaneously combust.

And then it happened.

Without breaking eye contact or interrupting the sexy little ditty he was playing, he leaned forward and placed a kiss right over my clit. My jaw hinged open as I sucked in a breath and held it while my legs jerked involuntarily. Of course that messed up his angelic song, what with my toes kerplunking on the keys under my feet and all, but Noah just gave me that smug smile and continued on. The only difference between what he was playing before and what he had begun to play was that the notes sounded heavier, more urgent.

He also continued to do that thing he was doing with those luscious lips and serpent-like tongue. His mouth was hot and wet, his lips softly caressing my south mouth while his tongue expertly manipulated every nerve ending in my body from that one spot between my legs.

It wasn't going to take me long.

The Cooch was warming up her vocal cords, preparing to give the concert of her life. Maybe she couldn't actually sing, but Noah had made her hum madly over the short amount of time that they'd known each other. All I'm saying is that he was one hell of a vocal coach.

And speaking of humming—Noah was doing just that against me, keeping in perfect harmony with the music he was playing, like he'd written the thing himself. Which he very well could have.

The muscles in my thighs shook uncontrollably and my hips bucked as I tried to get closer to the deliciousness that was his mouth. I ached for my release and found myself begging for it out loud. The music suddenly stopped and Noah latched on to that swollen little bundle of nerves between my legs, sucking like his life depended on it. I bolted upright and fisted his hair in my hands to force him to stay right where he was. At the same time my orgasm took over my body, and my head fell back and my thighs clamped around his head, followed by a string of indecipherable profanity from my lips in a voice that didn't in any way, shape, or form sound like mine. Swear to God—er, Noah—I think I'd become possessed by some evil orgasm-hoarding demon or something.

It wasn't until after the waves subsided and the tension in my body unwound a bit that I became legitimately concerned that I had cut off Noah's air supply. Death by aspussiation, as opposed to asphyxiation, was not exactly something they'd put on a death certificate, but how cool would it be if they did?

"Oh, my God! Are you okay?" I panicked and forcefully lifted him by the hair of his head to get a look at him.

He was wearing that "I'm a fucking god" smirk on his face, and then he licked the remnants of my orgasm from his lips and said, "No. But I sure as hell am about to be."

I didn't know how or when he'd had a chance to do it, but as he stood upright, his pants were already down to his ankles and his colossal cock was standing at attention, saluting me.

He lifted me off his piano and sat back down on the bench with me in his lap. It took all of two seconds for him to lift my ass, position himself at my entrance, and then slam me back down on top of him. And he didn't lose momentum from there. Over and over again he lifted my hips and brought me back down hard on him. His mouth clamped onto a nipple as I held him to me. Even though I was the one on top, I was in no way in control of the situation. It was all Noah. Inside me, around me, on me—he was everywhere.

With each thrust of his cock, he went deeper and harder until a light sheen of sweat coated his forehead and began to dampen his hair. My eyes started rolling to the back of my head, and I thought perhaps I really was possessed, but I wouldn't know for sure until my head started spinning or I felt the urge to vomit pea soup everywhere. I didn't actually think it would happen, though, because how could something that felt this good possibly be evil?

I came again, digging my nails into his back, and I didn't give a rat's ass if I was shredding his designer shirt or not. All I knew was that I needed to hold on and never let go. And I did just that, even after Noah let loose this feral growl that should've frightened me, and then came inside me. With a couple of strokes more, he was finally spent and exhausted.

Noah kept the side of his face pressed against my chest and his arms wrapped around my waist. He didn't even bother to pull out of me. And he was silent. The only sound in the room was the echo of our heavy breathing as we both tried to come down off our high, or maybe we were just trying to make it last longer.

I didn't let him go, either. I kept stroking his hair and kissing the top of his head until I finally laid my cheek against it and held on. I couldn't let him go. I couldn't *fucking* let him go. For the first time since I'd made the decision to do this, to sell myself into this whole messed-up thing, I was terrified.

When had that happened?

It was in that moment I realized how truly inexperienced

and foolish I really was, a small-town girl attempting to play in the major leagues with a man who was larger than life itself.

After what seemed like an eternity, we finally released each other and I retreated to the bathroom for yet another shower. I might have needed one, but more than that, I wanted the time alone to collect my thoughts. It wasn't until the hot water from the shower hit my skin that I began to silently cry.

The pretenses—oh, God, the pretenses I had been hiding behind, that wall of I-am-woman-hear-me-roar: it all started to crumble in rapid succession. I was nothing but a girl crushing madly on a man who saw me as nothing but his property. And he truly did own me in every sense of the word.

My mind wandered back to earlier in the day, after the romp in the limo. I had thought he'd said he loved me, and my heart had stuttered, felt like it had dropped to the pit of my abdomen, lying in wait to be birthed and handed over to the one person I felt I might actually be able to hand it over to willingly.

But that wasn't at all what he had said. Was it? Which proves how truly inexperienced I really was. Such a silly, foolish little girl.

Noah Crawford was a man who had the whole world sitting in the palm of his hand, and I had nothing to offer. But, God help me, I was falling madly in love with him.

From out of nowhere, Noah appeared, having opened the shower door and catching me by surprise. "Hey, I'm going to go shower in one of the guest suites. Just wanted to let you know in case you get done before—" He stopped talking abruptly and furrowed his brow. "Have you been crying?"

I turned my head away and started wiping my eyes. "Um, no. Of course not," I lied. "That's a silly question. Why would I be crying? I just got soap in my eye, that's all."

He slowly lifted my chin to look at my face and I saw something in his eyes, but before I could let my mind wander too far into the land of delusional idiots, I realized that it was just a mere reflection of what was in mine. And it scared the crap out of me. Again. Because I shuddered to think of the consequences if he saw what I felt. He'd probably take me and his receipt right back to Scott's customer service counter for an exchange or a full refund.

He didn't feel the same way about me. He never would. Never could.

"Okay, if you're sure, I'm just going to . . ." He jerked his head toward the direction of the bathroom door.

"Yeah, I'm good," I said with a fake smile. "Go ahead, you're freezing me to death."

"Well, we can't have that, now can we?" He leaned in, spray from the shower splashing against his bare chest as he gave each of the girls, and then my lips, a chaste kiss. With a wink and that crooked grin, he was gone.

Just like he would be gone if he ever found out I was developing feelings for him, which undoubtedly was not part of the contract. Kind of went against the whole no-strings-attached clause. I had to get my shit together and push past my moment of weakness. I could do it. I could get over him and be there in the capacity that he needed me and nothing more. I'd survived far worse.

I was not a vulnerable woman. I was strong. I was resilient.

I had done everything within my power to help my parents in the face of the impending loss of my mother, the foundation of all that we were. I had blindly sold myself to the highest bidder to make sure that she, that we all, had a fighting chance.

I could get over this. I had to.

Noah

The next morning, I found myself sitting at my desk with my hands tearing at my hair in frustration. I hadn't been able to sleep well the night before. I couldn't get that look on Delaine's face out of my head. It haunted me. Something was different about her eyes. I'd seen that look before. I just couldn't place my finger on it.

She'd lied to me. She had been crying, and since she wouldn't tell me why, I was left to draw my own conclusions. It didn't take me long to figure it out. She was a prisoner in my home. Although I'd pretty much given her free rein, she was still a prisoner who was forced to submit to my primal urges whenever the mood hit me. Why had it never crossed my mind before that she might actually find that demeaning? Sure, a lot of women threw themselves at me, but they did it of their own accord, not because they'd been paid to and therefore had no other choice.

I stood up and went into my private bath. I turned on the cold water and let it pool in my hands before splashing it across my face. I did that over and over again until I realized it was having no effect. Nothing was going to shake me from the numbness I felt. I grabbed a hand towel to dry my face, but I caught a glimpse of myself in the mirror and froze. I could see it then. I had become the one person that I despised most in the world: David Stone.

After all, what I'd done was something he might have done, except I paid for a long-term contract instead of using her as a one-night stand. I was using her for my own benefit and with total disregard for how this might affect her in the end. And I did it all with the safety net of telling myself that she had chosen to do this, so she knew what she was getting herself into. While that might have been true, it certainly didn't mean I should've taken advantage of that fact. What if she was mentally ill? She didn't really seem to be to me, but who in her right mind did something like this? Someone with her back to the wall, that's who.

If I was taking advantage of her desperation, how was I any different from David? Ignorance really wasn't a good excuse. I should've known that anyone, whether it was Delaine or some cracked-out whore, would only do something like this as a last resort. So, regardless, I was still in the wrong.

I went back into my office and looked at the phone sitting on my desk, willing it to ring. Like the masochist I apparently was, I wanted to know what had happened in her life to force her down this path. The savior in me wanted to help her. Truth of the matter was, I was no savior; I was an enabler.

I must have had some sort of super ESP, because it was at that moment that the damn phone actually did start ringing. All of a sudden, I wasn't too sure I wanted it to be Sherman, because if he told me what I suspected was true, that Delaine was in a wretched place when she decided to do this, I just didn't know how I would handle that.

I took a deep breath to calm myself and steady my nerves and then picked up the receiver. "Crawford."

"Hey, Crawford. Sherman here. Got that information you wanted. Hope I've caught you at a better time."

I sighed and it sounded despondent even to my own ears. "It's as good a time as any," I answered. And then I waited with bated breath.

"Yeah, well, got a pen and paper handy?" Sherman asked in his all business voice.

I grabbed a pen from my pocket and slid my notepad in front of me. "Shoot."

"Delaine Marie Talbot, aka Lanie Talbot." Like I needed to be reminded.

"She's twenty-four, lives at home in Hillsboro, Illinois, with her parents, Faye and Mack Talbot. I've got an address if you want it," he offered.

"Isn't that what I'm paying you for?" I asked, agitated.

Sherman rattled off the address and then got right back to it. "High school records show she was a straight-A student, but I couldn't find any record of her ever having attended college."

I wasn't surprised at all that she was smart; maybe she needed the money for tuition.

"Also doesn't look like she was much into the social scene. Not surprising with a straight-A kid. They tend to be recluses."

I had been one of those straight-A kids, so I knew damn well that nothing could be further from the truth.

"Seems pretty boring, if you ask me." I hadn't asked. "There really wasn't much more on her, so I went digging on her folks. Her father used to be a factory worker until he recently got fired for attendance issues. There were doctor excuses on file, but they weren't for him. Apparently he'd been taking care of his ailing wife, Faye. Faye Talbot is terminally ill, like at death's door terminally ill, and in need of a heart transplant," he said, and paused.

Memories of my mother's closed casket flashed before my eyes and I dropped my pen, suddenly losing control of my motor functions. I had lost the only two people I had ever truly loved at the same time, so I was all too familiar with how Delaine must be feeling. And she was there with me, instead of by her mother's side. Why?

I could hear Sherman shuffling papers in the background, and then he continued. "They recently came into a large sum of money, donated by an anonymous source. Before that, looks like they were going under fast. Lots of medical bills, maxed-out credit cards . . . You'd think health insurance would pay for some of this. But then again, no job usually means no insurance."

Son of a bitch.

"No police record on Delaine. That's all I've got." He sighed, and waited for me to say something. The problem was that I didn't know what to say. My brain was still processing the fact that Delaine's mother was dying. For the first time since my own mother passed away, I wanted to cry.

"Crawford? Crawford, do you hear me?" he repeated.

I couldn't say anything. I was choking back the flood of emotions that suddenly rushed at me and threatened to overtake the dam I had carefully constructed to keep those emotions in check, like it was made of twigs instead of 330 feet of reinforced concrete. The grief that I'd felt when I lost my parents had nearly destroyed me. I would've done anything to save them if it had been possible. Anything.

I barely even registered hanging up the phone in my state of shock.

Delaine had done the most selfless thing any human being on the face of the earth could have asked of her. She had given up her own body, her own life . . . to save her dying mother.

She was a goddamn saint, and I had treated her like a sex slave.

Guilt like none that I had ever felt before started eating away at me. Because knowing what she'd done, and the reason she'd done it, broke my fucking heart.

13

i feel froggy

Noah

I left work early. I just couldn't do it; I couldn't sit there acting like everything was fine, conducting business as usual when what we were doing was anything but.

"Yo, Crawford." Mason stopped me as I made my way toward the outer office door. "You heading out? What's up?"

Yeah, I probably should've told my assistant something, right? Everything in my goddamn head was a jumbled mess and getting messier by the second. Un-fucking-usual.

"Just send my calls to my voice mail. I'm checking out for the day. And if anyone asks, you don't know where I'm going."

"But I don't know where you're going."

"Exactly."

I turned on my heel and continued on my way, ignoring Mason's "Is everything okay?" No, everything was not okay. And no, I didn't want to talk about it. I just wanted to wallow in my own guilt for a while and then figure a way out of this mess.

I knew there was only one place where I was ever going to get the peace and serenity I needed to sort this shit out, and I wasn't going to let any Chatty Cathies delay me. Which meant I had to be rude, and I was . . . to several employees. But you know what? I didn't give a good goddamn if they felt slighted because I didn't smile politely when they asked how I was doing and give them a superficial "Fine, fine. And you?" I didn't fucking care how they were, or that little Johnny had a snotty nose, or that Susie made the cheerleading squad, or even that Bob finally got that promotion. I didn't fucking care.

I made my way out of the building and jumped into the first cab that answered my hail, because no way was I going to hitch a ride with Samuel. I didn't want anyone to know where I was. Was it irresponsible of me not to tell someone? Probably, but again, I didn't fucking care.

I flipped a fifty over the seat to the driver and said, "Sunset Memorial."

"Sure thing. Say, aren't you that Crawford kid?"

"Nope. Must have me confused with someone else." I sighed as I sat back in the seat. Of course he knew I was full of shit. He'd just picked me up in front of the very same building "that Crawford kid" owned, for Christ's sake. So it was his fault that I had to lie to him. He shouldn't have asked such a stupid question.

Before long, the heavy traffic of downtown Chicago faded from view and the sun broke through the cloud-laden sky. It was odd to see the rays streaking down through the minuscule opening, especially when the clouds surrounding them looked like they were about to pour down rain at any second, but it soothed me a tiny bit when I followed the beams straight down to the place where I was headed.

The Crawford crypt.

Well, I suppose *mausoleum* was the correct term, but *crypt* just sounded better. Either way, it was the final resting place for the only two people who had ever really gotten me, who had loved me for who I was. And one of them was probably going to walk out of that thing to smack me in the back of the head for what I had become.

"You want me to wait?" the cabby asked when he stopped at the walkway at the bottom of the hill that led to my family's burial ground.

"Nah. I'm good," I answered.

"Are you sure? Looks like it could start raining anytime now."

"All the better," I mumbled, then stepped out. Torrential rain would match the way I felt on the inside perfectly, anyway.

"Well, I wouldn't feel right leaving you out here by yourself without at least a little something to warm your bones," the cabby said as he reached across the seat and handed me a brown paper bag with an unopened bottle of Jose Cuervo inside. My father's favorite—how ironic.

"Thanks," I said, handing him another fifty and taking the bottle.

I walked up the hill to the family crypt and took a seat on the marble bench across from the door. Then I took the bottle out of the bag, twisted the top off, and poured a healthy dose onto the ground. After all, how rude would it have been for me to drink it in front of the old man without offering him a sip?

"Cheers," I said with a tilt of the bottle before I took a swig. It burned going down, and I winced, much like the very first time I'd swiped some from his liquor cabinet when I was thirteen. David had dared me to do it, and I didn't want to look like a pussy, so I choked back the cough my body had fought to let loose, hoping David wouldn't know I wasn't as tough as I made myself out to be. Funny thing was that when David took his turn, he coughed the shit out of his nose. I could still see him pinching his nostrils together and whining for a good hour after it happened about how much it burned.

I had to let out a chuckle at the memory, and then I took another hard swig before looking down at the ground. Fuck David. And fuck me.

I still remembered the night I'd lost my parents. Of course I remembered it; I'd murdered them, so it wasn't like I was ever going to be able to forget it. Maybe not by my own hand, but it was my fault nonetheless, and that made me a murderer.

David and I had been fucking off, as usual. Drunk out of our goddamn minds. I believe whiskey had been the culprit that night, and we were drinking that shit like it was water. The challenge? Who could drink a bottle faster—straight up, no chaser. We weren't the least bit concerned about alcohol poisoning, didn't give a fuck that we were graduating the next day and had to be up at the crack of dawn. And neither of us was in any shape to drive. My parents had been on their way home from a night out at the opera when I'd called them. I'd only meant for them to send our driver out to get me, but my father was furious, and my mom was worried. So they'd insisted on picking up David and me on their way home. They never made it. Some other drunk motherfucker who'd decided it would be a grand idea to get behind the wheel of a car instead of calling for his own goddamn ride that night hit my parents head-on. They were both dead at the scene, clutching each other's hands lifelessly. I knew, because I'd walked up to the accident when I saw the flashing lights. They'd been only three blocks away.

I'd won the drinking contest that night, but it had come at a very high price. That was my fault, but Delaine's mother? That wasn't anyone's fault, especially not Delaine's. She wasn't a spoiled brat born with a silver spoon in her mouth who had no idea just how good she had it. She wasn't a belligerent asshole who thought getting drunk and fucking everything that had a decent set of tits and a nice ass was the perfect recipe for a good time. So why was her price set so high?

I sighed and looked up toward the darkened clouds overhead. "Tell me what to do," I said, throwing my hands up in desperation and sending the tequila sloshing around inside the bottle. At that exact moment the rain clouds above me decided to let go of the load they'd been carrying.

I had my answer. I had to let her go. She needed to be with her mother and father, which was a whole hell of a lot easier said than done. I tilted the bottle back again, but before the liquid fire could scorch my tongue, I pulled the bottle away and threw it over the grassy knoll to the left of the mausoleum. I watched it roll until it stopped at the bottom of the hill and emptied the majority of its contents onto the ground, but not all of it.

The symbolism made me guffaw like a madman. Delaine was the devil's juice, capable of setting me on fire from the inside out. When I was around her, my mind was numb and my thoughts incoherent. And now she was free, but there would always be a small part of her that I would carry around with me. Because Delaine Talbot was not easy to get out of your system—at least, not mine.

I couldn't do it. I couldn't set her free.

~$~

I stayed there in the graveyard until well after the sun had set. It could have been hours after; I wasn't really sure because time seemed to stop while I wallowed in my own guilt. I was freezing, and my ass and both legs were numb from not having moved from that spot on the bench. Thankfully, the rain had only lasted for about half an hour, and I was completely dry again.

I ignored my growling stomach, my parched mouth, and my incessantly ringing cell phone. People were looking for me. I knew it. And it was only a matter of time before Polly brought out the bloodhounds to track me down. But the one name that flashed across my caller ID that made me curious was Delaine's.

Not gonna lie—I wanted to answer that damn call more than anything. I grabbed the phone on the first ring, stared at it through the second, and held it so hard through the third that I thought for sure I'd cracked the damn thing. But, I didn't answer it. What in the hell would I have said?

So I hired a PI to check into your background, because I'm a nosy motherfucker who might have a slight tendency toward being a control freak . . . Damn it, she was going to be beyond pissed when she found out what I'd done. I'd guaran-fucking-tee it.

And guess what I found out? That's right. I know that you sold your body to pay for your dying mother's heart transplant, but I'm going to keep fucking you regardless, because I'm sick and I need help—lots and lots of shock therapy to my dick might be just what the doctor ordered.

Yeah, that was so not going to happen.

My phone chimed the familiar notification that I had a text message, and I picked it up. A little flutter went through my chest when I saw that it was from Delaine, and before I knew it, I was opening the message. The digital clock told me that it was after ten o'clock already. Shit, had I been there that long?

Where r u? I'm all alone . . . in this big bed . . . naked.

My dick twitched in my pants at the image he and I both knew all too well. "Shut up. This mess we're in is all your fault, you horny little motherfucker," I scolded my lifelong friend.

Business meeting. Don't wait up.

Bullshit. Talked to Polly, but glad ur alive. I'll let her know.

Thank God she wasn't going to push it further than that for the time being. Of course I was perfectly aware that when I had to actually face her, all bets were off. At least she'd get Polly off my back.

Going to sleep. Feel free to wake me when you get home. If you want. ;)

Oh, I wanted. But I wouldn't.

I put my phone in my pocket and went back to staring at nothing at all. My mother's ghost hadn't appeared to smack me upside the head. My father's ghost hadn't come out to scold me for wasting good Cuervo or to tell me to get my shit together and stop acting liking an idiot. I hadn't had some great epiphany, or made any kind of decision about what I was going to do. All in all, it was a wasted day and night.

I pulled my phone back out and called my uncle. Daniel was a cardiologist, the best in Chicago. Not only that, but he seemed to know everyone. Probably because he was a huge supporter of everything that had anything to do with medicine. Just like how he'd bought Everett's practice. That medical building supported specialists from almost every field, and Daniel was like a sponge, constantly trying to soak up as much knowledge as he could. I knew calling him was a stab in the dark, but I wanted him to see what he could find out about Faye Talbot's condition and whether he could maybe help her out. No way was anyone going to give me any information with all that medical confidentiality bullshit—not that I'd understand one word of any of it even if they did. But Daniel could do anything.

After placing my call and getting Daniel to agree to help me out, I called Samuel for a pickup. It was time to go home, and even though I was dreading my body's reaction to seeing Delaine, my heart needed to.

Samuel knew better than to say anything to me on the way home. Clearly I was not in the mood for sharing. When we got to the house, I went in without a word and made my way toward the bedroom. Even though I knew the way by heart, it still felt like I was being pulled in that direction by some unseen force. She was there, and I was like a magnet drawn to her.

For the very first time in a long time, I climbed into my bed with every stitch of clothing still on, except the shoes of course. She was asleep, but she was turned toward my side of the bed, her angelic face looking peaceful even though I knew the hell that fate—and I—had imposed upon her.

Every molecule in my body wanted to reach out and touch her, but I couldn't. Because I was dirty and she was not. And I wasn't talking about the fact that I had spent the day in wet clothes and hadn't yet showered. I couldn't bring myself to smudge something so pristine. But my smudges were already all over her, weren't they? I had touched her everywhere, left no inch of her perfect skin unmarred by my branding.

So I did the only thing I could do. I lay there and watched her sleep, memorized her every feature, watched her breathe. And I knew right then that I would never treat her like a sex slave again.

Lanie

"Get your ass in gear or we're going to be late!" Polly had been barking orders at me from outside the bathroom door for the better part of an hour and it was seriously grating on me. I had just wrenched open the door to tell her off when all of a sudden a loud rumble shook the house and a meteor the size of Texas crashed through the ceiling and landed directly on

top of Polly's head before barreling through to the first floor
and landing with a thud. Her little arms and legs were all the
evidence I could see when I looked down through the mam-
moth hole in the floor, and they weren't moving—not even a
twitch. Ding, dong, the witch was dead . . .

"Well, it's about time!" Polly screeched, shaking me from
my hallucination. The hole in the ceiling was gone, as were the
hole in the floor, the debris, and the gigantic meteor. Serious
acid trip. Must do again.

Polly gasped, seemingly speechless. Really, that wasn't anything like her. "You're absolutely . . . God, I am so effing jealous of you right now," she said as she walked around me. "If
the sight of you in this dress doesn't knock Noah out of that
I'm-pissed-at-the-world mood of his, nothing will."

I walked over to the full-length mirror attached to the back
of Noah's closet door and looked at myself. The dress was
gorgeous—what there was of it, anyway. It was a navy blue
satin number, cut low in the back until it dipped just above the
curve of my ass. The chest area was basically a sash that criss-
crossed over my breasts and wrapped down and around my
hips. My stomach was bare down to the place where the skirt
began at my hips. And the skirt may have been floor length,
but what difference did that make when there was a slit all the
way up to the top of my thigh? At least the material was loose
and free-flowing.

Polly had swept my hair up into a twist, but she left elegant
little wispy locks strategically placed around my face. The
makeup was much bolder than anything I would have done
myself, but smoky eyes actually looked good on me. If only

Dez could have seen me now—she'd swear I was a different person altogether, and maybe she wouldn't be so embarrassed about being seen out in public with me.

But as pretty as I felt, I doubted Noah would notice. Polly was right—he seemed to be pissed off at the world, and I had no idea why. He hadn't even touched me since that night in the music room, the night we'd made the most beautiful music I'd ever had the pleasure of hearing, our bodies and his piano the only instruments in the orchestra. I had to giggle-snort at myself because that sounded corny as all get out even in my own head, but it was true.

I missed him.

When he'd come home from his "business meeting" he didn't wake me. Unusual for him, disheartening for me, devastating for the Cooch. Polly had told me that Mason had said he took off from his office like a bat out of hell with no indication whatsoever of where the fire was. He hadn't answered his calls, not even mine, until I'd texted him.

"Did you hear me?" Polly asked in that heeeellloooo-o tone. Oh, right, daydreaming again.

"Um, yeah?" I asked, rather than stated.

"What did I say?" Polly had her hands on her hips and her head tilted to the side with her "you're in big trouble if you don't come up with the right answer" look.

"Noah lost his sight because the dress knocked him out and he wrote the world into his will," I repeated. Okay, so maybe it wasn't spot on, but it had to have been close, right?

She narrowed her eyes at me. "Get your shoes on. The boys are waiting."

I slipped into my heels and grabbed my clutch before following the little yapping Chihuahua that was Polly out the door and down the first set of stairs. I stopped when I reached the first landing, stunned into silence when I saw Noah. He was perfect from head to toe. Black tux, white dress shirt, black shoes, and pretty face all present and accounted for. The man made it look so easy.

He looked up toward the landing where I stood. He almost turned back around, but did a double take instead. Ah, so I had caught his attention after all. He smiled awkwardly as I descended the staircase and ran his hands through his hair before he took my hand.

"You are stunning," he said, and then kissed the back of my hand like a real Prince Charming. I realized then just how much Cinderella and I had in common. Like her, I was just a girl from the working class living out a beautiful fantasy. Only instead of a fairy godmother I had a two-year contract.

Noah's smile broadened when he saw the Crawford cuff bracelet on my wrist, and then suddenly he dropped my hand and the smile was gone. He cleared his throat awkwardly and tucked his hands in his pockets before saying, "Okay, so we should go."

Polly cleared her throat in turn, totally inconspicuously—yeah, right—and when Noah looked in her direction, she quickly tilted her head toward me while patting her throat.

"Oh!" Noah said, finally getting the very obvious hint. "I got a little something for you." He reached into his pocket and brought out a thin platinum chain. When he held it up, I could see the simple blue diamond dangling from the center.

"Oh, Noah. You really shouldn't have." Jesus, I even sounded like Cinderella, but that was what the man did to me.

Noah shrugged but didn't look at me. Instead he focused his attention on the clasp of the chain. "It really isn't a big deal. You deserve . . ." He sighed and finally lifted his head with a look of certainty in his eyes, "so much more."

That was odd. Especially considering the way he'd been treating me for the past couple of days, as if I had the plague.

Noah walked behind me and lightly brushed the bare skin of my back with his chest as he clasped the necklace in place. Before he stepped away, his fingers swept across my naked shoulders, sending chills down my spine.

I put my hand on his forearm to stop him from walking away. "Thank you," I whispered, and then I stood on my tiptoes to give him a soft kiss. When I stepped back, I noticed the muscles in his jaw tensing like he was grinding his teeth.

I really didn't understand what his problem was. Until two days earlier he'd been all over me like he couldn't get enough. And now it was a complete one-eighty. I didn't know if he was disgusted with me, if I'd done something to tick him off, or what. But I knew one thing: he most certainly was starting to tick me off. Then again, maybe that was the point. Since finding out about Julie, I'd been trying to put my bitchy side away and play nice. Maybe he didn't like that side of me. Maybe he hadn't changed. Maybe I was the one who had, and the new me just didn't work the same for him.

Fine.

I stuck my chin out, dropped my hand from his arm, and started for the door. And then I realized no one was following.

So I turned, looked at them, and said, "Well? What are we waiting for? Let's get this over with."

~$~

The ride in the limo was quiet. Polly and Mason had driven themselves to the ball, in case either we or they wanted to leave early. Noah sat on one side of the limo, smoking a cigarette while he stared out the window. Translation: he was torturing me with the whole "watch me make love to this cigarette while I ignore you" vibe he had going on.

And then the real torture began.

People. Lots and lots of people. And cameras. Flashbulbs were going off everywhere as we walked down the red carpet to whatever fancy venue was hosting Chicago's elite. People were yelling and shoving, vying for position to get a better shot. And the center of attention? Noah Crawford—and his date. I kept my face hidden behind his wide shoulders or just turned away in general. Noah kept his arm around my waist as he smiled and posed, waved and greeted the hordes of people while still managing to completely ignore the probing question, "Who's the beautiful woman on your arm tonight, Noah?" until finally we were out of the chaos and inside, where the party was in full swing.

I was relieved, but then Polly took her place by my side and said, "You ready to go inside?"

"I thought we were inside," I asked, looking around.

"Silly girl. This," she said as she opened a set of double doors, "is the Scarlet Lotus Ball."

Wow. The place was huge, not that I was surprised. Everything Noah did was huge. There were red lotus flowers all over: floating in glass bowls filled with water and candles, in bouquets, everywhere. Silky red banners were draped from the ceiling, complementing red tablecloths and red bows; it looked like a beautiful massacre had taken place in the room. Champagne ran in fountains. No, seriously, there were champagne fountains, in addition to two dozen or so servers strategically roaming the open room with trays of flutes filled with liquid gold. Which probably explained why the people were so lively. Too damn lively.

The attendees were gorgeous, all of them dressed in elegant gowns and tuxedos worth more than the monthly household income of most of the residents in my hometown. It even smelled like money in there. The social hierarchy had a way of reminding people of their place when it came right down to it. Noah had never made me feel less than adequate, but then again, he and I had never really been out in plain sight like this before. Until tonight it had only been the two of us going at it like bunnies in the privacy of his gargantuan abode. Now, in the midst of his real-life friends, I saw the score clearly. If I hadn't felt completely out of Noah's league before, I most certainly did now.

"Welcome to my world," Noah whispered into my ear before taking my elbow and leading me through the crowd. "There are some people I want you to meet."

Jesus. I was going to screw up big-time. I just knew it.

"Noah! I was waiting for you," this little bouncing brunette screeched as she sidled up to him. She looked like she'd already had one too many drinky-poos, if you asked me. "Oh, you brought a date? I didn't realize you were seeing anyone."

"Mandy, just because we're outside the office, it doesn't mean I cease to be Mr. Crawford," Noah told her in a firm voice. Just then, a waiter came by with a tray of champagne. He grabbed one flute and handed it to me, then took another for himself.

"Oh, right. Sorry," Mandy said, chastened. And then the sizing up began. Judging by the way she scrunched up her nose and faked a smile, I'd say she'd seen through the illusion that I belonged on Noah's arm. "Who's she?"

"She is none of your business. Now, run along and find another drink, Miss Peters." He dismissed her with a wave of his hand.

She gave me one last nasty look, and I leaned into Noah with an adoring smile on my face to spite her.

"Oh! There's Lexi and Brad!" Polly squeaked, pointing toward a stunning couple a mere few feet away. I managed to snag another glass of champagne before she grabbed my wrist and practically yanked my arm out of the socket to make our way over to the world's most beautiful couple. Noah got stopped by some suits, but Polly, determined little shit that she was, kept chugging along.

"Lexi!" Polly squealed, finally dropping my arm to run up to the leggy redhead and hug her. This chick had to have been the woman they modeled Jessica Rabbit after. She was built like a brick shithouse: flawless skin, huge tits, tiny waist, pouty red lips. I almost expected to hear the Commodores interrupt the uppity snore music that was currently playing.

"Oh, Brad!" the gargantuan guy next to her trilled in a girly voice, mocking Polly as he batted his lashes and waved his wrists in the air. "I've missed you so, and you're my favorite person. Ooh! Let me feel you up, too!"

Polly broke the embrace with the brick shithouse and stared him down while said brick shithouse smacked him in the back of his head. "Don't be an ass, ass. We have company," she said, nodding toward me with a curious look.

"Oh, yeah. This is—"

Noah cut her off, suddenly appearing as if out of nowhere. "Delaine. My Delaine." He wrapped his arm around my waist and pulled me into him possessively. "Delaine, this is my favorite cousin, Alexis, and her husband, Brad Mavis."

"You can just call me the Gentle Giant," Brad said.

"He's a starting defensive tackle in the NFL," Noah clarified.

"Damn straight," Brad boasted, puffing out his chest.

"Lexi is his fearsome agent," Noah continued with a nod in her direction. "I think she scares him more than any of those blood-sucking contract negotiators."

"Someone's gotta keep him in line. Besides, he likes the rough stuff." Lexi smirked.

"Nice to meet you," I said as I offered my hand toward Lexi in greeting. "Noah has told me absolutely nothing about you." I laughed awkwardly.

"Likewise," Lexi said, shaking my hand. One might think the whole "likewise" bit was in regard to the pleasantries, but I had a feeling she meant that as an answer on both accounts—Noah hadn't said anything about me either, which made sense, just not to them.

"So, Patrick, have you seen Mom and Dad?" she asked Noah.

I looked at Noah with my brows raised in question.

He knew right away what the look was for. He rolled his eyes in embarrassment before saying with a shrug, "Everyone in my family has always called me by my middle name. It was just the easiest way to differentiate between me and my father without having to call us Noah senior and Noah junior."

"Of course," I said. Details like that were probably something he should've shared before introducing me to his family as "my Delaine," but who was I to say? I sucked back half of the champagne in my glass, my nerves getting the best of me.

"And no, Lexi, I haven't seen them yet," Noah continued, looking through the crowd as if trying to rectify that situation.

"Well, they're around. I'm sure they'll eventually make their way back over," she said with a wave of dismissal. "You know how Daddy can be at these functions."

Brad, Mason, and Noah started up a conversation about some sports team that I was paying absolutely no attention to because Noah was rubbing circles on the small of my back with his thumb while his pinky dipped beneath my dress to rest in the crevice of my ass. Polly and Lexi were chatting it up, a conversation to which I had nothing to contribute because I didn't have a clue about the gossip in their circle of friends. So I did the only thing I could: I preoccupied myself with a game of Let's See if I Can Drink All of My Champagne Before the Next Tray Comes Around with More, and I was winning. It was no small feat. There were lots and lots of trays.

Noah leaned down and whispered into my ear. "Pace yourself, kitten." Which made my head swim. Funny, I'd just had four, maybe five glasses of champagne, and I was fine. But the man called me "kitten," and I was suddenly unequivocally inebriated.

"I have to pee," I blurted out. The conversations around me came to a sudden halt and all eyes turned to me. I supposed that what I'd said wasn't very ladylike, and certainly not the sort of thing a woman dating Noah Crawford would say out loud. Noted.

Lexi laughed. "I have to pee, too. Come on, Polly. Sounds like we need to hit the head."

"I swear, Lexi," Polly said with a disapproving scowl, then turned to me. "She may look like a debutante, but don't let that fool you. She's a rude, crude dude underneath all that glitz and glamour."

"That's my girl," Brad crowed as he smacked her on the ass and sent her on her way.

"Hurry back," Noah's husky voice floated across the sensitive skin beneath my ear. "I want you by my side all night." He pressed his soft lips against my neck inconspicuously, but I definitely felt that kiss and it melted me like butter over a stack of hotcakes.

"Jesus, Patrick. We're just going to the damn bathroom. I promise not to scare her off," Lexi said with a roll of her eyes.

He scoffed. "Good luck with that. I think you'll find Delaine is quite capable of withstanding your witty charm."

"Fuck you," Lexi retorted.

"I love you, too, dear cousin." Noah smiled and then winked at me before he took a sip of his champagne and turned back to the guys.

As we made our way across the crowded hall to the ladies' room, Lexi stopped short. "Look what the dog dragged in," she said under her breath as she nodded to our right.

There was a huge mountain of a man with slick black hair, tanning-bed-bronzed skin, mutton chops, and super bright teeth standing in the middle of a crowd of people across the way. Women were fawning all over him, and somehow he managed to pay equal attention to each one. He certainly possessed a great deal of animal magnetism.

"Well, he's a cutie, if you like the whole Wolverine Ken thing," I said with a snort. "Who is he?"

"David," Lexi sneered.

"David who?"

Polly leaned in like she was about to tell me a dirty little secret. "Noah's former best friend David, that's who."

I gasped, and then I got impossibly hot—under the collar, definitely *not* under the skirt.

"He's also Patrick's business partner," Lexi mumbled, pushing the bathroom door open. "He's been trying to get Patrick to forfeit his share of Scarlet Lotus since my uncle and aunt died, the cunt fucker."

And so my love affair with Lexi Mavis began.

"Wait, Noah's parents died?" I asked before I realized I probably should have known that, too, but I was just so shocked. He'd never spoken of them before.

"Yeah, a car accident six years ago," Lexi answered. "He never talks about it, so I'm not really surprised you didn't know."

Polly's expression was solemn. "He lost them both at the

same time, and it has tortured him ever since, so don't bring it up to him. When he's ready, he'll tell you himself, okay?"

"Yeah, okay." I suddenly missed my own parents.

Lexi opened up a stall door and ushered me inside. "Hurry your ass up. I need to get my drink on. God, I love an open bar."

I took care of my business while Lexi and Polly got caught up. Having babies was their topic of choice: Polly wanted one, but Mason wasn't quite ready; Brad wanted one, but Lexi refused to be barefoot and pregnant while putting her career on the line.

"What about you and Noah, Delaine?" Lexi asked when I opened the stall door.

"Um . . ." I hesitated and walked over to the sinks to wash my hands. How was I supposed to answer that?

"Lanie," Polly interrupted. "She likes to be called Lanie, isn't that right?"

"Yeah, just Lanie," I said with an uneasy smile. "And, um, Noah and I haven't talked about babies. I mean, we're not really there in our relationship . . . yet."

"Mmm-hmm, I see," Lexi said and then she sighed in dramatic fashion. "Well, let's go ahead and get this out of the way, shall we?"

I turned the faucet off and dried my hands. "What exactly is *this*?"

"Look, Lanie. Noah has no mother, no father, and no siblings. So the whole overprotective warning bullshit falls on my shoulders," she started. "I don't really know you, but from first impressions, I like you. Regardless, I've gotta put you on notice. If you hurt my cousin, I'm going to kick your ass. And when I say I'm going to kick your ass, I mean you'll need an ass transplant by the time I'm done with you. We clear?"

I really admired her brass ovaries, but as the woman who everyone thought was truly dating Noah, I had to counter or else I'd look disingenuous. I threw my used paper towel in the trash receptacle and put my hands on my hips, facing off with her. Polly took a step back because she was a smart kid.

"Fair enough. But here's a little memo of my own from me to you and anyone else who wants to be in our business. I love that man more than I ever thought I could love another human being, unconditionally and irrevocably"—which wasn't a lie at all, I realized—"and if anyone has to worry about getting their heart broken in this deal, it's me. Having said that, if anything goes down between Noah and me and you feel the need to kick my ass, then you've got it to do. I'm not intimidated by you. So if you ever feel froggy . . . jump."

Polly sucked in a deep breath and I could actually hear her swallow. I kept my stare intense, never wavering as I faced Lexi down. She was an Amazon of a woman who very likely could've annihilated me, but I wasn't going to back down. That would have been a show of weakness, and although I felt vulnerable as a snail out of its shell when it came to Noah, I most certainly was not a weak person by nature.

Lexi's scowl broke and one corner of her mouth lifted up into a smile, Noah's smile. "I swear to God, if I weren't already married, you and I would be eloping tonight."

I smiled in turn and Polly let out the breath she was holding. "You two are a match made in heaven." She shook her head. "If we're done seeing whose ovaries are bigger than whose, can we get back out there to our men?"

"Absolutely," Lexi said, linking her arm through mine. "Mine are bigger, by the way."

"Well, that remains to be seen," I tossed back as we stepped through the door.

My smile dropped immediately when the sea of people in front of us parted and I caught a glimpse of Noah. He was standing across from an older dark-haired man who was very handsome, and he was smiling and nodding. But what made my stomach churn in knots was the woman hanging on Noah's arm. Draped like she was part of his wardrobe was a tall, strawberry-blond woman who reminded me a lot of Ginger from *Gilligan's Island*. She was movie star material, and she looked like she knew it, too.

"Lexi, please tell me that's your sister."

"Ugh, please! That hussy only wishes she shared the same gene pool."

"Then who is she?"

"That . . . would be Julie," Polly answered with disgust in her voice. "Aka the octopussy. Rumor has it she fucked eight guys at once—after she and Noah broke it off, of course. Don't ask me how she did it."

"Octopussy, huh? I guess that explains why she's got her slimy tentacles all over my man," I said, seeing a whole lot of red and, admittedly, a bit of green. My mind started drumming up all sorts of lethal maneuvers from Mortal Kombat, all of which I knew I could certainly pull off, given as pissed as I was.

"Want me to do the honors? I've been itching to cut that bitch for a long-ass time now," Lexi offered. I really adored Lexi. She was quickly becoming my sister from another mister.

"No, thanks. I've got this," I said as I threw my shoulders back and made my way toward my man.

I heard her laugh from behind me. "Ribbit, ribbit."

14
the dam breaks

Noah

I fucking hate Julie. As I stood there with my uncle Daniel and aunt Vanessa, there was nothing I could do about Julie's unwanted and unsolicited attention. Except to drink more, and quickly, so that my body would hopefully be numb to her repulsive touch. I would need to scour with an SOS pad or something as soon as I got home.

Not long after Delaine—who looked delectable in that gown, by the way—disappeared with Lexi and Polly to the bathroom, the traitorous bitch had made a beeline straight to where I stood. As if she thought I was champing at the bit to see her again. On the contrary, it had totally slipped my mind that she might be there, but like I said before, my mind hadn't been anywhere near right since Delaine walked into my life.

"Oh, fuck me," Mason had sighed as something behind me caught his eye.

Of course I had to turn around to see what all the fuss was about, but as soon as I did, I wished I hadn't.

"Well, as I live and breathe . . . Noah Crawford," the familiar sound of my ex's voice cooed. She was trying way too hard to sound sultry, and it didn't suit her—at all. She might have looked good, but I wouldn't know because all I could see was her bent over while her asshole was being plugged from behind repeatedly by David's cock.

"Well, as I suffocate myself and hope to die . . . Julie Frost," I replied in a bored tone.

"Aw, play nice, Noah, and I just might give you a second chance by the time the night is through." As if I was ever going to go back down that road again.

"Fuck you," I said simply, and turned my back on her.

"That's the plan."

She sounded so sure that shit was going to happen that all I could do was scoff and finish off my champagne. I was going to need something stronger to get through the night. "Who was stupid enough to bring a whore like you to something this classy anyway?"

"Watch your mouth, Crawford. That's my date you're insulting," David approached our little clan and slipped his arms around Julie's waist from behind. "Told you my date was a real looker."

I would have wagered my left nut that what he expected to gain from that little donkey punch of a move was one hell of a reaction out of me, one that would be explosive and detrimental to my position in the company. He expected me to lose it in the middle of a room filled with not only employees but clients—both current and prospective—not to mention board members. It was a good plan, but one that didn't stand a chance of working when a bitch like Julie Frost was involved. No way was I giving him the satisfaction. So I gritted my teeth and forced a smile.

"You're looking good tonight, David. Where'd you get the tux? Backstabber's Emporium?" I asked. To their credit, Brad and Mason did their best to cover their laughs.

"Very witty. Did you come up with that all on your own, or did your girlfriend help you? Oh, wait, that's right. Your girlfriend is with me." David's obnoxious laugh made me clench all my muscles to keep from knocking him the fuck out. "I'm going to the bar to get a real drink. Want to come, babe?"

"No, thank you. I think I'm going to hang out here for a bit and talk about old times with Noah." Julie kept her eyes glued to me. Not that I was looking at her in turn; I could just feel her eyes undressing me. Yeah, so not going down that road again. She'd had her chance, and blew it out her ass—literally.

Daniel and Vanessa joined our assemblage, effectively ending our little tête-à-tête and sending me catapulting into the deep, dark bottomless pit in which I found myself trapped.

"Patrick," my aunt sang in her motherly tone. She practically glided over to me and wrapped her arms around me for a hug. "Such a sight for sore eyes."

"Aunt Vanessa." I smiled broadly when she pulled back. "I'm so glad you could make it."

"Where else would I be? You know how your uncle is about these things," she said as she looked up at Daniel adoringly.

"Patrick," he greeted me, adding a nod and a friendly clap on the shoulder before shooting a glance toward Julie. "I hope you're behaving yourself tonight."

Yeah, they knew about the fuckery that had gone down between us, but they were big on taking the high road. I nodded with an innocent smile. "Absolutely."

Julie wrapped her arm around mine and leaned into my side. "Patrick and I were just about to reminisce about the good old days." The bitch was laying it on thick, even calling me by my middle name as if she was part of my family, which she goddamn wasn't.

"Wonder what's taking the girls so long?" Mason spoke up, doing his best to change the subject.

Fuck.

If Delaine came out and caught sight of Julie hanging all over me . . . I shuddered at the thought of the outcome. Especially if the way she'd reacted to Fernanda was any indication. We'd be lucky if the entire building wasn't left in a pile of rubble and ash by the time she was done going all fire-breathing Godzilla on the place.

That was about the time Delaine emerged from the bathroom with Lexi and Polly. Instigators by nature, those two, which didn't bode well for me.

They were laughing at first, until they looked up. Judging by the ferocious expression on Delaine's face, I had every reason to panic. So I did, but inwardly, because to show weakness would only make matters worse. I could do nothing but watch and wait as Lexi and Polly left Delaine's side and continued on their path, giving Julie the evil eye the whole way, but my million-dollar baby didn't follow. Instead she . . .

Oh, hell, no!

Lanie

I set my eyes on my target: Noah Patrick. My mind was focused, my determination was set, and my girls were looking perky and round. He was mine and I wasn't about to let that whore sink her talons into him. Julie had had her chance, and she'd blown it. It was time she realized what she'd given up, and I hoped Noah wouldn't be stupid enough to go back down that road again.

"Lanie, wait!" Polly said in a hurried whisper as she ran up from behind and pulled me back. "Daniel is there."

"So?"

"Julie is Everett's daughter, as in Dr. Everett Frost." She bobbed her head and rolled her hands, encouraging me to get the point. "Julie's father is one of Daniel's closest colleagues, not to mention a longtime family friend. You can't just barge in, grab Everett's daughter by her hair, and beat the shit out of her right in front of Daniel."

"Polly, give me a little credit," I said with my hands on my hips. "I wasn't going to beat her up unless she forced my hand. Or fist."

"As much as I hate to admit it, she's right," Lexi said, completely disgruntled. "Daddy will have an absolute fit. And you don't want to make a scene in front of everyone who works with Patrick. As entertaining as that might be, it wouldn't look good for him and would probably only turn out in David Stone's favor. Bastard's been itching to find a way to force Patrick out of the company ever since they inherited it from their fathers. Even though everyone knows Patrick's the one who does all the work."

"Besides, that dress is far too expensive to ruin for the likes of Julie Frost," Polly tacked on.

"You know what you should do? Kill her with kindness,"

Lexi suggested, and then a wicked smirk pulled at the corner of her mouth. "And it probably wouldn't hurt if you copped a feel or two of Patrick in the process. You know, just to remind him who he belongs to."

"That was the plan, Lexi. But, from the looks of it, Noah seems to be quite okay with the woman copping a feel at the moment." I was going to kill him as soon as I was done with Julie. I mean, how embarrassing was that? I was his date and he was letting her hang all over him like they were about to throw down some triple-X action right in front of everyone. It was a disgusting display, and it was clear the chick was good to go. Noah was embarrassing himself just as much by letting it continue.

But then the thought occurred to me that while Julie might be acting the part of the whore, I was the one playing it in real life. And I really had no claims on him. Noah wasn't mine. We had only been playing house, or *Penthouse* or whatever, but it wasn't real all the same. That wasn't the case with Julie.

He'd been in love with her once upon a time, and maybe he still was to some extent. Maybe she was more his type. Or maybe, having come from money herself and being way more familiar with Noah's lifestyle, she was just able to pull off the façade much better than me. My family only ever lived from paycheck to paycheck, and sometimes we'd had to stretch that more than was comfortable. We weren't cut from the same cloth, Noah and I, and I would always feel that difference. I was merely a hired hand, or body, as far as he was concerned. Maybe Noah and I weren't in a committed relationship in the traditional sense, but he'd come with me, and I was a real person with real feelings, and he was making me look and feel like quite the fool.

Polly stepped in front of me and grabbed both of my shoulders, giving me a little shake so that I would look at her and away from the free porn show happening across the room. Okay, maybe that was an exaggeration, but it was how I saw it. "Lanie, I know Noah. He's getting absolutely no enjoyment right now. He's merely keeping up appearances for appearances' sake. He's probably doing everything he can to keep his dinner down at this very moment. So go easy on him and give him the benefit of the doubt. Okay?"

"Yeah, okay," I lied. I wasn't going to make a scene, but I sure was going to make my presence known—with dignity and class. And if Noah had a problem with that, then it was his problem to solve. All my brain was processing was that Julie's hands were all over my man, and Noah was doing nothing to stop it. In fact, he was smiling, looking damn gorgeous, and seeming to be enjoying himself a little too much. And that in no way sat well with me.

I needed a drink so that I could get my head straight and figure out my plan of action. Marking my territory was a really good suggestion, but as angry as I was at Noah in that moment, I'd probably mess around and yank his nuts off with my bare hands. And that would get pretty gruesome, thereby defeating the purpose of not causing a scene.

As I turned to look toward the bar, I saw David Stone standing there. All alone. A plan started to formulate in my head, one that I fully intended to implement, because I knew that if there was even one ounce of Noah's possessive nature for me left, what I was about to do would most certainly force him to pay attention.

"You two go ahead," I said to Lexi and Polly. "I'm just going to grab a drink and take a moment to calm down before I hike up my skirt to piss on Noah's leg."

"Have I told you lately that I love you?" Lexi asked with a look of adoration on her face, and then she bumped her shoulder into mine. "Grab me a shot of Patrón, will ya?"

"Sure thing, and thanks," I said with a genuine smile before I turned and headed toward the bar. David Stone was my weapon of choice for making Noah Crawford feel just as insignificant as he'd made me feel.

"Patrón Silver, on the rocks, two," I told the bartender when he greeted me.

"Well, hello there, little lady," the scumball of an ass fucker said as he sidled up next to me—just as I'd hoped he would. He reeked of cologne that would have smelled good if it had been applied in a smaller dose. Plus, there was a lethal dose of obnoxygen spilling from his pores. I recognized the scent because Polly gave off a little bit of it, too. Luckily, she had been only mildly contaminated, whereas David Stone was obviously the poster child for it.

"Hi yourself," I answered him, turning on the charm.

He introduced himself, extending his hand. "David Stone."

I returned the cordial greeting, taking his offered hand. "Delaine Talbot."

"Wow! Nice bracelet. A gift?" He examined the cuff bracelet that marked Noah's territory like a jeweler sizing up its worth. "Crawford, huh? You related to Noah?"

"Thanks. And no, Noah is my boyfriend. You know him?" I asked, knowing he did, but playing the part oh so well.

"Yeah. We're the best of buds, practically family. Funny, he never mentioned you. Must be his dirty little secret," he said playfully.

"I guess you could say that. He doesn't like to share, so he keeps me hidden away."

"Such a shame. A diamond like you should be on display for the whole world to see."

I almost gagged at his lame attempt at complimenting me, but I kept the smile on my face as I looked over and made sure Noah was watching, which he most certainly was. So I stepped closer to David and ran my fingers under the lapel of his jacket. Never dropping the pretense I was putting on for Noah's benefit, I leaned in and said, "Well, see . . . I know all about you."

"Do you, now?" He moved in closer, his voice deep and seductive. "You can't believe everything you hear, you know. Jealousy can make some people very spiteful."

"Mmm. You're absolutely right," I agreed. "But I don't think that was the case here."

He inched even closer and put a hand on my hip while ogling my cleavage. "Well, now you've piqued my interest. Do tell. What have you heard?"

"You were Noah's best friend, but then you went and screwed that tramp over there behind his back. I guess technically it was from behind *her* back, but still," I said with a shrug as my fingers followed his lapel up and around the collar to his neck. "So it would seem that Noah is absolutely warranted in wanting to keep me his little secret. However, what he fails to realize is that not every woman is as easily susceptible to falling prey to the likes of you."

"Is that right?" he asked with a confident smile, baring his canines, which only proved my point.

I nodded, still maintaining a flirtatious smile. "I see you for what you really are."

"And what is that, exactly?"

"You're a leech, a parasite, a common remora."

He shifted from one foot to the other, clearly not liking my assessment. "What the hell is a remora?"

"Remoras are those little fish that cling to sharks and other stronger, more powerful species in the seas. They use them to get around that big ol' ocean without having to do any of the legwork themselves. They feed off the leftover scraps of food from their host, and sometimes even the host's feces," I explained in a voice that reminded me a lot of a kindergarten teacher talking to her students.

"See, in this equation, Noah would be the shark; working hard, fighting for every meal, making his own way. But you . . . you're the parasitic remora, feasting off his shit and doing your best to gather up his leftovers while you wait for everything to be handed to you." I smiled broadly, my expression a total contradiction to the words I spoke.

"You prey on a person's weaknesses and twist them until you find a way to capitalize on them, thereby filling the empty void in your own life, if only for a moment. I feel sorry for you, truly, I do. But if, for even a millisecond, you see me as a potential chink in Noah's armor that you can use against him, you better think again. Unlike you, and that ex of his, my loyalty to Noah Crawford knows no bounds. I live and breathe for him and him alone."

He swallowed hard and then chuckled. "Goddamn, woman. You just gave me a hard-on the size of California."

"California, huh? Not bad." I nodded. "But Noah wins again. He may not be Texan, but his cock obviously is. And you know what they say: everything's bigger in Texas, darlin'." I caught a glimpse from the corner of my eye of Noah on the fast track toward us, so I took a step back.

"I'm glad I got to meet you, David Stone. I wish I could say it was a pleasure, but I'd be lying. Toodles!" I tucked my purse under my arm and then grabbed my drink, along with Lexi's before I turned and walked away.

I'd only made it about ten feet before Noah reached me. And boy, was he pissed. His hazel eyes had turned steel gray and his nostrils flared slightly in anger as he gave me a death glare. He grabbed my arm and pulled me right next to him so that he could talk without being overheard by everyone around us. His body gave off waves of malice, and he shot daggers in David's direction. "What the fuck do you think you're doing?"

"You've got about two seconds to let go of my arm before I start screaming bloody murder," I warned in a calm voice.

He turned me loose and stuck his hands in his pockets. "Answer the goddamn question."

"I was thirsty. I went to the bar to get a drink. And that kind gentleman struck up a conversation," I said nonchalantly. "I didn't want to be rude."

"Yeah, well that kind gentleman . . . ," he growled, and then stopped.

"What?"

"Nothing," he said with a shake of his head. He looked down at the floor and then back at me. "Look, just . . . I don't want you to talk to him anymore. In fact, I don't want you to talk to any man here. Do you hear me? You're mine."

Well, well, well. And the little green monster comes out to play. My turn.

I narrowed my eyes at him. "You sure don't act like I'm yours," I snapped, and then stepped around him to walk back toward Polly and Lexi, whose rapt attention was on our little display.

He growled again, and then I heard his hurried footsteps as he attempted to keep up with me. "What's that supposed to mean?"

I huffed. "Oh, don't play me, Noah. You know exactly what it means. Who is she? Huh?"

"Who?"

I spun on him, nearly sloshing the liquid out of one of the low-balls I was holding. "Really, Noah? You think I can't see? And don't try to tell me she's another one of your relatives or some sort of business associate, because relatives and business associates don't feel you up like that unless you're from some messed-up colony of incest freaks."

He ran his hand through his hair, clearly frustrated. "She's . . . no one. Look, we'll talk about it later." He made a move to step around me, but I blocked his way.

"I want to talk about it now."

"Don't make a fucking scene, Delaine. I work with these people," he warned.

"Oh, well, since you put it that way, no worries. No scene

from me," I said, making a show of clamping my mouth shut while I continued on my merry, obedient way.

"It's about time," Lexi said when I handed her one of the glasses.

Polly looked at me with her brow furrowed in question, then back in the direction where David was now standing with Julie—who had apparently scurried away when Polly and Lexi made an appearance—and then back to me once more. I shook my head almost imperceptibly to let her know it wasn't a big deal.

"Here she is," Noah said, putting his hand on the small of my back. The scowl was gone, replaced by a beaming smile of pride as he introduced me to the beautiful couple who stood across from us. "Delaine, this is my uncle, Daniel, and his wife, Vanessa."

God, his family had to be directly descended from angels themselves. That's how gorgeous they were. Daniel's hazel eyes smiled just like Noah's, only they had a more pronounced version of the crinkles of time that had already begun to grace the corners of Noah's eyes. Their lips were the same shade of pink in the shape of a bow, and their hair was the same shade of chocolate, only Daniel's was peppered with gray at the temples. Distinguished and magnificent, not that I had expected anything less.

I put on a happy face, smiling as brightly as my cheeks would allow. "Hi. I'm so glad to meet you," I greeted Vanessa. I said nothing to Daniel. Noah had instructed me not to talk to any men, and he was most certainly a man. I was just following orders like a good little subordinate, after all.

Daniel cleared his throat, attempting to ignore the fact that I hadn't said anything to him in greeting. "So is Patrick being a gracious host?"

Oh, yeah. He took my virginity, threw out all my clothes and then purchased a whole new wardrobe for me—sans panties, of course—and allowed me to suck his cock on more than one occasion. But I have received multiple orgasms out of our little arrangement, and if that isn't the very definition of a gracious host, then I don't know what is.

That was what I could've said, but lucky for Noah, I wasn't allowed to talk to men, so I didn't. Instead I just nodded with a smile. Noah gave me a disapproving scowl. Polly stared at me bug-eyed. And Lexi covered her giggle with an inconspicuous cough.

"How do you like Chicago, dear?" Vanessa asked.

I perked up and answered. "Oh, I simply love it! What I've seen of it, that is. Noah keeps me preoccupied most of the time."

"Oh really?" Daniel asked. "And what exactly does he have you doing?"

Uh-oh. How was I going to answer that with a nod or shake of my head?

Aha! I shrugged my shoulders.

Daniel and Vanessa looked confused. Brad, Mason, Lexi, and Polly turned their backs like they were suddenly interested in the crowd. But I saw their shoulders shaking, a very clear indicator that they were laughing.

Noah cleared his throat. "Will you excuse us? I'd like to trip the light fantastic with my date."

"Yes, of course, sweetheart," Vanessa said with an uncomfortable smile.

Noah took the glass out of my hand and sat it on the table next to us. "Dance with me?" I caught the underlying tone. It was an order, not a request.

"Why, Mr. Crawford, it would be my honor," I said with my best southern belle impersonation.

Noah said nothing more as he took my hand and led me out onto the dance floor. We faded into the crowd and he spun me around, pressing me tightly to his body before leaning down so that his warm breath was at my ear. Then we began to sway back and forth.

"What the hell was that all about?"

"What?" I asked, his scent invading my senses and making me forget what he was talking about.

"You were being very rude to my uncle. If it weren't for the fact that you were actually talking to his wife, I'm sure he'd think you were a mute."

He lightly pressed his lips to the spot below my ear. It was a good thing he was holding me so tightly, because my knees suddenly turned to Jell-O, and I was sure I would have fallen.

"You told me not to talk to any men, and correct me if I'm wrong, but I do believe your uncle is a man," I answered breathlessly. "Either that or he's a very convincing cross-dresser. Or—gasp!—is he a hermaphrodite?"

"Very funny," he said in a dry tone, and then he playfully bit my earlobe. "Do me a favor, and knock off the sarcastic shit."

"Yes, sir. Whatever you say, Mr. Crawford, sir."

Noah pulled back and looked at me, obviously not amused by my tone. "What's your problem all of a sudden?"

"Problem? No problem." I shrugged. "Just being myself. The only one here with a problem is you."

He sighed. "Whatever. I should've known better than to bring you here. My fault."

"Why?" I asked, trying unsuccessfully to pull out of his hold. "Because I'm just something you purchased? One who doesn't quite fit into your social class?"

Noah pulled back and looked into my eyes. "You're kidding me, right?" When my expression didn't waver, he leaned down and whispered into my ear. "You're the most beautiful woman at the ball, Delaine."

It wasn't true in the least, but it would have been easier to believe if it hadn't been for that display I'd seen when I came out of the ladies' room. And so, true to form, I let him know about it.

"Yet you couldn't keep your eyes off that other woman," I mumbled. "Julie Frost, right? Your ex?"

I felt his body go rigid against mine, every muscle coiling like a viper ready to strike. "Who told you?"

"Does it matter? The point is that *you* didn't. Maybe it's because you still want her."

He pulled back again to look at me. At the same time, his hand moved further down my back until it was resting over my ass. "You couldn't be more wrong."

"Is that so?" I asked, meeting his gaze. My eyes immediately latched on to the sight of his tongue darting out to lick his luscious lips, and I struggled to keep my train of thought.

"Because you went from not being able to get enough of me to not touching me at all. You've been sleeping in your clothes; you don't talk or even *yell* at me. It's beyond obvious that you don't want me anymore. And I know I have no right to question any of this, but damn it, Noah, I don't like feeling like . . . like I don't matter."

He stopped moving and stared at me, his eyes shifting back and forth like he was looking for something. Then, without a word, he took my hand and started for one of the exit doors.

"Where are we going?" I asked, quick-stepping to keep up.

"Someplace more private," he answered as he opened the door.

I looked back at the crowded hall and noticed Julie and David huddled together under the chandelier, which was now shaking. Just as the wires broke loose and the ornate fixture began to fall, Noah jerked my arm, and me, out of my make-believe world again. Damn it all to hell.

He looked from left to right until he finally chose to go right. We turned the corner into another hallway, and then another, until all I could hear of the music from the party was a dull bass thud. There was a darkened stairwell to the left of where we had ended up, and Noah punched open the door and pulled me inside.

My back was pressed against the wall and Noah's body was flush against mine within a heartbeat. Before I could say anything at all, his hands were on my hips and his soft lips were moving over mine in a sensual kiss that I absolutely answered with every bit as much tenderness. And then, as quickly as it had begun, he broke the kiss, his hands cupping my face.

"What there is or isn't between Julie Frost and me doesn't matter. But you? You fucking matter, and don't you ever forget it." His voice was low and husky, seductively erotic. And he had a hard-on the size of . . . well, Texas.

I pushed my hips forward to rub against him. "Is that for her?"

He sighed and rolled his eyes. "Delaine . . ."

"Because if it is, it's okay. Just let me be the one to take care of it for you. It's what you paid me to do," I rambled. "I mean, I know I'm not her, but—"

"You could never be her," he said angrily. He backed away from me until the opposite wall made it impossible for him to go any farther.

No, I couldn't be her, could I? He used to love her. Apparently he still did. I would never measure up. She was from money, practically a member of his family. And I was the whore he had bought to get over her.

I slowly crossed the space between us. "No, I know that. And I would never try to fill her place," I assured him as I knelt before him.

"Delaine, don't." His voice was raspy, but he didn't move to stop me as I undid his pants and pulled out his cock.

"And I may not be the one you love, but I'm the one you're with. So let me fulfill my purpose," I said, nuzzling the head of his dick and then giving it a kiss.

"No!" He pushed me away, quickly tucking his cock back in his pants.

Never had I been so humiliated. I stood, my hands balled into fists at my sides. "Why?"

"Because this isn't what I want," he said, motioning back and forth between the floor and himself. "This isn't right."

"Well, fuck you, Noah! Maybe you forgot that you're the one who purchased me!" I was furious, and hurt, and . . . furious. Yes, in signing that contract I had done a desperate thing at a very desperate time, but that didn't make me any less of a person than Julie. What she had done was far worse than what I did. At least I wasn't a cheater. "I may not be Julie, but I sure as hell would never let your best friend fuck me in the ass!"

His head snapped up, and his stare was almost lethal. I guessed that was the proverbial slap across the face. I immediately regretted saying the words the second they left my mouth, but the bitch in me was rejoicing, simply because she needed to hurt and humiliate him the same way he had done to me.

I loved him, even though I knew he could never love me, that he was already in love with someone else. And there I was, on my knees before him in an elegant dress, willing and able to help take his mind off what he didn't have so that maybe he could focus on what was right in front of his stupid, beautiful face, and he'd pushed me away like I wasn't good enough for him.

Noah took his phone out of his pocket and dialed a number. After a moment he said, "Meet us on the south side, Samuel. We're leaving."

He snapped his phone shut and took my hand. "Let's go," he said and then paused. "Shit!" He opened his phone back up and pressed another number. "Polly, Delaine and I are leaving. Grab her purse and tell anyone who asks that she wasn't feeling well, so I took her home."

"I feel fine," I mumbled as he tugged me along.

"Funny, seems to me like you've lost your goddamn mind," he barked.

I didn't argue, because quite frankly, he was probably right. But I wasn't done with him, either. He was pissed. I was pissed. And that was when he and I were at our best. We got angry and then we fucked and made up. That was how we did things.

We made it through the labyrinth of halls without being noticed by any of the other partygoers, a miracle in and of itself, and then we were outside. I stopped short because it was storming like crazy—lightning, thunder, torrential downpour, the whole bit. Samuel was there with an umbrella to shield us from the rain and Noah dragged me into the back of the limo. The same limo, mind you, where he had fucked me as I looked on at all the other people living their mundane lives like they were the caged ones being gawked at by the one who was actually living freely. The same limo where he had told me that he was there for my pleasure, just as I was for his. The same limo where he had told me that he loved a woman who knew what she wanted.

He sat opposite me and lit up another one of those pornographic cigarettes, and I'd had enough.

"Look at me," I said authoritatively. He ignored me.

"I said, look at me!" I demanded. He exhaled a puff of smoke but never turned my way.

I reached across, took the cigarette from between his lips, and threw the thing out the window. Then I lifted my skirts, straddled him and grabbed two handfuls of his hair, forcing him to look at me. "Don't ignore me. I don't like to be ignored."

"Then stop acting like a bitch," he said with zero emotion. I should have smacked him, would have smacked him, except he was right. I was acting like a bitch. But again, that was how we did things.

"Fuck me."

"No."

"Because I'm not her?"

"No. Because I don't want to fuck you anymore."

It felt like whatever had been holding my godforsaken heart in place had just let go and allowed it to fall into the pit of my stomach, like a thrill seeker taking the plunge over the Royal Gorge Bridge without a bungee cord to yank them back to safety. Only I wasn't buying it.

"Bullshit. I don't believe you," I said, and then I forced a kiss on him. I could taste the tobacco that he had just smoked seconds earlier and the champagne that he had drunk before everything had gotten so out of control. I wanted him to want me, not her. I wanted him to fuck me, not her. I wanted him to love me, not her.

I . . . was delusional. And he . . . didn't kiss me back.

I pulled back to look at him, beyond confused because that wasn't supposed to happen.

"Get off me." His voice was eerily calm, unruffled, like he'd given up and had no fight left in him.

The car came to a stop and I kept looking at him. Then the door opened and Samuel was there with the umbrella again, getting soaked while he waited for us to make a move.

"Are you going to get out or not?" Noah asked me.

I finally got off his lap to step out, pushing past Samuel

because I didn't want the damn umbrella. I wanted to feel the rain against my skin, because at least then I'd be feeling something. I stalked toward the front door and barged inside the dark house with Noah following.

I had one more card to play, a bona fide ace up my sleeve. And if it didn't work, there was nothing left to do.

"You might not want to fuck me," I said, climbing the staircase in my ruined gown, "but there were at least a half dozen other men back at that party who did. In fact, one in particular springs to mind."

That was all it took.

Noah's hand shot forward in time with the clap of thunder that resonated through the night sky, and he grabbed me by the ankle, causing me to trip and lose my balance. He caught me before I could hit my head and laid me down on the stairs beneath him, hovering menacingly over my body. His face was hidden in shadow, the only light in the house coming from the lightning that spilled in through the massive windows.

"You want to fuck?" His voice was cold and rough as he yanked my skirt up and around my waist. "I'll fuck you." It took half a second for his pants to be undone and his cock exposed, but I was too focused on the hard lines of his face to pay much attention. In one swift, unforgiving motion, he entered me.

There was nothing gentle about what he did, nothing slow, nothing sensual. But it was everything I'd wanted because although there was no pleasure in it for me, he wasn't ignoring me anymore.

Noah pounded into me fast and furious, and I hung on for

dear life, digging my nails into his back and taking anything he would give me because at least it was something. He buried his face against my shoulder and relentlessly pumped into me, not giving me the satisfaction of seeing his expression or the dignity of looking into my eyes. There was no way to know what he was thinking, but I knew whom I didn't want to be on his mind.

"Don't think about her!" My voice cracked, but I held him to me. "Don't you dare think about her while you're inside me!"

His reply was nothing more than an occasional grunt and heavy breathing. He fucked me hard and with savage anger. A bolt of lightning flashed outside the window, followed closely by a loud boom of thunder that rattled the glass. The brief flash of white light cast shadows of our entwined bodies across the walls, and I realized we were those shadows. Just as empty, merely creating the illusion of a happy couple who were passionately in love when nothing could've been further from the truth.

That wasn't what I wanted. I wanted this to be real, a tangible thing I could touch, something that wouldn't disappear when we were suddenly shrouded in darkness and out of the spotlight.

Noah came, his whole body seizing up as he spilled his seed inside me with a strangled growl. I clung to him, not wanting to let him go because I knew I'd crossed the line and forced him to do something he hadn't really wanted to do. All I felt in that moment was Noah's heated body and his weight on top of me. It wasn't the furious pulse of my blood, not the edges of the stairs digging into my back, and it most certainly was not the cold that had seeped its way into my heart and threatened to spring tears to my eyes.

He was going to send me away. I was sure.

When he was done, he broke free of my hold and then stood to put his clothes back in order. His movements were calculated and mechanical. I remained unmoving and numb, but I refused to take my eyes off him.

"I can't take back what I just did. I can't take back any of it, for that matter. And it's fucking killing me . . ." Noah's voice trailed off until he sighed and looked at me. His face was twisted up in anguish, his hair wet and disheveled like his clothes, and I saw him clearly. He looked every bit as broken as I felt.

He ran his hands over his face with a frustrated growl. "I know, Delaine. I know about your mother, and I know she's the reason you did this. I didn't want to fuck you, because it wasn't right. I didn't want to *fuck* you anymore, because . . . somewhere along the way, I did the unthinkable," he said incredulously as he threw his hands up into the air. "Jesus, I fell in love with you. There. Are you happy? Now you know. And for the record, it was never about Julie. It was always about you."

He didn't wait for me to respond. Truthfully, I don't think I could have. It didn't matter that he loved me, just like it didn't matter that I loved him, too. We would never work. Maybe in another time, another life where we were equals, but that wasn't now. In this life he would forever be Noah Crawford the successful millionaire, and I would forever be the whore he had bought for his sexual pleasure.

He dropped his arms in exasperation, curled his shoulders in on himself, and walked up the stairs, cursing along the way. A rumble of thunder rolled across the sky like a solemn ovation for my enormous screw-up.

What the hell had I done? And how was I supposed to fix it?

15

*making love out of
nothing at all*

Noah

As I uttered the words that would forever change the dynamic between Delaine and me, I could hear my own voice breaking, the emotional turmoil on the inside seeping its way out. I tried to rein it back in, but when I looked down at her, her gown still shoved up around her waist and her fragile body lying on the hard stairs—how could I have done that to her? I had vowed to never treat her that way again, but I guess my word didn't mean anything, not even to myself.

I ran my hands over my face with a frustrated growl. Not telling Delaine about everything that I knew was exactly what had forced her hand and led us to that moment. And I couldn't hold it in any longer. I had to get it out. I had to purge the secret, because if I didn't, I was going to cross that thin line between guilt and insanity, and things between us would only get worse.

Fuck me, I'd done it. I'd told her everything.

She just looked at me, stunned.

And all I could do was sit and wait for the fallout, but not then, and not there. She would find me when she was ready, and I'd feel so much better about doing it in our room. At least within the relative safety of those four walls maybe she wouldn't get the urge to push me down the fucking stairs.

I dropped my arms in defeat and started the long trek up to the second floor. My legs felt heavy, my feet like cement blocks as I took one step at a time, willing myself to walk away. Everything inside me screamed to go the opposite direction, to sweep her up into my arms and run like a madman, carrying her away from everything to someplace where the outside world couldn't interfere anymore.

That was the dreamer in me. The realist, he knew we couldn't hide from anything anymore.

With every step I took down the corridor that led to our room, the distance to the door seemed to lengthen, but I finally made it. Leaden arms grasped the knob and gave it a turn, opening up to the place where we'd first consummated our relationship. Even I had to scoff at that. "Consummated"— the word sounded far too clean for what had actually happened there. More like I had damned it, doomed it to failure from the very fucking beginning.

I shed my jacket, throwing it to the side like it was a dirty washcloth instead of the expensive tailor-made masterpiece that it was. I didn't care. There was far more catastrophic shit going on in my life for me to worry about whether or not a jacket got a crease in it. Catastrophe number one: I owned a sex slave. Catastrophe number two: I'd fallen in love with said sex slave. Catastrophe number three: said sex slave had a dying mother whom I was keeping her away from. Catastrophe number four: I knew all of that and still fucked her like a goddamn animal on the stairs.

Grabbing my pack of cigarettes, I loped over to the couch and slumped onto the cushions. The flame from my lighter cast an orange glow over the otherwise darkened room as I lit my cigarette and exhaled the smoke in an exaggerated fashion. The nicotine calmed me, and God knew I needed it. I was ready to explode, ready to tear down my parents' home with my bare hands until there was nothing left but a pile of rubble. Because that was what my life had become. Fucking rubble.

I hauled my ass off the couch and stripped out of the rest of my clothes, badly in need of a shower. My clothes landed wherever I was when I discarded them, because again, they didn't matter. I made my way into the bathroom, not bothering with the light because I didn't want to see myself in the mirror. Images from that day in my bathroom were already on a constant replay in my hyperaware mind, reminding me of just how alike David Stone and I really were. I didn't need to see that again.

What was wrong with me? The more I tried not to be like him, the more I was. I'd fucked her on the goddamn stairs, for Christ's sake. Fucked her without any emotion, fucked her without giving her any pleasure, fucked her and then left her there, but not before I admitted how I'd fucked her over.

I stepped into the shower without first letting the water warm, because ice water on the boys was not a pleasant thing, but that was what I deserved. All I really wanted was to relax to the point where I could drift off into a coma, so I wouldn't have to feel the ache that had set up camp in my heart. But what I wanted and what I needed were two completely different things. I needed to face what I had done. I needed to stand before Delaine and take it like a man while she reamed my ass for snooping in her business. I needed to look her in the eye when I apologized for stealing her virtue. I needed to watch her walk out of my life with no hope of ever seeing her again. And I needed to feel the heartbreak of losing her.

Emotionally and mentally exhausted, I leaned my head against the wall, using my forearm as a prop, and just let the water cascade over my body. I'd hoped the shower would somehow wash away the filth that was festering on the inside, staining my soul, but that wasn't possible, unless I could somehow find a way to turn my skin inside out. Even still, mere soap and water would have never done the trick. Hell, I doubted bleach would have touched it.

All I could see was the way she'd looked as she stepped down those stairs earlier in the night. The way her hips had swayed and the slit of her dress had parted to reveal the creamy smoothness of her leg. How soft her skin had been when I'd put that necklace on her. The way she'd tasted when she brushed her lips against mine in gratitude. And I could still smell her. Jesus, the mere memory of it all gave me a hard-on. I wished things could've been different. I wished that instead of standing there, wallowing in my own guilt, I could have been holding her and she could have been holding me.

But I'd ruined it. I'd ruined her, and I'd ruined me.

In the darkness, my disoriented mind actually began to play tricks on me. I swear I felt her hands wrap around my chest from behind, and a gentle kiss being placed on the center of my back. And to make the mindfuckery even worse, her scent settled around me again, heavy and more potent in the hot steam. My cock naturally reacted to the presence that wasn't there, and I wondered how long it would take before he and I got over her.

"Please turn around." I would have thought she was actually there, except her voice sounded so meek and unsure. That was when I knew it had to be an illusion of her that I had only created in my mind. "Noah, please? You can't run away from me after ignoring me for days, making me think I'd done something wrong, and then telling me something like that."

Yeah, that was definitely Delaine. The only reason that she could possibly be there was to snap my dick off and shove it up my ass for snooping in her business. There was no running from her. I had to face her wrath because she had me cornered. And I deserved every single bit of what she was about to say and do to me.

I slowly turned around, my eyes having finally adjusted to the darkness, but no amount of adjustment was going to allow me to see her when there was absolutely no light source in the bathroom to begin with.

"I know, and I'm sor—"

I didn't even get a chance to finish my apology before I felt her body pressed against mine, and fuck me, she was naked. I might have expected that, because that was absolutely something she would have done, but I didn't expect that kiss. Her lips began to caress my own—delicate, tender, un-fuckingbelievable. It was the sweetest damn kiss I believe I'd ever received.

I threaded my fingers through her hair, deepening the connection and memorizing the way she tasted, the way she felt, the way she smelled, because I had no way of knowing if I'd ever get the chance to experience any of it again.

Christ, I loved her.

Her hands were all over me, her fingertips pressing into the skin of my chest, my back, my arms. It was like she was leaving permanent impressions everywhere she touched me. And at the same time she was trying to get closer. If it were possible, I would have opened up my goddamn chest and let her crawl inside, sealing her away and carrying her with me always.

The fucked-up thing was that I just didn't get why she was doing it.

And then she broke the kiss. I could feel her chest rising and falling, heard her labored breaths, felt the warmth of them against my wet skin.

She laid her head on the spot over my heart. "Make love to me, Noah. Just once, let me know what it feels like to be loved by you."

I knew I should've refused, but behind the façade I was a weak man—only for her—and I wanted her to know the truth of my words. But not in a damn shower, and not where I couldn't see her face.

I kissed the top of her head before nudging her back so that I could lift her chin for a soft kiss to her supple lips. Then I shut off the water, slid my hands over the curve of her ass, and lifted her to straddle my waist. Delaine linked her fingers behind my neck and pressed her forehead to mine as I stepped out of the shower and carried her into our room.

Her eyes never left mine as I walked her to the bed. It was still dark, but the storm outside had ceased and the clouds were sparse enough to allow her creamy skin to be bathed in the moonlight that filtered in through the windows. As I laid her upon the bed, I realized that she had so much in common with that heavenly body that hung so prominently in the pitch-black sky. She, alone, stood out amongst a sea of stars, outshining even the brightest of them. She was right there, but try as I might, I couldn't really reach her. I'd been given this one chance, this one rocket ship into outer space, and I wasn't going to waste it.

My heart pounded in my ears so loudly that I knew she could hear it. I was terrified, afraid that she would see me for the coward I really was and not the self-assured man I'd worked so hard to become. To give her what she wanted, I'd have to bare it all, strip down to nothing and leave myself completely vulnerable. And I would do it . . . for her. Hell, I would have given her anything that she asked for. If she wanted my arm, she could take it. My leg? She could have it. My heart? My soul? They were already hers.

As I crawled into the bed and lay on my side next to her, I stroked her cheek, letting my finger drift down the side of her neck. She shivered under my touch and I realized that I'd left her wet, like the moron that I was, and she was cold. When I reached for the sheets to cover her body, she stopped me with a hand to my forearm.

"It's not from the cold," she whispered with a delicate smile. My heart did a flip-flop in my chest.

I captured Delaine's lips with mine as I hovered over her,

careful to rest my weight on my elbow. The back of my hand continued its journey over her shoulder, sweeping past the curve of her breast and then down her side before coming to rest on her hip. Every dip, every curve reminded me of how truly precious she was, or at least should have been. She deserved to be worshipped, to be revered.

I covered her right thigh with mine, slipping my knee between her legs as she angled herself toward me. The palm of her hand slid over my ribs and she urged me closer as my tongue swept across her bottom lip, asking for entrance. She didn't hesitate. The tip of her tongue came out and greeted mine, like a woman embracing her lover after oceans and years of separation.

My knuckles ghosted over the soft skin of her stomach, traveling further upward to skim one hardened peak of her full breasts. She moaned into my mouth and arched her back, begging for more.

I broke from the kiss, my lips forging a trail over her delicate jaw line and down her slender neck to her collarbone where I sucked at her skin gently, because this wasn't about marking her. She wasn't my territory or my plaything. This was about loving her the way she deserved to be loved.

Delaine held on to my bicep, her fingertips dragging down my arm and onto my chest, leaving fire in their wake. Every nerve ending in my body was on high alert, each touch from her sending shock waves of pleasure straight to my nether region. She could do that to me; whether we were role-playing vamps in my entertainment room, making out like exhibitionists in the back of my limo, or cooking bacon in my kitchen;

she could do that to me. I was putty in her capable hands, and it would never be the same for me with anyone else.

I pulled her hand to my mouth and gave her palm an open-mouthed kiss before placing it over my heart so that she could feel the heavy thump, thump, thump. That was for her, and I conveyed as much with my eyes.

With one gentle kiss to her succulent lips, I dipped my head and captured one of her pert nipples with my mouth, swirling my tongue around the raised bud until she took in a deep breath, bringing herself even closer. I sucked the sensitive skin into my mouth and flicked at it with my tongue, nuzzling her. One of Delaine's hands was in my hair, the other gripping my shoulder and holding me to her. She was forced to relinquish her hold somewhat as I turned toward her other breast, wanting to shower it with equal attention.

I gave her nipple a soft kiss and then moved down her body, covering every inch of skin with my mouth and hands. No part of her would be left untouched. As I slipped my hand behind her knee and lifted her leg over my hip, I rolled my groin against her. It was an involuntary reaction to her closeness. I hadn't meant to do it, but judging from the moan that escaped her lips and the way she pushed back, she hadn't minded it at all. In fact, her hand slid down my back until she was cupping my ass and pressing me closer. The heat of her arousal coming into contact with my cock was nearly my undoing. So I pulled back, hushing her whimper of protest as I moved down her body and spread her legs to accommodate my shoulders.

I loved that she was always bare for me—bare, warm, and oh so wet. Keeping my gaze locked with hers, I placed a soft kiss at the apex of her folds. She closed her eyes, bit down on her lip, and let her head fall back into the pillow. A ripple effect went through her body; her back arched, her stomach rolled, and her hips surged forward to bring her center even closer to where I wanted her to be. So I took her offer, dipping my head and partaking of her delicious fruit while letting her juices coat my lips, my tongue, my face.

"Noah . . ."

My name sounded like a desperate plea as it fell from Delaine's lips. Her hips rose and fell and she laced her fingers through my hair, enclosing her thighs around my shoulders. Not to smother me, but to cocoon and keep me where she wanted. She propped a tiny foot on my shoulder and slid her soft sole down my back and over the curve of my ass before retracing her path again and again. I slipped two fingers inside her, curling them back and forth, in and out while I licked, sucked, and kissed every inch of her precious heaven. And then, all too soon, she shuddered under my manipulations. Her thighs went taut, her hips stopped moving, her hands tugged on my hair, and she let out this sound that I will never, *ever* forget. It wasn't loud—Delaine was never overtly loud when she came—but it was animalistic, like a lioness's purr as she bathed in the evening sun after having filled her belly.

I could feel the wetness gathering on the head of my cock, threatening to seep out prematurely, and that would never do. I ignored my own desire to satiate my needs, wanting to bring her to the brink once again so that I could watch as she fell over the edge of the cliff. My tongue and fingers continued to work her, guiding her through her orgasm until another one followed closely on its heels.

Slowly the muscles in her thighs relaxed, giving me permission to abandon my post. Not that I wanted to, but I had to stop eventually, or I feared I never would.

My eyes drifted over Delaine's form, her body writhing beneath my stare. She looked up at me, her gorgeous blue eyes full of expression. "You're so . . . beautiful," she all but whispered.

"Not nearly as beautiful as you." It was the truth. She didn't need a fancy house, expensive cars, or a high-profile job. She had everything she needed in that heart of pure gold. She was just as beautiful on the inside as she was on the out, and that was what made the difference between her and me.

That was what made her perfect.

Unable to look without touching any longer, I crawled up her body, hovering as I positioned myself against her center. Careful to maintain my weight on my forearms, I settled upon her and pushed a stray lock of hair behind her ear.

"This should have been our first time," I said, and then I slowly entered her.

She let out a soft mewl that I smothered when my mouth covered hers. Delaine's legs crossed at the small of my back as I moved back and forth inside her, oh so slowly. Her fingernails dug into my shoulder blades with each push and pull of our bodies. She answered my rocking motions with a purposeful grind of her hips. I pulled back from the kiss and went to her neck, lavishing her skin with kisses, licks, and sucks.

My hand palmed the pert globe of her ass and moved down her thigh. When I reached the bend behind her knee, I tenderly nudged it back, keeping my hand there and opening her up further to allow me to go even deeper. The need for her to feel me all the way into the depths of her soul took over and drove my every action. I angled myself a little to the side as both of her hands made their way down my back and she cupped my ass in turn. Delaine was definitely an ass chick. I made sure to flex the muscles there for her benefit, thrusting deeper inside her, rolling my hips to give her clit the friction I knew she craved.

Back and forth, our bodies rocked, like the ebb and flow of the ocean's current sending waves crashing against the rocky shore only to recede and do it all over again. It was magic in the making, the kind of stuff you only read about in those sappy romance novels. But never had two bodies been made to fit more perfectly together, whether in real life or make-believe.

It was the kind of thing that made you believe you'd finally found your other half. Too bad I was the only one who felt that way, but as much as it ached to know the truth of it, I didn't care. I was fated to love her, of this I was sure. Even if it was only meant to teach me a lesson, at least I knew what it was like to care more about someone else than I did about myself— for once.

I'd face the fallout of my decision later, but at that moment she was there, and she had to know how I really felt. I couldn't let her leave that room without knowing, beyond a shadow of a doubt, where my mind, my heart, my soul was. They were with her, and forever would be. And if she left when it was all said and done, she would take it all with her.

I nuzzled the spot below her ear, my words thick with passion and laced in pain. "I love you, Delaine. With my whole fucking heart."

"Oh, God, Noah." Her voice was so full of emotion that I had to look at her. Her bottom lip trembled and her eyes glassed over. A timid hand cradled my face, and the pad of her thumb swept over my bottom lip. "Please, call me Lanie. Just . . . Lanie."

I searched her face, and as one tear slipped down her cheek, I couldn't find one ounce of proof that she was merely saying it out of pity for me. If I thought my heart had been thumping and flip-flopping before, that was nothing compared to the acrobatics it was doing in that moment. My heart swelled, a gust of warmth shooting through my chest and radiating outward before going straight to my brain. I grew light-headed, yet I couldn't curve back the smile that spread across my face.

"Lanie," I repeated in a whisper.

She shivered in my arms. "Jesus, that sounds so sexy. Say it again." She pushed her fingers into my hair and lifted my head just enough so that she could see my face.

'I brought my lips closer, barely ghosting them over hers as I repeated her name, "Lanie . . . "

Her teeth tugged on my bottom lip, once, twice, and then she sucked it between hers, mumbling, "Again."

With more vigor than our last, I kissed her, saying her name over and over again because I goddamn could. Finally. My thrusts became more insistent, and I held on to the inside of her knee and rolled my hips against her. Harder, deeper, faster. I grasped the edge of the mattress above us in my hand and used it for momentum as I pulled myself back and forth, in and out. She clung to me, the sweat from our bodies intermingling as we slid against each other. The tendons in my arms and neck were taut, the muscles in my back, abs, and ass getting a serious workout while I gave her everything I had.

Delaine dragged her nails across my back and I prayed to God she left wounds there, wounds that would never heal—scars to rival the ones that would be left on my heart when she left me.

I pulled back to look at her, memorizing her every feature, and I couldn't help but notice the way the vein in her neck throbbed with her heavy heartbeat. Yet another vision that would haunt me for the rest of my life. So exquisite.

A drop of sweat dangled precariously on the tip of my nose until it fell onto her bottom lip, and I watched as she flicked her tongue out and tasted it. Her eyes closed and she hummed like she'd just popped the last gourmet chocolate into her mouth and was savoring the taste.

"Look at me, kitten," I whispered. She did as I said, her eyes forming an instant connection with mine. It was a connection that went so much deeper than outward appearances. "I love you, Lanie."

"Noah, I . . ." She moaned and then bit down on her bottom lip, tossing her head back. Her orgasm rippled through her body in waves and her body stretched tight beneath me.

That sight. Oh, God, that sight. The look on her face when I told her I loved her and she orgasmed . . . there simply were no words adequate enough to describe how it made me feel.

With one final thrust, I followed suit. I could feel her inner walls gripping and stroking, milking me as I throbbed and pulsed inside her until there was nothing left to give. I rolled onto my side and took her with me, using both arms to hold her against my chest, unwilling to let her go. And wasn't that the crux of the matter? I couldn't let her go, but I had to. Because to keep her there would just be cruel.

We lay there in our postcoital bliss for what seemed like a lifetime, but it still wasn't long enough. Neither of us said anything, neither of us relinquished our hold, both of us lost in our own thoughts. The sheets were drenched—soaked from our wet bodies, soaked by the sweat of our labor, soaked by the resulting release. And oh, what a sweet release it was.

And then she broke the silence.

"Noah." Her voice was so soft I barely heard her say my name. "We need to talk." That I heard loud and clear. And I didn't want to, because this was the part where everything got ruined, where I got bitch-slapped by reality . . . where she told me she was going to leave.

"Shh, not yet." I smoothed her hair back and kissed her forehead. "It can wait until the morning. For now, let's just stay here like this."

Delaine . . . Lanie nodded and nuzzled her face back into my chest without another word, giving me that one last night to hold her in my arms. It was the first and only night that everything was right in the goddamn world because she was there and she knew I loved her. No way was I going to sleep and waste one second of what precious little time I had left with her.

~$~

For the remainder of the night, I stayed right there. As she slept peacefully, I stroked her hair, rubbed her back, inhaled her scent. It wasn't until the first tinge of orange tinted the morning sky that I finally maneuvered my way out from under her. A soft kiss to her cheek and a whispered "I love you," and I was off to take my shower.

As I passed by the bedroom door, an invisible hand seemed to reach in from out of nowhere to grab hold of me. Down the hall and into my office it dragged me, until I found myself standing in front of an open drawer on my desk. With a shaky hand, I reached inside and pulled out my copy of the contract, the contract that bound Delaine to me for the next two years.

Lanie

I awoke the next morning and freaked for just a moment (okay, it was longer than a moment) when I couldn't feel and then didn't see Noah in the bed. But then I sat up and looked around, noticing that the bathroom door was closed, which meant he had to be there. I realized I was still naked, which wasn't too shocking since Noah had always insisted I sleep like that—truthfully, I kind of liked it—and the gown that I had discarded was still lying on the floor where I had stepped out of it last night before the shower. It hadn't all been another one of my delusional dreams. I floated back down to the bed and snuggled with Noah's pillow.

He loved me. He really loved me.

And he hadn't just said it. He'd shown me with every touch, every kiss, with every part of him until there could never be any doubt.

My thoughts flashed back to mere hours before, and I smiled

so hard that my cheeks hurt. I was soaring on the inside, my body vibrating on the out.

I knew the second he told me he loved me with his "whole fucking heart" that he meant it. But it just didn't sound right for him to say something like that, without using the name I had insisted he had no right to use. He'd more than earned the right to call me Lanie. Nothing could have been more right. And when I heard him say it, heard the *L* roll off his talented tongue—gah, it gave me goose bumps, and I trembled from the inside out, yearning to hear it over and over again.

Until that moment, I had been sure things could never work between Noah and me. We came from two completely different worlds, and regardless of how we felt about each other, those worlds could be unforgiving. But when I saw, felt, and heard his conviction, I knew we deserved a fighting chance, and I wasn't going to be the one who killed our shot of happiness. Not when I felt the same way he did. We could make it work. Maybe all those romantic comedies weren't just fantasies. Maybe Noah and I could have a little bit of that magic, too.

I was going to tell him that I loved him, but then he told me to look at him, and I saw what I could only imagine was how he truly felt on the inside. It was as plain as the sexy nose on his face, and then he said those three little words again, using the familiar version of my name. I couldn't hold back the orgasm that it evoked. Utter bliss.

I even tried to tell him again, once we each had a chance to cool our jets, so to speak. But he didn't want to talk. He just wanted to bask in the aftermath of what we'd done, and that was A-okay with me, too. Because we still had today, and tomorrow, and the next day, and every glorious day of our lives after that.

We were in love, and nothing or no one was going to be able to come between us.

I mean, what were the odds? Two strangers, both taking desperate measures to relieve the hardships we had to endure, and from all that mess, we found each other. We found love. We took nothing and made it into something. That would be the story we would one day tell our children and our children's children—leaving out the part about their mother and grandmother being a whore and all, of course, 'cause I really couldn't see that being an "awww" moment.

I was happy. I was giddy. It was a new day. The storm clouds had been pushed away. The sun was shining. Birds were chirping. I bet if I had gone over to the window, pushed it open, and leaned out, a little blue songbird would have even landed on my finger and sung me a song. Talk about a fairy-tale moment. Not that I had any intention of doing that, though. With my luck, I'd trip or something and fall two stories to go splat on the pristine concrete below with nothing to break my fall except that teeny-tiny songbird. It would look like a smushed blue M&M beneath me, and I couldn't have that on my conscience.

Nope, wasn't going to happen. Nothing was going to ruin the beauty of the day. So I mentally told that little blue bird to stay on his side of the window, and I would stay on mine. That way nobody had to get hurt.

Big sigh, huge stretch, and bingo! Brilliant-idea moment.

Breakfast. I was going to make him breakfast. I got a huge, cheese-eating grin on my face when I decided it would be bacon and eggs, and a devilish smirk when I thought about what could possibly come of that. Who'd have thought? Bacon, a cholesterol-filled aphrodisiac. Huh. Great for the Cooch— bad, bad, bad for the arteries.

The Cooch gave me two thumbs-up for my idea. But of course she would, little slut.

I shrugged her off and went to toss back the covers to get breakfast started—because the way to a man's heart was through his stomach, after all—but then the bathroom door opened and Noah stepped out. He was completely dressed and looked like pure sex, even with the slight shadows under his eyes. Guess I must have kept him up too late last night. My inner whore giggled like an innocent schoolgirl. Total contradiction, I know.

"Good morning." I smiled timidly, suddenly unsure if he would still feel the same way now as he had last night.

"Good morning," he answered, except his tone was a tad bit more sullen than I had anticipated. He dropped his eyes and started fussing with his tie, even though it was perfect as usual. I got the feeling that he didn't want to look at me.

Oh, crap. Okay, there was no need to panic. Maybe he was just thinking along the same line as I was and didn't know what my reaction was going to be this morning. Easily fixed.

"So, um, are you going to work?" I asked, because I wasn't really sure how to start.

"Yeah. I kind of left in a hurry last night and hadn't made all my rounds to prospective clients and the board members.

So I need to do some damage control." His unnecessary preening moved from his tie to the sleeves of his jacket.

"Oh. Sorry about that," I said, feeling a pang of guilt over my behavior. "Do we have time to talk first?"

He shrugged. "No need to, really. I already know everything you're going to say, and the solution to the problem is simple."

Well, that sort of pissed me off. How dared he presume to know what I was thinking? And what solution? To what problem? As far as I was concerned, everything was perfect.

Noah walked toward the bed and pulled a folded paper from his inside pocket, opened it up, and then ripped it in half. He let the two halves drift onto the bed beside me. "Go be with your mother and father. They need you far more than I do. Besides, it would've never worked between us. Not in the real world."

As I looked down at the paper, he turned his back on me and headed toward the door. It didn't take a great deal of studying to realize that the sheet he had destroyed was our contract. What once served as a tether that kept me bound to the man I loved was now an insignificant donation to the Earth Day cause: recyclable material.

"Noah, I—" I started, but he cut me off.

"I have to go," he said, pausing at the door with his back to me. "You should, too."

With that, he opened the door and walked out on me.

They need you far more than I do . . . it would've never worked between us. His words were almost deafening as they rang in my ears. And why was I so shocked? He'd only confirmed what I'd known to be true all along anyway.

My heart, which had been about to bust with giddiness mere seconds before, was now much like the useless document that lay beside me: destroyed, shredded, torn in two.

"But . . . I love you, too," I whispered to the now empty room. I couldn't let him leave without making sure that he at least heard the words.

I jumped out of the bed to run after him, but when a rush of cold air caused me to shiver, I realized I was still naked. So I grabbed one of his T-shirts and threw it over my head, then ran for the door and down the long corridor. I nearly fell head-first down the stairs, but I somehow managed to stay upright long enough to reach the foyer. Then I wrenched open the front door and opened my mouth to shout the words just in time to see taillights of the limousine as it pulled down the drive.

Too late. He was gone. And I was all alone.

To be continued . . .

acknowledgments

My decision to publish the Million Dollar Duet did not come quickly or easily, but I'm glad I did it. Obviously, this page is dedicated to acknowledging those people who gave a little bit of their blood, sweat, and tears to help me make that happen. So let's get on with it, shall we?

First and foremost, I simply must thank my incredibly talented friend and mentor, Darynda Jones. If it hadn't been for you, this adventure would have taken an entirely different direction. I am convinced people are put into our lives for a reason. Lady, you were put in mine to help make my dreams come true. I love your luscious face.

I still can't believe how lucky I am to have scored my very remarkable agent, Alexandra Machinist, and my extraordinary editor, Shauna Summers. You are two of my most favorite people in the world. Thank you for taking a chance on me.

Huge thanks to my pre-readers: Patricia Dechant, Melanie Edwards, Maureen Morgan, and Janell Ramos. You are my anchors, my sounding boards, and my biggest cheerleaders. Love you. Mean it.

A special shout-out to my street team, Parker's Pimpin' Posse, and the members of PNSS. Most important, my loyal readers, thank you. I wish I could call you all out by name because it is your support that keeps me doing what I'm doing.

Will Noah and Lanie finally get their happily-ever-after?
You don't have to wait long to find out in the shocking and
seductive conclusion to their story,

A Million Guilty Pleasures.

Coming soon from Bantam Books.

Read on for a sneak peek . . .

I am a man who paid for sex. Not that I needed to, mind you, but it was the only way to be sure I wouldn't get fucked. Well, getting fucked was kind of the point, but not the one I'm trying to make. Bottom line: I paid an insane amount of money, two million dollars to be exact, to own a woman for two years. She was a virgin, and well worth the trade, but then I did the unthinkable.

I fell in love with her.

To make matters worse, I found out the truth behind why she put her body up for sale in the first place. She did it to save a life. I had purchased her to get laid. Clearly, I was the ass in the equation, but I was going to make it up to her or die trying.

My name is Noah Crawford, and this is the continuation of my story.

1

jinx

Noah

Walking away from Delaine Talbot was the hardest thing I've ever had to do in my life. And that was saying a lot considering I'd been responsible for the death of my parents and had subsequently inherited a multi-billion-dollar corporation, Scarlet Lotus, that I ran alongside my mortal enemy, David Stone.

David had once been my best friend until I came home from a business trip to find him fucking my girl, Julie, in the bathtub. Needless to say, Julie was no longer my girl. A pariah, yes, but my girl, no. All of those events inadvertently led me to Lanie. I still wasn't sure if I should be bitter or happy about that fact.

I'd heard about an underground organization that procured women to auction off to the highest bidder. It was all very illegal, of course, as human trafficking—voluntary or not—should be. However, these women agreed to become the property of the winner in whatever manner they required. I might not have trusted women after the Julie/David debacle, but I was a man, and I had needs like every other man. So when I'd heard about the auction, it seemed the best route to take.

Scott Christopher was the proprietor of Foreplay, a club that, on the face of it, catered to the shenanigans of college students, but hosted the auction underground. I didn't like Christopher in the least, but I hadn't gone there to make friends. I'd had a single purpose in mind, and I'd always gotten what I wanted.

Delaine Talbot was a twenty-four-year-old virgin. Unsullied, untamed. Perfect. The two million dollars I paid to own her for two years was a very fine investment, indeed. Two years for me to have my very wicked way with her whenever and however I wanted. And I did. Although I hadn't expected her to have zero experience with sex, I was pleased that I'd be the one to teach her. She was a star pupil, accelerating in her lessons to the point that I thought she might actually be the death of me. An added bonus, she came equipped with an attitude. You'd think that would be a turnoff, but it had only made my cock even harder for her.

We went round and round, butted heads like nobody's business, but in the end, it always landed with my cock buried deep inside her exquisite pussy while she moaned my name. I was a sex god and she was every bit the goddess. That was until I found out she was actually an angel and I, the devil in disguise.

Had I been half as smart as I'd thought I was, I would've hired someone to do a background check on her from the beginning. But no. I was a horny fucker without morals, hence the purchase of a human being in the first goddamn place.

It turned out Lanie Talbot had made the ultimate sacrifice. She'd sold herself to save her dying mother's life.

Faye Talbot was in need of a heart transplant. The problem was that the Talbot family couldn't afford the transplant, nor did they have health insurance. Mack, Lanie's father, had lost his job after having missed so much work tending to his wife. Corporate America could be a cold bastard at times, caring more about the bottom line than the people who made it to begin with. But what had been done had been done. All they could do was trudge forward and hold out for hope.

That hope came in the sum of two million dollars that I'd paid to have my very wicked way with Lanie.

Charitable of me, huh? I didn't think that had been what my dearly departed mother, Elizabeth, had in mind when she'd first started the charity campaign at Scarlet Lotus. Noah Sr. would've disapproved greatly as well.

Once I'd found out what I'd done to Lanie, I knew I couldn't do it to her anymore. I'd fallen for her. Big-time. And although it nearly killed me to admit it, I knew I had to let her go. She belonged at her mother's side, not in my bed.

I'll admit I hadn't thought I could actually follow through on it, so I'd hedged. It was the night of the annual Scarlet Lotus Ball that the dam had finally broken. First of all, Julie had shown up and shown out. She had been all over me like a second skin and there wasn't a damn thing I could do about it at the time because of all the board members and potential clients who were in attendance. Add to that the fact that Lanie had been openly flirting with David Stone and you had a catastrophe in the making. So I'd been forced to drag Lanie out of there before I lost all composure and made a horrific scene from which I'd never be able to recover. It was what David had been hoping for, I was sure.

Lanie and I had argued on the ride home. Well, she had argued. I ignored her. Which had only pissed her off more. She wanted me to fuck her, expected it, because that was what we'd always done. Only I hadn't wanted to fuck her anymore. I couldn't. Not after everything I'd learned. Don't get me wrong; I wanted her. Goddamn, did I ever. But I couldn't do that to her anymore.

She wouldn't leave well enough alone, though. Nope. Not Lanie. When I'd spurned her advances, she'd bolted from the limousine and into the rain toward the house. I'd followed after her, of course, but she was crazed, spewing anything at all to get a rise out of me.

She hit the proverbial jackpot when she told me if I wouldn't fuck her, someone else back at the ball would, and one person in particular sprang to mind. David Stone.

My possessive nature kicked in. Admittedly, I was angry, but it was no excuse for what I'd done. None too gently, I'd grabbed her and fucked her senseless, right there on the stair-case. I hadn't cared if it felt good to her. I hadn't cared if she was uncomfortable. I hadn't cared about anything other than claiming what I'd considered mine.

Only she wasn't mine. Sure, maybe I owned her body, but I didn't own her soul or her heart, and those were the parts of her that I'd wanted the most. Those were the parts of me that I'd given her without even realizing it. And they hadn't cost her one red penny.

After fucking her like a goddamn animal, I'd finally forced myself to confess everything I'd been keeping from her. I told her that I knew about her mother, about why she had to auction herself off to the highest bidder. And as fucked up as I knew it was, I told her that I'd fallen in love with her. And then I left her there without another word.

To my utter amazement, Lanie had come to find me in the shower. Imagine my surprise when instead of cutting my balls off, she asked me to make love to her, to let her know what it felt like to be loved by me. Just once. That was all she'd wanted. And I would've given her anything she asked for, so of course I gave her my heart, bloody but still beating, on a platter.

I'd known while I was making love to her, while I was baring my fucking soul to her, that it was the last time. I'd known it, and still I managed to push all of that to the side and revere her the way she should've been revered from day one. I loved her freely and completely, with all of my might and all of my being. There had been no room to doubt how I had felt about her, how I still felt about her.

I loved her. God help me, I fucking loved her.

Afterward, she made it a point to state the obvious, that we needed to talk. But I'd known everything she was going to say already, so I claimed the night and just held her. I knew it would be the last time I'd ever be able to do so. That had been last night.

This morning, it had taken every ounce of strength I had to leave the measured serenity of that bed. It had to be done. So I'd nuzzled her neck and softly kissed the bare skin of her shoulder before whispering one last "I love you" into her ear.

She'd stirred and smiled in her sleep, which made it even harder to leave her side, but I somehow did.

The shower was quick, my dressing time even quicker. And when I'd come out, there she was, my million-dollar baby, looking even more beautiful than I'd ever thought her to be before. She'd wanted to talk, but again, I knew the score, and I just didn't think I could handle hearing her say the words. So I did the right thing.

I ripped up the contract and told her to go be with her family. And then I willed my shaky legs to take me away from her. She didn't follow after or try to stop me, which was as it should've been. The fantasy I'd tried to buy was over, and it was time for me to get back to the real world.

As the limousine pulled away, I refused to let myself look back at the front door. I didn't want to see that she wasn't there. It was hard enough knowing she wouldn't be when I got home. Maybe the day would eventually come that she'd think about me and not hate my guts. Maybe she'd even smile warmly. Maybe, but I wasn't counting on it. As long as she was happy, that was all that mattered to me.

And so I found myself in my limousine, alone and fucking dying on the inside. I'd turn to the only thing that had gotten me through every other tragedy in my life, Scarlet Lotus.

Lanie

As I watched the limousine disappear from sight, something came over me. I expected it to be defeat, agony, betrayal, or heartache, but it wasn't.

Rage. Rage and more rage.

How dare he? Stupid man with his stupid big house, and his stupid big ego, and his stupid big head thinking he knew what was best for me. He said it wouldn't work, but I didn't believe he meant it. I saw that look in his eyes. It was killing him. So why do it? Why go through all he had the night before to prove how he felt for me only to turn me loose at dawn's first light? Because he had control issues, that was the reason. Well, he couldn't tell me what to do. I wasn't one of his employees anymore. The shredded piece of paper he had discarded onto the bed was the end of that contract.

Discarded . . . just like me.

I was going to tell him I loved him, too, to put an end to his ridiculousness, but no such luck. Before letting me get the words out of my mouth that were sure to prove him wrong, the control freak told me to get lost.

How was it fair that he got to say all he wanted when I didn't? I mean, sure, I could've echoed his declaration while in the throes of passion, but that passion was pretty epic and I'd had a hard enough time remembering to breathe let alone being able to say anything that would have sounded in the least bit coherent or endearing. Besides, I really thought I had all kinds of time to tell him how I felt. I mean, hello? I told him to call me Lanie, for Christ's sake. Plus, I didn't want him to think I was saying those three little words just because he did. I wanted a separate moment to do the whole shout-it-from-the-highest-mountaintop-for-the-whole-world-to-hear thing so there was no doubting the sincerity of my declaration because a declaration of that magnitude was a pretty serious thing. But I was prepared to make that leap—for him, for me . . . for us.

And then he had to go and ruin it with his caveman crap. Men are jackasses.

But at least I could do something about my jackass because I really had nothing to lose by confronting him. I was going to make him listen to me, whether he wanted to or not. He was going to know that I loved him, and he was going to feel like a total jerk for dismissing me the way he did, because I was going down to that posh little office of his to demand his attention. He was going to see how wrong he was to make the assumptions he had made, and he would never jump to conclusions again. I was a woman who had given up everything to save her dying mother's life, and I had a voice that was screaming to be heard. I'd be damned if everything I'd been through since I entered Noah Crawford's world was going to be for nothing.

Resigned to that plan, I turned on my heel and stalked back into the house with my shoulders back and my head held high. After a quick shower and a tour through Polly's wonderland of inappropriate clothing, I dressed and grabbed my cell phone from the table before leaving.

I was really quite impressed with myself as I scurried down the stairs, again avoiding a neck-breaking, skull-crushing fall. When I reached the first floor, I heard a car pull up. It had to be Samuel returning from dropping Noah off, and I gave myself a healthy dose of see-this-was-meant-to-be because how perfect was that timing?

And then there was an insistent pounding on the door, followed by, "Lanie Marie Talbot, I know you're in there! Get your fat ass out of bed and open the door!"

That was my bestie, Dez.

I sprinted for the door and yanked it open just as Dez was about to pound her fist against it again. For a girl she was pretty strong, and I was lucky that she narrowly missed cold-cocking me in the forehead. Like I needed to look like a uni-corn when I went to confront Noah.

"Dez!" I shrieked as I ducked her fist. We both took a step back and eyed each other from head to toe.

"What the hell are you wearing?" we both asked simultane-ously. "Jinx! You owe me a Coke!" I yelled at the same time that Dez yelled, "Jinx! You owe me a cock!"

Every time we played this game, I never got my Coke. Dez, however, always got her cock—without my help.

Dez was dressed head-to-toe in black on black. Well, mostly. Black skinny jeans, black turtleneck, black snakeskin boots. One larger-than-life skull belt buckle adorned the center of her low-slung hip-huggers, and she was wearing a black cap embroi-dered with yet another skull just over her perfectly sculpted eyebrows.

I tackled my best friend, wrapping my arms around her torso and pinning her arms to her sides. "Oh my God! I've missed you so much!" It wasn't until she was right in front of me that I realized just how badly.

"Get the fuck off me! Damn, what are they feeding you here, steroids?" she asked, trying to wriggle out of my hold.

I turned her loose, realizing my hug was probably border-line bone-shattering and stepped aside to invite her in. "What's with the *Mission Impossible* getup?"

"I'm breaking you out." She turned to look me over once

again with an approving smile. "Boyfriend sure did trick you out, huh? Look at you with the little red minidress, Slutty McSlutterson." Then she suddenly gasped, her eyes going wide. "You have been thoroughly scrogged! Spill!"

I felt my face go red. "What? No!"

"Yes, you were, Lanie Talbot! Don't forget who you're talking to. I think I know that just-been-fucked look."

I wanted nothing more than to gush to my best friend, but I needed to catch up to Noah, and Dez's arrival was keeping me from doing that. Speaking of . . . "Wait, what did you mean by the whole breaking-me-out thing."

"I meant, get your shit and let's go. I'm on a covert mission to bail your ass out of sex-slave prison," she said, and then looked around in awe. "Although, I don't think I'd exactly call these digs a prison. This is a freakin' palace!"

"Okay, seriously. Why are you here, and how did you know where I was?"

Dez rolled her eyes. "You said Noah Crawford bought you, and it didn't dawn on me at first, but then it hit me like a whore getting bitch-slapped by her pimp in a dark alley: The Noah Crawford of Scarlet Lotus. Right? I mean, because how many Noah Crawfords could there be in the world, much less in this corner of the country and with enough money to pay two million little cha-chings for his own personal little *oh-yes-daddy-milk-me-papi*?" she asked with all the great acting skills of a porn star destined for the silver screen.

"Yes, but that still doesn't explain why you're here insisting on breaking me out. I'm fine, and really, it's not exactly like I'm a prisoner. Noah treats me very well."

My best friend took a deep breath and sighed. "I have something to tell you, sweetie," she started. Sweetie. She never called me that unless she was about to lay something heavy on me. My heart jumped into my throat and tried to claw its way out.

"Faye has taken a turn for the worse. She's been admitted to University Hospital, and they've called in the family. I promised Mack I'd get you there. It doesn't look good, babe."

Just then, the front door opened and Polly bounced over the threshold. "Good morning, Lanie!" she greeted me in her usual bubbly voice as if my whole world hadn't just been turned upside down. The smile immediately dropped from her face once she saw what I assumed was my paled expression. "Oh, God. What's wrong?"

"Noah was right." My chest constricted like an anaconda was squeezing the life out of it in preparation to swallow it whole. "My parents do need me more than he does."

ABOUT THE AUTHOR

C. L. PARKER is a romance author who writes stories that sizzle. She's a small-town girl with big-city dreams and enough tenacity to see them come to fruition.

Since she's been the outgoing sort all her life—which translates to "she just wouldn't shut the hell up"—it's no wonder Parker eventually turned to writing as a way to let her voice, and those of the people living inside her head, be heard. She loves hard, laughs until it hurts, and lives like there's no tomorrow. In her world, everything truly does happen for a reason.

clparkerofficial.com
Facebook.com/CLParkerOfficial
@theclparker